SKELETAL

BY

EMMA PULLAR

www.bloodhoundbooks.com

Print ISBN : 978-1-912175-69-7

For The Weirdos

FACT
Crows recognise individual human faces
and can hold a grudge if you treat them badly.

People think there are choices. They think they have life and a reason to breathe. I don't. My choices are black and white; remain inside the darkness or walk into the light. Live and be dead or die and be dead. That's it.

I've always wondered what the world was like before. Elders tell of a time when everyone was free but that can't be true. No Skels? Don't think so. Central control everything. I've never seen one but I know I hate them all. They alone hold the power to give or take away life in this city – the last city.

I stare into the abyss, mesmerised by the gentle lap of the trench water. My head empties of thoughts and I try to keep it that way, aware of only my reflection, my brown eyes like two black pebbles in the dark, dirty water. With the back of my hand, I scrub the last remnants of glittery makeup from my hollow cheek, the last indication that I was ever a host. I'm a Skel, and that's what I'll always be, no matter what labels they stick on me. Skels are named so because of the way our bones jut out. I've not felt starved in days yet I still look sickly, skeletal.

Overhead, wings flap. Drawn to the sound, I follow the crow in flight with watchful eyes. It settles on the single streetlamp which shines down on the bolted entrance to Rock Vault. The stony castle's sharp edges blend into the night sky, causing the lit door to look as if it's a floating entrance to a place beyond our world. It's not, of course. Rock Vault is the end of the line. The door doesn't lead to some magical place, it leads to nowhere worth being and nothing good. It's a door I never want to go through, a door no Skel ever wants to go through.

The trenches surrounding Rock Vault (the city prison) are always deserted. No one ever comes down to the water's edge and most never venture out of their cubes after dark but I couldn't help it. I felt suffocated when confined to my cube. Confined but not locked in, none of us are. No privacy, no locks; at least not for

Skels. Central forbid us to leave after lights out, we must never leave once the stars appear, and night crawlers aside, I'm the only one that does, as far as I know.

The stench from the trenches is sometimes unbearable. No need for my snood, pulled up over my nose, but the odour is still strong enough that it stings my eyes. The air tastes as vile as ever and the breeze is thick with flies. Gale City is silent, still as the grave.

Today, I'm in more trouble than I've ever been in, all because I can't stand being controlled. They tried to control every aspect of my life, sent me to the Morb complex. The guards will have orders to capture me, make an example of me. I don't care. I'm not scared of them, or death ... my biggest fear is living a lie, to only exist for the purpose of aiding the privileged. At twenty, my adult life has only just begun and already I want a way out of it. Each night I wish it and each night the Dark Angel never grants my wish, never comes for me, only for them. However, I would not want to die the way they did.

Unblinking eyes stare down at me; some of them dangling from the sockets of their skewered heads. There's at least a dozen, squashed ear against ear, along the thick cable over the trenches; like rotten tomatoes, their putrid flesh hangs down. Crows peck at the decaying faces and once the skin falls, the birds will no longer be the only ones' feasting. I pick up a stone and toss it into the murky water. *Plink*. It sinks into the grey. I should never have come here, should never have agreed to take him with me. Why did I? Feathers ruffle in the trees behind me. Those creepy crows are always watching.

'Skyla?'

Over my shoulder I see a chubby boy wearing the face of a ghost. To look at, we do not seem the same age, but we are. He looks much younger than me, more like twelve. I stare up at Bunce, our hair the same sandy blond, yet mine's like dust and his like silk. I look long and hard into those bright blue eyes, so childlike, almost innocent. He's scared and he should be. For today we run, today we change our future, today ... we live.

ACT I
THE PLAN

Chapter One

End Day

THIRTEEN DAYS EARLIER

The two long beams of light at the back flicker out, to signal that there's only ten minutes left of my shift. Gears grind, machines clatter their metal parts together and the smell of meat clings to everything. My legs are stiff, calf muscles tight as knotted rope. I squat down – I do this every half hour or so to alleviate the stiffness – knees poking out either side of my long apron, the front of which is stained pink. My joints cringe as I straighten up. I tug at the wristband of my blue, bloodstained, plastic gloves and wriggle my fingers in a little further. One size fits all, yeah right! I grab a cut of cold meat and mindlessly toss it into the grinder, watching as it slides down the silver funnel, leaving a trail of red before butting against the cuts of meat already waiting to be chewed up.

I left the logical part of my brain at home today; the whimsical and fretful part in full control. I can think of nothing but Showcase, of how I'm going to be judged like a grade of meat, and every time I picture myself inside that glass box, my stomach swallows itself. I've never seen the Showcase process; the pictures inside my head are born from gossip and the yearly spectacle of at least fifty girls lined up outside City Hall. Younger Skels dream about their life of manual labour coming to an end, even those who have only been labouring a few years. They pity the elders, all bent and broken, shuffling along, dull eyes reflecting the wings of the Dark Angel, which will come to carry them to their final resting place soon enough. The young don't want to become elders. They all want to stop being a Skel. Not me. The only change I've ever contemplated is running off into the desert, or, like the elders, into the arms of the Dark Angel. Which ... when I think about it, is the same thing.

The elders talk of 'going to glory' which I'm told means 'God in heaven'. No one uses the term 'God' anymore because no one believes we are made in 'God's likeness'. They believe the Dark Angel (which some elders still refer to as the 'Grim Reaper') comes for you when you die and takes you to the glory in the sky. A popular street drug was named after it and shortened to 'glory'. Users often describe the high as being heavenly and many say they feel glorious after smoking it. I've often thought of spiking the meat with it. I never would, it's not worth the punishment.

Minutes drag by like hours before the ear-splitting whistle screams out of the far wall speaker and echoes around the high ceiling. All Skels down tools, in my case, meat. It's always tempting to stop work a little early or slow down. I never do. I've seen Skels beaten bloody by guards for stopping to chat for only a few seconds before the whistle. At least the work isn't hard. It's tiring and monotonous; the gloves rub, my eyes often feel strained under the harsh light and my feet ache by the end of the day but it isn't back-breaking. Not like skyway maintenance, or any maintenance, for that matter. I work alone, keep myself to myself and that's how I like it. Most days I work the grinder. I feed the meat into the big industrial machine and it comes out as mince. Then it's mixed with vegetables and vitamins by nutrient control, and the different coloured slop is pumped into meal sized tubs. When I work the belt, I never get too close to the stuff. It's unnatural to me. The Morbihan who eat it are unnatural to me.

'End Daaaayyy! Come on, Sky.'

A scrawny Skel, whose name escapes me, grabs my arm and tugs me towards the exit. I allow her to drag me along by the elbow while I peel my plastic gloves off my shrivelled hands. I dump them in the glove bin as the sanitation crew sweep past and quickly get to work cleaning the machines, eager to get finished and join in the celebrations. I whip off my apron and fitted hat. Hair free, it drops to my shoulders. I join the queue of Skels heading towards the exit, robotically throwing my hat and apron in the laundry bin after the person in front has done the same, then in turn we each press our palms to the pad and clock out.

End Day is the last day on the Central calendar and at midnight, New Year begins. Every year begins with Showcase and every year I've been too young to worry about it. I'm now of age and that bothers me. It doesn't bother any of the other girls my age, they look forward to it. Excited and hopeful, they chatter mindlessly about what their host families might be like. I don't talk about it, it grates on me.

I live only a few blocks from the meat factory. I arrive home in minutes and to a package on my doorstep. Above, the black drone that dropped it buzzes off into the purple night, like a giant, flying spider. I scoop up the shoe-sized box and push open the front door. I'm lucky to live on the ground floor. Some Skels have to wearily trudge up seven flights of stairs after a twelve-hour shift. I slip inside and the front door closes behind me triggering the ceiling light. I toss the package to the table, made visible by the dim glow from the single bulb. I'll have electricity for only an hour, so before opening the box, I heat up the leftover pumpkin soup in a pot on the stove top.

It doesn't take long for the orange liquid to bubble up. I grab the metal pot from the stove, no need for a bowl – not that I have one – and perch on the stool at my battered wooden table. I inhale the steam from the hot, creamy soup. My mouth waters and my mind wanders to a time when my grandfather would make soup for me. He'd make it in the cold season, when the grey clouds would burst without warning. I would always push it too far, ignoring the angry clouds, I'd only head back once the first raindrops hit my cheeks. He expected nothing less and would open the door to me, soaked through and jittering. I used to love the smell of cool rain followed by the warm aroma of pumpkin soup, the spicy scent inviting me in out of the cold. Now, when I come home, my cube is cold, dark, devoid of comfort. It's as dead inside as I am.

I dunk husks of bread into the metal pot, the warm orange sinks into the grains and runs down the sides of the crust. I eat slowly, savouring the moist bread on my tongue, reliving my childhood memories. Bread gone, I scrape my battered spoon around the sides of the pot and, with every spoonful, I take a sideways glance at the package beside me, hoping it will somehow disappear. My teeth clench at the scraping sound of metal on metal. I carefully spoon the last drop into my mouth. I could eat two pots more but there isn't any more and it will probably be a long time before I get my hands on another pumpkin. I throw the spoon down onto the small wobbly table, snatch up the package, walk two steps to my bed and sit down. I sink into the lumpy mattress, the old springs creak and cry in protest.

My cube is ten feet by ten feet; everything in one room, including the toilet … a bucket. I use the facilities in the bathing block before lights out, otherwise my only option is the bucket, and trying to pee into a bucket in the dark can be problematic.

'Let's get this over with,' I mutter to myself, tearing open the box.

Inside, neatly placed on top of sheer fabric, is a small metal square, tied with a gold ribbon. *What? No dress?* I scoop up the square, pull off the ribbon and turn the device over in my hands. Light comes out of it and words appear on the screen:

Ms Skyla,

Congratulations on turning twenty. Now that your teenage years are behind you, it's time to think about the many wonderful opportunities presented in adulthood.

Showcase will begin at ten sharp and finish at midnight. Make sure to look your very best and be ready to compete for likeability, especially if you are challenged in curves, dark skin, or beauty.

You will arrive at City Hall no later than nine thirty. Wait outside until you are summoned. In the event of rain or dust storm you may wait on the steps. You must wear the dress provided, failure to do so will result in severe punishment.

We wish you the best of luck.
Grandly,
Chester Stout HHL
Esteemed member of the Gale City Official Guild

The city's emblem is on the bottom right of the screen in the shape of a wax seal. A blood-red blob with an impression of letters pushed into it, the words, 'Gale City: The System Works', circle an impression of a crow holding the sun in its claws. *The system works. Ha! Only for Central and Morbihan.* I set down the tiny touchpad and push my fingers around inside the box. *Where's the damn dress?* Not that I want to wear a fucking dress, but I don't want to be punished either. The bulb above me flickers and becomes dull. It's almost lights out. I reach into the box a second time and pull out the sheer material. I hold it up to the light. Wait, what? They can't expect me to wear this! I might as well go naked! The light flickers out.

I sigh and snatch up my snood from the end of the bed, pull it over my head and the darkness gets darker until my head pops out and my eyes adjust. I know my room well. I walk a few paces, around the table, towards the door and reach down. I stuff the '*dress*' into the side-pocket of my knapsack and feel around inside for my comb and stick; my fingers find their sharp edges. Confident I have everything I need, I push through my front door and back out into the cool air. Tonight's the only night guards are not on curfew duty and people may walk the streets as they please, and they do.

The air vibrates with New Year celebrations: laughter, music and singing mix together, creating the sound of joy. High above me strings of gold-glowing lanterns crisscross between lampposts. The clear string holding them up seems invisible, and an intermittent breeze pushes the golden balls of light around, making them look as if they're floating on a dark river in the sky.

Everyone has come out of their cubes to share what little they have. The feast is a rainbow of colour, yet Skels still dress in their black, city-issue clothes. Some have boldly added a ribbon to their hair or bowtie around their neck. I would never wear ribbons or bows, but the joyous atmosphere is not lost on me. I smile at the sound of the children's laughter as they run through the crowd playing tag. Once upon a time I did the same. I used to dance unashamedly to the drummed music beating boldly into the night.

CAW!

I flinch, that awful squawk a reminder of where I am, of what they did. Could still do. The horizon is thick with crows silently circling. I study the ill-omened feathered rings. The lack of cloud cover makes it look as if the navy sky is filled with swirling black holes threatening to swallow up the city, along with its inhabitants. The birds are waiting for the Mutil to arrive and start the carnage, they'll be waiting all night; the brain-dead Mutil never venture into the streets on New Year. Terrifying as most of them are, I often feel sorry for the Mutil; it could happen to any one of us and this is why Skels are reluctant to put a foot wrong. Central mutilate the person's mind as well as the body, in the name of research, yet these monsters must have some thought patterns because they consciously choose to stay away. Even so, the crows are always hopeful. I don't know why the Mutil don't come, and because they don't, it is the only time of year we can truly feel safe.

As I negotiate the packed streets, sidestepping my way through the New Year revellers, I spy a table of food which is different from the others: a few elders have brought bare-cupboard cake. Where they got the sweetener is a mystery. There is nothing more sought after than sweetener and nothing harder to obtain. I've never seen it in its purest form. I wish I had time to stop for cake. I don't. I start to jog, I have to hurry but I can't bring myself to run, I'm weary from long hours at the factory, blistered feet protesting. I force my aching legs to carry my tired body a little faster. I sprint past Mr Lotus – an elder who lives in my cube complex.

'Good luck at Showcase, Sky!' he shouts, waving.

I want to shout back something aggressive. I want to yell *Screw Showcase! I hope no one picks me!* But I don't. The shock of my little secret would raise too many questions and if I don't have time for once-a-year cake, I certainly don't have time for questions.

'Thank you!' I yell back, without stopping.

I stick to the sides of towering cube blocks, hidden by their shadows, keen to avoid more New Year's revellers. I prefer not to be seen, hidden away from the judgemental eyes of others. I've been labelled as aloof. I guess that's because I don't share in the frivolities, and I care least of all about the New Year celebrations. In fact, I haven't been excited about anything since my grandfather died. That goes for all city ceremonies, or noted achievements, for that matter. I don't want to be 'Skel of the Month', living for pats on the back for being the best at working myself to death. None of that matters. It's all pointless – puerile.

I need to cross the street but the surging crowds unnerve me. I don't want to go through them, too close to others, I don't like strangers touching me. A gust of wind rustles through the leaves of the tree beside me, throwing my long hair into my eyes; I claw it from my face, gather it up and hold on to it before stepping away from the shadows and into the stream of human traffic. Skels hurry past me on either side like ants avoiding an obstacle in their path. Some bump and brush me, apologising profusely but never stopping. The trees on the other side of the street sway in the wind. I squint … what's that? A red dot glows beneath the creaking branches. My muscles lock and my heart crawls up into my mouth. Thump, thump, thump. Spit it out. It'll draw their attention to me. Another red dot appears. Two lenses? They don't hunt in packs, do they? The celebratory music drums faster, keeping up with my accelerating pulse. I try to calm myself with a gentle reminder. Mutil don't come tonight, they don't! Another glowing dot appears, four, five. I take a cautious step back and a rush of black feathers shoots towards me.

'CAW! CAW!'

I duck down and throw my arms over my head, trembling. Children with toy torches set to the red filter run out from behind the tree screaming and giggling. They laugh at me as they pass. I want to yell at them, *little shits*! I breathe out, letting my heart slide back down my throat and into position. Their silly prank can be forgiven; they weren't born when it happened. I wonder if the birds remember things as we do. Do they remember that day? The day Kian was the only one left standing. I watch as the tree crows join the circling ones and I conclude that they do remember. They know what they did. Central say they're dumb birds, they don't remember anything. I don't believe that.

I hurry towards the bathing block, which stands like a last thought. Builder: *What next?* Central: *Better build somewhere for the workers to wash, I suppose.* So, they built a concrete box and plonked down in the middle of the road, splitting it, forcing traffic (if there was any) to go around either side. Vehicles can be used as weapons. Central banned them too. The Sky Train is the only transportation.

I yank open the nearest door. The pungent smell, of a bathroom seldom cleaned, assaults my nose – this is one of the cleaner blocks. Inside, the fluorescent tube is so dirty the light struggles to shine through. The power remains on even though Skels don't use the block at night, it's bait for those who break the law. Runners are wise to it, yet some still risk dealing from the blocks. If Skels do try to use the blocks at night, Central come for us – except for tonight. I throw my bag to the floor and stare at the brown girl in the cracked mirror above the grubby basin. Dark circles mark her fresh face. The sharp jaw line enforces her undernourished existence. I don't really know this girl. I never see her much. I prefer not to see her. She reminds me that I'm a slave to the system. No choice in my occupation. I'm a Skel – assigned to the meat factory and that's where I'll work, from now until the day I die. Unless I impress at Showcase and I have no intention of doing that.

I turn on the stubborn tap and splash my face awake with cold, rust-coloured water. I shake off the smell of corroded pipes and slip out of my snood and work clothes, reach into my bag and pull out a cake of soap wrapped in a face cloth.

This block doesn't have a lock. Most palm-pads have been removed, or deactivated. I don't use the blocks that still have working pads, they're not reliable. Faulty is what they are, and I don't fancy spending the night locked in a filthy bathroom, although part of me thinks it would be better than attending Showcase. Sometimes I find a wooden stick that people use to jam the door. Tonight, there isn't one. I'll have to be quick.

I soak the cloth with the rusty water, rub it with soap, wring it out and then scrub it over my exposed flesh until I'm satisfied that the meat smell from the factory is eradicated. I wash the suds from the cloth and wipe the perfumed residue from my goose-fleshed skin, then wrap the soap back up, fold my clothes around it and stuff everything except my snood into my bag. I reach into the side pocket and carefully pull out the flimsy dress. I go to slip it over my head and realise my bra doesn't match my knickers. I only own one bra. It's badly fitted, the elastic is worn in places and it's black. My knickers are tan! I can't wear the bra. They'll make me take it off. I've heard of girls being told to remove dark-coloured underwear. Oh, why didn't I ask someone if I could borrow a light-coloured bra? My lip trembles, I don't want to do this. I already feel violated.

'Suck it up, Skyla; you've survived a lot more than this minor humiliation,' I whisper to myself.

Truth is, I would rather suffer torture, or starvation than walk around semi-naked in public. My body is mine. It's all I have.

Hands shaking with cold and anxiety, I slip the golden material over my head. It drops down over my skin and I feel like I'm caught in a net. The dress pulls in at the waist and strokes over my nipples when I move. They stand to attention and my cheeks flush. It isn't long enough either; the hem dusts my crotch; my long legs are completely exposed. I already feel self-conscious and there's no one staring at me, or judging me. I reach into my bag for the last time to retrieve the comb and stick. I scrape my sandy hair up into a ponytail, then wind it around and force the hand-made wooden pin though it. The bun isn't perfect, but it'll do.

I pinch my cheeks and my olive skin pinks. I have to look as if I've made some effort even if I don't want to. Then I fasten my bag and gently push the snood over my hair, careful not to unravel the bun. I tug the hem of the black snood down as far as it will go – not far enough for my liking, I can do nothing about my knickers showing. I leave the bathing block as another girl hurries in. I've seen her before, I think she works as an attendant on the Sky Train. She's cutting it fine.

I always take note of people around me, but I don't make friends. Skels don't have much time to socialise and when I do, I always choose Kian as company. It's easier than hanging out with the girls in my community and pretending to be excited about becoming a host. There's a chance Kian will be at Showcase, he's been looking into guard training. I despise guards but it would be good to have someone on the inside. Nearly all the guards and potentials will be at the hall tonight.

Before long I'm standing, shivering with dozens of other young women at the bottom of the sandstone steps. The night is calm. The warm midday breeze which gave way to a chilly evening gust has long retreated beyond the wall and into the desert, leaving the giant flags that flank City Hall's glass-fronted double doors, limp. The squat building normally looks ridged, stark lines carved with an air of importance. This changes for one night only, when City Hall is given a New Year makeover. Gold banners and strings of stars are draped over the triangular roof. If I was to liken the building to a person's face it would be my grandfather's on 'The Day of the Bird'. He'd sit at the dinner table, forehead twisted in a bumpy frown, an imaginary storm cloud brewing over his head, bony arms folded across his chest, unamused by the weaved hat placed on his head (usually by me) and say: 'To celebrate such a day is ridiculous! We don't celebrate the land wars so why this?'

He's right, to celebrate a day famed for the murder of hundreds of Skels is insane. Perhaps this is why it's called a 'murder of crows'? I blank the killer crows from my mind and smile to myself at the thought of my grandfather's grumpy old face. Then my lip trembles and my eyes sting. I miss him so much.

I blink away pending tears and look beyond City Hall to the towering Morbihan apartments which chisel into the dark sky like silver missiles aimed at a far-off planet. Squares of light are dotted up and down the high-rise buildings. I wonder what the inhabitants are doing. Excited twittering erupts as more young women join the group. Reality crashes into my daydream and my eyes track back down to the dwarfed sandstone hall and linger on the city emblem, the same one as on the wax seal. A crow holding the sun is carved into the stone, along with the words: GALE CITY HALL.

Two guards stand on the topmost steps, hands fastened behind their backs, still as statues and in full uniform: knee-high black boots, tan jacket and trousers, belt and beaked helmet, patched with the city emblem. They wear their crimson desert scarves wrapped tight across the nose and mouth. I'm curious as to why their mouths are covered, there's no dust storm. Maybe it's so they don't feel the urge to talk – but guards don't need to be gagged, they do as they're told. I search their bodies with my eyes, what weapons are they packing this evening? Peeking out from behind the right shoulder I see the handle of a sabre sword, and behind the left, a long baton. They don't often have guns, as guns are hazardous in the wrong hands and guards are still bred from Skels. If Central were guards, I'd bet they would always carry a shooter. Since the gangs have guns, it seems a bit unfair not to arm the guards, but then guards are disposable, Central doesn't care how many are shot; there'll always be more to take their place. I know guards carry a bowie knife, only because I once felt the sharp edge of one when caught sneaking out of my front door at night. I rub my arm. The scar from the knife wound reminds me of my place in this city. My throat tightens. I'm starting to feel uncomfortable about entering a room full of guards. A room full of puppets, their strings pulled tight, they do the dirty work of the repressors, enforcers, and punishers.

My head turns when the crowd hushes, a gap widens between City Hall's front doors. The crowd falls silent. A small man with a snake's smile steps out and, either side of his short shadow, the orange light from inside spills over the steps. I know who he is, even though I've never laid eyes on him before. His name is Chester Stout – a High-Host Central suck-up. He stands in-between the guards, shoulders back, pot-belly forcing the touchpad he's hugging to stick out diagonally. High-Host family members are over-fed and over-confident about their place in the system. Chester is, by his own admission, very high up in the ranks of society.

'Welcome potential hosts!' he bellows importantly, holding out a porky hand in a triumphant gesture. 'Form a line and follow me.'

I close my eyes for a second and swallow my pride. The other girls immediately do as they're told. I'm soon sandwiched between excited young hopefuls, the sheer material we all wear one degree away from nakedness. I'm glad of my snood.

'Hi, Sky!'

The girl in front of me turns and accidentally elbows me in the breast, then almost blinds me in one eye as her long braids lash my face like a cat o' nine tails. Ouch. I wince.

'Oh sorry,' she says sweetly.

'Hey, Andia,' I say, cupping my stinging eye.

'Isn't this exciting?' She beams, broad grin exposing her big front teeth.

Andia works at the factory. A simple soul, slightly annoying and incredibly awkward. She frustrates the hell out of me, in an itchy rash kind of way, irritating at first and then a sense of relief and almost enjoyment once you scratch it. It's hard not to like her.

'Sure is.' I try to sound enthusiastic.

We ascend the steps in single file, my reluctance to enter the building unnoticed. My unease is swallowed up by the elated mutterings coming from the line of shimmery dresses, sparkling in the moonlight.

'Just think,' Andia squeaks over her shoulder, 'in a few hours, our lives could change forever!'

She skips through the huge double doors.

'Forever ...' I mutter miserably to myself as I'm nudged over the threshold by the pile-up of girls behind me. I don't particularly like my job but I know I'll like being a host even less.

Chapter Two

Showcase

Outside, City Hall is immaculate. Skels paint it twice year because it's close to the Morbihan side of town, it's what links the two sides of the city. Inside, City Hall is old. Clean but worn. It reeks of lost generations. The tired wooden floors are polished but well-trodden and uneven, and despite every effort with the perfectly placed vases of flowers around the room, the smell of mothballs and musk manages to win through.

I shuffle forwards, my personal space invaded by bodies in front and behind as we are prodded along like cattle by the officials. Once at the front desk, a guard orders me to remove my boots and snood and to hand over my knapsack. I can hardly hear his voice over the roaring chatter and shuffling noises of potential guards and hosts finding their way to their registration points. I do as I'm told, removing my snood (security blanket) last. I cross my arms over my breasts before being pushed along by a short, darker-skinned girl with her finger in my back. I pull my body away from her jabbing finger and push up onto my toes but I can't see much, only heads bobbing up and down. Potential hosts like a pack of nervous rats, twitching around, surveying their surroundings.

Guards stride around the room making sure potentials find their way, with the exception of about a dozen muscular bodies up near the stage; a wall of tan uniform, locked shoulder to shoulder. Sometimes, I think they're as mindless as the Mutil, and as I walk past stony face after stony face, I wonder if they've been conditioned. Mind fucked and broken. Kian isn't a troublemaker but he isn't compliant either, would he cope as a guard?

There's a whistle behind me, I turn my head to the sound. It's as if Kian has walked out of mind and into reality. Tucked away in the corner nearest the front doors, Kian sits smiling at me, touchpad on his lap, guards in training on either side of him. I unfold my arms to wave and he raises his thick eyebrows, runs his fingers through his wavy hair then shoots me an uncomfortable frown. The young man beside him nudges him in the ribs and smirks, the crooked-nosed one on Kian's right winks at me. My face burns. I flick them my middle finger, then cup my breasts in my hands. They laugh and hoot. I ignore them, immature little boys. Nose in the air, determined not to let my nakedness overpower me with anxiety, I stride forward until I've bridged the gap in the line left by stopping to wave at my friend. I realise that soon enough everyone will be staring at my breasts. I swallow my insecurities. I can't let things get to me. It'll be over soon, and life will resume as usual.

Once we are in the centre of the room, Chester strolls past us, moustache twitching like a restless slug glued above his lip, touchpad under one arm as if he's captain of the guard. He orders Skels to different tables around the room. I take the opportunity to look around at my supposed competition. Most are darker than me. I have one of the lightest skin tones in the room. They won't want me. Morbihan favour the darker-skinned, they think they're healthier than lighter Skels. Morbs are so pale, and in a way, they envy our sun-kissed skin. I bet they'd burn up in the sunlight, spontaneously combust, or something. Our skin is the only thing they envy about us but they would never admit it. The lighter a Skel's skin, the less desirable, and although my skin is brown, it's more like sandstone at sunset than beautiful bark. I'm bottom of the pile. Good!

A freakishly tall girl barges past, knocking my shoulder; she takes her position next to me. My hand instinctively reaches for the knife I keep in my boot, of course, it's not there and neither are my boots. I straighten up and compose myself. The girl beside me is older, she must be coming to the end of her ideal fertile age and she has a desperate look etched into her hard features. She also has light-brown skin and her hopes of being chosen will fade with age. I feel a guilty fish swim in my stomach, she really wants this and I don't. I should want it too. I shuffle on the spot. I want to leave. Behind me, any hope of running is gone; a wall of guards blocks the exit. Unblinking. Interlocked. Immovable.

The short girl in front of me, a puff of dark hair making her seem an inch taller than she is, leans back and whispers.

'She's been fed.'

'Excuse me?'

'You know, her folks gave her their rations and any fruit and veg they could barter for at market … or they might have used sweetener, to feed her up. Make her look more fertile.'

I glance over my shoulder at the curvy beauty behind me.

'Oh,' I say, unaware of this 'feeding' practise. People really will do anything to be picked.

'So many have been fed this year.' She turns around and continues to whisper, her hot breath depressing the flimsy material covering my chest, 'It's just me and my kid brother, I couldn't bring myself to eat half of his food in the run up to Showcase, just to gain a few pounds. They've got an unfair advantage over scrawny girls like us. Look at the curves on her! She'll get picked.'

She turns back to the front, her puff of hair bobbing as she strains on tiptoe to get a glimpse of the other girls. I stare back at the only girl in the room who seems to have hips.

'Pink!'

I snap out of my daydream. Did Chester point to me? I look around nervously for help but the other girls are walking away, towards their stations. I hurry to catch up with Chester, who is half my height and yelling colours at girls as he passes down the line.

'Um … Mr Stout.' I say, not loud enough for even an ant to hear.

I awkwardly bump into three girls trying to get past me and to their table.

'Chester!' I say, a bit louder.

'Yes, young lady?' He cranes his short neck backwards to look up at me.

'I didn't hear my colour.'

He looks down at the pad.

'Ms Skyla, isn't it?'

I nod.

'Pink.' he says and walks off.

I glance around like a nervous mouse. Potential guards are seated at different stations, hosts line up at others. I see a large glittery pink sign and hurry through the crowd, excusing my way to the table. I'm the last one there.

High-Host families sit huddled together behind the tables, smiling, pointing at the crowd of hopefuls, quietly nattering amongst themselves. They ooze over each other's clothes and jewellery. They wear conservative colours, not nearly as flamboyant as Morbs yet they disgust me just as much. Traitorous try-hards! Some have even bleached their children's skin as well as their own, desperate to fit in with the Morbs, to be more like them and less like Skels.

Andia once told me that after the host duties have been carried out, the host and her link partner are reassigned to 'higher jobs' or 'clean jobs', like teachers, shop assistants, or librarians, while Skels continue to do the dirty work. If you don't become a host, the next big career leap you can hope for is to work as a servant inside the Morb complex – a system of apartments interconnected by tubes. Somewhere in there is 'The Hub', a swanky estate where the High-Hosts live. I've already decided I don't want to live with those people. I'd decided before I left work, but the sight of them has confirmed my position. I'd rather blow my brains out than associate with these fakes.

I watch the other hopefuls and imagine them all swollen-bellied and useless. Some die in childbirth, the kids kill them on the way out. The Morb maternity unit is safer than birthing at home like Skels do, there's a higher chance of survival but nothing is 100% and I've heard stories of pain so bad girls think they're dying, some are ripped almost in two by the new life forcing themselves free of them. Post-pregnancy, some girls shit or piss themselves every time they sneeze or their bowels open without warning. Not to mention the sagging sack of stomach flesh you're left with. Some are untouched, no sagging, no tears, but most are not.

Why would anyone in their right mind want this? Who cares if Morbs live or die. We don't need them. Though I wouldn't want to be pregnant, even without Showcase. Kids are cute, but a curse. I've never wanted them and I don't want to carry them. I've seen mothers starve themselves to feed their young, and how are they repaid? If they're lucky the kid will grow up decent and look after them in their old age; if not, their sacrifice was for nothing.

If I get picked, what spawns from me will not be my child. The creature that slithers from my body, the screaming white blob, it won't belong to me, it'll belong to them, my masters. I don't want that thing inside me. I already feel used. Using hosts seems wrong to me, like using someone else's oven so you don't have to dirty your own. The dirt will be baked on. I'll have to live with whatever mess my body is in afterwards. Morb ovens don't work and that's why I'm here. I'm secretly hoping mine won't work either and they'll let me go back to the factory, but then, I don't know what happens to a host who can't conceive. I've never heard that talked about. They might punish me. A new wave of anxiety washes over me.

I flinch when a High-Host link, dressed in a garish, puce suit, slaps a round sticker on my chest with a number ten on it. He smiles, keyboard teeth so white you'd think he scrubbed them with cleaning chemicals. He sweeps his hand over his shiny brown hair, which looks as if it's made of plastic.

'Good luck, honey.' he says in a deep, gravelly voice.

I force a smile, then jump as a chirpy female voice echoes through the hall, I instantly recognise it as belonging to Delia Gold, the city announcer.

'Welcome to Showcase!' she says with a gleeful sigh.

I can't see what's going on. I stand on tiptoes again and stretch my neck above the crowds of girls. Two figures stand in the middle of the stage. Little and large. Delia: tall and curvy in bright red. Chester: short and squat in his green suit. I decide he doesn't look like a snake, he looks like a fat, little toad. Delia looks down lovingly at her counterpart and he gazes up at her, returning the warmth. Then they look out at the sea of people and Chester addresses the audience.

'Good evening, hopeful hosts!' he says in that familiar, jovial, yet superior tone that makes me cringe when it rings out from the city speakers.

The crowd cheers and claps. Chester the toad smiles widely as he scans the room, his thin lips a smear across his smarmy face. I'm not convinced he cares about any of this. All I see is a slimy amphibian who should go back to the polluted pond where he belongs.

I half-listen as he bleats on about the honour and responsibility of being a host, the land wars, survival of the human race, and the importance of extending the Morbihan community in order for them to create new technologies to enhance our way of life. *Their way of life*, I think to myself. Then Delia chimes in, her sugary voice makes me want to vomit.

'Now girls, line up behind the High-Host link dressed in the colour Chester assigned to you and then you will approach the stage when I call your name.'

We shuffle around and squeeze into lines in front of the suited freaks wearing our given colour. I wonder why we've been put into groups but quickly realise we have been sorted by skin shade, lightest to darkest, pink being the lightest group. This is humiliating beyond words.

'In no particular order,' Delia yells in her poshest voice, 'from the purple group, Ms A. Bellasen.'

A squeal of excitement sounds two girls down from me. At least someone's happy. Tension mounts as I watch Andia slink up the steps and onto the stage. She stands tall; an athletic, dark beauty wearing her gold dress with pride. Unlike me, she has remembered to wear matching underwear. My shoulders scrunch up by my ears. They start to ache and I force them to lower. *Deep breath, Sky, try to relax.*

One excited girl after another hurries to the stage while I apprehensively wait for my turn. Delia says the word 'pink' and my pulse thunders through my veins. I don't want to go up there. I can't do this. I study the girls carefully as they pass by. Many wear home-made makeup and they do their best to strut across the stage like they're the most desirable creatures in the world. Some are a little reserved, but not the ones that are gunning for the prize – a life of luxury and safety, living in an apartment with their host family until their job as host is complete. Then they get to move to the comfort of The Hub.

'Ms M. Skyla.' Delia's loud, formal voice resonates around the hall.

I take a deep breath before making my way to the stage. Around a hundred eyes are on me. Their hot stares cause my skin to heat. I want them to stop looking at me, but I know they won't, and they don't. As I move, the material draped over my body shimmers like it's made of stardust. The strong hall lights reflect silver dots over faces as I pass; now I really feel intimidated. It's like I'm twelve-years-old again on the first day of work. I remember walking through those factory doors, heart racing faster than the Sky Train, fretful about the unknown and wishing I could turn invisible. That's how I feel right now.

I try to hold my head high but really, I'm quivering inside. I manage the steps without tripping and move past a line of nine girls already standing on the stage, their checks done. Chester rests the large silver pad on his pot belly and prepares to read, while Delia Gold moves me one step to the side so I'm on the marker – a painted black cross. Delia is a voluptuous middle-aged woman with botched bleached skin. Lightening of the skin isn't an exact science and Delia is a good example of this – her face is two shades lighter than her blotchy burnt orange arms. Her skin clashes with her bright red dress, which not only matches her lipstick but also her fingernails and long magenta hair, which erupts from the top of her head like lava from a volcano. Her crimson claws click a small microphone to the neck of my dress. She back-steps and then speaks into something clipped on the shoulder strap of her dress.

'Can you hear me, number ten?'

The voice vibrates from my neckline.

'Yes.' I say, into the mic.

Delia shuffles back to my side.

'Parasites?' Chester says in a robotic tone.

Delia reaches up to check my head, releasing my hair from the bun, it drops gracefully to my shoulders. She places the fastener on a table behind her and proceeds to feel through my scalp with her sharp nails. I shiver at the tingling feeling, a creepy but welcome sensation.

'No.' she finally replies.

'Skin rash?'

She walks around my body, pressing her cold fingers against my skin in places.

'No.' she replies.

'Broken teeth, gingivitis?' he asks.

Her eyes are level with mine. She does not smile or blink. She's so close I can smell jasmine on her skin. I note the diamond-encrusted tiara on her head and several gold chains around her long neck. I'm surprised she can hold her head up with what looks like my body weight in gold draped over her. She squeezes my cheeks and I stick out my tongue. She nods and I grin widely so she can check my teeth.

'One slightly chipped tooth, hardly visible.' She slides her hands down my arms, picks up my hands and turning them over she says, 'Nails not bitten, cut short, good condition.'

'Thank you,' replies Chester. He clears his throat.

'Vision or hearing problems?'

His words go unanswered. He clears his throat again.

'Any vision or hearing problems?' he asks, staring at me expectantly.

'Pardon?' I say.

The stage erupts with staggered laughter. The short city official glares at the other nine girls and they fall silent again.

'Do you have any hearing problems, or issues with sight?' he says, through gritted teeth.

'Oh sorry! You were talking to me,' I say nervously. 'No.'

'Digestion or respiratory problems?' he continues.

I shake my head.

'Addiction to illegal substances not on your record?'

When I don't answer right away his beady little eyes open wide, 'We can check,' he says.

I look away. If I lie they will force the truth from me. I guess most are not going to lie to get out of Showcase and say they take drugs when they don't.

'No.' I whisper.

He strikes his pen across the pad.

'Ever had broken bones or mobility issues?'

I shake my head.

'Are your periods regular?'

I nod and blush a little.

'Let's see you walk,' he says, and gestures for me to walk the length of the stage.

After watching the other girls sashay daintily across the stage, this might be my last opportunity to blow my chances. I trudge across the stage, heavy footed like a Mutil, stamping past shimmering dress after shimmering dress, my bare feet slapping against the shiny wooden floor. Then, instead of turning around gracefully and walking back, I remain with my back to Chester the inquisitor, and I don't know what possesses me to do it, but I raise my arms and tilt forwards. Blood rushes to my face and life pumps in my limbs. I cartwheel and flip until I'm standing breathless and exhilarated next to Delia. A roar of cheering explodes from the potential guards, accompanied by giggles from the hopeful hosts. They're quickly silenced by Delia who makes a 'settle down' hand gesture, like she's quieting a group of toddlers. I tug down my sheer dress and smile at the crowd.

'Have you quite finished acting the clown?' spits Chester.

I nod. Delia flicks her magenta locks over her shoulder and smooths down her red dress.

'Right girls, show time!'

Starting with Andia, she leads the line of girls offstage and behind heavy, velvet curtains. I bring up the rear. I tuck myself behind the curtain and blink in the darkness. In front of the curtain, Chester's voice booms for the next girl to take to the stage. Behind the curtain, Delia lines us up, hands on our shoulders, one at a time she moves each of us into place. I lean forwards and look down the line. Every one of us is stood in front of a black door, palm-pad on the right of it. Delia disappears and we all look round at each other, not sure what's going to happen next.

'On the count of three …' Delia's voice vibrates from each of our microphones. 'You will press the palm-pad and step into your box.'

My body shakes with apprehension, heart pounding. I will my arms and legs still.

'This is your chance to impress the masters and mistresses,' she says sternly. 'Use the props, use your personality. For some of you this is your last chance, no room for mistakes! One, two, three, go!'

We simultaneously press our hands to the silver palm-pad. To my surprise, the door doesn't swing open, or inward, or shift into the wall. The black door starts to rise, releasing light which falls across my bare feet. When the door is almost all the way up, I step down onto the pink light coming from the floor of the glass box. I'm dazed by the floodlights shining down on us, the city beyond is shrouded in darkness. My eyes adjust. I spot Delia. She's in a tube opposite our glass boxes, along with about forty Morbihan in hover-chairs. Delia, all in red, like head devil, weaves up and down the tube, stopping to lean down and chat to each couple.

I don't want them staring at my semi-naked body, and I don't want to dance around for them like a glorified Glo-Girl.

Beside me, there are nine other boxes in a semi-circle, the girls inside them stand on different coloured spotlights. The girl in box seven holds silver pompoms and is doing her best to strike cute poses with them. Another girl has some sort of confetti she is throwing playfully in the air. Andia is in the purple-lit box. Are those bubbles? Yep, she's blowing bubbles. Not a good prop to use in a glass display box. One pops near her eye, she turns her back and rubs both eyes in an attempt to style it out. I scan my display case, on the floor is my prop – a teddy bear. I roll my eyes, cross my arms and lean my shoulder against the glass. Screw this.

'Uncross your arms!' Delia's shrill voice sounds below my chin. 'That's not a good way to sell yourself, Ms Skyla!'

I quickly uncross my arms. Not because she told me to, but because I have an idea. Not a good way to sell myself, huh? Well, I don't want to sell myself to anyone! But I can't do anything too drastic. Dry-humping the teddy bear or ripping its head off, will result in a painful punishment.

I reach down and pick up the brown bear. Cuddling it at first; I then hold it away from me and twist my face up in terror; place its paws around my neck and act as if it is strangling me. I flail about my glass box trying to escape the killer teddy. Delia's voice screams through the microphone for me to stop this nonsense. I ignore her and with teddy held behind my head, I slam my cheek into the glass, holding its paws as if I'm trying to stop it strangling me to death. I slide down the front of the glass box and then slump over on the floor, head hanging, dead. Teddy bear sitting on my lap, triumphant.

'Time's up, girls, please exit the box and make your way to the waiting room backstage.'

I stand and throw the teddy on the floor. But before I can exit the box, ready for the next girl to come in and try her luck, Delia's blotchy face appears in front of me.

'That will cost you!' she hisses, and I know it will. I'm counting on it.

Chapter Three

An Unwanted Win

The sun's rays are too hot for the city. It melts. The apartment windows seem to slide, the tarmac ripples and twenty feet down, below the tracks, Skels edge around buildings, passing through shadows like vampires afraid of the sunlight. Skels have no choice but to brave the elements and make sure the Morbihan have everything they need. Morbs are of the utmost priority in this city, precious to all but me. I despise them, the disgusting hover-chairs of blubber. And now I'll be surrounded by them. The thought sickens me.

The sun beats down on my head and heats up a question that's been torturing me for days; *How did I get chosen?* Someone must have made a mistake. I tried my best to be unappealing. I was so sure no one would pick me. I kick the Sky Train shelter and then quickly bend to rub the scuff mark from the tip of my polished shoe. I straighten up, puff out the tension and backhand a bead of sweat from my brow, fanning my face with my other hand so I don't accidentally (on purpose) smudge my caked-on makeup.

I'm tense. My body wound up like cotton around a finger, blood rushing to the tip like it rushes to my head and throbs. I know this feeling well, fight or flight, I'm on high alert. Usually it's the Mutil who cause me this kind of anxiety. They're a constant threat during darkness, but they don't come out during the day, they've learned to be nocturnal, learned their place in the city. Their brains are damaged, their bodies a mess but they know better than to brave the daylight and I know better than to meet this family.

There's nothing I can do about it. I have no say in this decision. Skels have no say in anything. The good fortune of being one of the chosen few has been bestowed upon me. I don't know how. There were so many better candidates then me; every candidate was better in my opinion, yet I have the honour of becoming a host. For me, it is no honour and there is nothing good about this.

'Why the sad face?' Kian walks up beside me, dark hair shining in the sun, tan guard uniform pressed and crisp. I try on a smile, he smiles back. 'Soon you'll be living the dream. All that food, nice home, the honour of ...'

'Kian!' I snap. 'There's no honour in pushing Morb brats out of your -'

'Flower?'

I laugh. He's always known how to make me laugh. I would never use that word in that context. Kian is working as a trainee guard. Central decided he's trustworthy and strong enough to be trialled. They don't know him like I do. He can beat any lie detector test, or memory sweep. He's strong but he'll never be trustworthy, not to them.

'Why do I have to wear this?' I sigh, holding out the pretty, pink silk as if it is a dirty rag, 'it's worse than the Showcase outfit.'

'But you look so cute.' Kian says, in a baby voice.

I glare at him.

'How about you wear the dress?'

He raises a dark eyebrow at me, mild amusement in his stare, or impatience? I can't tell. He thinks this is a good thing, like everyone else, he thinks I lucked in. I narrow my eyes at the imposter reflecting in the shelter glass. This isn't me, this isn't who I am. I blink, and false eyelashes, like glued-on spider's legs, curl upwards and touch my eyebrows. I'm afraid if I blink too much I'll blink them off. The lashes have three tiny diamantes spaced out on each one. I blink again and my brown eyes water. I wipe away the water with my index finger, careful not to smudge the liner. Silver glitter from the tip of my pink polished nail rubs off, leaving a snail-trail under my eye.

'Dammit!'

'Need some help?' Kian offers.

'No, I'm fine.'

I carefully wipe away the excess glitter with the tip of my thumb then smear it down the shelter pole. I glance back at myself, lips pursed in frustration; shiny, pink gloss making my mouth look like a piglet's snout. I part my lips and the sticky gloss tries to pull them back together. Yuck. I resist the urge to rip off the feathered lashes and rub the pink from my mouth. Morbihan like to dress up and it's customary for those chosen to wear 'meet the host family' outfits. Central forbids you to turn up in your dark city issue clothes.

'It's not that bad, Sky.'

Kian pulls one of my forced ringlets down and watches as it springs back up.

'I'm wearing a dress designed for a toddler. It's *that* bad.' I pout, crossing my arms.

Kian shrugs but I know I look ridiculous. My mirrored image mocks me. Mocks my blond curls tied up with a ribbon at my crown, the baby-doll dress, pink and frilly with a matching oversized bow at my back, but the worst part was when the dresser rubbed her shrivelled hands all over me, coating my skin with a strange gel. Its fragrance is sickly sweet, and my arms and the top of my exposed chest all shimmer with glitter.

It's as if I'm a present not a person. Yes, that's exactly how they see me! A gift. But I'm not *the* gift, I'm only the wrapping; to be ripped, torn, screwed up and discarded. I'm to give the gift of life and in turn, that life is their present. Skyla: the bronzed treat in pretty, pink wrapping, the disposable incubator – the host. I'm also a bad choice, like the shiny material that looked so nice at the market but is unforgiving when trying to wrap a present; too slippery, not compliant. I'll never forgive myself if I let the Morbs use and abuse my body, and for what? Luxuries, trinkets, and treasure – these things aren't important to me. Trees are important, trees and plants and people – life. I choose life. My own! I cross my arms.

'It'll be okay,' Kian says, scooping my knapsack from the platform floor, 'come on, the train's here.'

The sun dances across the tall, metal face of the Sky Train as it approaches. I've never been on the train before and an unexpected rush of excitement teases my nervous stomach. Sometimes, at dusk, I watch for the last train. I wait for the headlamps to glide over the city, silver body weaving between buildings like a kite-tail across the sky. My stomach backflips. I don't want to get on the train alone. I touch Kian's shoulder.

'Come with me?' I ask, hopeful.

'I can't, I'm not a guard yet,' he says, nudging me forwards.

I dig in my heels then stumble as his hand presses into my back, forcing me along the platform.

'But you passed the tests.' I say.

A cool breeze fans through my curled hair as the enormous metal snake swooshes past.

'Yeah, but I have to pass the trial too.' He yells over the noise of the train clacking down the track.

A thought strikes my mind, bang! As if I'd stepped out in front of the train. I grab a fistful of Kian's shirt sleeve.

'What about Tess!' I yell.

Tess is like my little sister. She lives in the slums with Skels who opted out of the system. They're called Eremites, Central gave them this name and, as far as I know, it means religious recluse. They don't worship the glory in the sky like other Skels, they worship the birds. They think The Day of the Bird was a warning. That the birds tried to cleanse the city, eradicating sinners who work for Central. Fearing civil war, Central banished all Skels who refused to conform to city law but instead of sending them into the desert to die, they allowed them to reside in the dump at the edge of the city, and after a beating from guards the Eremites decided the dump was a better option than death. Over time, the dump developed into a plastic slum, Eremites using anything they found as housing materials; though they consider themselves free, the slum dwellers are not completely out of Central control.

Life is hard for them and that's why I took Tess under my wing. She will worry when I don't turn up. Who else is there to take care of her? Bring her the extra food she needs?

'I'll keep an eye on little red.' Kian yells back, handing me my knapsack.

I shoulder it on and breathe out a momentary sigh of relief, then smooth down the front of my silky dress, wobbling to one side, not used to heels. My toes feel crowded, ankles insecure. Kian stares at the towering metal beast, as if the train won't stop if he doesn't. I study my best friend; his glowing brown skin, his shoulders relaxed. His body is his own and will never be anyone else's. For a moment, I envy him. He'll never need to do this, men don't – they can't. I don't let the injustice swallow me, I know men carry other burdens and Kian carries his well. He takes my hand and squeezes it gently.

'Are you ready?' He asks.

The train slows, gears grinding to a halt. I square my shoulders, my doll-like reflection stares back at me from the silver surface, I slump. *You can do this, Sky. Stop being such a baby.* A baby. I'm not ready to have a baby and I won't ever be. I take a deep breath and my breasts rise, pushed up like two round coconuts. The dress tightens, I breathe out, worried I might split a seam. Fingers laced with the person I trust most in the whole world, I squeeze Kian's rough hand back and whisper to him.

'I'll never be ready.'

The journey to Mr and Mrs Vable's apartment takes ten minutes, but it feels like seconds. The approaching view from my window is an illusion of utopia. Skyscrapers stretch into the clear, blue sky like glittering knives and, with every second click-clack down the track, the sun shines out from between the gaps in the silver and pokes me in the eyes with its pointy orange fingers. Behind us, my side of the city is a dark festering pit; even the sun tries to avoid it. Cube blocks are piled high like coal, no sense of order, no attention to detail. The streets are overrun with bone-tired Skels held together by a thread; along with the many crows, rats, and serpents. The city has an invisible line drawn down the middle and no one wants to live in my part, they all want to live with the fakers in their fakery.

I press my face up against the window, the glass warms my cheek. As the gleaming buildings get closer, the outlines on the spotless apartment windows become clear; the blinds are drawn. I can't see in, yet my mind sees them – those disgusting, self-indulgent hermits I'm about to meet.

I exhale and my breath fogs the glass. I peel my face away and lean over to touch the red cushioned seat beside me. Spongy, soft like a pillow. I yawn. I want to lie down, but I don't, instead I look over my shoulder. I'm somewhat surprised by how well maintained the train is. Windows streak-free, chrome polished so you can see your face in it, or in my case, someone else's face painted over mine.

Because Morbs don't use the train I expected it to be in disrepair. Why keep it nice for Skels? I decide it is probably because the train passes through the Morbihan side of town and needs to be in keeping with their high standards of cleanliness. Also, many guards use it and I'm told their training complex is something to behold. Central look after hosts and guards in a way they do not for the average Skel.

I twist my body around further so that I can see the very back of the carriage. It's empty. The only passengers are myself and my guard; a tall, black lamppost of a woman who was already on the train when I boarded. The guard stands over me, holding on to a silver pole with one hand. She doesn't look at me, she stands 'pole up her back' ridged, blank-faced, involuntarily swaying from side to side with the train's propulsion. There's a strange peacefulness in the motion of the train, like a mother rocking a child to sleep. I wish I'd known my mother, or my father for that matter. I remember the tenderness of my grandfather.

He always made me feel safe and loved. My eyelids droop, the Sky Train slows, my eyes close, shocked open seconds later when the great metal engine jolts to a stop.

When we disembark, the guard leads me down concrete steps. I struggle to keep up with her, she wears guard issue boots and doesn't give any regard to me toppling down the steps behind her in these silly heels. I step out on to the immaculate streets and the warm breeze sweeps past, bringing with it the smell of sweet flowers. It's like a dream. Lured by the comfort, stars shine in my eyes and my skin tingles. I catch myself. *Remember, Skyla, this is an illusion of happiness and comfort. Yes, the smell of flowers and the cleanness is nicer than the smell of dirt and decay but it can't induce happiness. Can it?*

As the guard strides and I totter through the quiet streets, Sky Train rattling away in the distance, I note that the Morbihan side of town isn't gated, guarded, or surrounded by a vector ring and it doesn't need to be. Morbs don't move around the streets like we do. The glittering pavements have hardly seen a footstep. Yet workers *must* tend to the streets, washing the windows and pruning the shrubs into works of art.

'Look at that one!' I say to the guard's back, my voice loud against the emptiness. I point to the shrub, she doesn't look round, 'It looks like a tall mushroom …' I tilt my head, 'Actually, don't look, it looks rude.'

The guard's head moves slightly to the left. Ha! Made her look. We turn the corner and the one mushroom turns into a row of tall mushrooms. To me, they look like giant, green penises growing out of the ground. Was that what they were going for? Oh hell, what if it's a freaky fertility garden; hosts on their knees, surrounded by dick shrubs, everyone chanting while the masters wash our hair with jizz!

I see someone, not a Skel, one of *them*. There's a tube tunnel beyond the cock shrubs. The guard has doubled back and is standing beside me, she pokes me in the ribs to get me moving again. I smack her hand away and her jaw clenches. Inside the tube, a Morb glides along in a hover-chair. Sunshine blinks across the glass and the memory of Showcase shudders through my mind.

Tubes run through this side of the city like dozens of see-through snakes, but on my side of the city there aren't many and I don't remember being able to see inside them. Maybe the tubes on our side are dirty? I succumb to the guard's prodding but move as slowly as possible. The Morb hovers slowly through the clear tunnel, disappearing every few seconds behind a shrub; it makes me think of a boa constrictor digesting a greedy rat that has eaten his body weight in bare-cupboard cake.

The guard shoves me towards a secure door.

'Hey!' I say and step away from her reach. 'Can't you speak?'

She says nothing, lips pressed firmly together as if glued shut, face set in stone. Do her facial muscles even work? In front of us is a solid-steel door. A secure door. A door I don't want to go through. A vision plays out in my mind, of me kicking off my heels, one flies off into a penis shrub and the other hits the guard in the face as I run for it. The idea dies when sunlight strikes the large blade in the guard's utility belt.

In front of me, the guard spreads her long fingers and presses her palm to the pad beside the door. I stare at her hand, wondering if her skin will melt. I know it won't but part of me wants it to – wills it to. An incorrect hand-map means unauthorised personnel. Secure doors can only be opened by a guard. They aren't locked, but if I tried to open one, the skin on my palm would definitely be melted ... probably. Actually, I don't know if the melting part is true or made up to scare us. To my knowledge, no Skel has ever touched a secure door. There isn't anyone crazy enough to test that theory. Am I crazy enough? I get a strong urge to test the theory; *go on, Skyla, shove the guard out of the way and touch the pad*. It's a strange sensation, that nagging urge to do something insane; jump from the sky track, or kiss an attractive stranger, or punch Delia Gold in her blotchy orange face.

Before my grandfather died, the palm-pads worked on every door; only our hand-map could open the door to our cube and there was no melting of the skin if you tried to open someone else's door, it just wouldn't unlock. Central disabled the locking mechanisms on most buildings, most 'unimportant' buildings.

The secure door swishes open, disappears into the wall cavity and the guard steps over the threshold. On the other side of the door is a holding chamber, the walls are silver, like the inside of a tin. I'm ordered to sanitise my hands with a harsh chemical gel. It burns. I wince when it almost peels off a layer of skin. I may as well have touched the palm-pad.

A tall, gangly woman checks my knapsack, while a short weasel of a man, in a surgical face mask, traces a gloved hand over and around my body. My guess is he's scanning for weapons or drugs. He lingers on my breasts for longer than I'm comfortable with. My eyes narrow and he draws back his hand sharply, as if my cold stare violated him! He waves us on, signalling we're cleared to enter. The second door opens and I immediately shiver. The air-conditioning is up high. My silk dress is inadequate for the cool temperature but I dare not ask for warmer clothes. I must keep up the polite pretence, keep my mouth shut and do as I'm told. I don't want a beating from the guard. A bruised and bloodied host would not be the guard's fault, it would be mine and, however unfair, turning up in that kind of a state would probably result in being beaten some more.

The chilly corridor is made colder by its grey walls, sucking warmth from every corner and the strong smell of disinfectant stings the inside my nostrils as I breathe through my nose. I clip-clop down the marble stretch after the guard, past doors and stairwells and shafts. My heels want to go in their own direction. I struggle to stay upright. I'm going to break my bloody neck in a minute.

'Is it much further?' I ask the guard, on behalf of my complaining feet.

The guard's eyebrows knit into a V and this time she growls at me. I don't speak again.

I've been invited to stay at the Vable's family home, two weeks before implantation. I use the word 'invited' loosely. I was told to pack and move. You cannot be a host and live outside the complex; full control over your food, health, and who you interact with must be exercised at all times.

The silent guard stops abruptly. I stagger sideways to stop myself from colliding with her, I manage to fall into the door rather than my escort, who scowls at me. The guard raps on door twelve with her large fist. Without a word – she hasn't said a word since I met her on the train, unless you count the growl – she marches off back down the corridor and I'm left at the mercy of my new family. I press my ear to the door and a faint hum grows louder the longer I listen. The humming gets louder and louder, blood thumps in my ears. Inhale, exhale, inhale ... the door slides open. I flinch, then remember to stand tall, hands by my sides. I quietly exhale.

Chapter Four

Hover-Chairs of Blubber

'Oh, my goodness, don't you look a doll!' shrieks the tripled-chinned face, framed by a blond bob. My first thought; wig on a giant pig. I can only assume this is Mistress Vable. 'Hello, Ms Skyla. Now, how are you feeling on this very important day?'

I weave my short fingers into my forcibly curled hair and try on a fake smile, glad she didn't use my first name.

'I'm fine,' I say.

The three layers of face tilt upwards and she glares at me through one sunken blue eye and one lens. The lens blinks separately to the natural eye, it reminds me of automatic double-doors opening and closing. My captor is exactly as I imagined she would be: a beanbag body draped in sunset coloured silk; all head, no neck. The host mother's uneven painted eyebrows are raised expectantly, her thin lips turn down at the corners. It's then I remember.

'I'm fine, thank you, Mistress Vable,' I say, quickly.

I hate myself.

'Much better,' she says, in a sickly-sweet contralto. 'You may be able to get away with ignoring courtesy when working in that awful factory, my dear,' she pauses and takes a few breaths, her large frame deflating and inflating, as if someone has a device in her back and is hand-pumping air into her. 'But here,' her voice rattles out, 'common courtesy is to be upheld at all times.'

The hover-chair carrying the host mother turns and glides away from me, air holding it inches from the ground. You wouldn't think something as light as air could hold the weight of someone as heavy as Mistress Vable. The mechanics and scientists are the true heart of our society, without them the Morbs would die. *The Morbs would die.* The thought pushes a broad smile to my lips. Am I really that cruel? So twisted that I wish death on people? I am. I imagine myself plunging a knife into the soft skin where her neck should be. I'll take her life like she's taken mine. Die, bitch, die!

'Come along, my dear.'

Inside the apartment is rich with extravagance, right from the front door. On either side of the hallway, paintings in gilt frames take up every inch of wall space, almost as far as my feet, although I can't imagine the Morbs can see anything beneath their hover-chairs, even at a distance. I nudge the painting at ankle height with the tip of my high-heel. How useless. Most of the paintings are abstract, block colours of randomness. Some are portraits of real life, not real life as I know it, rather the fakery of Morbihan life.

'Master Vable and I like you very much,' says the host mother.

Her hover-chair hums as it glides further away from me.

'You do?' I say before I can stop myself. 'I mean, thank you,' I whisper like a child who has lost her voice.

'We do! That piece of theatre you performed at Showcase was most inspired,' she rasps, 'for a Skel.'

I bite my lip. Dammit! That was meant to put Morbs off, not inspire them! I reluctantly follow the hover-chair into what must be the lounge. I say 'must be' because there isn't any defining furniture. Sharp lines, golden walls, not a smudge, not a smear, more paintings, jewel-encrusted frames, it's like the inside of a treasure chest, not that I've seen the inside of a treasure chest but grandfather used to tell stories of pirates and this apartment is ripe for a plunder. It's the vision screen which gives the room away, silent as the stone it's mounted on. They have one at City Hall but I've never seen it working. Mistress Vable takes a deep breath and motions to a couple of small stools next to the only other piece of furniture in the room, a high oval table which sprouts out of the marble floor like a flower. I carefully tuck my dress underneath me and sit down, discreetly rubbing my arms, my skin so cold I'm starting to get goosebumps.

'The rest of the family will be along momentarily,' she says, jowls wobbling.

The sound of her artificial organs pumping blood and oxygen around her huge body, reminds me of a fruit fly buzzing high up in an olive tree. I nod politely but continue to stare at the screen on the wall, wondering if it will come to life.

'Would you like to watch something?' she asks me, psychotic smile smeared across her face, round cheeks rising over her eyes.

I nod and she taps the arm of her chair. Startled by the booming voices echoing around the room, I almost slip off the stool; the mistress lowers the volume and I push my backside back up onto the seat. The words: 'Gale One News' are cast over the top right-hand corner of the screen and a High-Host is sitting in an armchair across from a regal and insane-looking Morb in a hover-chair. The projection plays with my eyes, the background flat yet the two people seem as if they're in the room with me. I know they're not, but still, I reach out to touch them. My hand falls through the air, distorting the 3D image. I shuffle forwards on my stool, enough that my head is level with the projected Morb. Amazing. It's as if they're sitting at the table with me, but what's more amazing is the fact that a former Skel and a Morb are chatting like old friends. Like equals.

'I'll take your bag to your room,' Mistress Vable says. I try to protest (no doubt she will snoop through my bag) but I can't tear my eyes from the spectacle in front of me.

The chair hums as Mistress Vable hovers from the room. I study the projection of the Skel. It's Delia Gold; red trouser suit, red lips, red nails, gold jewellery, mountain of magenta hair. There's no mistaking her. When the male Morb on the right speaks, I find out from a caption scrolling across the bottom of the projection that his name is Hatti Bloomfield and he is a professor of science and technology. His name is strangely fitting, for he wears a tall rainbow-flowered top hat on his head. He also wears peculiar lenses that have been made to look like real eyes, which is discernibly creepy, his fake eyes look as if they're about to pop out of his head, while his trimmed beard has been sprayed with tiny, glittering stars. The conversation between Delia and Hatti includes advances in science and mechanics, research into Morbihan health and crime statistics, or so it says on the right-hand side of the screen, along with the option to choose each topic by pressing the assigned colour on the hover-chair control panel.

'There is growing concern over the possibility of street gangs and drug dealers spilling into our side of the city.'

The pompous Hatti talks with a plum in his mouth.

'These criminals must be punished. We can no longer rely on Mutil to clean up the streets. My sources tell me a task force will be assigned to bring in these lawbreakers and serve them justice and not a moment too soon, if you ask me.'

My fists clench at his words, anger boiling my blood. *You Morbs made the streets dirty with crime, you and Central. You divided the city. You are responsible for the creation of Mutil, Slum Lords, Gangs, Glory Runners, and Glo-Girls! The Morbihan cannot survive without Skels, Central would never function without us either but do they treat us well? If there's a rise in street crime, it's your fault! Surely you idiots know that!* It takes all my mental strength to stop my voice from firing at the screen. If they do know, they're playing dumb because Delia continues to prattle on about the need for more control over the wild races; the city rats and the savages. There must be tighter control on these 'degenerates', she says. *Race traitor!*

My gaze is drawn to a servant who skulks across the room, head down. She does not speak. Like the guard, her brown lips are sealed with imaginary glue. My eyes follow the girl's movements. She snatches a look at me, dark eyes stabbing me with jealousy. She is as thin as I am and dressed in a black maid's uniform, complete with bowler hat, which looks to have been forced down on her head, a bush of tight curls bunched up beneath it. Her bony hips are covered by a long pinny but she cannot hide the sharp lines of her clavicle. Morbs are both delighted and disgusted by us. To them, our brown skin is beautiful but we are essentially ugly. Everything about us screams poverty: our dry sun-damaged hair, our chipped teeth and protruding bones. Workers reek of poverty and poverty is ugly in the eyes of a Morb.

The maid places a tray of food on the table and backs out of the room. I reach for a tub and lift the corner of the nearest lid, inside is a brownish green mince. The same gloop we make at the factory. Revolting. I can't believe they eat this stuff. I turn my attention back to the vision screen and Delia.

'Now, I must ask you about a sensitive subject, this rumoured "cure". Is it true a scientist, who remains anonymous for legal reasons, has created a miracle serum that he claims will halt the genetic weight gain?'

Delia leans forward to give Hatti her undivided attention. I do the same, my eyes transfixed on Hatti's huge painted lips.

'I'm sorry to disappoint but the rumoured "cure" is just that, a rumour. I'm told the scientist in question was experimenting on a cloned rat. At first it seemed to be losing weight but then it died. Not a cure, I'm afraid. Serum 574 turned out to be deadly and every batch has been destroyed.'

I shiver, as if the tip of a feather has been stroked down my spine. I can't quite believe what I'm hearing. A scientist was working on a cure for the Morbihan condition. Working on a serum to stop their obesity? Delia's chirpy voice interrupts my train of thought.

'Quite ... thank you for clearing that up ...'

Mistress Vable hovers in front of the screen, distorting the projection and blocking my view. Not thinking, I lean to one side to look round the enormous hover-chair. She shifts her chair into my line of sight and smiles smugly, silencing the voices coming from behind her with a push of a button.

'That's enough of that.'

I nod, but really, I want to spit in her face. I was watching that!

'You may begin. We can't have you wasting away.' She lifts her hand in an open palm gesture towards the tray. I try not to look horrified. I hope she doesn't expect me to eat that slop. 'It's okay, you don't have to wait; hosts often eat before their masters.'

I reach out, hand shaking and it's then I notice a lone tub labelled 'Host'. I snatch up the tub and rip off the lid. Fruit salad. Thank the Dark Angel. The sweet smell is intoxicating. I plunge the spoon in deep, ready to shovel the fruit into my mouth … she's watching me. I delicately lift a helping of grapefruit, strawberries, and orange segments to my lips, push the spoon through them and then chew politely with my mouth closed. The tart flavours dance across my tongue. I eat slowly, trying not to gobble. I don't want to slop berries down the front of my pretty pink dress. Berry stains would surely ruin it, which would be an awful shame. Not.

I scoop every last piece of fruit from the tub and replace it on the tray. My bony backside aches. I fidget, unable to get comfortable on the hard stool. I'm not used to sitting for so long, unlike the Morbs who are bound to their hover-chairs.

'Good afternoon, Ms Skyla.'

A husky voice that must belong to Master Vable drifts through the lounge, followed by the faint hum of his hover-chair. Out of the corner of my eye I see Master Vable's thick finger press a button upon his chair and the blinds slowly start to open, allowing orange sun to tiger-stripe the marble floor.

I slide gracefully off my stool, (as gracefully as I can) and totter, clumsy on my high-heels towards Master Vable, who has stationed his hover-chair in front of the huge window, which is actually an entire wall of glass. The blinds slowly fold away, giving me full access to the magnificent view. The sun drops a copper blanket over the mountain range and brushes the silver Morb apartments with diamonds.

I can see my block. I mean, the block I used to live in, in my one-person box. The mass of dark buildings seems far away. The blocks of cubes are half the size of the sleek Morb skyscrapers and all the buildings in the city are dwarfed by The Spiral, the glory of Gale City, as Central call it. The glass ball atop a long silver pole, sparkles like the most ostentatious jewel in the crown but I've heard the stories, I know its secrets. On the outside, it shines like a glorious ripe fruit but on the inside, it's a maggot infested apple, rotten to the core. The Spiral is filled with selfish people making selfish decisions. I find it laughable that they call the Central nerve centre the 'glory' of Gale City, they mean it as something divine but I think of it as the highly addictive drug, a destroyer of lives. I hear a rattling back breath beside me. I forgot to speak when spoken to. I smooth down my dress and side-step closer to the hover-chair.

'Nice to meet you, Master Vable,' I say sweetly, and I kind of mean it.

Strangely, I instantly warm to the master's kind face. He smiles at me and deep lines draw down his drooping cheeks. I turn back to the view and silently stare through the glass, tracing the path of the city wall with my eyes. I feel his dark-blue lenses trace my profile. I glance sideways again but Master Vable's huge head faces the window.

'Do you know why we have the wall, Skyla?' Master Vable asks.

I flinch at being asked a question. I don't like questions when I'm likely to give a non-Morbihan answer, which is probably wrong. I think for a moment and then look up into his mechanical eyes. Unlike the host mother's, his eyes are comforting, even though they're metal lenses; they're somehow trustworthy. The master's weathered face hints that he is much older than his link, Mistress Vable. Morb faces don't age quickly, lines and wrinkles only start to form around the age of sixty. Skels age at different rates and Mutil always look like they have one foot in the grave. I clear my throat.

'To keep us from leaving ... master?' I answer.

'To keep us safe,' he replies.

'Safe from what?' I ask. 'Sand?'

I cover my mouth with my hand. Crap! I hope he doesn't take offence at the sarcasm in my voice.

'Safe from ourselves,' he rasps, unfazed by my lack of manners. He draws in a rattling breath. 'Many Skels, and even young

Morbihan, have been struck with the desire to scale the wall. It is folly, not freedom. Even those who are permitted to explore for scientific research,' he draws another breath, 'who are carefully instructed, sometimes don't come back.'

'Some people don't want to come back.' I say, without thinking.

'Suicide is never a solution.' He says, shutters blinking at me.

Maybe not for you, I think, other people's lives are hard, their minds tortured, how can a Morb relate to that? He can't. Look at him, look how fat he is. He'll never know starvation, that stomach pain when the body tries to eat itself. The fear of Runners and gangs breaking in at night and stealing what little you have. The fear of being raped or killed. Sleeping with one hand under the pillow, grasping a knife. Master Vable goes back to staring out of the window in silence. I try to speak, my mind and mouth struggling to form words, words that won't get me into trouble, that is.

'Master, I …'

'The system can work for you too, Skyla.'

Oh no, he senses I don't want to be here. Even though life as a Skel is no picnic, I think he can tell I don't want to live here; dressed like this, preparing to be impregnated, or rather, have his sperm and her eggs mixed together in some lab then inserted into my womb. Why don't they invent an artificial incubator? They can invent artificial organs but not a womb. I stare at my master's bulbous head, neck hidden under a mound of folds. Does he truly believe the system can work for me? I'd like to think I'm here because the desert would kill me and that I'm better off being a host, but the system doesn't work and Morbs are everything I hate and if Master Vable believes the lies on the vision screen, then I have no business believing a word he says.

Our moment alone is broken by voices coming from the hallway. The light hum of multiple hover-chairs is accompanied by something I did not expect; footsteps.

'Bunce, you know we haven't any facilities for you h-here,' Mistress Vable stammers. 'Did you not go before you left home?'

'I did but I have to go again, can't I use the staff toilet?' says a young male voice, his tone notably higher than the others.

'Certainly not! You will go all the way home and come back again,' shouts a stern, decrepit old Morb, as her chair glides into the room. Her face is heavily made-up, like an oversized, retired Glo-Girl; large painted lips taking up most of her face, her body sparkle-covered – a jiggling pudding in a hovering bowl. She's followed by Mistress Vable and a stocky young man with sandy blond hair. Behind him, an elderly male hovers through the wide doorway, his head lolling to one side. He looks dead. His large chest rises and falls, he's asleep. How can he be sleeping? He'll crash his hover-chair.

'Not wanting to sound crude, Mother, but I can't hold it that long,' says the young, upwardly mobile Morb. He faces Mistress Vable, but his eyes settle on me. 'Anyway, why haven't you installed a toilet for the baby yet?'

'Because we don't need one yet!' Roars Mistress Vable. 'Honestly, it's so disgusting and unhygienic. I'm putting it off as long as possible. I don't know why we can't hook them up to chairs as soon as they're old enough, better still, baby chairs, toilet training is such a waste of time.'

'Learning to crawl and walk is a big part of brain development.' Bunce says, crossing his arms like a head boy schooling his class mates.

'Our brains develop significantly through puberty, little brother,' Mistress Vable hisses, 'we are not like Skels and we need not develop the same way,' sharp intake of breath, 'that is why we do not have the urge to make babies, all our biological urges are channelled into achievement and advancement.

Bunce opens his mouth, 'But ...'

Bunce's makeup-slavered mother talks over him. 'We grow our brains, not babies, that is best left to the brainless ...'

'Ahem.'

Master Vable clears his throat and the family immediately stop bickering. I stand tall, and clasp my hands together in front of me like a good dolly.

'Bunce …' says Master Vable softly. 'Please show our lovely host where the servant toilet is. You can use it just this once.'

The older Morb opens her big fish lips to protest but Master Vable raises his hand, the skin around his arm hanging like limp lettuce.

'Just this once,' he repeats. 'Bunce will have no need for it soon enough.'

'Fine,' huffs Mistress Vable, beckoning me with her ring-laden fingers.

I move at once. She takes my bony hand; her plump fingers feel like the cuts of meat I throw into the grinder, except they're warm.

'Bunce will show you to the …' she stops and swallows, as if mouldy bread is stuck in her throat, '… staff facilities. Do hurry back, my little brother has a tendency to flounder.'

I smile sweetly, nod, and gently pull my fingers from her porky hand. I sicken myself. Why am I doing this? I should slash the wires hooking the foul beast up to her life support and run for my freedom. I don't know why I don't. I've stabbed people worthier of life than this woman. Maybe I do what she says because deep down, even though I'm not scared to die, I actually want to keep on living or maybe it's simply because I don't have my knife. It was confiscated by the dresser before she violated me with glitter and silk.

The young Morb called Bunce locks me with a laser stare, like I'm a wild animal loose in his sister's lounge. His eyes haven't moved from me since he stepped into the room; his gaze penetrating and curious. Maybe he's mirroring my expression. I've never seen a young Morbihan before. Apart from the freakishly pale skin, he looks almost normal.

He moves towards the door without saying a word. I follow. Outside the apartment, Bunce stops and stares at me expectantly. I raise my eyebrows. He doesn't move. Does he need winding up or something? Mechanical parts already inserted? After a minute of uncomfortable silence, I risk speaking.

'You lead the way.'

Without a word, he starts off down the corridor. We don't go far before I see a blue door with STAFF written on it in bold, black lettering. Instead of going through the door, Bunce leans against the wall beside it, takes a wrapped stick from his pocket and tears away the packaging. It looks like some sort of compressed meat. I recognise it. We make them in the factory.

I wait and watch while he chomps on the meat stick. I cross my arms, growing impatient. Why isn't he going in? Why am I standing here like an idiot watching him eat? The noise of his chewing and swallowing echoes around the empty corridor. Smack, smack, smack go his pink lips. I uncross my arms and point to the door.

'Are you going in?'

'No,' he says, casually.

I wait a few seconds. Pondering how to respond, I don't want him running back to tell his sister and brother-in-link how the host was rude to him.

'Then what are we doing here?' I say, struggling to repress the irritation in my voice.

'I didn't want to sit there listening to them jabber on about useless junk,' Bunce says. His hand back at his chubby face, he rips another mouthful from the stick. He chews and swallows. 'To be honest, my brother-in-link looked rather upset that I didn't invite him to escape with us.'

My shoulders relax, I almost feel grateful he got me out of there. The pressure to behave myself was getting a bit much. I take a step closer to the wall and lean back beside him. Not too close, I don't want any part of his body touching mine.

'I feel like I should introduce myself or something,' I say, 'but you already know my name, right?'

Bunce looks at me and smiles. A nervous grin. He switches the meat stick to his left hand and reaches out with his right.

'It's a pleasure to finally meet you, Ms Skyla.'

When I don't respond, he takes my hand in his, grips firmly and shakes. How odd. At first, I want to snatch back my hand in disgust, the Dark Angel only knows where his hand has been, meat products aren't the half of it. I stop myself from recoiling. His touch is weird, foreign. The Morb's skin is smooth, soft like a baby's. On impulse, I bring my other hand up and hold his plump wrist, I run my fingers across his silky skin, up his arm. He flinches and I release his hand, aware that what I did was probably stepping over a line.

'Sorry, I didn't mean to …'

'It's fine,' he says, smiling, 'I must seem pretty strange to you.'

I laugh.

'Yeah, well … this whole place is pretty strange to me.'

I look into his pale round face. No scars, no bruises; behind his watery, blue eyes I see no sign of mental laceration. Has he lived his childhood in a protective bubble? I don't imagine he has ever climbed a tree, wrestled a friend, or run a race. I want to touch his cheek, his hair; pull at him, poke at him. I knew young Morbs existed, but seeing one in the flesh is surreal. I'm guessing he's about my age but he's so unlike me, it's like we're from different planets. I always thought I'd feel resentment towards someone like Bunce but I don't. Coming face to face with a Central would be different. I'd definitely feel anger. Anger that they put me in here.

'So, Bunce,' I say. 'Is it ok to call you that? Or is there some term used to address the brother of my mistress?'

'Bunce is fine.' He smiles.

I'm almost amused at what I'm about to imply.

'Isn't lying breaking some Morbihan code of conduct?' I ask.

'Yes.' he says, through a mouth full of jerky.

'Why'd you lie?' I ask. 'Morbihan don't often lie, do they?'

'Truth-stretching is not lying,' he says, ripping another chunk of dried meat from the bar.

'Truth-stretching, huh?'

I smile. Then I remember I hate Morbs. The smile melts from my lips. I want to hate them all. I should. I did an hour ago; greedy, insular, metal race. Why do I feel warmth from Bunce? *Don't let your guard down, Sky. Never trust a Morb.*

Chapter Five

Be a Good Dolly

The weeks before implantation is a time for the host to get used to their new surroundings and integrate into the Morbihan way of life – so we are told. From what I've experienced this is not the case. I think it's a test. To see if the chosen host will be suitable or whether the host family feel they need to change up.

I'm three days into my 'stay' with the Vables, and even though I'm not paying much attention to the High-Host co-ordinator, who chatters on about the most boring shit, I did notice one of the girls sitting behind me has changed her face.

The tall, twenty-something who always wore a determined expression is now a short, twinkly-eyed girl in her mid-twenties, wearing a painted-on smile. If one dolly doesn't play nice then she is easily replaced by another, more obedient dolly.

I slip into daydreams of being outside, breathing, if not fresh, natural unfiltered air. With my pencil, I twirl a blond ringlet round and round until it's caught and I have to rip it free. I play with the lock of forcibly curled hair and think of ways I can free myself. What would it take to be replaced?

'Ms Skyla, are you listening?'

I don't look up at the co-ordinator. I haven't even bothered to learn her name. I really don't care. I'm bored out of my skull.

'I wasn't, but I am now,' I say, picking at a blemish in the wooden desk.

Gasps rush like wind around me. The High-Host walks towards me, heels clicking confidently against the polished floor; slowly, steadily, as if she's been wearing heels from the moment she could walk. She places her blotchy hands on my desk and leans forward until her face is level with mine and I'm forced to meet her gaze.

'Why weren't you listening?' she asks, sternly.

I don't shy away red-face and ashamed, like other girls would. I stare back at her, taking in every inch of her peculiar face. It's as if her original skin melted off and she's glued synthetic skin over the top. I cross my arms.

'To be honest, this all seems a bit pointless ...' the fine hairs on my arms prickle with the shear horror emitted from the other hosts, the air filling up with their discomfort at what I'm saying, but the co-ordinator's expression doesn't twitch, she waits, blank-faced for me to finish, '... are we actually going to learn about birthing the baby or how to take care of it? Do we need to prepare our bodies before they're ripped apart by the new life?'

The High-Host draws herself up to full height and clears her throat.

'To answer your first question, Ms Skyla,' she slinks around my desk, trailing her long fingernails across the corners of it, 'birthing is natural. Your body knows what to do. Second, you won't be taking care of *it*,' she drops that last word like a rock, 'your mistress and master will, you will feed and clean the baby, and third,' her eyes smile wickedly, 'you will be examined.'

'Examined?' I say, alarmed.

'Enough!' she yells and slams her hands down on my desk. I flinch. 'It is not your place to question our methods,' she glares around the room, addressing all of us, 'understand?'

The High-Host's face is as red as the setting sun, the rage drains from her skin when a chorus of 'yes co-ordinator' ripples around the room.

'Right then, being a host requires many skills, we are not merely incubators ...'

I lower my eyes and keep my head down, concerned about that word 'examined.' It could mean anything. Finger resting on the touchpad, I swipe the screen until I reach page seven, the page I was meant to be studying. Being educated by family members means many Skels only have the most basic reading and writing skills. My grandfather was a great teacher but I wonder how many girls in this room can read? The words are simple enough; it's a lot like a comic, with speech bubbles and simplistic sentences.

Page seven depicts a hover-chair bound mistress smiling at an equally smiley pregnant-bellied host. As speech bubbles appear, the mistress touches the host's ball-shaped belly affectionately. I don't want my mistress touching me like that. Yuck! The animated host seems familiar; braided hair, sharp blue eyes. She looks like Andia, who didn't get picked. I think of her back at the factory, as miserable there as I am here. What I wouldn't give to trade places. I didn't think much of my life as a factory worker, but this is so much worse. I wonder who's taken my place at the grinder? What's happened to my cube? Today would have been my recoup day. I bet Kian is at the market. I try not to let the bitterness turn down the corners of my mouth. I have to at least try and blend in.

The classroom buzzes with excitement as hosts point 'interesting' things out to each other as they read. No one talks to me. I begin to wish I was like the others, happy to be here, happy in my pretty dress and extreme makeup. My eyes wander from the touchpad and I spy a hover-chair-shaped shadow moving past the frosted glass doors at the front of the classroom. A fantasy forms in my head. I envision secretly packing a hover-chair with explosives and blowing the complex to smithereens. I smile to myself.

I'm snapped out of my fantasy by the heavy clip-clop of the co-ordinator's heels stomping towards me. She towers over my desk like she is about to breathe fire.

'Still not concentrating, I see.'

'I was, I ...' I stumble over my words.

She grips my arm and yanks me up out of my seat, and to my horror, pulls up the back of my dress, exposing my knickers to the class then whips the back of my legs with a cane. I cry out with the third stinging strike; she drops my dress and stalks away.

I hold the pain with both hands, my eyes water but I don't let tears fall, I'll not give her the satisfaction of seeing me cry.

'Sit!' She orders.

I gingerly lower myself onto the chair, the back of my thighs throb against the hard surface and the classroom is deathly quiet, as if the other hosts died of shock.

'Now, girls,' the High-Host says enthusiastically, 'I want you to practise polite conversation with each other, as if you are talking to your mistress or master. There are some sample conversation starters at the back of the handbook, but only use them if you need help to get going. Right, everyone, find a partner.'

There's a scraping of chairs. I don't think I can stand, the pain is excruciating. I look to the cane in the co-ordinator's hand, sure it has spikes on it. I find I don't have to get up, for the grinning new girl has moved her chair opposite me. Oh joy.

'I'm Ara,' she says, straightening the glitter bow at her crown.

'Skyla.' I mutter in reply.

She looks like she'll burst if we don't start the role-play this second. I roll my eyes. The High-Host claps her hands.

'Begin!'

The round ceiling light in the waiting area is brighter than the sun, the walls are orange and the chairs are too close together, so close that my bare arm is touching that of the girls either side of me, my skin sticking to their skin. Every so often I peel my arm from each of the girls next to me, and every so often the girl to my left scowls at me for daring to move. There are no windows or ventilation. The waiting room is a hot box. This part of the complex doesn't involve Morbihan, I guess they don't feel there's any need to keep it cool for the staff.

The door to my right swishes open and Ara reappears in a surgical gown, frilly pink dress draped over her arms which are wrapped tight around her body, a small drawstring bag dangles from her wrist. She was called by the High-Host doctor half an hour ago. She limps back to her seat, like a wounded animal, red-faced, puffy eyes. Hell, what did they do to her?

'Ms Skyla.'

My body stiffens. The doctor looks around expectantly at the sea of dollies in bright dresses until I finally stand.

'Come through.' He smiles.

I side-step past the seated hosts, the hem of my dress brushing their knees and as I approach the doctor, a bad feeling crawls over my skin. His smile is predatory and his beady, bespectacled eyes undress me, as if his glasses have the power to see through clothes. Did he just lick his lips?

'Right this way.' He puts his hand on the small of my back and guides me through the door, his creepy long fingers send a shiver through my bones.

The doctor's office is as expected; Posters on the wall about pregnancy, one showing the inside of a pregnant woman, a cluttered desk, drawers of supplies, an examination table and a plastic chair. I don't like this room.

'Right,' the doctor says, swishing his white coat-tail behind him and settling at his desk, 'Ms Skyla, have you ever been examined before, at the Skel hospital or by a healer?'

I slowly shake my head.

'Good,' he says, 'now, the host examinations are a little intrusive and you may endure some discomfort but it's to make sure you're fit to carry a baby, and you want to please your master and mistress, now don't you?'

I nod slowly.

'Today, we're going to do an external and internal examination, to make sure your body is in top condition, okay?'

Internal? Eyes wide, body ridged with apprehension, I can't even bring myself to move my head. It's not okay! None of this is okay! But I can't answer with that, can I?

'I've got your notes here.' He consults a touchpad. 'From the information Chester has gathered, you're in pretty good shape, let's see if we can't get you a 100% pass mark today, hmm. Take off your dress.'

He swivels on his chair and starts scribbling on the touchpad with a jotter.

'What?' I say, in a small voice.

'Your dress,' he says without looking up at me, 'remove it.'

I search the room.

'Do I get a gown to put on?' I ask timidly.

'Once we're done.' He says, yanking open one desk drawer after another and rummaging around, 'Remove your underwear as well, then leave your clothes on the chair and stand in front of the bed.'

Hands shaking, I slip off my heels one at a time and place them under the plastic chair. I unzip and shimmy out of my shiny mauve dress and drape it over the chair so as not to crinkle it. I then reluctantly unclip and pull off my bra before I pull down and wriggle out of my knickers. I place them on the chair with my dress and stand with my hands clasped in front of my womanhood, head down.

The clop of the doctor's footsteps is loud against the silence. His polished, black shoes appear opposite my bare feet.

'I'm going to start with the external, nothing to worry about.'

I can't look at him, he's about ten years older than me and although he hasn't tried to bleach his skin, he still has that strange *fed* look about him, the weird features Skels acquire once they've lived in luxury with the Morbihan for a certain number of years.

'Stand with your legs apart, hands by your sides,' he says softly, 'I'm going to rotate your hips, they're not a particularly good width for child bearing but let's just see ...'

Cold hands grab a hold of my bony waist and the doctor starts to manipulate my hips, rotating them round like a Glo-Girl would, seductively dancing for business. He drops to his knees; his face is in line with my vagina. To take my mind of this invasion of privacy, I scan a poster on the wall but as soon as I start reading in my head, the doctor is upright and talking.

'You're doing very well, Ms Skyla,' he smiles, a greedy smile, he loves his job, 'now I'm going to check your breasts for any abnormalities.'

I instinctively lean away from him.

'Not to worry, it won't hurt,' he says, sweeping my hair, (which fell forwards during the 'hip testing') behind my back, his fingers dust my shoulder and my stomach turns. I don't want his creepy hands on me. I take a deep breath. It will be over soon enough.

The doctor rubs his hands together, in delight or to warm them up, who knows, and then gently cups both my breasts. I stare back at the poster while he gropes me. Hands squeezing; thumbs rubbing over my nipples. He steps back and leans in, his face too close to my chest, his hot breath shushing onto my skin.

He wants to fuck me, I can feel it. He wants to bend me over and shove his cock into me. If he does that, I'll break his neck. It's not the way I want to escape this place but it's a choice and, with little else in the way of options, I'm not afraid to make that final decision. His lips are almost touching my nipples. What's he going to do next? Suck them to see if they'll be adequate enough for a baby to latch? He drops my breasts and stands.

'Half way there.' My shoulders relax, relieved, he walks over to the drawer and pulls out a clear box, he pushes his fingers around in it as he walks back over to me, then pulls out something clear, 'I'm just going to fit you for suction cups, they're designed to get your nipples ready for feeding the baby and I'll also give you a buffer.'

Suction cups and a buffer?

He places a plastic cone over my right nipple and then pulls it away quickly. Takes out another size, holds my breast in one hand and pushes a smaller cup over my nipple.

'Size 3B,' he mutters to himself as he walks back over to his desk, 'lie down on the bed, if you will, Ms Skyla.'

I hoist my naked body up onto the bed and lie down, again I clasp my hands over my modesty. I've never felt so humiliated and violated in my life but I'm almost through it. To stand any chance of getting out of the Morb complex, I must play the game.

The doctor crosses the room again and places a small drawstring bag, I assume it has the cups and buffer inside, on the chair with my clothes. He then goes back to his desk, sits on his swivel chair and rolls himself and the drawers over to the bedside. He slaps on some white surgical gloves.

'Now, this might be uncomfortable, but the more you relax, the less it will hurt, okay.'

'Okay.' I nod and take a deep breath.

He takes out an instrument from the bottom drawer, a long silver rod, round at the top like a bullet. I gulp. He pushes a button at its base and five prongs spring from the tip. No fucking way! I try to slide of the bed. Pre-empting this, the doctor grabs the top of my arm.

'Ms Skyla!' he says sternly, 'do you know what the punishment is for not having the internal?'

I sigh and swing my legs back onto the bed. If there is a punishment for not taking the punishment the doctor is about to give out using that silver torture device, you can bet it will be something much worse.

'Now, bring your knees up and then drop your legs so your knees are facing outwards, like a frog's legs,' he says, dipping his gloved fingers into a pot on the top of the drawers. He scoops out some clear jelly and slathers the pole with it. I do as he says, legs open, knees bent, soles of my feet touching each other.

He pushes off with his legs and the swivel chair takes him to the end of the bed. He stands and leans forward. I close my eyes and grimace at the feeling between my legs as two slimy, gloved fingers are inserted into me. He pushes them in and out four times, obviously trying to stimulate my body so he can guide that thing inside me with ease. I do my best to think about something else, not to concentrate on what he's doing down that end but it's useless, he pushes the thick metal into me, further and further, I start to relax, it doesn't hurt.

He stops, waits. Click … I scream in agony and grip the sides of the bed, it's all I can do not to kick the fucker in the face. I start to sob, the pain is like nothing I've ever felt, as if he shot me up the vagina with a harpoon. I cringe at the sloping sound of the lube-slathered rod being removed, I don't feel it come out because all I can feel is the throbbing pain.

'All done,' he says, in a chirpy voice.

I roll over onto my side and bring my legs up into the foetal position and hold my stomach. Fuck this shit. I'm getting out of here.

Chapter Six

The Life of a Host

Day Eight. Arms crossed, I lean on the ledge and stare out of my bedroom window. The black silhouette of the city leans against the dark sky. Moon absent, three lonely stars aren't enough to light up the night. There's a faint glow in the distance, I can't imagine what it is, the slums, maybe, but they wouldn't have power, would they? A lot can change in eight days, I wonder what I've missed. I sense movement. I can't quite see it, yet I know it's the drones, whizzing about the sky, delivering parts, parcels, and protocols to Skels around the city. Skels who aren't even awake yet.

Every day my motivator wakes me before sunrise, I haul myself out of a mountain of duvet and start the ritual. Today, I struggled to get out of bed, still tender from what they did to me. I managed the shower; showering is the only part of the routine I enjoy – hot water running over my back – it's the one and only thing I'll miss when I leave here. It would have been easier to scrub the meat stench out of my hair and skin if I'd had access to showers, instead of having to wash at the kitchen sink or in a filthy bathing block.

The hygiene routine, like everything in Morbihan life, is excessive. I dread chemical scrub the most. I can only liken the blistering pain to sunburn. It's to stop blemishes and unwanted hair growth, it holds back imperfections. Flays the skin off along with them, more like. Who knows what it's doing to my skin.

I head to the basin and reluctantly pick up the tube marked 'facial scrub' and squeeze a capful onto my fingers. It instantly burns and, shaking, I close my eyes and slop the gloopy grit onto my cheek, I quickly rub it over my face and then remember my dresser's words, 'circular motions.' I wince as the grit tears at my skin. My eyes water, hot tears mixing in, it burns even more. I grit my teeth and hold in a scream. I don't want to wake my masters. I splash cold water on my face and reach around for the hand towel. Every day I have to purposely burn myself! Every damn day! I gently dab my swollen skin.

I lower the towel and stare at my reflection in the mirror. After wearing so much makeup every day, my naked face looks like a blank canvas; dull and boring and almost sickening for a splash of colour. Although I've been prodded, poked, and pulled about, others have it worse. I overheard a girl talking about injections yesterday. Her stylist wanted to reduce the dark circles under her eyes. The Skel admitted to being an insomniac. For Showcase, she hid the bags under her eyes with makeup, but up close her masters noticed. They've been injecting a toning agent under her eyes, and while she was having that done, her masters decided they'd like her breasts to be a bit larger. They want the baby to have plenty of milk when it arrives, so now she's being injected there, too. It's noticeable and although the girl was smiling, and saying how happy she was with her new bigger breasts, she's stooped over, clearly in pain, her back bent like a buckled chair leg under a growing Morb teenager. She always stands slightly apart from everyone, and yesterday, when I moved past her, she turned her body to make sure I didn't accidentally knock into her ample breasts, which, like mine and everyone's, were partially on display and covered in glittering moisturiser.

I've already moisturised this morning, slopped the cold gel all over my body and let it sink in. The floral smell is overpowering and sometimes causes me to feel nauseous, but what's really gross is that my skin feels like it has a sticky film covering it, as if a hundred snails went for a trek across my naked body while I slept. Next, I spray my underarms with a sickly perfume and then I'm to dress in the clothes laid out for me. That's what I'm meant to be doing now, but instead I'm standing free from my material constraints, staring longingly out of the window, pining for my old life.

I've always felt suffocated by my existence, yet now I feel strangled. I used to daydream about far off places, better places. I wished I was a bird so I could fly away. The crows of Gale City never seem to leave. I wonder why they don't? Maybe, like all of us, they're scared to move too far from the guaranteed food source. I need the freedom to spread my wings. Being caged like this means I can't even stretch, let alone fly. The cage is too small, the bars are too close together, the control too tight.

I drag my shimmery body over to the dressing table and pull on the purple mess of silk which is today's outfit. I smooth the skirt down, adjust my breasts in the bodice, and then tie the ribbon tight around my waist. The next step is hair and makeup. I've practised with my stylist, a High-Host called Angellyn, but I still can't get used to applying all this slop to my face and twisting my hair in different ways to make it look appealing to my masters. I sit down on the cushioned chair and open the drawer containing brushes and colour palettes. I fish them out and begrudgingly finish the rest of my morning ritual.

As I apply the eyeshadow I sigh to myself; I don't think I can take another day in that cold classroom. It's miserable. The other hosts talk about what they used to do: orchard worker, solar assistant, Sky Train attendant. They never talk to me – most won't even look at me, even Ara. It's like my misery is an infectious disease and if they get too close, I'll suck the happiness right out of them. Being ignored I can handle; people never really talked to me much at the factory, but being singled out is different. The co-ordinator seems to have it in for me, she hasn't forgotten my outburst, the bitch even asked me if I enjoyed my examination.

Yesterday, because I wasn't perky enough, she made take extra lessons in the evening, which involved putting on a mousy voice and repeating phases over and over while smiling until my cheeks ached.

Yes, Mistress.
Yes, Master.
How clever of you.
How interesting.
I'm very well, thank you for asking.
My pleasure.
How do you do?

I had to hold back the urge to add, *go fuck yourself*, in there somewhere, I don't want another caning. The backs of my legs are bruised from all the whipping the co-ordinator dishes out, mostly to me. I have to behave, even though it's frustrating as hell.

In one lesson, we were given a thick book, not a touchpad, an old-style tree book. I love those. The first thing I did when it was handed to me was smell it. It smelled like forgotten happiness. I thought it was a 'real' handbook, not about politeness and correctness but about becoming a vessel for the creation of life, or a guide about new-born babies. It wasn't. The yellow book had no words in it, or pictures, for that matter. The pages were blank. We were then made to walk around the classroom in single file with the heavy books on our heads.

Apparently, walking as if you have a carrot shoved up your backside is important. I dropped my book more than the co-ordinator could tolerate, and was caned around the back of the legs each time she heard the thud of the heavy hardback hitting the floor. She would make a point of lifting my dress to strike me, so the marks wouldn't be seen by my host family. It took all my strength not to snatch the cane and whip her around the face with it. I can't stand being treated like a naughty child.

Mistress Vable pretends to be happy with my efforts but I know she's not, she's regretting her choice. I expect she makes allowances because she knows Master Vable is fond of me.

When I'm satisfied I've done a good enough job of 'making myself up', I enter the lounge to find my mistress finishing breakfast. She's up early, Mistress Vable's not usually awake before I leave but I can't ask her why she's up, hosts don't ask questions.

One side of her enormous face is bathed in the soft glow of light coming from a wall lamp and the other is the dark side of the moon. She spies me, puts down her utensils and beckons to me with her fat fingers, flush with gold. She won't be able to bend them if she piles on any more rings.

'Ms Skyla,' she says, followed by a rattling back-breath. 'First day dressing yourself, is it?' I nod. 'Come closer to me.'

I hesitate and pull down a curl near my cheek. I accidentally burned myself with the curler and I don't want her to see the red mark on my face. She beckons more vigorously, meat-hand waving about, hanging arm-skin jiggling. I totter towards my mistress, baby steps, terrified I'll slip on the shiny floor. I'll never get used to these heels.

'Hmm …'

Her mechanical eye shifts around in its socket, taking in every inch of my face. I remain as still as possible, goosebumps rise on my arms, not only from the freezing air-conditioning, but also in fear of being found inadequate. It's taken me hours to create this fakery. I had to re-do the eyeliner four times. I couldn't get the swirls from the corners of my eyes right, and I'm sure I used too much glitter. I also poked myself in the eye, which watered and caused streaks through the foundation. I couldn't bear to start again from scratch so I patched it up as best I could. I hope she doesn't notice. I bring my hand up absentmindedly to chew on a nail and Mistress Vable's painted eyebrows merge into a frown. I lower my hand. I've only been here eight days and suddenly I care about what I look like and what others think of me. I'm losing myself.

'Turn!' Mistress Vable shoves my bare arm with her plump fingers, scraping my skin with her false nails. 'This bow is a mess!'

There it is. She loves to find fault, even the smallest thing. Yesterday, I wasn't sitting properly, I thought having my legs crossed was the right thing to do but apparently not. *Never cross your legs, my dear, when you're carrying you won't be able to, instead sit with your knees together and legs gracefully swept to one side.*

I feel a tug at my sides. I stumble backwards a little as she pulls the ribbon tight around my waist. Her thick fingers find my arm again and I'm whirled back round to face her. I stand still, arms at my sides, unmoving, like a guard at inspection.

'I suppose you'll do.'

Two hours of work and I'll do? I can't stand this woman. My foot twitches, my brain telling it to kick her off her hover-chair. I envision the ball of blubber falling to the floor, wires connecting her to her life support severed, she flails around like a helpless squid. My smile fades. Do that, and I'll be executed.

'Have some breakfast and then see to it you get to your morning class before anyone else.'

She takes a mechanical breath and hovers out from behind the table.

'Mistress Turnly thinks her host is superior to all, but we're going to prove her wrong now, aren't we?'

I nod.

'Yes, Mistress.'

When the hover-chair is out of the room, I swipe the apple from the top of the tub marked "Host" and shove it in my knapsack. I leave the lounge, and rush out of the front door. The corridor is silent, as if the building slumbers along with its occupants. I move swiftly, light steps, trying not to clip-clop too loudly past the other apartments. But no matter how softly I tread, my shoes still make an irritating clacking sound on the marble.

I turn the corner and in front of me are the glass doors of the shafts. The large glass doors are meant for adult Morbs; the smaller, for us. I always lean forward and look down the lit-up hover-shaft. If the doors were to open I would fall to my death. Bunce says they only open when a hover-chair approaches, so there must be some sort of sensor attached to the door that can tell the difference between legs and a hover-chair. As I move towards the smaller shaft, the doors slide open and I'm at eye-level with Bunce's chubby face.

'Morning,' he beams.

Bunce wears his usual rainbow inspired, Morbihan outfit. Meticulously ironed. Not a crease in his bright, headache-inducing shirt.

'Stop doing this,' I spit, as I enter the lift.

'Stop doing what?' he asks innocently, blond eyebrows rising. He knows what I'm referring to.

'Walking me to class.' I scowl, 'just because I tolerate you doesn't mean I like you.'

I lean up against the cold wall opposite him. It's creepy the way he meets me every morning without fail. Other Morbs don't do this. I never see any other hosts being walked to class by members of their master's family.

'It's on my way,' he says, cheerful. 'I thought you could do with some company.'

'You thought wrong.' The doors shush shut. 'In future, leave me the fuck alone.' Bunce's cheeks flush.

'You mustn't swear!'

'Don't tell me what to do!' I snap, 'I have enough people ordering me around.'

'But if they hear you …'

His eyes dart around the lift chamber, searching for a hidden camera or microphone.

'They'll what?' I chew at my nail and the bitter, pink polish flakes off into my mouth. I flick it from my lip with my tongue. 'Chuck me out or send me to Rock Vault? Gag me so I can't run my smart mouth no more?'

'What's wrong with you?'

Bunce hugs his backpack tight to his chest. He's curious about me, like a small child is curious about an older child. He knows I'm not like the others, I'm a wild animal he's been studying for the past week. He's not meeting me out of kindness or for his sister, who he seems to despise, he truly does think there's something wrong with me and that interests him.

'Nothing's wrong with me,' I say bitterly, 'that's the problem.'

The lift bumps and my body is jarred against the hard metal wall.

'The problem ...' Bunce whispers, 'is if you keep acting like this you'll lose your host privileges.'

'Privileges! Ha!'

My right heel slips forward, I steady myself.

'I'm serious,' Bunce says as he lowers his voice further. 'I heard about your shenanigans in class, my sister won't take kindly if she's made to look a fool.'

I lean forward, right into Bunce's personal space. I grit my teeth inches from his piggy nose.

'Fuck your sister and fuck you!'

Bunce gasps.

We stand in silence, Bunce staring down at his green sneakers. Afraid to look at me. I watch spectrums of light glide across his pale forehead. The metal box we ride in jolts to a stop and the doors swish open.

'After you, Ms Skyla,' he says, in a small voice.

Eyes diverted, body hunched over, he waits for me to pass like a servant would wait for their master. I step out of the lift. I feel bad. Why do I feel bad?

'Call me Skyla,' I say, turning to look behind me, almost slipping as I step onto the marble. Damn heels!

'Okay.' Bunce perks up. 'But ...'

'But?' I say.

He draws into himself again, nervousness radiates from him like heat from a fire. I really do unnerve this Morb, yet he still comes to meet me every morning.

'Wouldn't you prefer I call you by your first name?' he says.

'No!'

I grab hold of Bunce's arm to steady myself, he shudders under my touch. I've scared him, the little mouse. He's frightened of me. The guilt surges. I soften my tone.

'Everyone calls me Skyla, drop the Ms, okay? It's driving me nuts.'

'How do you do that?' he says, holding me steady.

'Do what?' I ask as I carefully place one wobbling foot after the other. My left heel slides, Bunce's grip tightens. My knapsack swings down onto my forearm. They've polished the floor. It's definitely more slippery than usual.

'Say how you feel ... so freely.'

I hold Bunce's arm. His solid frame gives me confidence and I walk a little easier. I pat his hand as a thank you for keeping me from falling, then straighten up and tug my knapsack back up onto my shoulder.

'I move my lips and words come out, simple.'

'I wish I could do that,' he says woefully, 'I can't even bring myself to tell this girl that keeps pestering me that I don't like her.' Bunce looks hangdog. 'Her name's Kally and if I'm completely honest, she kind of repulses me ... I shouldn't have said that, please don't tell anyone I said that.'

He holds his hands together in a begging motion. I smile. I haven't felt like smiling in days. I pat Bunce on the back. He tenses. Not used to human contact, or at least, not used to Skels touching him or maybe it's just me?

'I'll keep your secrets and you keep mine, okay?'

Under my hand, I feel his shoulders relax.

'Okay,' he smiles.

We stay close to one another as we enter the tube, Bunce walking slowly so as not to leave me behind. I struggle along, the slippery floor and the pain from my blisters cripples my walk. Orange sunshine streams through the transparent tube and the brightness brings temporarily blindness, sunlight swallowing the city outside.

'Can I tell you something ... Skyla?'

I keep my eyes down and heel-toe slowly. I'm not going to fall.

'I dunno, can you?'

This is the first time he's used my name without the Ms. It sounds odd coming from a Morb. My stomach growls. I reach into my knapsack and pull out the shiny, green apple. Bunce nervously hitches his backpack higher over his shoulders.

'It's difficult to say.'

'Did we not just agree to keep each other's secrets?' I say, biting into the apple. My lips close around the pierced, green skin and I suck hard, careful not to let the juice run down my painted face.

'Yes but …'

'Spit it out, Bunce.' I say, taking another bite.

His cheeks pink.

'I don't want to never see my penis again.'

I almost choke on the apple, spraying half-chewed, green pieces across the floor. I repress a snort of laughter.

'Why?' I swallow. 'Where's it going?'

'It's not going anywhere!' Bunce scowls.

I sweep the apple-spit to the side of the tube with the tip of my shoes in an attempt to hide it.

'Then what's the problem?' I ask.

The tube snakes around to the right and the sun's rays bounce into my eyes again, making it difficult to see where I'm going. I lower my eyelids like a sun shield.

'The problem is when I change, you know, get to the end of puberty …' Bunce scratches his head, he can't find the right words. '… I imagine adult Morbihan might not be able to find their genitals under all their extra body mass.'

I press my finger to my lips, pretending to be deep in thought when really, I'm surprising a giggle.

'I see what you mean.'

'I mean, that's why you're here. Morbihan can't reproduce, even if they wanted to. You can't make babies if you can't find your equipment, right?'

He's whispering again. I guess this is a subject he can't talk about with other Morbs.

'I'm not sure it's as simple as all that.'

He turns his head away to hide his almost permanent crimson face.

'I don't want to become one of them,' he sighs.

I take another bite of the juicy apple and push the chunk into my cheek.

'No choice, Bunce, that's your future.'

'Yes, it is,' his voice lowers, spite-laced, 'and being a host is yours.'

The words cut. I swallow hard and the sharp edges of apple scratch my throat on the way down. Bunce has walked me to and from class for over a week and I've never heard him talk like this before. A sudden pain punctures my abdomen. I double over.

'You okay?' Bunce asks, fretful.

'I'm fine.'

I'm not fine, I haven't been fine since the doctor shoved that rod up me. Bleeding on and off, sudden pains. Fuck knows what they'll do to me next, this place is going to kill me, I have to get out. Perhaps Bunce can help? Hand pressed against the tube, I take my mind off the pain by watching the clouds move across the sun, the brightness shrinks away and shadows drop over the perfectly pruned dick-hedges and benches that are never used. I throw the apple core into the bin next to me and glance up at the numbers projected above our heads on the hologrammatic clock. It's ten minutes to seven. I have an hour before I have to be in class. This is my chance.

Chapter Seven

The Cure

Next to my classroom is a library. Hosts and Morbs are both permitted, it's one of the only spaces we are allowed to share but it's mostly used by hosts wanting to swot up on Morbihan way of life. I browsed the shelves a few nights ago and found the touchpads were full of inaccurate historical accounts and fictional tales of Morbihan bravery. Nothing worth my time. It's a quiet room though, where hosts and young Morbs don't look out of place together.

'I hope I haven't offended you.' Bunce says, and I remember he's beside me.

I have just told him 'fuck your sister and fuck you' and he's worried about offending me? The pain subsides enough that I can straighten up, and just in time, as a humming travels towards us and we press our backs up against the curves of the tube to let a hover-chair pass by. The floating blubbery being tips his cowboy hat.

'Bunce.'

'Mr Seeker,' Bunce replies.

I wait until the hover-chair has disappeared round the bend in the tube then grab Bunce by the strap of his backpack.

'What time does school start?'

'It's not school! I'm twenty, not twelve!'

Bunce crosses his arms and pouts like a two-year-old.

'What time's your first class?' I tap my foot, impatient.

'My physics class is at eight, why?'

I pull Bunce by the arm strap of his backpack and he stumbles after me. I shoulder my way into the library, dragging Bunce in with me. The door is old, it doesn't disappear into the wall automatically, it swings back and almost hits Bunce in the face. He holds out a chubby hand and stops it. Inside is carpeted and the sound of my heels softens against the stretch of navy threads. The library doesn't have an old smell of wood and centuries gone by, like City Hall does, it smells of newness and cleaning agents. Bunce whispers to me, not wanting to disturb the five hosts and two young Morbs quietly reading in a corner.

'What are we doing in here, Ms ... I mean, Skyla?'

I lead him over to two chairs in the furthermost corner, plucking two touchpads from the closest shelves as we pass. Above us, the library alcoves have been decorated with elaborate carvings that look like wood but aren't, they're metal, sprayed brown, and on the other side of the room a grand fireplace dominates, flickering fire alight in the grate. Except there's no heat, no burning smell, no aroma of old ash yet the crackling sound is there. It's a good imitation, as are the fake bookshelves. I prod the spine of a leather-bound book at eye-level and the image distorts, more holography, like the vision screen projection in the Vable's lounge.

'We can talk in here without being overheard.' I say, carefully lowering myself into a chair. As I bend in the middle, there's a pinch to my abdomen, I twist and turn in my seat, trying to find a comfortable way to hold my body, a position that won't cause me so much discomfort. I sit straight-backed, turn on the slimline device and it lights up my face. Bunce copies me. I lean over the arm of my chair and pretend I want to show him something on the touchpad.

'I saw a programme on the vision screen the day we met,' I say, in a low voice.

'You were watching the VS?' Bunce asks with a tone like I'm the biggest liar he's ever met.

'Yeah, your sister put it on for me. Not for long, for a few minutes before you arrived.'

I point to the touchpad and Bunce nods in interest at the blank screen. He's on board with the charade.

'I'm surprised she let you do that,' he says. He doesn't believe me.

'Shhh.' I press my painted nail to my lips; my mind racing to access the memory I need. 'Let me think …'

Bunce immediately falls silent and my thoughts ring loud inside my head: *Bunce doesn't want to be hover-chair bound, I don't want to be a host. We have a common interest. What if he's my ticket out of here? Help myself by helping him? Cure the Morbs of their weight gain and there'll be no need for me to be here, I can go home.*

'… serum,' I say, trying to recall the conversation Hatti and Delia were having.

'Serum?' Bunce repeats.

'That's right, a scientist created a serum, a type of cure but it was dangerous or something. What if we find that scientist and ask him about it?'

'A cure for the weight gain?'

Bunce frowns and I wonder how he can be so thick.

'No,' I scowl, 'a cure for your insufferable ignorance … yes, of course for the weight gain!'

Two hosts, one dressed in a lime green poodle skirt and boned bodice, the other in a ruby red silk dress, both with matching bows tied at their crown, glance up at my raised voice. Bunce and I stop talking for a moment, then Bunce mouths to me.

'Are you sure? I haven't heard anything about that.'

'I'm sure,' I whisper back, 'maybe they're working on new cures all the time.'

I lean closer to Bunce and we huddle.

'Do you know what would happen if the weight gain was cured?' Bunce shakes his head. Unlike me, he obviously hasn't given much thought to the notion of a world without hover-chair bound, organ-enabled Morbs. 'No more hosts. No disappearing penises. Freedom, Bunce! Freedom!'

Bunce's mouth hangs open as a light switches on in his head.

'I wouldn't be bound to a hover-chair for the rest of my life?'

'Nope.' I grin.

'Maybe I could even go outside!'

I accidentally tap the cover of a book on my screen and the projection of a teal rose blooms out of it.

Bunce's eyes light up, rose mirrored inside the blue. He can see it – see himself setting foot in the real world for the very first time.

'Yep,' I nod, and tap the screen, the rose shrinks away.

'I can't imagine it,' he says solemnly, his eyes dull, light fading.

How quickly Bunce has gone from hopeful to defeated.

'Do you know where the labs are?' I ask.

Bunce stares into space.

'Bunce, the labs?'

'I do, but we're not permitted …'

'Forget the rules for a moment. Can we get into the labs?'

'I suppose, they're not guarded.' His voice sounds far away, like he's talking to someone in another dimension. 'We could pretend to interview scientists for a project or something … but we mustn't, our lives wouldn't be worth living if we're found out.'

'They're not worth living now!' I tell him. The young Morbs look up this time, holograms dancing from their screens, suspicion in their eyes at a host and a Morb talking in close quarters. Bunce doesn't notice them staring.

'We can't walk in there and demand information. We need a plan,' Bunce says in a hushed voice.

'Then let's make one.'

Our eyes lock.

'Seriously?' he says, wide-eyed.

The cringeworthy twitters of my classmates lining up outside starts to build, the hosts in the library with us gather their bags and slink towards the door. I watch them shimmer past, and know I have never been more serious about anything in my life. I have to get out of here, now.

'Shake on it?' I say.

I hold out my hand in the Morbihan custom. Bunce nervously grasps it and his warmth melts the cold from my frozen fingers.

We're so different, Bunce and I, and it's not only the colour of our skin and eyes and the shape of our bodies that's different, it's the colour of our consciousness, mine burns orange like the sun, his sways green like the leaves of a tree. Will I burn him down or will he keep me alight? A twinkle of sunshine reflects in the calm aqua of his eyes. I have an ally. An ignorant, insulated, immature ally but an ally none the less. My skin tingles with a new-found hope.

Chapter Eight

Lab B

Day Ten

Mistress Vable permitted Bunce to take me on a 'tour' of the complex when he told her how interested in Morbihan life I was after seeing the gardens. He's getting good at this 'truth-stretching.' This pleased my fat-headed mistress. She thinks of it as one-upmanship. Her host will have the most knowledge of the Morbihan way of life, thanks to her little brother's forward thinking and eagerness to help his big sis. Bunce told her he'd be happy to show me more of the complex and then, before bringing me back, he would stop off at the labs to do research for his 'science project.' The lie was bought – clips, comb, and curler. I'm finding that even though fully grown adult Morbs value truth, younger Morbs don't hold those same values as dearly. I wait outside my classroom and replay my last encounter with Bunce.

The gardens are under a glass dome. The dome is packed with hundreds of species of plants and flowers. After that blue rose popped up on the touchpad in the library, Bunce took it as a sign the gardens would be a safer place for us to talk. One plant that caught my eye, (and I can't stop thinking about the gruesome thing) was the Giant Sundew – a great octopus of vines, with several pitchers. It's roped off, behind a warning sign which reads: 'DANGER: Keep your distance!' Bunce says it's carnivorous and that he's seen botanists feed it rats. I wish I could feed it half the population of Gale City.

It was humid in the gardens, and this was the reason we could hatch our plan there; no one else was around. Adult Morbs would overheat, which meant they could only visit the gardens at certain times of the day, when air conditioning is permitted. The heat wasn't uncomfortable for me, I'm used to it; in the city it can reach unbearable temperatures in the summer, but Bunce isn't used to it and was sweating like a Runner with a score of glory, trying to escape capture. I liked the gardens; to me they felt like a little slice of heaven planted in the middle of Hell.

Strolling amongst the plants, Bunce told me that a Morbihan scientist *is* still working on a cure and that his experiments are top secret. Bunce got this information straight from the source, or as good as; the scientist's granddaughter. I haven't felt this excited since my grandfather gave me a necklace for my tenth birthday. That necklace was a secret he kept from Central and a secret I've hidden under the floorboards of my cube for years. The serum is a secret I must steal.

The sound of sneakers squeaking their rubber soles down the corridor grows closer. He hasn't backed out. Good. I've only known Bunce a little over a week, so I don't really know him at all. A week isn't long enough to get to know anyone. I'm not sure if he's as serious as I am about changing the future. I wonder if he's bored and looking for a bit of excitement. If it's the latter, he'll be in for a shock. Skels do what they mean to do. When we put our mind to something, it gets done. One way or another.

'We set?' I ask, dropping into a steady stride beside him.

'Yes.' Bunce nods.

I look him over. If we hadn't dressed ourselves anyone would think the dressers had chosen our clothes to complement each other. I wear a marigold yellow baby-doll dress with gold trim, and he wears a garish, gold sequin smattered shirt, ruffed at the neck and arms. We turn a corner and enter a dim tube; the see-through chamber is darkened by the charcoal clouds outside.

'And you know which lab it is?' I ask. His clothes are distracting. Who pairs a gold top with yellow, plaid trousers and spring-green sneakers? What was he thinking when he put that on?

'It's Lab B ...' Bunce says, nerves shaking his voice. Has he got tiny gold clips in his hair? He spots me staring. I quickly turn to face the direction we're heading. 'Kally said Lab B is where her grandfather works and it's primarily used for creating vaccines and medicines. She also said …'

Bunce glances around nervously. I draw closer to him.

'What is it?'

'Someone's coming…'

He takes my hand and drags me. I stumble along on my gold stilettos, Bunce strides on, looking over his shoulder every few seconds, ignoring the jolts to his hand every time I slip and stagger. A whooshing noise, like wind in a tunnel, draws closer and Bunce throws out his arm, flattening me to the curved wall. Three young Morbs speed past us like lightning, rush of air freeing wisps of hair from my updo. Bunce glares at them as they disappear down the corridor, in an echo of laughing and whooping.

'Air-Soles aren't permitted in CORRIDORS OR TUBES!' he yells.

I smirk.

'Assholes aren't permitted … and you have a go at me for swearing!'

Bunce chuckles.

'Air-Soles,' he lowers his voice, 'not assholes!'

'What are Air-Soles?'

'Did you not notice how fast they were moving?' Bunce says, pointing in the direction the Morbs had rushed.

'Yeah, but everything is so weird here, I never know what's going on.'

'They were using Air-Soles, a connective plastic that you stick to the sole of your shoe, they carry you at speed across any surface, with the exception of water and sand.'

'How come you can't use them on sand …?'

'Maybe they do work on sand …' Bunce is lost in thought, 'No way to know. I mean, none of us have been outside to test them. Maybe they only work inside the complex …'

I wave my hand up and down in front of Bunce's face.

'Bunce … hello.'

'Huh?' He snaps out of the trance, 'Oh, sorry. You were saying.'

'I was going to ask how they work.'

'I don't know the exact science,' he scratches the back of his head, a nervous habit, 'they work like hover-chairs except you can travel much faster and they're controlled by movement rather than a control pad. You push your legs out in a skating motion to propel them and then use your arms in a swinging motion to increase and decrease speed, there are these sensor bracelets that come with the pack,' Bunce imitates the movement, slow running on the spot. 'Top speed is about thirty miles per hour. People do tricks on them and race each other. There are strict zones for their use.' His eyes linger where the group had passed by. 'Reckless, they could really hurt someone.'

'Do you have some?' I ask, hopeful.

Bunce shoots me a quizzical look.

'Why? Want to try it?'

I shrug but in truth, I'm desperate to try it. Bunce takes my hand again and tugs me forwards. I'm taken aback by the contact. When we first met, he was weirded out when I invaded his space and if he'd held my hand like this back then, I might have pulled away; holding hands with a Morb should feel unnatural, but strangely, it doesn't.

'We'd better go,' he says, nervousness back in his voice, 'we're running out of time.'

Another whooshing sound echoes down the tube and we again flatten our backs to the clear wall. Two more young Morbs whizz past. This time they see Bunce. The one in front slows, his dayglo orange shirt hard to look at, it's 'stare at the sun' bright. The Morb's dark green, messy locks come to rest on his shoulders. He wears an air of confidence not in keeping with the fact he resembles a carrot.

'Hey Bunce! Nice link!' he throws his head back and laughs.

The carrot then pumps his legs up the side of the tube, lights flashing on the bottom of his orange boots, he skates sideways, shirt flapping around his waist.

'Weirdo!' Shouts the girl behind him in stripy, pink knee-high socks and blue tutu, which bounces as she rushes past us.

They disappear round a bend, their spiteful laughs echo off the tubular walls, fading as they get further away. Bunce glances down at our linked fingers. He says nothing and pulls me into a jog. I totter after him.

'Maybe you shouldn't hold my hand …'

'They were poking fun at me, Skyla.' Bunce's voice wobbles as we hurry faster down the tube. 'They'd believe we're plotting to change life as we know it before any notion that we might be together.'

He drops my hand and I feel a tiny pinch of rejection. Strange. He walks off and I follow. I hate following. I'm not a follower. But he knows the complex and I don't so I allow myself to be led. The tube expands into an elaborate foyer, wall sculpted in flowers. I drink in the decorative, high ceilings and see through the oval windows that dusk has fallen. Sun well and truly set, bulbs on several miniature chandeliers blossom gold. The light from the chandeliers pushes shadows out from beneath the marble columns which circle around to gem encrusted double doors. The word 'MALL' is written in shimmering letters above the entrance. I squint and skim-read a sign which states the mall closed at 6.00 p.m. and would re-open at 8.00 p.m. for late night shoppers.

We cross the vast glittering floor, which looks as if an explosion of stars is trapped beneath the surface. I find myself wondering how it stays clean. Then I remember, hover-chairs and shoes that never tread on the dirty streets outside are the reasons, and with people using Air-Soles it's a wonder Morbs bother using their feet at all. A few more strides and I feel an urge to cut through the silence.

'Let's go over things one last time.'

Bunce takes a deep breath.

'Okay … we do our interview with Kally's grandfather as planned. He thinks it's about illness and immunisation. We work in some questions about the serum and try to get as much information out of him as possible.' Bunce rubs the back of his head again, he's doing this more frequently, clearly stressed, 'It might take a few months to get him to talk but …'

'A few months?' I say, alarmed. 'Bunce, I'm days away from implantation.'

Bunce shakes his head.

'Did you think it would happen overnight? We walk in there and he hands us the file marked 'cure'?'

We enter an even darker tube on the other side of the foyer. A path of glowing dots, triggered by the onset of night, lights the way.

'No,' I say, struggling to keep up as Bunce strides onward, 'I thought the plan was that you keep him busy asking questions while I poke around the lab!'

'Don't you think he'll notice you poking around?' Bunce says over his shoulder.

'Not unless his head swivels three hundred and sixty degrees. I pocket the serum, job done.'

I nod to myself. I'm sure I could find it. It's probably in a fridge labelled, 'The Cure.' Morbs are highly intelligent, but they have no common sense.

'I can't even begin to tell you how impossible that would be. He'll expect you to sit and take notes for me.'

'Most Skels don't even know how to read, let alone write, why would he expect that of me?'

Through the tube glass, the city streets, (not my city, theirs) are lit up by pools of lamplight; palm trees swaying in the gentle breeze. A breeze I wish I could feel. Everything is uniform here, nothing left to chance, a predictable life; safety and comfort paramount. No one takes risks, except those Air-Sole Morbs who insulted Bunce just now. The closest I've come to feeling the wind in my hair was when that handful of rebels rushed past. Rebels. I smile to myself. That's as rebellious as Morbs get, I suppose. What Bunce is doing with me right now must be difficult for him. Way more rebellious than racing around corridors and tubes. This is so far out of Bunce's comfort zone. Kian is my comfort zone. I miss him. I wonder what he's doing. Marching around. Learning how to use weapons and fight in close combat. On patrol, observing fully fledged guards arresting Runners and wacked-out users. Bunce slows down to walk beside me, blocking my view. Irritating.

'If that's the case, why would he expect you to be there at all?' Bunce says, equally as irritated with me, 'This is never going to work.'

I ignore Bunce. He thinks everything is too difficult.

'If I can't find it, we'll have to decide whether or not we have time to use blackmail.'

'Blackmail!' Bunce spits, 'That's insane! I can't agree to that.'

I scowl at him, Morbs are insane. Why shouldn't that work?

'Look,' I say sweetly, 'I need to get out of here and I can't go back to my job, so I have one option left. Change. Once we've cured a large amount of the Morbihan population there'll be no going back. I'm getting that cure! And anyway, you need it as much as I do, you could explode into a mountain of blubber at any moment!'

'It doesn't work that way.' He shakes his head.

'Whatever, are we doing this or not?'

We stop outside the entrance to the science labs. Bunce hesitates, I push past him and the frosted glass doors swish open. Inside, the ceiling is low and hanging lights dangle; any taller and I'd have to stoop so as not to bang my head on one. At the elaborate front desk – a great wave of mahogany – sits a High-Host receptionist. My heart skips a beat. She'll ask questions, what if she sees through us? Bunce's posture has changed, he stands tall, confident. It's like he's stepped onto the stage and into character.

'Jennavive, how are you?'

He knows everyone.

'Bunce, how nice to see you. I'm well, and yourself?'

Bunce leans over the desk and bats his blond eyelashes, flirtatious.

'All the better for seeing you.'

I raise an eyebrow. What's he doing? Who is this guy and where is Bunce? The woman, in her forties, touches her beehive hairdo, coyly.

'Such a charmer.'

'I try.'

Bunce props himself up on his elbow and rests his chin in his palm, he gazes up at Jennavive like she's his long-lost lover.

'What brings you here this evening?' she asks, lapping up the attention.

'Science homework. Can you point me in the direction of Lab B? Don't bother buzzing me though, they know we're coming.'

Jennavive looks me up and down.

'Is there a reason you have a host with you?' she asks, eyes loaded with suspicion.

Bunce casually pushes his fingers through his sandy hair, he seems to be enjoying all this truth-stretching, he's quite the actor.

'Ms Skyla came up with the idea of interviewing a scientist. My sister said she could tag along.'

'She did, huh?'

The receptionist narrows her heavily painted eyes at me. Bunce clears his throat so she has no choice but to look at him again.

'She's a bit star-stuck being here,' he nods in my direction. 'About to become a wonderful success like yourself.'

'Oh stop,' the receptionist giggles like a school girl, the composes herself, 'I thought you might have come down to find Cara.'

Jennavive taps at her monitor; long, rainbow-painted nails making a clicking sound on the screen.

'Cara?' Bunce frowns.

'Yes, she was just here, sent down by Master Vable. When I saw you, I thought she might have forgotten something.'

'Coincidence, I guess,' Bunce brings his withering smile back to full bloom. 'Just don't tell my sister that Cara was down here. She hates it when my brother-in-link sends the maid to run errands that aren't in her job description.'

'My lips are sealed,' she says, passing her rainbow-painted finger and thumb nails across her lips like she's zipping them shut. 'Lab B is right through there.'

Jennavive points to the first door on the right. We head there. The door to Lab B is white, clinically clean, not a smudge or smear on it. I can see my painted face in it. There's a palm-pad. I raise my hand and then think better of it, this palm-pad could map my hand and tell Central I was here, Bunce should press it. It's then I notice the door is bowed. That's odd. I back away, and bump into Bunce.

'What is it?'

I open my mouth to answer with *I don't know* but the words don't come. I stand slack jawed and wide-eyed as the lab door warps and depresses in the middle, like a vacuum is stuck to the other side, sucking the door into it. I narrow my eyes. *What's doing that?* On the other side of the stressed door, macabre voices murmur, glass shatters, beside me Bunce flinches and then there's a subtle click. A trigger?

'Quick!' I yell, and grab the front of Bunce's spangled shirt, dragging him backwards; he stubbles over his surprised feet, we need to get to the reception desk ...

A blast as loud as thunder sends a shock wave of dust, metal, and debris through the reception area and the force knocks us down like skittles.

I lie still for a moment, head pounding but thankful I'm still conscious. I slowly roll onto my back, smoke collects in my throat and I start to cough, then choke, when water fills up my open mouth. I spit and splutter. Ceiling sprinklers triggered, water showers over me in a relentless downpour. I push my elbows backwards, arms sliding across shallow surface water. I force my aching body up into a sitting position, lean my ear to my shoulder and three cracks rip though the back of my neck. I shiver, jittery; my dress is soaked, a sheet of ice against my skin. Eyes unglued, droplets of water hang from my eyelashes, weighing them down and making the destroyed reception look as if it's under a black feathered fringe. I rip off the false lashes and wipe away grit and stinging eye makeup, with the back of my hands. I blink my vision clear.

Bunce lies a few feet from me, face down, motionless, water splashing against his back. I kick off my heels, roll over onto all fours and scramble towards Bunce, my hands and knees slapping through the water.

'Bunce?' I shake his shoulders. No response. His head is turned towards me, his skin paler than usual.

Water pools around his body and I catch my refection in it. Pretty hair I spent hours on, now a tangled, dripping mess, I look like I have two black eyes, and my dress is a dirty dishcloth. What a pretty dolly for my masters. I pick at the frayed trim on my sopping yellow dress. Why am I even worried about what I look like when Bunce looks as if he's dead? What's wrong with me, brainwashed after just ten days trapped inside this nightmare.

'You okay?' I yell and poke Bunce in the side with one finger.

Bunce lifts his head and then turns to look the other way. A few seconds pass and he rolls over; his heavy arm splashing down in the surface water.

'I'm okay, you?' he says, droplets startling his eyelids, squeezed shut.

I stand up, soles of my feet wrinkled against the water-logged floor.

'Fine. Take my hand.'

Bunce opens one eye and grabs my hand. I tug hard but I can't pull him up, my feet hop forwards as I try to resist falling. He turns sideways and heaves himself up onto one knee. A buzzing noise draws our faces to the ceiling. A battered black drone hovers above us, struggling to stay in the air, it shudders towards the reception doors, which are blown wide open, frosted glass fractured in the pattern of a spider's web. Like a large mechanical bee, lost on its way back to the hive, the drone buzzes along above our heads and disappears into the tube. Bunce frowns, he's as confused as I am and that's not good. I skid across the floor in a hydroplane and lean over the reception desk, the wet, silk dress causing me to slip back down off the rolled wood. Jennavive is unconscious, slumped against the wall, beehive hair squashed into a pear shape, her right leg at an impossible angle.

'What was that?' Bunce asks, as he joins me at the desk, gold shirt glossy, hugging his curves, plaid pants a shade darker.

'A drone.'

I drag myself over and drop down behind the desk. I crouch beside Jennavive and search through her jacket pockets, she might have something useful I can swipe, security ID or something that will get us out of here. Nothing. I pop back up and I'm met with Bunce's twisted white face, blond hair dripping water into his eyes. He doesn't approve of me robbing an unconscious woman.

'I know it's a drone,' he says, ignoring my actions with his words while judging me with his eyes, 'what caused that explosion?'

I don't answer that stupid question. Who knows what caused it? I climb back over the desk, my dress snags on a protruding nail and as I jump down, the material rips up the side. I sigh and stride past Bunce.

'Where are you going?'

'Lab B.'

'Skyla, wait! We have to get out of here.'

His heavy sloshing steps lumber after me. The door to Lab B hangs open, scorch marks around the frame, smoke drifting out like someone opened the oven door after burning dinner. A sharp smell of burnt flesh, singed hair, and chemicals wrinkles my nose. The cooked meat smell takes me back to a memory I'd rather forget; when they burned the bodies after The Day of the Bird. A huge flaming mountain. The guards only put the fire out once the bones were black, fretful that the birds might have transferred some kind of disease to the bodies.

I study the scene. Did an experiment go wrong? I step over the threshold and unwittingly onto shattered glass. A piece embeds in my toe; I suck in air through my teeth at the spike of pain. I step away from the glass, reach down, and yank out the shard, blood pooling on the tip of my big toe. The room is blackened and, judging by the overturned equipment and furniture, which looks to have been shunted towards the back of the lab, I'd guess the blast came from near the door. Chemicals drip off the furthest bench, oozing from a beaker turned on its side. Not a scientist in sight. Dread brushes over my head and shivers through my hair.

Bunce is right. We have to go. Something strange is going on. People were working in here, I heard them before the blast, so where are the bodies? Then, I see a body – a Skel. The charred remains of a lab assistant lie face down in the corner – a skeletal body, skin flayed from the bones. If batches of the serum 574 was in there, it's gone now. Everything is destroyed.

'This is bad.' Bunce says, large head peeking into the room as far as his courage will allow.

I turn around and stare past him at the sprinkler rain showering over reception. Droplets ping off the mahogany desk and plink onto the marble floor. Beside the sprinkler heads, the dangling lights swing gently, no longer lit. Emergency wall lighting keeps the place from total darkness. I check the other lab doors. No one has come out. Not one Morb has moved from their lab to see what happened. Unlike Skels, they'll stay put and wait for assistance. No curiosity or desire to help others. Self-preservation top of the list. Anger flushes my cheeks. They only care about themselves. Time for me to do something selfish. I motion to Bunce, and point at the exit.

'Let's go.'

Chapter Nine

Lockdown

I grab Bunce's arm and yank him to come with me; water rushes around our ankles as we slosh towards the way out, the sprinklers show no sign of slowing. Glass flakes out of the frosted doors as I use both hands to try and tug them apart. Bunce kicks the fractured glass and it caves in, dropping through to the other side. He ducks through first and brushes away the shards scattered across the floor with the side of his sneaker. I carefully climb through, dress catching, glass scratching, bare feet again treading on sharpness.

We take off back down the dark tube, stopping every so often so I can pull nuggets of glass from the bottom of my foot. My hands shoot over my ears when they're shot with the high pitch wail of the siren; it screeches down the transparent tunnel like a bird squawking over missing chicks, stolen by rats. The alarm has been raised and the ominous sound of boots marching adds to the din. A drumbeat of guards heads our way, we must hide. We arrive in the Mall foyer before the guards do and hide behind a column. A squad stamps past. We keep quiet and still and wait for the tan and red uniforms to disappear into the tube leading to the labs.

We're out of sight and out of mind, for now, but they'll come for us soon enough. They'll question us both and something tells me Bunce won't be as good at lying to the authorities as he is to his family. If they force the truth from him, we're both screwed. Crouched beside me, Bunce is hyperventilating. I sigh, *giant baby.* I pinch his arm and he takes the hint, concentrates and slows his breathing.

'What do we do now?' he pants.

'I dunno,' I hold out my tattered dress, can't explain this away, 'we're screwed.'

'That's not helpful.' he stands and taps my bare shoulder with his damp fingers, I flinch. I hate being tapped. He whispers hot breath into my ear. 'What's our next step?'

'You Morbs are meant to be super fucking smart,' I say, irritated. I hold the two ripped sides of my dress together. It's ruined, no way it can be sewn back together. I drop the silk, 'what do you think we should do?'

His eyes widen at something behind me.

'You should get the hell out of here.'

Strong fingers squeeze my shoulders. I whirl around.

'Kian!'

I throw my arms around my friend and nestle into his firm chest, he holds me for a moment before I pull back, a little embarrassed at my surge of affection. I've never been so glad to see anyone. I smile up at him, he doesn't smile back. He has that arduous look in his green eyes, the same one he gave me when I told him I didn't want to be a host. My gaze drops to the stripe on his shoulder. I reach up to touch it, and as my fingers meet the material, the siren cuts out.

'Real guard now, huh?' I say, voice lowered.

'Yes.' he says flatly.

His posture is stiff, back straight, shoulders square, like a guard would stand.

'Here to turn us in?' I ask.

He relaxes and leans up against the column.

'Would I do that?'

I shake my head. Of course, he wouldn't. He may be a guard but he's still my friend.

'Do you know what caused the explosion?' I ask, pushing wet strands of hair off my face.

'I thought you might have an idea.'

Kian eyes my sopping clothes and dishevelled appearance.

'We were there for a science project,' Bunce blurts out, stepping away from his hiding place in the shadows behind me.

I knew it. He's already breaking into a sweat and Kian hasn't even begun to question us.

'Allow me to escort you home, young master,' Kian speaks gently to Bunce, as if he is a little boy, 'it's not safe here.'

'I stay with her.' Bunce says, defiantly crossing his arms over his patchy shirt, which is still dry in places.

'As you wish,' Kian says, blank-faced.

He turns his attention back to me.

'My guess is an experiment gone wrong. ERU took a scientist out of there.'

'ERU?' Bunce says.

Kian glares at him as if he is a child interrupting an adult conversation.

'Emergency Response Unit,' he says to Bunce. 'My team has been sent to secure the area and clean up the mess.'

'They know we were there?' I say.

Kian lowers his voice.

'You're not their main concern, they're looking for someone, a maid.'

'A maid?' I say confused. Surely, they don't think a maid blew up the lab.

'Cara!' Bunce chimes in.

A bolt of lightning strikes my mind.

'Kian,' I slap both hands on his chest, 'I think I know why they want Cara, can you help me get out of here?'

'Why do you want to leave? You're doing so well.' He frowns.

'I'm not! I hate the place!' I say, louder than I should have.

'Sky, please, we've been over this, this is the best place for you.'

Bunce stays quiet. I lean in close to Kian.

'I think Cara has this serum, that's why they want her, I'd bet a month of food rations that she's stolen the cure for the Morbs genetic obesity.'

Bunce gasps.

'What?' Kian scoffs, 'Surely you didn't buy into that crap about the rat?'

I grasp Kian's pressed shirt with both hands.

'Can you get me out of here or not?'

'No, Skyla!'

He backs away, his shirt yanked from my grip.

'Please,' I beg, grabbing his sleeve, 'I'm going out of my mind in here! Do me this favour. I've done enough for you over the years.'

Bunce still hasn't said a word, apart from that gasp about Cara being a thief. He keeps his eyes down, hands clasped behind his back like he's already a prisoner, waiting for Kian to bind his wrists together and take him away.

A crash shakes the floor, I grab hold of Kian's arm to steady myself. It's sounds as if the tube ceiling has caved in.

Kian brushes my hand away and peers around the column.

'Shit!'

'What was that?' I whisper.

'Lockdown.' Kian grunts, 'come on, I'm taking you both back to your apartments before we're all stuck here.'

He grips my bare arm, pinching the skin.

'Kian, let go!'

I struggle against his grip as he tugs me along, into the tube, Bunce follows, shrieking when a heavy shutter comes down behind him, sealing off the Mall area.

'Sky, don't fight me,' Kian says, striding along the tube, while I trip over my bare feet, pulling away from him. I look back at Bunce and plead for help with my eyes. He looks away. 'You need to tell your master and mistress that you had nothing to do with that explosion. Run away and they'll think you're involved.'

I stumble along beside Kian, clawing at his thick fingers which are cutting off the circulation in my arm, bruising it. I'm gonna boot him in the nuts if he doesn't let go. Except I don't have any boots on and my bare foot isn't going to make much of an impact. I twist and tug, he tightens his hold on me.

'Perhaps you should loosen your grip,' Bunce says in a mousy voice as he scampers along behind us.

'Perhaps you should let me do my job, young master,' Kian snarls over his shoulder. We reach a shaft, the one close to the Vable's apartment. Kian bears down on Bunce who shrinks down, 'or shall I tell your mother you were obstructing a guard on duty?'

Eyes on the floor, Bunce shakes his head.

'Cowardly little bitch,' I spit at him through gritted teeth.

'It doesn't matter,' Bunce sighs, hurrying to keep up with Kian's long strides, 'I know Cara, she'd never steal anything, she'd die before she'd betray my brother-in-link.'

'What was she doing there then, Bunce?' I growl back, allowing Kian to drag me along.

He shrugs.

'She's always back and forth from the labs.'

'Why didn't you say this before?' I spit, 'We could have asked *her* to find the cure!'

'Like I said, Cara is loyal,' Bunce frowns, 'She'd turn us in in a second.'

A voice springs from Kian's wrist.

'23-06 where are you?'

Kian doesn't stop moving, he drags me along while he speaks into his talking wrist.

'On my way, shutter came down and separated me from the squad, I'll have to take the long way around.'

'Copy that.'

'I have to get back to work,' Kian stops in front of the shaft, 'Can I trust you to go back to your apartments?'

I nod, but I don't intend to do any such thing. Kian lets go of my arm then drops his hand down to catch mine before I can get away.

'More shutters could drop, I need you to go home and stay home, okay?' He says, his green eyes flit around my face, trying to read me like a book.

'Why are they dropping shutters?' I ask, 'Bit dangerous.'

'Morbs stop moving when the siren sounds and wait for an announcement. They don't move during lockdown, never been a case of one being crushed to death by a shutter,' he grins at Bunce, '… yet.'

'That's true,' Bunce says in agreement, not picking up on the fact Kian was insinuating he'd be amused if Bunce was crushed to death, 'we're the only dummies moving about, and the guards, but they're skilled,' he quickly adds before rambling on about how fantastic guards are, clearly trying to impress Kian. It has the opposite effect.

'I mean it, Sky,' Kian says as he strides away, 'go home.'

I scowl. He knows he can't tell me what to do. *Go home, he says. I intend to.* A few days ago, I saw a way out, what I hope is an exit out of the complex. That's where I'm going.

'Well, goodbye, Bunce.' I say, chirpily as I step into the lift, 'I hope I never see you again.'

I press the button for the Vable's floor and he wedges his large frame between the doors.

'Wait!' he says, lips quivering, clearly hurt by what I said, 'We made this plan together and we'll see it through to the end, together.'

I shake my head.

'Not a good idea.'

I push against his fleshy arm and try to force him back through the doors.

'I'm coming with you!' he says sternly.

I push harder, my hands sinking into his soft body. I can't budge him.

'You're not!'

I lean my body away from him and up on tiptoes, I push my hands into his side, throwing all my weight into it.

'I can help,' he says, and forces more of his body firmly in between the half-closed metal doors.

'With … what?' I strain, slamming my bony shoulder into his large frame, 'Would you move already!'

'I want to be the first to take the cure.'

I stop pushing but leave my hands resting against his shoulder. I grin at the idiot Morb. He's off his head.

'We don't know if it even works, the serum could kill you, if the city doesn't first. You don't know what it's like out there, Bunce,' I puff, and shove him in the ribs.

'You need me. If Cara has 'stolen' the cure, she'll talk to me. She trusts me.'

'I'm not going after Cara,' I say, agitated, why won't he take no for an answer? 'I'm going into hiding. I can't help you, Bunce.'

'You can't hide from Central,' he says.

I stop trying to shove him back through the door and stand, hands on hips.

'I can't stay here.'

I don't want to talk to him anymore, I just want to go! Things happen, circumstances change, a new direction is needed. Why does he need to plan every little detail?

'Neither can I, not when there's hope for a better future.' he says, eyes like steel, determined.

'What about the unfiltered air?' I say. I'll say anything to get him to move. 'What if you get outside and can't breathe?'

'I would rather look into the sun just once and risk blindness than live my life without ever feeling its warmth on my face.'

I'm silenced by this sentence. A sentence I know well. The last words my grandfather ever spoke. I fall back into the lift, to the floor. Bunce squeezes through the doors, which swish closed behind him.

'How do you know those words?' I ask.

I fall into a daydream. I'm not in the lift with Bunce anymore, I'm back in the centre of town, black clouds above me, a waterfall of tears falling down my cheeks.

'I heard it when I was a boy, on the VS, I think, a documentary or something.'

'A documentary?'

I lean back, head clonking against the cold metal, damp dress hanging on me the same way it would if it was draped over the back of a chair. The lift begins its ascent. My limp body rocks with it. The emptiness inside me is like a river run dry.

'I didn't get to see the end,' Bunce goes on. 'My mother switched it off.'

He leans against the metal wall, opposite me.

'It wasn't a documentary,' I say, flatly. 'It was my grandfather's execution.'

I choke back the sorrow. My grandfather's death is still difficult to talk about. In fact, I don't think I've ever talked about it with anyone. Not even Kian.

'Your grandfather was executed?' Bunce frowns.

'What you said just now ... about the sun ... those were his last words to me, before they killed him.' My eyes water.

'I'm sorry,' Bunce says. 'I didn't know.'

I hold my forehead.

'I can't believe it was broadcast.'

Bunce shifts over to my side of the lift and picks up a strand of my sodden blond hair. He lets it drop though his fingers.

'That little girl, who ran out to him, that was you?'

I nod.

'He died for what he believed in. It took years for me to accept that,' I say, and it did. I still haven't fully forgiven him for leaving me but I have at least managed to accept why he did what he did.

'What did he do wrong?' Bunce asks.

I can't stop the rage, it bubbles up, spills over and erupts. I lunge for him, grabbing him by the scruff of the neck.

'What did he do wrong? Automatically, you think it was his fault! Skel turned criminal, fucking scumbag, right! You over-privileged little bastard! What do you know about it? What do you know about anything? NOTHING! That's what!'

'Skyla, my apologies, I didn't mean to ...'

He squirms. I let go of him before I choke him to death. I scream with frustration and punch the floor of the lift with my fists.

'I can't take anymore!'

Angry tears gush. All the stress, all the pressure, it rushes from me, my body convulsing with the expulsion of emotion.

My shoulders heave. I'm losing my mind. I can feel it – it's all slipping away.

'Skyla …'

A pudgy hand is on my shoulder. I look up, and Bunce's eyebrows bow, his mouth turned down in sympathy and regret for what he said.

'He didn't do anything wrong.' I sniff. 'He organised a protest outside City Hall. Central tried to shut it down, there was some conflict and my grandfather was accused of assaulting a High-Host.'

Bunce gasps and clamps his chubby hand over his mouth.

'The bastards were trying to take our market away. Thanks to my grandfather we got to keep it … the cost was his life.'

We sit in silence for what seems like an eternity, our bodies swaying with the upward motion.

'That's exactly why you must let me come with you,' Bunce says, his voice soft as a lullaby. 'Your grandfather wouldn't want you to hide, on the run for the rest of your life. I'll take the cure and then if it works, I can give it to others.'

'You'd risk your life for something that might not even work?' I say, 'that's not very Morbihan of you.'

Bunce struggles to his feet, he's nowhere near the size of a fully grown adult Morb but his frame is a lot larger than any Skel's and thus he's not as nimble or light-footed. He leans against the opposite wall. I push my trembling body up the inside of the cold metal lift to face him.

'Morbihan are fascinated by statistics,' he says, matter-of-factly. 'Sixty percent chance this artificial organ will be effective, eighty percent chance the body will reject that one and so on. I know the odds of success aren't in our favour but you're right, there's more to life than being stuck inside a bubble, acting out the same boring routine every single day. There's got to be more … and I want to find out how much.'

The lift jolts to a stop and I'm flung forwards. Bunce catches me by the arms and I slip down, my face level with his crotch. I glance up at him.

'Thanks.'

He blushes and pulls me up onto my feet. The lift lights blink off and a robotic voice rings out of the speakers. We stand perfectly still in the darkness and listen.

'This is an announcement. The complex is in lockdown. Please remain calm. All shafts have been temporarily deactivated and tube entrance will be denied. This is for your own safety. The cooling system will be unaffected. Stay inside your apartment. If you are outside your apartment, please refrain from any unnecessary movement about the complex. Once the guards have completed their objective, all power will be restored. We apologise for any inconvenience this may have caused and thank you for your patience.'

'Help me with the door,' I say, pushing my fingers into the gap in the metal, the gold paint on my nails chipping off.

Bunce squeezes in behind me and we pull the door back. Bunce grunts as he forces the left one back, the right one opens on its own as its twin is shifted. We're between floors. My floor at the bottom and Bunce's above. The gap to Bunce's floor is too small for him to fit through. I slip down and my bare feet slap against the cool marble. Bunce follows behind me but is less graceful, he lands on his feet and stumbles a few steps forwards, managing to keep his balance.

'There's an emergency stairwell a few apartments down from my sister's, I'll go get my stuff and then meet you at the bottom of it, do you know the one?'

'Yes,' I say. I was right, there is a way out.

We set off in different directions. I stop and look back.

'Bunce.'

Bunce skids to a halt, his sneakers squeaking against the polished marble floor.

'If things don't work out ...'

'I understand.'

'There's no going back ... for either of us.'

'I know,' he says, determined.

I nod and I sprint away, dress flapping around my legs in tatters, makeup smeared in clumps down my cheeks. He'll probably have second thoughts once he gets back to his apartment. He won't come with me. I relax a little at the thought of doing this alone but part of me feels relieved to have someone fighting my corner, someone who also doesn't believe that the system works. I try to think of a lie to tell my masters. Nothing comes to me.

I arrive at door twelve in seconds and once inside, I still haven't thought up a lie. I creep past the loud paintings which are quiet in the lockdown forced darkness. They can't see me but if they could and if they could talk, I imagine they'd be shouting, *she's here! She's here! She's done something terrible!'* I peer round the doorframe and into the minimalist lounge. It's dark, strips of moonlight sneak through the closed blinds and zebra stripe the floor. It's too quiet. Where are they?

I make my way to my room and as soon as I've closed the door I tear the yellow rag-doll dress from my body, change into my work uniform – black pants and shirt – then quickly dash into the shower room and turn on the cold tap. I splash my face with the fresh water. Aware I will never have access to clear water like this again, I cup my hands tight, let the water fill up and greedily drink it before it drains away through my fingers. I splash more on my face and my makeup slides off, running black and pink into the sink and down the plughole.

As I leave the shower room I pull my lank hair up into a high ponytail. I reach for my knapsack, then decide I don't need it – if they find out it's gone, they'll know I ran. I pull socks and the snood from it then wonder if my mistress will know I kept my Skel uniform? She might check my bag. I shove the bag and the torn dress under my mattress. That way they'll take longer to figure out what happened to me. I carefully pull each sock over my blistered and glass splintered feet. I didn't bring my boots, and heels will be useless on the streets. There is nothing else, all I have are twenty pairs of different coloured foot cripplers. I decide on socks only.

Outside the apartment, I tiptoe back past the shaft until I reach a door marked 'Stairs'. No palm-pad, I push it open, and sure enough, there's a flight of winding stairs before me. I hurry down in my socks, feet making no sound. I pull open the door at the bottom of the stairs and thump! My body bounces off a guard. Not Kian. Not good.

'What you doing down 'ere?' she yells, and grabs both my wrists.

I struggle, but as I do I size her up. Female guards are picked only if they can challenge a male guard to a fist-fight and win. This guard and I are the same height, the difference is, she's extremely muscular. I'm not sure I can take her, but then looks can be deceiving.

I force my wrists free and grab hold of her, driving my knee upwards. It connects with her hard-pelvic bone. She shouts in pain, folds over and staggers backwards, her baton clatters to the ground. I grab it. Thwack! Blood spits from her nose, she falls forward and her skull thuds against the floor. I don't hesitate. I ditch the baton and start unlacing her boots, all the while wondering where the fuck Bunce is. I knew this was a step too far for him; he's chickened out, typical Morb.

I pull on the freshly polished boots. They fit. I step over the body then double-back. I can't go outside without a weapon. There's a dagger in her belt. I snatch it and shove it into my right boot. I instantly feel secure. I've always carried a knife and the euphoria I feel that I might actually walk out of the Morb complex and into the open air is intoxicating. Excitement mixed with apprehension carries my body towards a far tube. I note there are no apartment doors on this level, only the stairwell, and further down there are shaft doors, only one set, for hover-chairs. Kian is at the tube entrance waiting for me. He knew I wouldn't do as he told me.

'What took you so long?' He smiles, amused at how predictable I am.

'Bumped into a guard,' I pant and move past him.

'Who?' Kian grabs my arm. The one he bruised earlier. I wish he would stop doing that. I tug away.

'I don't know! She's unconscious on the floor back there.'

I glance down and wiggle my toes in my new boots. The floor down here is grubby, not in keeping with the rest of the complex at all.

'Great, more of your mess to clean up.'

He reaches over and rubs something from my temple – blood. That guard's blood.

'Oh, and I do nothing for you?'

I wipe my cheek with my palm, transferring blood mixed with remnants of glitter to it.

'Name one thing you've done to help me in the last month.'

I clean my palm down the front of my cargo pants and try to think of something but he's right, every time he's asked for my help I've said no. Mental note, be a better friend to Kian.

'Bunce didn't show, then?'

I peer round Kian, over his right shoulder then left.

'Don't change the subject.'

He folds his arms over his chest.

'I knew he wouldn't come.' I say.

'Actually, he did.'

I raise my eyebrows.

'I'm as surprised as you are,' Kian says with a grin.

'Where is he, then?'

I peer around Kian once more and squint into the dark tube.

'I sent him on ahead.'

'You what?'

I glare at him, of all the stupid things to do.

'I told him to meet you at Rock Vault.'

I slap my hand to my forehead.

'He'll be dead before I get there!'

'No, he won't. I told him to hide until you arrive.'

'Hide? His skin is as white as the clouds.'

Kian pushes me towards the tube entrance.

'Better go then! You won't have long before they realise you're gone and I better go figure out what to do with that guard you beat up.'

He jogs away from me and I sprint in the opposite direction, down the dark tube, each step echoing off the long cylinder. My concern for Bunce's safety drops away as I dash for my freedom, almost giddy. I run and run and soon my legs tire, muscles shaky, when is this tube going to end? I slow down and a stuffy smell hits me, like old socks. The glass is dark, unlike the other tubes, I can't see the outside. I don't know where I am and that unnerves me. I pick up speed, sprinting faster than I did before despite my protesting muscles. A stitch pinches my side, I hold on to it.

My cheeks go from warm and puffy to cold. I start to shiver. The temperature has changed, this end of the tube is an ice tunnel. Ancient air-con units clatter to life and shush out more cold air. I can't think who would use this tube. Guards only, I imagine, so why run the air-con at all? After I've walked for what seems like an hour, the end of the tunnel is in sight. How did Bunce manage this trek? I was half expecting to find him keeled over a few miles back.

There's movement to my left, a rat? I stand still, now the air-con has quietened down to a low shushing, a faint clicking coming from the floor can be heard – a travelator rolls along. Bunce must have used it to travel all the way to the end. I shoot the track a look of contempt; *my legs ache and it's your fault.* When I reach the end of the tunnel I'm faced with double doors with a palm-pad and a side exit without one. I take the side exit, and as the door swings open the cool 'real' air strikes my lungs. I drink deep, breathing in the stench-ridden air. Above me, the star-speckled sky stretches over the city; no glass, real sky. I might be free from the complex but I'm still not free from the system. I stroll up to Rock Vault and crouch down by the dirty water. I'm thirsty, but there's no way I would drink trench water, with rotting flesh floating in it. The euphoria of escaping my cage quickly evaporates. In the blink of an eye my emotions have changed from elated to anxious. I've swapped one cage for another. The journey has only just begun.

Chapter Ten

Blood Block

There's a scuffing noise behind me, probably a rat. I ignore it, my eyes locked onto the faraway stare of the centremost rotting head on the line.

'Skyla?'

I turn around at the sound of my name. Shoulders hunched, worry carved into his pale face, Bunce trembles like a child afraid of the monsters under his bed, or rather, the monsters hiding in the many filth-ridden cracks and crevices of Gale City. I'm thankful he can't see what's lying in wait; if he saw a Mutil or met a Runner, he'd probably shit his pants. I'm sure he knows about them, the fear twisting his face is enough to tell me that. Perhaps he's heard stories of the streets. The *real* Gale City. I wonder what he's been taught about my world. I'd guess not much, otherwise he wouldn't have come. I'm shocked he didn't back out. Actually, I'm surprised he's not dead already. He's got guts, I'll give him that.

'You look a little green,' I say, standing to face my accomplice. 'Sure you want to do this?'

'I have to,' he says, squaring his broad shoulders and pressing his thin lips together until all trace of pink disappears from them. He doesn't have to come but he wants to believe he does. I attempt a reassuring smile but only manage to twitch my cheeks.

'I can get Kian to take you back, there's still time …'

He shakes his head like a defiant child.

'No! I'm perfectly fine. It's a little overwhelming and it smells funky out here,' he wrinkles his nose, 'that's all … I can't believe I'm actually outside.'

He tilts his head to the sky. He's seen it so many times but always through glass. It must be weird for him. I join him in watching the twinkling stars.

'It's pretty amazing out here,' he sighs. 'Don't you think?'

I look at the dirty ground and then up at the crows sailing down like burnt leaves falling from a lightning-scorched tree, they land on the tips of the black building before us, and blend. No, I don't think it's amazing out here, it's dangerous but a damn sight better than being held prisoner in the Morb complex.

Bunce's wanderlust turns to unease when he notices the black castle that is Rock Vault. It blocks the moonlight, giving the sharp, mountain-like edges an eerie glow and an ominous feel, as if the place is cursed. The only other source of light comes from the single lamp, which shines down on the bolted entrance. The lamp was not placed there so people can see where they're going; it's there so Skels can *see where they're going*. Half the streetlamps on our side of the city are dull or broken but not this one. Central makes sure the prison light is always on and at its brightest. It's there as a reminder, it's there to highlight the heavy doors from which there is no escape, it's a statement. 'Don't step out of line. You don't want to end up here.'

'Are we going in there?' Bunce asks, voice muffled, he has his nose buried in the crook of his arm, the stench from the trenches is obviously getting to him.

What a ridiculous question. No Skel would ever willingly enter Rock Vault; dragged in kicking and screaming, for sure, but willingly walk through the front doors, NEVER. Oh hell, I hope Kian doesn't get into trouble. If Central finds out he allowed us to leave, he'll be thrown head first into a cell.

Bunce waits wide-eyed for an answer, nose still buried behind his elbow.

'Relax, we're not breaking into the city prison,' I say, amused at his naivety. 'Rock Vault is a one-way ticket, people don't come back out, at least, not the same as they went in.'

'Do you think Cara's in there?'

'She might be,' I shrug, 'if she got caught.'

'Do you think she's been caught?' Bunce says, worry driving lines across his forehead.

'We'll soon find out,' I say. 'Our first stop is a guy who knows everything that goes on in this city. It's the only thing that rat-faced, glory gorger is good for and it's what keeps him from being stabbed in the face, by me anyway. He'll know where Cara is. He knows where everyone is.'

'He doesn't know where I am,' Bunce says raising an eyebrow.

'No,' I say, smiling at this oversight, 'he doesn't.'

Bunce coughs and holds his throat as he retches and splutters, struggling to breathe, not used to the natural air, not used to the foul city smells. I hold my hand up to pat him on the back but he's choking on air so there's no use in slapping him, no matter how strong the urge is to belt him about a bit. I withdraw my hand. It's as if he is learning to use his lungs all over again. I hope he doesn't get sick. I hope he can keep up.

Our plan to find the serum was foolhardy at best, suicidal at worst and now I think about it, leaving the complex and taking Bunce with me was downright idiotic, but what else could I do? Bunce, to my knowledge, is the first of his race to ever venture outside. The Morbihan never breathe unfiltered air and I'm not sure what prolonged exposure to the elements might do to his lungs. I need him healthy. I can't be dragging him along. Time is short. If Cara does have the serum, I need to get to her before the guards do. I try to think where she might take it and why, but nothing is making any sense. I untangle my thoughts, one at a time; I'll find out what Tinny knows first and go from there.

Bunce takes a deep breath and again chokes on it. He holds up his right hand, to indicate he's okay. Like he knows what I'm thinking. He doesn't know. I don't want to help him. I want to shut him up. His loud coughing is going to draw attention to us.

'Give me a minute.' He says gasping, 'I'll be fine in a minute.'

Bent over, hands on his knees, Bunce takes great gulping breaths. I imagine his body exploding into a wobbling mess of meat, which is what will happen if we don't hurry. Morbihan puberty comes to an end at twenty-one, I didn't think to ask how close he is to his twenty-first birthday. It could be days away for all I know. He could fat out at any moment. Maybe it's happening now! I envision his trousers splitting and his shirt tearing at the seams – his blindingly bright shirt …

'That's a problem.' I say pointing to his shirt.

'What's a problem?' Bunce splutters.

Hands on hips, I tip my head to my shoulder.

'You look like a rainbow puked on you. Not very inconspicuous, is it.'

Bunce straightens up and his quick breaths ease into a natural rhythm. He tugs his multi-coloured t-shirt out in front of him and inspects it, oblivious to the problem his top could pose. Dumb Morb. He might as well paint a bullseye on his face walking around in clothes brighter than the sun.

'I don't have any dark clothes,' he says, hurt. 'You know that. Morbihan don't wear …'

'Shhh … hear that?'

I pull Bunce down into the shadows beside me and concentrate on listening. He opens his mouth to speak and I touch my index finger to my lips, my hands smell of dry dirt and nail polish. Real life and fake life mixed together. Bunce crouches beside me, fretful, listening. A faint sound builds. A mechanical sound. A pumping sound. An artificial organ pumping blood haphazardly around a rotting body.

'Don't move,' I whisper in Bunce's ear.

I will my mind and body to remain calm; slow my breathing, empty the panic out of my head. It's no use, anxiety rises in my chest as the pumping sound grows nearer and louder, soon accompanied by heavy robotic stamps. Beside me, the Morb is trembling. Bunce's fear leaches into the cool air. Can it smell fear? Will it find us? Bare, blistered feet with chipped, yellowing toenails slap down on the concrete, inches from the shadow we hide in. I keep my breaths shallow, but I can't stop my heart galloping against my rib cage. The horrible wheezing of struggling artificial organs is right above us. The sound reminds me of the factory, when the conveyer belt gets stuck and judders, gears sticking, forcibly grinding together. The Mutil sniffs the air. Fresh meat. What a feast it would have! Bunce would be its best catch ever.

Bunce has no idea how close we are to death. If he did, I'm sure he'd have passed out already, and with little knowledge of the city, out here, alone, he would die within days. Knowledge is a dangerous necessity for me. I could not roam the streets at night without it, and instinct – instinct is survival. Heads full of emptiness don't survive in this city unless you are a Mutil. Although, they are not so much empty-headed as they are wiring gone wrong. Of all the night crawlers in Gale City the Mutil would seem to be the most dangerous, but I know better. I know my enemy and it doesn't roam the streets at night. Knowledge equals alive and empty head equals death, unless you have instincts, and Bunce has neither.

I grab him by the arm. His pulse races against my grip. We're going to have to run. I've never seen Bunce run before, I mean really run. I don't even know if he can, especially with that large backpack he's carrying, but there's no choice. Mutil can run if they have to, fast if they're starved. If only he did own some Air-Soles. They'd come in handy right about now. There's a bathing block about ten metres away. I think Bunce could make it but it's not one that I use, I don't know if it houses squatters or not. Outcasts of the outcasts, they'd slit our throats the moment we opened the door. The drone of the city siren sounds to my left, the Mutil doesn't move, it's caught the scent of flesh. The siren means nothing to it.

'The guards … they know we're missing.'

Bunce's whisper is almost silent, his breath falters on my cheek, his fear infecting me. If they already know we're missing then it's my fault. The guard that I battered and then stole her boots, has probably reported me. I shuffle into a start position, ready to run. Bunce copies, sort of, chin tucked to his chest, body rolled into a ball shape, he shakes all over.

'When I say move, move. Got it?'

He doesn't reply. Did he hear me? I'm not repeating myself. If he didn't hear me, that's his problem.

I wait for the siren to get louder; the noise will muffle our steps. I can't wait too long, if the Mutil doesn't find us, the guards will. *Wait ...* I tell myself. The Mutil grunts and stamps his slab of a foot closer to us. *Wait ...* Fingers spread, I press my hands down hard against concrete, knees bent, muscles tense, lines creasing across my leather boots, poised on the balls of my feet, heels off the ground. *Not yet ...*

'Move!'

I grab a handful of Bunce's chubby arm and yank him up onto his feet and out of the shadows. The Mutil sees us – smells us! I chance a look over my shoulder and my eyes are met with a moulded mess of flesh and machine. Wires hang from a gouged eye socket, remnants of a faded, grey shirt which would have once been black, draped over a skin-coloured skeleton. The shirt is stained with blood, pus, and worse. Cracked lips part and the howl of a wounded beast, held together by the thought of a good meal, wails along with the siren. Bunce whimpers at the sound of the Mutil's cry. Desperate footsteps pound after us, artificial heart pumping harder, faster.

Fist full of Bunce's rainbow shirt, I drag him to keep up the pace. He clumsily staggers along in my wake. Charging footsteps join the ungainly stomps of the Mutil that hunts us. But the brain-dead creature behind me is now a secondary concern. If the guards find us I don't know what they'll do. To my knowledge, Central have never executed a Morb but then no Morb has ever ventured outside before. They could choose to make an example of Bunce, or kill us both on sight. They will, they'll kill us, they'll kill us! The mantra beats to the tune of my quickened pulse.

I skid to a halt and throw Bunce through the first door. The effort it takes to propel his large body forwards knocks me off balance, the metal slips through my fingers and the door slams shut. He yells from the other side. I push the tips of my fingers into the gap between the door and the frame and attempt to peel back the metal. It budges then bites back and I snatch back my hand and shake the sting away. No time. I slip inside the door next to it and press my back up against the cold metal. My heart thumps violently against its cage of bones, my chest heaving. I knew he shouldn't have come. If there are Runners or squatters in that bathing block – he's dead. If the Mutil gets in – he's dead. If the guards find him – he's dead. As much as he drives me insane, I did not bring him along to die.

I press my ear to the cold door. The siren has stopped. I listen for the Mutil. Silence. Thwack! My face is shocked away from the reverberating metal. The Mutil bangs its fists angrily against the door but can't get in. Angry fists crash against the metal three times. I stare at the door, fists clenched. Ready for a fight I can't win.

My boots slip on the grubby tiled floor, I regain my balance and something hard presses against my leg. The guard's knife; I don't draw it, I wait. Seconds turn into a minute. It's gone. When I don't hear Bunce's screams on the other side of the block wall, the rise and fall of my chest slows. I take a cautious step closer to the door and reach out with my shaky fingers. I touch the grimy, square edges of a panel beside the door. Crap! I never use this block. The 'deactivated' palm-pads can sometimes reactivate and lock on the inside, only to be opened from the outside. Lucky for me, the Mutil couldn't work that one out. No locks, no secrets. I wonder if Central knows that this block locks? They said deactivating the locking mechanisms was for our own safety, but I know it was for theirs. I hope upon hope that Bunce's door is locked too.

The bathroom is cold, urine-saturated, empty, and safe. Dirty white tiles cover everything except the ceiling and the bath is stained brown. I imagine an elephant took a dump in it and then smeared it around with his trunk. The beam of light above the one cracked mirror is broken, and it flickers.

Glug, gurgle …

The toilet is talking. I step forward a few paces, lean over and peer into the off-white pot. Is the drain blocked? The water at the bottom of the bowl is rusty orange and rising. It thickens, darkens, emitting a wave of stench into the air, a stink worse than the trenches. Rats stuck in the u-bend?

The putrid liquid starts to rush, bubbling over the rim. Bits of dead rat float to the surface and crimson gloop spills over the edge. My nose wrinkles. I step back. Red water explodes upwards, spraying my face. The stink is a cocktail of excrement, blood, and stale urine. My stomach spasms and I dry retch as I feverishly scrap the splatters of rot from my face, dragging my nails down my cheeks, I want to scrape my skin off. The liquid oozes faster, gallons heaving up and out of the bowl. The dirty, white tiles awash with death from the sewers. Disgusting! I shuffle backwards and try the door – it won't open.

Sweat panics through my skin, hands slippery with bloodied toilet water, my fingers slide across the palm-pad.

'Dammit!'

I wipe my palms down the front of my cargo pants and position both hands up against the palm-pad. I push my body weight onto the panel. I shove and shove at it, scream and slap at the grimy pad until my hands redden and sting. Nothing happens, I can't get out. The rancid river reaches my heels. I pivot on tip-toe, expecting to find the bodies of hundreds of rats flushed over the stained floor. Bile touches the back of my throat. The odour is dizzying and the blood-drenched floor grips me with fear. Not rats … thumbs, fingers, a floating ear, a severed hand; a slithering eel of intestine trail over the bowl and into the blood water lapping at my boots. I clamp my hand over my mouth and nose. *What the hell?* The damp of my socks makes me retch again. I have to get out … I don't want to drown in this, my body a sponge for the liquid dead.

I scan the room, even though I know there are no windows, only vents in the high ceiling that I can't reach. The door is my only hope. I slosh backwards, red water threatening my knees. I boot the door. Not even a dent. I wade backwards again. This time I line up my shoulder. Thud – splash. *Fuck!* I stumble backwards holding the pain to my upper arm. The door is rock solid. Despite the throbbing, I line up and run at the door again and again. Thud, splash, thud, splash; the door flies open, thump – whoosh. The water escapes with me, rushing around my battered body and mixing with the dirty ground to create a new vile odour.

I spit out dirt and the metallic taste of my own blood. My bottom lip ripped across the gritty ground and split, the delicate flesh burst open the way a grape does when pinched between the fingers. I crane my neck to look behind me. Bunce holds the heavy door open. A decaying ear floats up beside his green sneakers. He jumps backwards, releasing the door, it crashes shut. I push up onto my knees and brush the imbedded grit out of my palms, by wiping them down my thighs. Bunce reaches down and I reach up, his meaty hand encases my slender fingers and he pulls me to my feet in one swift motion. He almost lifts me into the air. He's strong. Why does this surprise me? After all, he's never been starved or sleep-deprived or worked to the bone. Why wouldn't he be strong? Because I see him as weak? Weak mind does not mean weak body. Imagine what Bunce could do with a strong mind to go with his strong body.

'What is that stuff?' he asks, in disgust. 'You smell terrible.'

'Beauty treatment of course,' I say, flicking a slither of rotten flesh from my shoulder. 'All Skels wash in blood and severed body parts, didn't you know that?'

'Excuse me?' he says, wrinkling his piggy nose.

'I don't know what the fuck it is, Bunce, okay!' I say, while I wring out my sopping pony tail, my blond hair now a dirty pink.

'Okay,' he says defensively, 'You don't have to swear.'

I roll my eyes.

'Guards? Mutil?'

'Gone, I heard the guards beat the Mutil and drag it away,' He shrugs, but the casual movement doesn't cover up his nervous shuffling from one foot to the other. *Stay still!* He shoves his hands into his pockets in an attempt to stop his twitchy legs. 'W-what happened in there?'

'I dunno,' I say, and I don't. I look down at the trail of blood water coming from the closed block door. I kick at some entrails with my boot. 'The sewer backed up or something and suddenly, river of death. I'm never washing in a block again. I'm going to the pond.'

I stride away. An aching pain in my ribs stops me for a moment, I hold my right side and carry on walking but Bunce doesn't move. I turn around.

'Come on!'

'I can't go there!' Bunce wrings his chubby hands. 'It's in the slums, isn't it?'

'Yeah, so?'

'Eremites don't like outsiders and they hate Morb ...'

'Everyone hates Morbs!' I say it with more malice than I intended.

Bunce looks away. I don't have time for this.

'We're not going to tell them you're a Morb, are we,' I say, softening my tone. 'We'll say you're from a High-Host family.'

'No one will believe that!' Bunce says, kicking at the ground as I did. Red jelly from the blood water sticks to the tip of his sneaker; he hops about and flicks his foot around, flinging off the bloody inners. 'Look at me, I'm paler than the moon.'

'No one'll believe a Morb is outside!' I say impatiently, the guy is the same age as me yet he acts like a giant toddler. 'We'll tell people you've been sick or something. Let's go.'

The patter of Bunce's sneakers joins the rhythmic clonk of my boots as we cross the deserted road. He stays close to me, taking struggled breaths every so often. It's getting easier for him to breath out here. He's adapting quickly. He gasps and ducks down when crows caw overhead. I whisper that it's okay but I wonder if he has been taught about the past. About the birds?

Hundreds of beady-eyed, black crows plague the city skyline, constantly staring, making my skin crawl. They perch on cubes, bridges, and the sky track, in trees, on fences and on severed heads at Rock Vault prison, but never on Morbihan apartments or Central buildings. They only dare to perch on buildings of little importance, ones they can shit on without getting shot.

Apart from us, the crows and rats are the only other creatures around. Still, I should use a little more stealth; the guards will be looking for us by morning if they aren't already. That siren clearly wasn't for us, we'd be on our way back to Rock Vault and through the front doors if it was. I can only imagine the siren sounded in order to scare Cara into giving herself up. I wring out the last drops of blood from my shirt and snood as we head towards the tip. My cargo pants stick to my legs like a second skin, I peel them away but they snap back and cling to me. Misty rain hangs over the silent streets. I sense a storm and pick up speed. Bunce keeps up, wiping his face every few seconds, the moisture in the air new to him.

The pond is roughly six blocks away. The quickest route is through the park, but we can't go that way, the park is always crawling with Mutil. I peer down the dark alleys and unused roads as we pass, so as we don't get jumped by anyone, or anything, lurking in the shadows. Our footsteps echo and there's a manic flapping of wings above us as the crows hurry for cover. Guards ignore most night crawlers, patrols are usually sent to find hard-working useful Skels who Central do not want becoming back-alley dealers. I wonder why they attacked that Mutil? For fun? Guards can be cruel but they don't normally go around beating up Mutil. They need them to keep the gangs and Eremites under control, heaven forbid the guards have to do any real work.

The stars are slowly being blocked out by a layer of fog and the Sky Train tracks are hidden in the gloom. There aren't any night trains, no one is at the controls until first light. Control. I hate being out of control. That's why I hated being a host. I cannot control the city, I tell myself, I can only control my own actions and thoughts. I glance down at the storm drains, beneath are the sewers. I shudder. I don't know what caused that vile toilet explosion or where it came from, or why.

It feels like things have gotten worse since I've been away. I've been gone just ten days and even so the city feels more deprived, more dangerous, deadlier. Maybe it seems that way because I've been living in a different world, a safer world, where people aren't mutilated, beaten, or worked to death. My confidence wanders off. I haven't been away that long, so why do I feel like an outsider? I've changed but I mustn't let my emotions consume me. I hold my head high. Even though we don't control it, Skels run this city and I will not feel intimidated by the impossible situation I find myself in, or the task ahead.

Chapter Eleven

Clover

Eremites are normally up past midnight, after that, Slum Lords take it in turns to guard the place. As we near the top of the grassy knoll which overlooks a sea of ramshackle, plastic houses, the floodlights shoot stars into my eyes. I blink and hold my right hand to my eyebrows in a permanent salute, it's enough of a shade that I can just about see through the blinding light, while Bunce makes a binoculars shape around his eyes with his porky hands. The unusual brightness and stillness puts me on edge. I scan the town, once completely white, the plastic houses stained orange from the years of violent dust storms. It reminds me of the white tubs I steal from the factory and use to store pumpkin soup in, forever stained orange no matter how much I wash them.

The slum is ringed, to keep out wild animals, except these days, the Vector Ring isn't live and there aren't any animals around. I'm sure there must be some somewhere because I work at the meat factory but I've never seen anything other than dogs, snakes, rats, and crows. Eremites don't live by the same moral code as Skels. They'll kill anyone who dares set foot on their territory uninvited. That's why the gruesome Mutil – those disfigured Skels who have been experimented on until their bodies can't take no more – don't come here. Even at night they don't come. Another example of instinct prevailing over lack of brain-power.

I draw my snood around me, a shield against the cold. In the daytime, it serves to keep the harsh sun from my head and during the night, the cold from my bones. Tonight, the air is brisk, not cold, but still I shiver. Probably because I've spent the last few hours soaking wet; first from the sprinklers, next the menstruating toilet, not counting the wispy rain which lingers, spotlighted as it passes by the floodlight bulbs and now I'm about to hit the pond. I hope I don't catch cold. That's all I need.

There's a strange atmosphere, different from the last time I was here. Something's not right. Nothing is ever right but just now, something is very wrong. The drizzle turns to the odd droplet of fine rain, and I'm disappointed, a downpour would have helped wash the filth off. Eyes adjusted to the light, Bunce inches forwards to get a better look at the makeshift homes, slanted at different angles.

'Stop!'

I throw out my arm and Bunce's chest rebounds off it.

'What is it?'

'Not sure.'

He stands perfectly still while I survey the compound. The air smells burnt. I stare hard into nothingness. Unfocusing my eyes, I squint. It's no use, I can't see or hear anything but I can sense it. How did they get enough to charge the VR? Gale City is surrounded by desert, the sun providing a limitless supply of energy, but it's controlled by Central. The solar grids are for Morb use. Skels can use electricity during the day, but it's lights out by nightfall. The only reason the tip is illuminated is so Central can spy on the Slum Lords. An alarm sounds in my head. We should leave… I can't. I stink. I need to wash the blood and guts off. The pungent smell clinging to my clothes is making me want to heave.

'The ring is live,' I tell Bunce.

'Pardon?' he says, confused.

'The –VR – is – live,' I say, stressing the words. 'You know what a VR is, right?'

'Yes, I know what a Vector Ring is,' he says, crossing his arms and huffing, 'but you must be mistaken, it was turned off years ago, and Eremites can't generate power, can they?'

'No, they can't … at least, not enough for the VR.'

I search over my shoulder and under my arms, then crouch down and brush my hands around the slightly damp yet brittle grass, unable to grow, shrinking in the dry ground, waiting for a storm that didn't come. I spot something grey; a dead rat. I pick up the maggot-infested rotten pile of fur by the tail.

'Don't touch that, it's not sanitary. Think of the germs!'

'Germs?' I say, holding the rat up close to his face, 'But this is our dinner.'

'What?' He covers his mouth, in case I might shove the maggoty-rat in there. 'You can't be serious,' he says, voice muffled by his fingers.

I glare at Bunce.

'Of course I'm not serious! You don't actually think I'll eat this?' I say, indignantly. 'Do I look like a Mutil?'

Bunce eyes the bits of flesh and entrails stuck in my hair.

'Um …'

'Um?'

His face flushes darker shades of scarlet with every passing second.

Rat held out, away from my body, the maggots wriggle from the gaping hole in its side, hit the yellow grass below and writhe around. I flick my lank ponytail over my shoulder with my free hand; cringing at its straw-like texture, damp and stiff, same as the grass, and as my hair flips behind me, a slither of toilet-vomited skin flies off and slaps against Bunce's round cheek. Not wanting to touch it with his bare hands he uses the sleeve of his shirt to rub the putrid skin away, continuing to rub his cheek even after the skin has dropped to the ground. The fallen maggots immediately inch towards it.

Bunce thinks we're all the same; the Skels, Eremites, and the Mutil. I suppose he's right in a way, we all started out as slaves to the system. I broke Central law every night I refused to stay in my cube. It's pure luck that I'm not a Mutil or living in the slums, which might be a reality if I don't find the serum. I sniff. I may not be a Mutil but I am starting to smell like one. I squeeze the dead rat in my hand and bits of fur and a claw drop down beside my boots.

'You Morbs are so ignorant,' I say. 'Why bother spending your days in an education unit if you're going to come out dumber than when you went in?'

I squeeze the ball of fur in my hands and more maggots drop out. I draw back my arm and throw it straight ahead. It impacts with the invisible wall, sizzles and drops to the ground emitting a rancid smoky smell. Bunce stares at the crispy rat.

'Yep, the ring is live.'

'How did you – I can't see anything.'

Bunce stares and stares at the place where the rat hit the invisible barrier.

'Kian,' I say, crouching to tie my unravelled bootlace, 'he taught me never to rely on my eyes and ears alone and showed me how to tap into my intuition. It's kind of a sixth sense.'

I think of Kian. My one true friend. I wish he was here with me now. My mother died giving birth to me, my grandfather went twelve years later, and I have no idea who my father is or was, he could be dead for all I know. Kian is all I have. Others helped in my survival, giving me a job at the factory, trading with me at the market but Kian has always been the only person (apart from little Tess and my grandfather) who I've ever truly cared about. Except now I have a new purpose, someone I need to make sure survives, someone who could help bring about change for the entire city and who's given me a reason to keep on living.

'BUNCE!'

'Hooo-weee! I gots me a Morb. What are the chances? How much you reckon this one'll fetch when I 'and him over eh, Skyla?'

I don't move from my crouched position, I lock eyes with the tin-hatted freak show. Tinny holds Bunce by the throat and grins a toothless grin, tin cap tipped to one side, neck veins protruding, jerky body movements. He's been using; high on glory, eyes all pupils. More colour drains from Bunce's face with each slip and press of the makeshift cheese grater knife at his neck. Tinny's long nose is always in everyone's business, but I can't believe he'd know a Morb was walking about the city. The only other person who knows about us is Kian and if Central has already worked it out, they wouldn't want the rest of the city to find out. They'd keep that a secret at all costs.

'Tinny,' I say calmly. 'Think about it. Morbs don't go outside, he's a High-Host. I found him, he's my prisoner.'

'Your prisoner, pfft!' shrieks Tinny. 'I is hearing things about 'choo. Heard you is a host. Steal him from the complex, did ya? This Morb ain't no more your prisoner than I am your friend, so don't talk like we friends, coz we ain't, and he's mine!'

I touch the knife handle that protrudes from the top of my boot and look for the best place to strike. My options are limited. I need to know where Cara is but I cannot risk Bunce's throat being slit. One false move and this unpredictable junky will plunge that jagged metal grater into my 'ticket' to a better life. I decide against brandishing the knife.

'Hand him back,' I say, slowly straightening up, staring into Tinny's sunken face. 'You're on the wrong side of the slums this late at night.'

'You'd like that wouldn't cha, keep this prize all for your ...'

Warm droplets spray across my cheek, I close my eyes and turn my face but my ears catch it; the desperate back breath of someone drowning in their own blood. *No, I need Bunce alive. This can't happen.* I couldn't even get him a few blocks past Rock Vault before walking into trouble. I knew he shouldn't have come and now he's ... alive, he's alive! Eyes wide, I stare into a smiling charcoal face then glance down at Bunce, who is kneeling beside his backpack at his saviour's feet. Bunce holds his neck, probably more to stop himself from being sick than holding the pain where the blade pierced his skin. I doubt he has ever seen death, not like this – real death. Clover holds Tinny up like the catch of the day. Clover; black as night and twice as deadly, arms like boulders, teeth like pearls, how is it he has not succumbed to other Eremites' dependence on glory? I stand to face Bunce's rescuer.

'Clover, you killed the Slum Lord.' I say, trying not to sound alarmed.

'I killed *a* Slum Lord, not *the* Slum Lord,' Clover says calmly, his voice as smooth as silk.

He throws Tinny to the ground like spoils and with one giant boot on the corpse's back, he pulls the blade from the body. The scrawny tin-capped addict leaks his life's blood over the water-starved grass. Thoughts grow inside my head. *No Tinny, we are not friends and I don't care that you're dead.*

Clover stabs the sword into the ground and leans lightly on the hilt. For an Eremite, he is dressed well. Slum Lords are only slightly better presented then the rest of the Eremite population but Clover always looks clean and healthy, coursing with vitality. I admire his strength – mental and physical. I always have. When my grandfather died and I was left a skinny, undernourished twelve-year-old wretch, Clover reached out to me – watched over me, in a way. He will ask questions about Bunce. What do I tell him? If I tell him the truth, he'll kill Bunce, but he'll know if I'm lying. Those piercing dark eyes never miss a trick.

Bunce coughs, snatches up his backpack and stumbles to his feet. He holds out his hand. Clover frowns at me. My eyes flick to the ground. It's not customary to shake hands in our society, it spreads illness and disease. We're exposed by this Morb's silly gesture of thanks or greeting or politeness, I never know which. Clover's face softens, he yanks the sword from the ground.

'Sure, take a look,' he holds out the hilt. 'Since I saved your life, I'm guessing you won't try to kill me.'

Smooth, brown lips curl and hug white teeth, pushing Clover's strong cheekbones up into soft peaks. Bunce's pink cheeks quiver as he nervously takes the sleek sword. My sigh of relief goes unnoticed.

'Ha ha, never held a sword, huh?' Booms Clover. 'Lift it a little higher, feel the weight, it's a weapon of beauty.'

Bunce lifts the blade, too heavy for him, he struggles to keep his hands steady. The metal gleams under the harsh floodlights. Red stains the bottom half of the sword. Bunce's eyes are focused on the blood. Unlike the trembling Bunce, Clover stands with his shoulders back, hands on hips, relaxed. Like killing someone on an evening stroll is as common as saying hello to a friend at the market. He watches Bunce closely.

'Tell me, what is a High-Host doing out here at this hour?'

Bunce shoots me a look of corncern then stares back at the sword in his hands. Holding the blood-smeared metal isn't helping his fear of the dead body a few feet away. Why does he fear Tinny? He can't hurt him now, he's dead. Bunce looked less scared with a knife at his throat. I dust dry grass from my knees. The dried-on, bloody toilet water makes my pants feel as though they are made of cardboard.

'Bunce accidentally locked himself in a bathing block and I was trying to get him out. He was checking the blocks for squatters.' I say, which isn't entirely untrue. Will Clover notice my half-lie?

'Isn't that a job for the guards?'

I think quickly.

'They're busy investigating an explosion in the Morb complex. Bunce is a volunteer.'

'Ah, a volunteer! Good man! We Eremites pride ourselves on volunteering.' Clover grips Bunce's shoulder. 'You got a real job, unlike those other High-Host pussies.'

'Y-yes.' Bunce stammers.

'So, what are you doing in my neck of the woods?' Clover asks me. 'You're covered in more than that tin-can man's blood, Skyla. Want to tell me what happened?'

'It's a long story,' I say, dismissively. 'I really need to wash this stuff off.'

Bunce awkwardly passes the sword back to Clover and breathes 'thank you.'

Clover takes it. His eyes stay on me as he wipes the metal clean on the dry grass and then slides the blade back into the sheath at his belt. He places his thick hand on my shoulder and squeezes.

'Don't lie to me, little Sky. I know when you're hiding something.'

I suddenly remember how brutal Clover can be, even to those he calls friend. The Slum Lord's accusing stare sends a nervous tingle to my stomach. The VR is dangerous but I would rather take a volt from that than cross Clover.

'It's nothing, I just need to get clean,' I say. 'I've never hidden anything from you and I never will, and now you've saved Bunce's life, we're both in your debt.'

Bunce bows, a custom that is recognised. Clover nods.

'Okay,' he says softly, suspicion still etched on his face. 'Follow me.'

We follow Clover. I check Bunce's neck as we walk side by side. A few red marks from the jagged edge of the knife, nothing serious. We follow Clover to a line of palm trees. One is bent so far over its long palms almost touch the ground on the other side of the VR.

'I can't climb that!' Bunce says, backing away.

Clover laughs heartily.

'It's not something I would attempt either, Bunce.'

Clover is broad and muscular while Bunce is stocky, more meaty than muscly. I could scale the tree but I'm not dumb enough to do it. Not with the floodlights highlighting our position and spilling shadows beyond; shadows anyone could be hiding in. The guards would easily spot me, no branches to hide in up a palm tree. Clover reaches down and pulls up a looped rope. It's attached to the grass and he lifts up a large circle of dirt along with it.

'A tunnel,' I say, surprised.

I've been coming to the slums to visit Tess for years and in all those years she's never mentioned this tunnel, and she'd surely know of its existence. Or maybe not. At ten years old, I doubt she would have ever experienced a time when the VR was used.

'Yes, a secret tunnel,' Clover reaffirms, 'and if I find out others have heard about this, I will know who to blame.'

Clover leers at us. Now I know why Tess didn't tell me. Clover's threats are not to be taken lightly.

I duck into the tunnel. The earth walls have nothing reinforcing them, as if a large animal burrowed through. It's dark for only a moment before I pop out the other side. Clover nudges Bunce forward and the Morb stumbles towards me, brushing dirt from his hair where he didn't crouch low enough in the tunnel. He looks longingly up at the palm tree, not keen on being this side of the VR.

'You're always welcome to use the pond, Sky, you know that,' Clover smiles. 'Shall I take care of your friend here?'

Bunce fretfully shakes his head at me.

'Yes,' I say, 'Bunce would love to learn all about Eremite culture, wouldn't you, Bunce?'

My Morb companion gulps, half-nods, and allows Clover to lead him away. He looks over his shoulder at me, worried eyes pleading with me to reconsider. I smile. He will be safer with Clover than he is with me even if *he* doesn't know that.

Chapter Twelve

Crow in the Shadow

The pond is not far beyond the plastic shanty town. I make my way quickly through litter-carved streets, and to each side of me the shacks are lifeless or rather, the people inside them are playing dead. A tingling feeling shivers through my hair, I'm being watched. Rag curtains twitch, are they hiding from something? Staying inside because Central have turned on the floodlights?

Beyond a thick treeline, the vast pond appears. Twin moons face each other on sheets of black, the only difference between them is that the bottom one ripples. Cicadas hide in the thick weeds and trees around the side of the pond, their clicking song the only indicator of their existence.

I strip down to my underwear, careful to place my boots where I can see them. Last thing I want is for someone to steal my knife. I step into the pond then flinch. The water is colder than I expected and mud squelches between my toes. I cross my arms over my frozen breasts and wade in, holding tight to my filthy clothes. The chilly ripples of water shock my skin, goose-pimples instantly rising all over my body. I submerge up to my waist, hard stones replace the mud beneath my feet, at least I hope they're stones. I get a foothold and reach over and rip off the head of a pink lotus flower.

Shaking uncontrollably with the cold, I crush the petals into the material and scrub the dirt and grime from my shirt, snood, pants, and socks then throw them next to my boots. My body temperature regulates, I stop shivering and let down my hair, then lean back to rinse out the putrid bloody water and entrails. I use more petals, rubbing them into my scalp. It won't get rid of the smell completely but it should at least mask it. With my head tipped back, ears blocked with water, I watch the slow movement of the shaggy trees in the breeze. The centremost one is lined with crows, more than is usual. The birds darken the tree, making it seem sinister, a swaying, feathered monster, its many beady eyes staring down at me.

I sense a different set of eyes on me and wade out of the water, underwear and hair dripping. I wring out my clothes and dress, all the while keeping my eyes on the tree. My cargo pants are especially troublesome. Nothing to dry myself with, I jump and struggle to pull them over my damp legs. My shirt slides on with ease but immediately sticks to my bony body, outlining what little curves I have. I bring my snood to my nose. It still smells rancid. I tie it around my waist instead of wearing it then slip into my boots, and replace the knife. I smooth back my hair, and stare up at the crow-laden tree. Little birdy heads twitch about.

'Have you been watching me the whole time?' I ask.

The thud of heavy boots hits the dry ground.

'Yep, spying on half-naked girls is a hobby of mine.'

Kian steps out of the shadows, moonlight twinkling in his emerald eyes.

'Shouldn't you be on duty or something?' I say. What's he doing here?

'I have to report back on the lab explosion,' he says, stepping closer. 'But, I wasn't there, I was making sure a guard who passed out, probably from exhaustion,' he winks, 'got back to the barracks.'

He shrugs. He's tried to tame his wavy hair by sweeping it back with some sort of styling product. He does look smart in his guard uniform. Red scarf tied around his neck, tan jacket and trousers, pressed and dirt-free. A far cry from the scruffy teenage boy I met at the pond eight years ago.

'Yeah, sorry about that.'

I kneel down, adjust the knife and pull my bootlaces a little tighter.

'If you'd listened to me, I wouldn't have had to ask Fingers to cover for me and you wouldn't be out here freezing your arse off!'

He holds out his arms, expecting me to rush to him. Instead I hug my arms around me. I'm cold but I don't want his warmth. He's going to ask me to go back.

'What do you want from me, Kian?'

'All I want is for you to be happy.'

Kian takes another step closer and reaches for my hand. I let him take it. Water runs down from my arm, he doesn't move. He reaches up and brushes my swollen lip with his thumb. I heal quickly. It's sealed up and doesn't hurt anymore. It must look worse than it is.

'What happened to your lip?'

'I fell and kissed the ground.'

'Some kiss.' He smiles.

Our eyes lock, in a way they never have before. I turn my cheek to his stare, heat flushing my skin. He senses my discomfort, drops my hand and steps back, wiping his palm down the sides of his trousers, pretending the dripping water was the reason he retreated.

'Where is he? Dead already?' he asks.

'Where's who?' I say, still in a daze from Kian's tenderness. What was that? Maybe I'm making too big a deal of it. We're close friends. That's all.

'Your pet Morb.'

'He's with Clover.'

'Clover! You trying to scare him to death?'

Kian looks amused as if he'd like nothing better.

'At least I didn't send him out into the city alone, like you did.'

'He survived, didn't he? Although he might be dead now. Clover won't tolerate insults and I can't imagine your Morb knows how not to insult an Eremite. He could say anything.'

A rush of concern slaps my face.

'See you around, Kian.'

I turn to leave.

'What about our ...'

Kian trails off.

'Our what?' I ask, confused.

'Forget it, go back to your Morb,' Kian shakes his head dismissively. 'If you'd stayed at the complex you couldn't have come. We should probably stop coming here every year anyway. Our lives are different now.'

'I didn't forget,' I say, but I did and I feel bad.

Being trapped inside the Morb complex has caused me to lose track of time. I might not have remembered the anniversary, but the day we first met is fresh in my memory.

I was a wiry twelve-year-old girl when I first bumped into Kian. I'd been caught stealing apples. The orchard guards let me off lightly. No broken bones, just a black eye and bloody nose. Kian found me at the edge of the pond, washing the red from my bleeding face, and here I am washing blood from myself again, at least this time it isn't mine.

I remember staring at my pitiful reflection, droplets of salty tears adding to the murky pond water. My sadness turned to alarm at the sudden appearance of a rippling male face over my shoulder. I tried to scramble away but Kian caught me up, said he wouldn't harm me. I instantly fell into his embrace, sobbing. He cradled me and I felt safe, wrapped in my Kian cocoon, my new-found friend. We talked for the longest time, secure in our stillness, for hours, peacefully watching the sun disappear and the moon arrive. From then on, every year we would meet back at the pond and eat stolen apples. After a while, security tightened around the food supply and we agreed not to risk going into the orchard again. He never kept his end of the bargain.

I'm brought back from my daydream by the sound of feathers ruffling.

'Why is that thing on your shoulder?'

A crow is nestled lovingly next to Kian's cheek.

'This is Glider,' he says, scratching the back of the winged beast's head.

'Glider?'

The bird nips at Kian's cheek, spreads his black wings, springs from his shoulder, flaps into the air and glides down onto a nearby branch.

'He's kinda taken to me,' Kian says. 'Follows me everywhere.'

'That's creepy, Kian,' I say, in a hushed voice.

'Why is it?' Kian crosses his arms.

'It just is. Why don't you use your influence on the birds for something useful?'

'Like what?' he snaps. 'We've talked about this before. There's nothing I can do.'

'Kian, that kind of power could change everything. It's not just that you can charm the birds ...'

'... the birds, the birds, that's all you ever go on about!' he yells, throwing his arms into the air. 'When all I've ever wanted to do is charm you!'

This admission cuts off my voice, slices right through my retort. We fall silent. The cicada's chatter grows louder, as if they're gossiping about us. Kian's eyebrows knit, the angles of his chiselled face are dipped in shadow, and moonlight shines over his emerald stare but not within it. The light is stolen from behind his eyes by his frustration with me. I've known him forever, and I love him dearly but ... Has he always felt this way about me or has he only just realised? Maybe deep down I've always known and chosen to ignore it – or I chose not to see it? As much as he is handsome, in a dark and brooding kind of ... oh, maybe I do feel something for him? No, I've been cooped up in that Morb complex for too long, I'm desperate for affection. I stare at his smooth caramel skin, his Cupid bow lips. He stares back. Never blushing, never faltering, always confident – over-confident.

'Kian, I'm sorry,' I say, stepping towards him, I reach out and rub his arm. 'I don't feel ...'

His lips are on mine, soft, moist. I can't move. Warm kisses move over my stunned mouth and his hand is suddenly at the small of my back. I flinch, but I don't pull away. Instead I close my eyes and move my mouth in rhythm with his. He tastes like apple. Did he steal them or did they give them to him, now he's a guard? My thoughts disappear when his rough, strong hand grasps the back of my neck and a tingle shivers down my spine. I press my lips against his, and push my fingers into his dark hair. He responds. My waist is tugged towards him, tight up against his pelvis. My heart jumps. What am I doing? I should stop. I can't stop. Everything aches. A breathless urge, my chest heaves, *kiss him harder*. The taste of apple teases my tongue and words whisper inside my head. *Let it happen. How long has it been since you've had a man?* He pulls me into the shadows and presses me against the rough bark of a tree. I want this, I want Kian to touch me – taste me. We kiss passionately, my lip stings, I ignore it, my senses in favour of the rush of excitement. The world evaporates and I run my hands down his back as he pushes his up the back of my shirt, fingers pressed firm against my damp skin. My body says *take him*. My mind arrives just in time. I press my hands to his firm chest and push until his lips disengage with mine. He holds my arms. I hang my head.

'I can't do this, Kian.' I gently give him back his arms, like I am giving back a borrowed touchpad.

'Why?' he says. His eyes sting with hurt. They threaten to rip out my heart. I rub my arm, the guilt all-consuming.

'You're like a brother to me,' I say.

'Really?' he says, aghast. 'See, I have three brothers and I don't kiss them, and definitely not like that!'

'Why are you being like this?'

'Like what? You're a fine one to talk. You're screwed up. Kiss me and then back off. Don't want to be a host, running from your responsibilities. You do my head in.'

I stare at the ground. When I first told Kian that I didn't want to do Showcase, that I would run away into the desert and never come back, he made me promise to never go near the wall. He said going into the desert was a death sentence and begged me to stay, told me I might like being a host and to give it some thought. I said I would think about it. I didn't. My mind was made up. Subconsciously, I was never going to be a host. I will not conform. Anger spikes in my throat. I clench my jaw.

'And what do you suggest I do?' I ask him. 'Go back and enjoy being impregnated with some Morb bitch's baby? Do you know what they do to hosts? Do you know about the examinations?'

'It's gotta be better than being on the run,' he says. 'You act like you'd rather starve.'

'Is that all life is about for you?' I say, blood thumping in my ears. 'Surviving? Doesn't matter how you live, just make sure you survive, right? Well guess what, Crow? The goal of life is death! But I guess you wouldn't know that, since you were the only one left.'

'Don't call me that!' he snaps back. His pet bird glides down to his defence, lands on his shoulder and squawks at me. I glare at the bird. He can snap his beak at me all he likes. I'm not afraid, much.

'Why? That's what everyone calls you!' I shout. 'That's what you are! Look at them, at your beck and call!'

I point at the crow on his shoulder then at the tree behind us where at least twenty crows fidget, waiting for a command from Kian. I'm annoyed at him for not wanting to change things, for not using his strange influence over the birds. I can't stop myself from raging at him.

'You survived and yet you've done nothing to help our people, avenge those who were killed, to build a better life for the rest of us!'

'You're so self-righteous!' He shouts. The crow caws and adjusts itself on Kian's shoulder so as not to fall. 'You think you have all the fucking answers! Are you saying I should kill all the birds in the city? Or maybe I should train them to attack Morbs and Central? These people don't go outside, Sky! What can I do?'

'You could do something, anything! But you don't!' I yell, fury flushing my cheeks. 'You didn't come here because of the anniversary; you came because you have orders to capture me and Bunce!'

Kian's eyes sharpen.

'You really know how to stick it in and break it off! Is that how little you think of me? That I would allow you to escape only to take you back hours later? Risk everything to get a reward, a pat on the back, is that it? You think accolades are important to me!'

I realise my mistake but it's too late, the damage is done. I try to grab his hand.

'Kian …'

'Don't!' he says, backing away.

'Kian, please!' I beg.

The crows flap from tree to tree following their master as he disappears into the night. He doesn't look back; his words throw the hurt back at me.

'You've changed,' he says, a bitterness in his voice I've never heard before. 'That Morb boy has changed you. I hope you'll be very happy together.'

'What are you talking about?' I shout.

'Good luck with your new life.'

'Kian, wait!'

He doesn't wait, he walks into the night, disappearing from sight, and from my life.

Chapter Thirteen

Tess

I find Clover and Bunce outside Clover's hut, playing a game of cards with Tess. Bunce sits uncomfortably on the edge of his chair. I'm not sure what's bothering him the most; the dirty chair and flop table; the ugly shacks and the filthy, makeshift streets; or the company he's keeping. It's probably a mixture of all those things. At least he's still in one piece. I guess that's because he's with Clover, no one would dare question his presence in front of a Slum Lord.

The Eremite welcome me and a handful of others, but not all Skels would have the same warm reception if they wandered into the slums. Eremite barter with Skels at the market but that's where the pleasantries stop. Inviting such city puppets and sinners against nature into their homes would be another matter.

Skels are a close-knit community. They look after their own first. They'd never watch a child starve, any child, even an outsider, but they won't reach out either. Don't let everyone in, there won't be enough food, we might starve. Better them than us. That's how Skels think. Eremites are different.

They work under the guidance of Slum Lords. There are four – three, now Tinny is dead. Each protect their corner of the slum, or they're meant to, some abuse their power; they rape girls and steal food from the weak. Clover is Tess's lord and I'm thankful for that. He treats his people well, but he's not always around to make sure they don't go hungry. That's why I look out for Tess, as Kian used to look out for me. I touch my lips. Kian kissed me. My mind gives me pictures of Kian's face, lips, and the intense feeling of his strong body pressed to mine.

'Everything alright, Skyla?' asks Clover, his face mirroring my bafflement.

'Everything's fine,' I say, ducking behind Tess to check her cards. I whisper the winning hand in her ear. She smiles, hazel eyes lighting up the freckles on her nose. She lays her cards down on the dirty, plastic table.

'Read 'em and weep!' she says, scraping her winnings towards her, which consist of a Central bag charm, obviously Bunce's, one of her hair clips, and a red cactus fruit – Clover's bet. I hug Tess's shoulders and she wraps her thin arms around my neck, she's in her night clothes.

'Does your mother know you're out of bed?'

'Not exactly,' she says, frowning.

'Come here,' I say, turning Tess sideways. 'Right side again, huh?'

An 'I'm loved' smile spreads across my young friend's face.

'I don't know how it happens,' she says, bashful.

I re-braid her hair and turn her round to face me, holding her plaits out either side of her head.

'Getting long. Soon we'll be able to use them as jump ropes!'

I spin the long copper plaits and Tess giggles. Clover smiles at us.

'Your mother will start to worry, young Tess,' he says warmly. 'Hurry back now.'

Tess gathers her prizes and bobs out from behind the table.

'Will you take me back? I'm scared,' she whispers.

'Of what?'

'Please! I'll tell you when we get there.' Her eyes dart to Clover.

'I'm gonna walk Tess home.' I say causally, 'Back soon.'

Bunce exhales and nods nervously.

'Just me and you this round then, Bunce!' Clover booms and deals the cards at speed.

Tess scurries off. I follow her round a plastic corner and straight into a huddle of Eremites; plastic hats on their heads, crow feather earrings, one wearing a spoon necklace. Their cold stares startle me, the place has been deserted until now. Their suspicious eyes follow me; sunken, bloodshot, the harsh floodlights must be keeping them up. I hurry after Tess; she's quick and nimble, swiftly weaving between people and ducking under their arms. I struggle to keep up. I don't look directly at faces as I excuse my way through the whispering slum dwellers. They talk in close quarters, glancing up every so often, eyes shifty. Up ahead, I catch sight of Tess's long plaits as she disappears into a shack with toilet seats for windows. The makeshift homes around me are made out of tubs, circuit boards, cables, doors, broken glass and all manner of refuse; the shack opposite Tess's has a tall pipe sticking out of the top, billowing with smoke like an oversized glory stick.

When I duck into the interlocking plastic junk house, the first thing I notice is Tess's mother's porcelain bed. It's a bathtub. There's a discoloured beanbag devoid of most of its beans next to it, I guess that is where Tess sleeps. All these years I've been visiting her, bringing her food, and I have never been inside Tess's home, I've never met her mother and now I have, I wish I hadn't. I peer into the tub. The woman inside is nothing more than skin pulled over bones. There's a strange beauty in her sickness, a peacefulness that she will die soon, on not quite her own terms but not on Central's terms either. She looks as if she is already in the afterlife, but then the hazel eyes, which have sunk deep into her skull, shift to look at me. She recognises me. Although we haven't met before, we know each other, and I understand the stare. I'm Tess's guardian. I nod. She blinks in thanks and closes her eyes.

Tess leaps into my arms, like she always does when I'm not expecting it. I stagger and hug the tiny bag of bones whose mother is dying, with no one to protect her ... tears threaten. She is younger than I was when I lost my only living guardian. I don't want to see her dragged out of the slums and put to work, but I don't want to see her stay and starve to death, either. She strokes a strand of my damp hair behind my ear with her delicate fingers.

'Are you staying with me this time?'

I cradle the back of her head and hold her close so she won't see my sorrow.

'Not this time, sweetheart,' I say, a lump in my throat. I wish I could stay.

'A Mutil was here,' Tess says softly into my cheek.

My body stiffens, like a poisonous caterpillar is inching up my spine.

'When?' I ask calmly.

'A few days ago, before they switched on the ring,' Tess whispers, her hot breath tickling my ear. 'I heard its cry. It woke me up.'

'What happened to it?' I ask Tess. 'Did one of the lords get rid of it?'

'I don't know but I'm scared more will ...'

'They won't.'

'But what if ...'

'Tess. I'll always be here when you need me.' I say, holding her a little tighter. 'I won't let the monsters get you, okay?'

Tess nods and her chin bumps against my shoulder. I hate lying to her. I can no more protect Tess from Mutil than I can protect myself, but I want her to feel safe. It's no good telling a child that there's a very good chance the monster will come back and rip her to shreds. She'd never sleep again. I wonder how it got in, and why would a Mutil risk being killed by Eremites? If they work out there's strength in numbers, the Eremites will be in real trouble when Central switch off the VR.

Mutil never hunt in packs, I tell myself, but anything's possible. Tess could have been woken by the Mutil calling for others, waiting for the signal to ambush the slum dwellers. It would be a bloodbath and I'm not sure the Eremites would come off better.

I lower the starved ten-year-old girl down onto her beanbag, where she curls up. A torn, threadbare nightgown hangs off her body like an old pillowcase, it might actually be an old pillowcase. She's small for ten, her frame suggesting she's only been alive for seven years or less. I tug the rag that is her blanket around her, kiss her forehead, and slip out onto the makeshift streets. Perhaps Tinny was out checking for Mutil when he came across me and Bunce.

In a daze, I shoulder my way through the huddled residents, they're clearly rattled by the Mutil intrusion. I knock into people and they protest, I ignore them and turn the corner. I wonder if I should ask Clover about Cara? Central will know by now that we're missing and soon we'll have to deal with guards on top of everything else. I'm certain Kian wasn't sent to capture us, he probably thought he could persuade me to hand myself in, or at least abandon my plan to find the cure. He failed on both counts.

'We'd better leave,' I say to Bunce as I reach the table. 'Daylight is coming and it is not our friend.'

'Daylight might not be your friend, Sky,' says Clover, pushing his chair out from the table. 'However, you have a good friend in Bunce, here.'

Bunce smiles at me and I catch it, smiling back. I send it on to the Slum Lord.

'As are you, Clover,' I say warmly. 'The shade protecting me from the sun.'

'Dear child, you honour me with your words,' Clover replies, glancing back at Bunce. 'The sun's not something you see much of, eh? I'm sure there are many hosts who would love to know your skin whitening secret. What are you doing? Injecting yourself with white paint? You're as pale as a Morb!'

The Slum Lord laughs heartily and Bunce adds a weak 'ha ha'. Clover doesn't notice the alarm in the young Morb's face.

'Now, what's all this about a serum?'

'What?' I say, startled.

'Bunce tells me there's a rumour around The Hub that someone has created a cure for the Morbihan condition.'

I glare at Bunce, who is smiling and wincing at the same time, as if he's going to be hit on the head with something. My fist, if he isn't careful! Clover looks up at me, floodlights illuminating his strong bone structure, his face glowing, blessed from above. When I don't answer right away, his smile fades. I'm going to have to offer some sort of explanation.

'We met at Showcase. I was standing next to his family. There was some sort of technical delay and we got talking, joking really, about how weird it would be if the Morbihan stopped piling on the pounds.'

Why did I do that? Why didn't I tell Clover the truth? He raises an eyebrow.

'When I helped him out of the bathing block, he mentioned he saw a news report about a serum, didn't you, Bunce?'

Bunce nods vigorously.

'A-and I said we should ask Tinny what he knew about it. I thought it might be valuable. If I could get some of this serum, it might help with Tess, you know, I could trade it for more food, or something.'

More lies. Can he sense it?

'Yes, I believe such a thing would be valuable,' Clover says, eyeballing me suspiciously. 'But I doubt you will find what you seek in the slums. Tinny was a gossip, nothing more.'

Bunce's eyes dart over to me.

'It's just a rumour. It probably doesn't even exist. I should be getting back,' he says.

'You're probably right, young Bunce. Skyla often gets carried away, she's a dreamer.' The muscular mountain of a man winks at me, then stands. Bunce also gets to his feet. 'Allow me to escort you both safely back to the other side of the Vector Ring. Our community is a little jumpy at the moment. What with Central using the lights and the ring. They're worried about being spied on and strangers won't be tolerated.'

'Thank you, Clover,' I say.

Bunce nods politely and shoulders on his backpack. I pull my hair back into a ponytail and follow behind. We reach the bent palm tree and quickly scurry through the short tunnel. Once back on the other side, Clover turns to me and bows his head.

Pain slams into the side of my face, I hold on to it. Did Clover and I butt heads? My temples pound, lids heavy, I allow my eyes to close. I force them open again, vision blurry, I can just make out Clover; his robes whirl around him as he searches for the attackers. Bunce's big eyes flash with fear as bodies close in around him. Tan uniform. Guards! No! No! My eyes roll back, the black pulling them under. My body goes limp. Thud.

Chapter Fourteen

Captured

My memory is being swept. I can feel it. Like someone thumbing pages inside my mind. It prickles. No interrogation? Straight to the mind manipulating. Where's Bunce? That Morb has dodged death without any skill. Luck has been on his side, but this time there's no escape. The Dark Angel of death must have found him. If not, people will start calling him Clover, so named is the Slum Lord because of his incredible good luck. Did Clover's luck finally run out or did he manage to escape the guards?

Hard metal throws pain through my back. I can't open my eyes, it's as if they've been sewn shut.

'She's coming around. Her thought patterns are replacing the memories.'

A woman's voice, I don't recognise it. Lemons sprinkled with sugar. Not a nurse.

'Give her another shot,' a droning male voice sounds to my right.

I start to shiver, convulse, consciousness knocking at a door I can't answer.

'Ouch!'

A thick needle is jabbed into my temple, I accidentally bite down on my tongue and warm blood swims over it, metallic taste strong in my mouth.

The last few days flash through my mind in a blur, like smeared paint. Everything happened so quickly. My life went from the usual to unusual, from bad to hopeless. I attempt to break into the real, my eyelids flicker but won't open. It's futile.

'What are you looking for, dammit!' I yell to nothingness.

The side of my head throbs. Cognition starts to fade and I'm surrounded by the past, which feels like the present. The blackness becomes brighter and brighter until my lids flicker open and unnatural light stabs my eyes. I squint, reality forgotten, memories made real. My mind throws up a place I'd rather not remember.

The sign above the store in front of me flashes in a continuous rhythm, lighting up the words: Hyper Market. I stare until I feel my eyes un-focus. Blink. Spots appear. A male maid sweeps past me and into the shop. I take a step forward. I know I shouldn't, I really mustn't, but curiosity has control of my feet and before I know it I'm on the other side of the doors. I jump when a chirpy voice echoes around me.

'*Welcome to the Hyper Market, all your nutritional needs under one roof.*'

I follow the maid, who is dressed in the usual black suit and bowler hat. I note he hasn't brought a knapsack to carry food back in. I scan other shoppers up ahead, none of whom carry bags. Why would anyone visit a market without bags? I walk in the maid's footsteps, he strides down the narrow aisle, reaching from right to left pressing squares on the walls. Every so often he stops and looks at his wrist and then carries on walking and pressing. I turn to the right wall; it's a mess of moving colours all fighting for my attention. I focus on a square at eye-level and read the words in bold.

'ZING!'

The picture is of a revolving pot. I reach out and tap it. A cheerful male voice fires.

'*ZING! A pot of pleasure, a taste you'll treasure! Never feel hungry between meals with this super snack!*'

I gingerly press the tip of my finger to a rectangle which says 'Ingredients'. I flinch, expecting another audio announcement, but instead a drop-box appears. My eyes trace over the smaller writing: 'contains meat, vegetables, enhancers and vitamins'. I frown, that really doesn't tell me anything. What meat? Rat?

Snake? The farm animals Central keep hidden somewhere? What veg is in it? What the hell are enhancers? An arm stretches out in front of me and skinny fingers tap the word select on the picture of the pot of ZING. I look round to see a female maid, curls squashed down beneath her round hat. My eyes are drawn back to the wall when the maid presses the next picture along and a high-pitched female voice chimes out.

'Delicious Burst is full of flavour, it's our number one bestseller!'

An explosion of stars lights up the square. I look closer, as I can't figure out what it is, exactly. Do we make this stuff in the factory? I've never worked in packaging and labelling. Where's the actual product? I look down, it hasn't materialised at the bottom of the wall from a secret compartment.

'You ain't meant to be in 'ere, Ms Skyla.'

I glance back at the young maid. This time I recognise her, she's the Vable's maid, Cara. I don't see her often, she keeps out of sight. Like glory smoke in the mist, she's around but she's not always visible. I have so many questions; one leaps from my lips before I have the sense to stop it.

'How does the food get to the apartment?'

Cara stares at me; lips tight, hands resting on her bony hips. Her face softens, giving into my question.

'Pickers pick it, packers pack it, placers place it.

Now I'm totally confused. The Vable's maid taps a select button on a lower product square.

'But how do they know where to place it?'

Cara lets out a long sigh. She points to the entrance where a group of Morb children, about eleven and twelve years old, amble through the doors, giggling and hanging off one another.

'A palm-pad inside the doors,' she explains, 'I press me hand to it, it scans, then when I press the select button, me prints are scanned again and the pickers know what the Vables 'ave ordered. They pick from the warehouse, some other Skel packs and then another Skel delivers. Got any more questions or are we done?'

The maid looks me up and down before allowing her eyes to settle on my exposed chest. I yank up the silk material.

'I hate this dress.'

'Wanna swap?' she asks.

I consider it. The maid's pressed uniform looks more comfortable than my waist-squeezing, breast-bursting, leg-exposing outfit; not enough material in some places, too much ruffled up in others. I'm about to say, 'yeah, let's swap,' when she grasps my arm.

'Those kids,' Cara points to the Morb kids, gathered around a large monitor. 'They're using the quick-shop screen, they press what snacks they want and it comes out the bottom.'

I watch and sure enough, a boy reaches into what looks like a tray at the bottom of the monitor and pulls out a packet.

'Cara!'

A shrill voice comes out of nowhere. Cara looks down at her wrist.

'Yes, mistress.'

'Don't forget the Tangy Paste.'

I peer over at Cara's wrist. There's a small, square screen embedded in it, and filling up the entire screen is the pudgy, one-lensed face of Mistress Vable.

'Yes, mistress.'

The screen goes black.

'Hosts don't belong in 'ere.' Cara glares. 'Go before you get us both in trouble.'

'Did it hurt when they put that in?'

I grab hold of her wrist and brush the smooth screen with the tips of my fingers, she snatches her arm away.

'You should leave now.'

I know she's right, but I don't want to leave. The feeling of disgust at this unnatural spectacle is overridden by intrigue. I want to stay.

'Fine. I guess I'll go back to the apartment and do pretty much nothing then.'

Beneath the rim of her hat, Cara's eyebrows knit.

'You're a strange chick.'

'I'm strange? Look at this place.'

I lift my arms and motion to the walls. A smile touches Cara's smooth lips. She turns her back and carries on shopping.

'Wait! Cara! Can you tell me how to get back to the apartment?'

She doesn't look back and I struggle to hear her instructions over the noise of product advertisements pinging out from the aisles beyond.

'Turn left, walk a few steps, there's a shaft. You know which floor, right?'

'Yeah, but …'

I watch her stride away. I suddenly don't want to be alone.

'Cara! Cara!'

The light starts to fade, and the pictures inside my head begin to blur. Tug of nausea. Images flash before my eyes and merge into flashes of light. I'm blinded. I squint, trying to focus, almost giving myself a headache as I struggle to concentrate on present time. A person in a long white coat stands in front of a blank screen. Flash. Bunce's face appears in my head. I shake my head, shake the vision away but when I open my eyes it's still there, this time, on the screen. The white coat is reading at high speed and I can no longer hold on to the room I'm in, the reality of it. My mind is a mess with voices from the past.

'*You don't own your womb, Ms Skyla, I do. I own your entire body, is that clear?*'

'*Eat up, Ms Skyla. We need you strong and healthy.*'

'*We made this plan together …*'

'No, no plan! There is no plan!' I croak, my throat as dry as the desert.

I don't know how much of my mind they've read but I know I've given away too many memories. The floodgates open and my thoughts rush in. I manage to hold back my past. Push it deep inside my mind, lock it away for none to read. It's probably too late for that.

'Where's Bunce?'

My eyes stay closed but my voice comes out strong.

'I need that Morb!' I scream, and thrash about.

My legs! I can feel them. I can move them. I kick out, aggravated, annoyed with myself, my choices, at the situation I've landed myself in. Bunce was my ticket to a better life, dammit! Morbs that step out of line aren't executed. To my knowledge it's never happened, and I don't want Bunce to be the first or worse, the first mutilated Morb. An image forms in my mind of an enormous mess of blubber and machine, crawling on all fours, dragging its useless body through the streets.

'BUNCE!'

'There's no point in shouting, my dear.'

I gasp. That's a strange voice. Am I back at the complex? I'm tired, what's happening …? My eyes roll back. Black out.

Chapter Fifteen

Rock Vault

'Are you awake, my dear?'

Shaky voice to my right. Is it real or not? My dreams and memories have bled together. This happens with prolonged mind invasion. They did it to my grandfather before his execution. After he was released – before they decided to murder him – he struggled to string words together. How long was I under? My brain feels scrambled. I force my heavy eyelids upwards, my eyes struggle to focus. When they finally do, it's not much different to when they were closed. Grey walls, grey floor, grey ceiling ... grey Morb? Old and shrivelled, slumped beside me in a hover-chair that has clearly lost its hover.

I grab my nose and try not to retch. The elder Morb stinks of stale sweat and hopelessness. I can't decide which I despise more, the smell of a body struggling to regulate its temperature or the self-pity oozing into the musty air.

My brain might be full of wool but it's clear where I am – Rock Vault, and vault cells are no place for a Morb. I'm amazed this old-timer is able to breathe. Even though he isn't breathing well, his rasps are drawn out like a death rattle, his artificial organs must be failing. Not dead yet but he soon will be. The noise is nauseating. If he doesn't croak in the next hour, I might put him out of his misery. I sit up slowly and cross my legs over the lumpy mattress that is my prison bed. I'm in the same clothes that I washed in the pond after the toilet threw up on me. I feel more than dirty, like I'm covered in the rat shit which has piled up behind my kitchen cupboard or what was my cupboard, since some other Skel is housed there now.

'Who are you?' I splutter.

My throat, dry and sore from screaming, feels like I've swallowed a mountain of sand.

'I'm not sure, I was hoping you might tell me,' the old Morb splutters through his suffocating larynx.

My head throbs like scalding lava is running through the channels of my brain. Did he say he's not sure who he is? Do I even know who I am anymore?

'What are you doing in here?' I ask, no courtesy in my tone, no grovelling, he'll not be addressed as master by me.

'Sitting,' he says plainly, and then mumbles under his breath, 'stupid, slow-minded Skel.'

'Fine, keep your secrets,' I snap.

Slow-minded, ha! Rather a little slow-minded and mobile than ultra-intelligent and immobile, or insane and immobile as seems the case with this Morb.

The Morb holds out a shaky hand and gestures for me to move closer. I hesitate. Whatever lands a Morb in Rock Vault has to be a horrific crime, much worse than anything a Skel is sentenced to. This Morb has obviously gone nuts! I stare at him. Is he a threat? He's ancient, rolls of wrinkled flab barely holding him together. He's weak and he must be almost blind, for he wears what looks like binoculars strapped over his eyes. I've taken a beating mentally by the mind sweeps, but he doesn't look strong enough to perform the handshake greeting, let alone overpower me.

I drop onto my knees and lean forward. I wrinkle my nose, not wanting to inhale his personal airspace. I manage to stop the assault on my nostrils and inadvertently taste his stench. I swallow and my eyes water.

'I have a secret,' he whispers, then shouts at the door, 'BUT I'LL NEVER TELL THEM!'

He coughs and splutters. I pull back from the spray of germs.

'What is it?' I say quietly.

'What is what?' he croaks.

I sit back down. Crazy old coot, he's probably in here because he's lost his mind and there's nowhere else to put an insane Morb.

'I'm a scientist, you know,' he wheezes.

Yeah, a mad scientist I think, and laugh inwardly.

'I do miss being in my lab.' He sniffs.

Lab? The shock of this word sends a pulse up into my skull, and the fine hairs on my arms feel like birds' feathers being stroked the wrong way.

'The cure?' I mouth.

'Some people call me Bins, is that my name?'

I don't know his bloody name. I need this Morb to think straight. I crawl closer to the Morb's hover-chair and stare up at him from the filthy floor.

'Lab B, is that your lab?'

I'm startled when he starts shouting again.

'I KNEW IT! I – KNEW – IT!' he yells, in between gulps of air, 'You're one of them! You'd be the same age as Kally. Is that why they sent you in here? To play with my emotions, get me to talk?'

I shake my head and try to say no, but the Morb isn't listening.

'They think I'll tell you where I hid it! You're not my Kally! I'm not so far gone that I can't tell the difference between a young Skel and a young Morbihan!' His face reddens. 'They want it so badly, aha! It's right under their snooty Central noses. They'll never find it.' He looks like he's going to pass out, he takes a deep breath and screams. 'YOU'LL NEVER FIND IT! YOU HEAR ME?'

The coughing fit that follows should have been backed up by his last breath, but the old Morb shakes his fists at the walls and clings to life. All the while, inside my muddled mind I've worked out who this Morb is. The scientist, the one who created the serum, the one who created a potential cure for the Morbihan's obesity, the one we were meant to interview back at Lab B.

'The explosion ... Central did that, right?'

'Central did what now?' He says, face wobbling.

I can't take much more of this.

'Blew up your lab!' I say, irritated.

'You want to blow up my lab? My life's work!'

The layered face of the Morb, apparently called Bins, (I'll take a wild guess it's a nickname associated with the binocular lenses strapped over his huge face), wrinkles into a sorrowful mountain threatening an avalanche of tears, if he can cry through those 'bins'.

'No,' I shake my head, 'I'm a prisoner like you.'

Bins slumps in his chair.

'I'm sorry, child. They've been sweeping my mind for hours,' he rasps. 'I'm weak. My thoughts are not what they once were.'

'Was the drone yours?' I whisper.

'Yes.' He pants. 'You know things, don't you, Skel. How do you know about the drone?'

'I saw it leave the lab,' Bins perks up, 'it was battered by the explosion but it got out.'

'Explosion?' He mutters and again, if he could cry, he'd have filled a bucket with tears by now.

'I'm not sure what happened … I say gently, 'your lab was destroyed.'

'And Tyris?' He asks, fretful, 'Cara left before they came but Tyris was with me when they shot me with a tranquiliser.'

If Cara swiped the cure then what was the drone for? An image of the blackened body on the lab floor flits into my head. That must have been Tyris.

'Is there a back door to the lab?'

'The back door leads to the hospital.' Bins says, annoyed I'm avoiding his question. 'Tell me what happened to Tyris!'

I sigh.

'I think he's dead, there was a body – a Skel.'

That explosion was no accident. The guards took Bins and then blew up the lab. They're sweeping his mind to find out if there's any more cure. Except I don't understand why they would ask Bins to create the serum in the first place? And what happened to Cara, where does she fit in all this?

'Oh, Tyris,' Bins sighs.

I raise my eyebrows. A Morb morns a Skel. Unheard of. How strange.

'Were you very close?' I ask, pity picking at my heart.

'I spent months training him, what a waste of time!' He rasps. 'And worse, my lab is gone, my life's work all gone.'

'Is that all you care about?' I growl, 'Tyris died!'

'Skels die all the time.' He says, waving his hand in dismissal, underside of his saggy arm wobbling.

'You think we're animals!' I yell at him.

'You are animals.'

What is he talking about now? Ugh! I've had enough. I climb back onto the lumpy mattress, cross my arms, and turn my back. Fat stinking pig! He's the animal, not me. We sit in silence. Minutes drag with the sound of his struggling breaths and I think about whether my hands are big enough to wring his thick neck. After what seems like an hour; him sat unmoving, breathing loudly, staring at the dark walls, me thinking about events passed, picking at the wall, a pile of plaster gathering on the mattress; he speaks.

'Skel,' he whispers. 'Talk to me, Skel.'

I ignore him.

'Do you want to know why I created the cure?'

I glance over my shoulder.

'Because you were told to.' I say firmly.

'No,' he replies.

No? I turn around and stare at his big moon face.

'You make stuff up as you go along, nothing you say makes sense,' I say, gripping the edge of the mattress to stop myself from punching him. 'Central asks you to create a cure, then they sling you in here and destroy your lab. Why?'

'Because ...,' he pants, 'they didn't ask me to make it.'

Artificial parts groan and Bins continues to wheeze. I'm dumbfounded. Morbs never do anything without authorisation. At least I don't think they do. But then ... Bunce did.

'The rat didn't die,' he coughs, 'they said it did but it didn't. The serum isn't deadly.'

'It isn't?' I ask, surprised.

'What isn't?'

'The serum, the damn cure!' I growl through gritted teeth.

The lowest of Bins' chin-folds trembles.

'You know about the cure?' I roll my eyes, it's like trying to have a rational conversation with a two-year-old. 'Central ordered me to stop but I didn't, they destroyed my samples …' he says, voice wobbling along with the loose skin under his arms as he buries his face in his hands. 'But I kept a vial for my granddaughter, she wanted to carry a baby so badly.'

I gasp.

'What?'

'Yes,' Bins says, lenses peering down at me from beneath his chubby fingers. 'I know it was wrong of me,' he breathes, 'but it pains me to see her so unhappy. That's all I wanted for her – happiness, and now I shall never see her again.'

Bins makes a weeping sound, crying dry tears. I can't find anything to say, let alone words of comfort. I'm shocked. It never occurred to me that Morbihan girls would want to carry a baby. Kally wants the choice to carry and I want the choice not to.

I feel a little sorry for this pitiful creature before me. He risked his life to try and make his granddaughter's dreams come true. Why would he do that? Morbs are selfish, self-indulgent, self-centred and anything else beginning with the word self! But not this Morb, he's fighting the system. Fighting Central! Not for Skels, but still. After hours of mind invasion, he should be a vegetable, his brain should be pulp. I'm surprised he can even talk, albeit he isn't making much sense.

'Why didn't they use the lie detectors on you, instead of sweeping?' I ask, and wait for Bins to muster the strength to answer.

His jowls wobble as he shakes his head.

'What a stupid question,' Bins chuckles. 'You can't use emotional detectors on Morbihan, my dear. We are an advanced species and cannot be manipulated in that way.'

The superior tone in his grainy voice puts my back up. Even though thrown in a cell, festering, demented, and almost dead, this Morb still thinks he's better than me. They didn't use detectors on me either, I think to myself. You're no better than me. I try to hide my contempt. I need him on my side.

'Bins,' I say softly, flicking my lank ponytail over my shoulder. 'I know your granddaughter.'

Bins looks straight at my face. I can't see the intensity in his eyes because they're lenses but I know it's there.

'You know my Kally?'

'Yes,' I lie. 'I was selected as a host. She's a friend of my mistress's brother.'

Bins doesn't respond. I hope I haven't confused him. I hope he's listening.

'So that's how you know about my lab.'

'Yes, I ran away from the complex.'

'No, you didn't,' he scoffs. 'Skels don't do that.'

My impatience is growing.

'Tell me where the cure is, does Cara have it?'

'Cara? Don't be silly.'

'Then tell me how to make it, and I'll get it to Kally …'

'You can't make it,' he splutters. 'You're not a scientist, and a rare desert ingredient is needed. Many died to bring it to the city.'

'What is it? I'll scale the wall, I'll give it to a scientist who can …'

'Are you listening to me?' he spits. 'I said it's not something you can get. I'll have some more soup, thank you, Tracy.'

I rest my head in my hands and try to keep calm. Who the fuck is Tracy? This Morb is impossible. Why'd they put me in here with him? To break me? Let him drive me insane with his bullshit?

'Look, the cure is this rancid city's last hope. We can't let Central win!' I say, frustrated.

The heavy iron door swings open, light spills in, and a guard throws in a new body. A curly-haired girl I recognise. It's Mistress Vable's maid. Is this real or a memory? Deja vu? Have I done this before? I shake my head. No. This is new. The girl lies bruised and broken on the stone floor, the iron door slams shut and we are in semi-darkness again.

'Hey,' I say, getting to my feet, I step cautiously towards the silent body. 'You okay?'

The girl pushes her skeletal frame up into a sitting position and sweeps back her tight black curls, her hollow eyes search the gloom. She spots me.

'You!' she shouts, and scrambles towards me.

I step back and she leaps up, punching both fists at me, I grab her bony wrists.

'Stop!' I shout. 'What's wrong with you?'

'You did this. It's your fault I'm in 'ere!' she screams, struggling against my grasp.

'Me?' I growl back. 'What did I do? You were at the labs too.'

'You kidnapped Bunce!' she screams in my face.

'I didn't kidnap him, he left off his own back.'

'The spooks think I helped 'cha escape. Damn spooks!' She shouts at the walls. 'Let me out of 'ere, I've done nothing wrong!'

I throw the maid to the ground and she curls up in a ball, arms wrapped around her knees. The only people who use the term 'spook' instead of guard come from the roughest parts of the city, where Mutil slaughter people on a regular basis. It must have taken all her strength to get the position of maid with Bunce's sister. She stares dark daggers up at me. It's clear she knows nothing about what's happened. Bins doesn't say a word. He gawps at us both.

'I'm sorry,' I say, and I am. 'I'll tell them you weren't involved.'

The maid buries her head in her knees, and even though I cannot see her face, I can sense her silent tears.

'It won' make no difference,' her voice quivers. 'I've been shamed, me masters'll never 'ave me back now. I'll be mutilated for sure.'

Her shoulders heave as she sobs. I glance at Bins; his head hangs down. Guilt throws acid at the walls of my stomach.

'Cara, isn't it?' I say, kneeling beside her.

I drape my arm loosely around her shoulders. Her skin is like ice, her black uniform is thin, not the pristine maid's uniform she was wearing the day I saw her in the Hyper Market. No bowler hat taming her wild hair.

'Yeah,' she sniffs, using her thumb to wipe away a tear from beneath her long eyelashes. 'And you're Ms Skyla. The run-away host.'

'It's Skyla, you can drop the Ms ... Cara, look at me,' I lift the trembling curls away from her face. 'We're going to get out of here.'

She looks deep into my eyes, searching for truth. Her full lips twitch and she tries on a smile. It's not convincing, but it is there. I ruined her life, inadvertently, but still it's my fault she's in here. I will take her with me when I go, it is the least I can do. How we'll escape I do not know but we must. Cara looks over at Bins.

'What's that old Morb doing in 'ere?' she whispers in my ear, her stiff curls tickling my nose as her head whips around to gawk at Bins.

'Er ...'

Before I can think of a good lie, Cara is up on her feet and strolling towards Bins.

'Excuse me for the assertiveness, master, but what you doin' in 'ere?' she says softly.

Bins smiles at Cara and his binocular eyes blink.

'Dear child,' he wheezes. 'I don't really know.'

Cara looks closer.

'Master Roven?'

'That's my name, isn't it?'

A broad grin exposes the Morb's stubby yellowing teeth.

'What's wrong with him?' Cara asks me.

I shrug. Bins whimpers again. 'Oh, what could I have done to deserve such punishment?'

He starts to cough and splutter.

'There, there,' Cara says, patting his pudgy hand empathetically. 'I'm sure it's a mistake, someone'll take you home soon.'

Why would Cara comfort this man? She's had a life of poverty, neglect, and hardship; unlike him. Why would she feel this pathetic creature deserves her pity? He's had a life of riches, comfort, and opportunity. I don't get it. Why doesn't she despise him? He's old and will die soon anyway. She has a lot more to lose; she's young and if not executed she will be mutilated for the sake of his kind, experimented on so that Morbs like him can have better working parts for their dilapidated bodies, while her body is hacked to bits. If there were no Morbihan, there would be no need to mutilate Skels to test new artificial organs on and prolong Morb's lives. Why doesn't Cara hate him? I do.

'Thank you, my dear,' he whispers to Cara sweetly. 'I need to speak to the other you now, the lighter one.'

'Yes, master.'

Cara bows her head to him and raises her eyebrows at me, quizzically. She's never encountered a Morb who's lost his mind, the mind is a Morb's biggest asset.

Bins' face is shiny with sweat, all the talking is taking it out of him. Cara and I switch places and the former maid sits quietly on top of a stained mattress pushed up against the dingy, grey wall opposite us, she twirls her black curls around her spindly fingers. She doesn't look up, she doesn't try to eavesdrop on our conversation. She is compliant like all Skels should be. I sit back down on the bed beside Bins and lend him my ear.

'You are friends with my granddaughter, yes?'

I'm not, but I nod.

'Will you take Kally the serum?'

I nod again.

'Yes.'

He stares at me for the longest time, until I feel uncomfortable enough to want to look away, but I don't. I hold his goggle-eyed gaze. He finally speaks.

'The maid,' he whispers, nodding his head towards Cara. 'She doesn't know anything, she helped with many experiments but not 574.' His breathing becomes deathly shallow. 'I used the drone to get the cure out of the building, when the guards came in. Tyris had the drone ready, he programmed it to wait up on a high shelf and only leave once the lab was void of people. I was tipped off, we knew they were coming, of course, what I did not know is that they would bring me in here.'

'Where is the drone?' I ask, elated.

Bins gasps, his voice rattles.

'I don't know.'

I rephrase the question.

'Where did the drone take the serum?' I ask.

'The serum is in the office.' Bins hisses. 'I need to walk the sausage. If I don't walk it regularly, it'll break down.'

He's losing it again. I glance up. I can't see any cameras or audio devices in this cell, but that doesn't mean there aren't any. Bins gasps for air, his movements shaky.

'Which office?' I whisper.

'Third from the lift,' he says, 'twentieth floor.'

'What twentieth floor? Where?' I ask, my voice becoming testy.

He drops his head. I sense the last twenty minutes has taken a toll on him, like twelve hours of hard labour does to me. He rattles out another breath and the words I least want to hear drift into my ears.

'The Spiral.'

I drop down on my prison bed. Impossible, that's impossible. How did he manage to hide it there? And in whose office did he hide it? He must have had help. They'd notice a drone flying around. I swallow my frustration, it sticks in my throat and I hang my head, staring down at my grubby hands, dirt collected in the creases of my palms. Bins is silent and still. Dead? No, rhythmic breathing sets in – asleep. Just like that, his body shut down, his circuitry has gone into hibernation. Why would he hide the cure in Central headquarters? How the hell am I going to get inside, let alone out again? I don't care for Morbs, but if Bins is telling the truth and he's been trying to hide this information from Central, we're on the same side and for his sake, I hope he doesn't wake up.

Chapter Sixteen

Revolting Secrets

There are no windows inside our cell. I can't tell if it's day or night and I don't know how long I've been in here. Twenty-four hours, for sure. A few days, maybe. I don't even know what day it is or whether Bunce is still alive. Cara has been asleep for a few hours, she makes little more than shallow breathing sounds. Bins more than makes up for Cara's quiet; his snores bounce off the walls in shattering echoes, aggravating my already tense shoulders. Even if he wasn't making such a racket, I couldn't lay my mind to rest, it's noisier inside my head than it is inside this cell, each thought fighting another for the spotlight. I think of how I might get past security inside The Spiral. How many guards are in there? Maybe it's full of secure doors. Touch my hand to a palm-pad and a pack of Ruinous pounce on me. No, that's ridiculous, they wouldn't keep dangerous animals inside The Spiral. Actually, they do. Central are the most dangerous animals of them all.

My non-Spiral thoughts revolve around my 'pet Morb' as Kian put it. I wonder what abrasive tests he's been subjected to. I need him back. I need to find a way to get out of here first but then I need to find Bunce. I then need to find the serum and … This is impossible! They've probably killed him and strung his head on the line, and if he's dead, then what? Give the serum to Bins' granddaughter, Kally, like he asked me? That's not such a bad idea, is it? Providing I can get to her. Providing I can get to the serum. The heavy cell door creaks and light pours across the floor, growing towards my stolen boots. I touch the rim; the knife is gone. I know it is, yet I can't help reacting and reaching for it. I touch my waist.

My snood is gone too, I hadn't noticed. A tall shadow fills the light, darkening the room again.

'Food,' the guard grunts. A metal tray is sent spinning across the floor towards me. I stop it with the tip of my boot.

I leave the brown salad and snatch up the stale bread, tearing great chunks from it with my teeth. It's like chewing cardboard but it's food and my stomach is grateful for it. Another tray is sent skidding towards Cara, who squints as she opens her eyes. Bins doesn't wake, not even with the sound of his tray clattering into the edge of his hover-chair. The guard bearing food moves on and someone behind him enters the room. The tall, broad figure, cast in shadow, walks over to Bins. He bends to speak to the old Morb.

'I'm going to empty your cylinder, okay, Bins?'

I recognise the voice.

'Kian!' I cry, almost rousing Bins from his slumber.

'Skyla!' he whispers, opening a compartment inside Bins' hover-chair. 'There are surveillance systems everywhere. Act like you don't know me.'

'Sorry,' I say loudly. 'Thought you were someone else.'

Kian frowns.

'Yep,' he whispers, 'I'm sure that'll fool them.'

He takes two thick cylinders from the inside of Bins' chair, replaces them with the ones he brought in and slams the compartment door shut. Bins jumps and his jowls wobble.

'What is it now?' he murmurs. 'I told you. I don't know what you're talking about, oh … er … hello, Crow.'

'Good morning, old-timer,' Kian says, warmly. 'How you feeling today?'

'Like death,' croaks Bins.

'So, better than yesterday, eh?' Kian winks.

Bins chuckles, which brings on a coughing fit. Kian scoops up the tray of food and places it in the old Morb's hands, then lowers his face close to mine, his nose almost touching my cheek. I inhale his smooth neck, he smells like soap. His breath is hot near my ear and my skin tingles as his lips move closer. I'm suddenly horrified. I must smell like dirt and blood and grime and …

'Skyla, are you listening to me?'

'Huh?'

'I said …' he speaks so softly I can barely hear his words. '… Try and get some rest. I can get you out of here but you'll need your strength. I'll be back for you in a few hours.'

He turns to leave. I grab his sleeve and pull him down to my level.

'Where's Bunce?' I whisper.

'He's safe.'

The relief that plays out on my face seems to anger Kian. He snatches his arm from my grasp and heads for the door.

'Wait!'

'What is it?' he says, through gritted teeth.

'We need to take her, too.'

I nod towards Cara, who has been quietly and quickly tucking into her prison food. She gulps the water from a small lidded cup on the tray. Kian looks down at her and back at me.

'No,' he says bluntly, and turns his back.

'Then I don't leave.'

'Fine,' he says, savagely. 'Stay here and die.'

The door slams shut behind him, taking the bright light away with it. I flop down on the lumpy mattress, appetite gone. I close my eyes and concentrate on shutting off the loudness inside my head. Slowly, it quietens.

I'm woken by a hand over my mouth. My body reacts before my mind and instinctively I jerk upright and claw at the stranger's arm.

'Shhh, it's me.'

Kian's deep tones are just audible over Bins' loud snoring. The cell is dank and dark, and the light beyond the open iron door is dim. A bulb flickers in the corridor, flickering words into my mind. Flicker: You're going to die. Flicker: Die screaming for mercy. Flicker: Everyone you care about will die because of you. I'm already dead, I tell myself. What I do from this point makes no difference. It's only a matter of time before Central send me to the Dark Angel. Yet it feels wrong to endanger Kian's life. He was against me leaving the complex. He told me to stop and I chose not to listen. I'm such an asshole. Why didn't I listen? Kian peels his hand from my mouth.

'I can't do this, Kian,' I say as soon as my lips are able to move. 'I'm putting too many lives at risk.'

'Don't use my name!' He whispers through gritted teeth. 'The camera's in here aren't great and some don't work but I don't know which ones. Playback and you can't tell one guard from the next but they might be able to work it out from the audio.'

'Sorry,' I whisper, 'But I can't let you do this.'

'You want to save Bunce, don't you?'

'Not if it means endangering you!'

Even with the door open, the darkness swallows everything. I can't see Kian's facial expression but I sense his relief. Calmness washes over me with the touch of Kian's soft lips to my clammy forehead.

'That's good to know,' he says, warmth back in his voice. 'Wake the girl and let's go.'

I don't need to wake Cara, she'd been silently listening. Her flat shoes shuffle on the concrete floor and seconds later her silhouette is cut out in the doorway. She knows all too well what will happen to her if she stays. I glance over to where the sound of snoring is coming from. I'll never see Bins again and he'll never know if I succeeded. He'll never see the changes his cure could make to his granddaughter's life, to Gale City. I decide he doesn't need to see what happens next, he can rest easy – take the hand of the Dark Angel and be flown to peace, safe in the knowledge that his secret is out, providing that I escape Rock Vault in one piece.

'Girl! Don't step out yet. We have strict patrol perimeters but some guards still break the rules.'

'I 'ave a name you know.'

'Most people do.' Kian says, pushing past Cara and out into the passage.

I've never seen the inside of the prison, only guards and prisoners have, and I had no desire to be either, yet here I am. Kian is behind us, he prods us every so often, to make it look as if he's escorting prisoners, or because he enjoys having the upper hand, controlling me. Cara and I walk shoulder to shoulder down the long stretch of grey, our steps echo in sync and with every closed door we pass, I wonder who is in there and what they did. How many are Runners, gang members, addicts, or guard killers, sitting in darkness, awaiting their punishment. The cobweb-covered cylinders of light above buzz and flicker. Kian whispers 'turn right' and we turn the corner. More greyness. Central seems to like everything to be grey. Except the Morb complex, which was colourful and clean. It smells like rat shit in here, I scan the narrow passage and see it's because there are rat droppings all along the skirting board. Gross! Ten steps down a new passage that looks like the last one, a dreadful scream hits me with the speed of a train. I stop. My heart pounds and I press my back to the wall. Cara copies me.

'Keep going.' Kian urges.

Neither of us move. Paralysed by a chorus of male and female voices up ahead, yelling in agony, some hysterical. What's happening behind those doors? Screams for help are all around us; No, please! Don't! Somebody!

'What the fuck is that?' Cara utters.

'We can't stop here.' Kian growls.

'You're taking us to be mutilated!' She screams.

'Don't be stupid! If I were, you'd be in chains.' Kian snaps at Cara and strides away, 'Let's go!'

I don't speak, I don't move, every bone in my body, every fibre, *says do something, stop their suffering* but I can't. I can't answer their pleas, if I do, I'll be next. Back at the complex, we were given a tour of the birthing centre. I couldn't take in anything the midwives were saying, the examination fresh in my mind and I thought that was bad enough. The screaming hosts fill every inch of my head space. The agony-induced screams of young women in childbirth comes back to me in waves, only instead of determination, the screams inside Rock Vault are of terror. Kian stops ten feet away and hurries back.

'What are you doing? Come on!' he yells in my face.

'Don't they at least anaesthetise them?' I ask, tears rolling down my dirty cheeks.

Cara leans against the dusty grey wall, head down, she clamps her hands over her ears. This was her fate and might still be if we can't escape, mine too. Kian still hasn't answered me. He stares at his city issue black boots. The screaming dies down.

'Well?' I demand.

Cara cautiously lifts her hands from over her ears.

'Sometimes, sometimes not,' he mutters to the floor.

'Fuck!' Cara shrieks, hand over her mouth.

Kian rubs his forehead. I can tell he hasn't become desensitised to the horrors that he knows go on behind those heavy doors.

'Please! I can't take it, I can't, don't, DON'T!'

The voice comes from the door opposite us.

'Kian, give me your knife,' I order.

'Why? What are you gonna do?'

I hold my hand out, staring at him.

'You can't help them.' He snarls.

Cara's eyes shift around nervously, frightened, wondering which way to run.

'Ever tried?' I snarl.

'Of course, I haven't! I'm not fucking crazy!'

This is why I could never be a guard. I could never betray people like that. Listening to their screams of torture day after day, and doing nothing. I can feel it coming, the impulse to act.

Do it Skyla, do something, don't be a coward. Here's your chance to throw yourself on your sword!

'I guess I am.' I say, hotly.

I throw my body weight into the nearest door, expecting to come up against resistance. Instead, it swings open and crashes into the wall, startling the people beyond it. I stagger into a trolley full of medical instruments. Crash. Clatter. I grab the legs of the trolley and almost bring it down with me. Silence. My eyes struggle to adjust to the bright operating lights. Ouch. Something sharp from the table has cut my arm. Squinty-eyed I force my vision to adjust, the fuzzy outline of a moonfaced, masked Morb in surgical scrubs comes into sharp focus. Cruel mechanical eyes rotate and shift forwards and back from within the swollen head like self-focusing telescopes, he stares down at me – a wild beast lose in his operating room.

The Morbs are upright – how is that possible? Not in a normal hover-chair, they're held up vertically by a hovering splint. The one nearest to me reaches out his blue-gloved hands, dripping with red. I shuffle away, scooting backwards on the instrument-scattered floor. To my left, there's another one, with robotic arms where his hands should be, blood streaking the silver; giant scissors and knives and pincers all soldered together in one metal nightmare. No one moves. None of us have ever been in a situation like this before and no one knows what to do. A Skel in scrubs stands confidently beside the Morbs, as if he's their equal. I'm stunned. Distressed breaths come from the operating table. I gather myself and get to my feet.

'Don't touch him,' the Skel says, his voice muffled by his surgical mask.

I glare. Swipe a scalpel from the dishevelled tray and brandish it at them.

'Or what?' I snarl.

Blood thumps in my ears. The Morb surgeons hover backwards, as I kneel beside the table and get to work loosening the straps holding the person down.

'Please,' A small voice comes from the table, 'hurry.'

'It's okay,' I say, 'I'm getting you out of here.'

'Not wise.' The Skel says through his mask, his masters don't speak. Are they mute?

I tug at the stubborn straps, saw at them with the scalpel, it's useless. I throw the thin knife and it clatters to the floor. My eyes frantically search the room for something else, something larger, sharper, but what I need to cut through this thick, cloth strap is the scissor handed Morb. The walls and floor are spattered with dried-on blood. This is nothing like the hospital. My thoughts are ridiculous. Of course, it's nothing like the hospital! This is a torture chamber. There's no heart monitor, because they don't care if the person dies, they'll try again on another victim. They have an endless supply of prisoners. I spot a glass-fronted cabinet full of hanging metal instruments: dirty saws and rib crackers; strange looking pliers and screwdrivers and a drill! How does anyone survive this room?

The realisation that most do not survive shudders through me, thoughts turn to pictures in my head; memories of the Mutil I've encountered over the years – rotting flesh, bone, artificial parts, some with half their face eaten away by disease. The walking dead. They say the Mutil are a result of organ testing, to make sure the artificial organs and lenses work before they implant them into Morbs. From what I can see, they also mutilate people for fun. This is a playroom …

'Skyla,'

Cara stands in the doorway. She won't cross the threshold. Tears streak her brown cheeks, not as full of colour as they once were, skin grey like the walls. Kian does not appear next to her. Her eyes flit over the three surgeons.

'The spook scarpered, we gotta get out of 'ere.' she says, desperately.

'Just a minute.'

The three blood-splattered mutilators remain still. They don't try to approach me. They do nothing. I frantically pull on the thick material. I can't unfasten it. It's too tight. I wrinkle my nose. The smell coming from the body is repugnant. The surgical team don't speak, don't attempt to talk me down. They watch me, the Skel wide-eyed in disbelief. Then a sound I know all too well explodes in my eardrums – the ominous wail of the siren. Every guard in the prison will be on us in minutes. I yank at the strap and it snaps. I stumble backwards and an arm flops over the side of the operating table.

'Skyla, let's go!' Cara screeches.

I stand up.

'Almost ... there.'

I stare at the lifeless body. I'm too late. Way too late. How did this man mange to talk to me? How was he even conscious? I don't know the corpse; the face is badly mutilated. Tubes and wires stick out from the victim's nose. Deep holes ooze pink where the eyeballs should be, what did they do, scoop them out with a dessert spoon? The skin around them is pulled back by small hooks, exposing the bone.

'Are you happy now?' The Skel shouts over the wailing siren.

He has pulled his mask down around his neck. His masters don't utter a word. It's as if they are subordinate to the Skel.

'Are *you* happy, traitor!' I yell at him.

'I was until you arrived and killed this subject!' he shouts back.

'Oh, I killed him? I stuffed wires and tubes up his nose and gouged out his eyes?' I shout viciously, backing towards the door.

'He would have lived!' spits the Skel.

'No,' I yell and point at the body, 'He wouldn't have. Call that living? Mutil suffer until they die. He would have suffered, more than he already has.'

'I'm going,' Cara shouts over the siren. 'I'm alive and I want to stay that way!'

I dash for the door, take one last look behind me, blood runs down the lifeless arm hanging from the operating table. That could have easily been my arm, I think. It's not and I have to go, I was never going to save him. My guilt is misplaced. I duck out the door after Cara. We sprint down dim passages, stopping every so often to look around corners. Visions of the mutilated body flash through my head. The suffocating despair I feel for the victim I couldn't save almost overwhelms me. I won't let my emotions cripple my mind and shut down my legs. I have to keep going. I have to get out.

Each junction we come to is deserted, there's no one around. The place seems abandoned and the siren has stopped. Why aren't they coming for us? There's no way they haven't noticed us. What's their game?

Rats scurry along the edge of the skirting, hurrying over little brown balls of shit. The rats keep up with me, four hurried steps to one thud of my boot. Rock Vault is a maze of corridors. I don't know how we're going to escape without Kian's help. Where is he, dammit! I run past a clean metal door, different from all the other doors. I double back. There's a seal around it and a long metal handle.

'Cara, wait!'

Cara hurries back. I grip the cold handle and tug it down. The sound of pressure releasing escapes and the door unsticks. I pull the heavy metal forwards and slip through to the other side, Cara follows and it closes behind us, sticking shut. Behind Cara, I notice there's no handle. Wherever we are, we're trapped.

'What's this place?' she asks.

'I don't know,' I say, and I don't.

There is another door up ahead and the small, clear plastic-lined room we are in smells like the Morb complex. A boulder sinks to the pit of my stomach. Please, don't let me be back at the complex. I shake that ridiculous thought from my head. Rock Vault isn't part of the complex and that tube I used to get out, that led me to … wait, there were two doors. I went through the side one, where did the other one lead to? Here?

I take three steps and grasp the next handle which feels even colder than the first. I push it down and the door opens inwards this time. I push the door, it's heavy and I have to throw all my body weight behind it. Cara presses her hands against the metal, her slim body up close to me, we push back the door, she's a lot stronger than she looks.

Beyond the door are metal steps, beams of light above spring and stutter to life as the door behind us closes. The stairs lead down in a steep incline to a factory. High ceiling and white walls, same as the meat-works, but instead of conveyor belts and grinder, this place has racks and racks of animal carcasses covered in a protective plastic. In front of the racks are several long, white benches, and unlike the torture room we ran from, the huge space is clean and sterile. The freezing air sneaks up on us, my skin goosepimples and my teeth chatter.

'Butchery?' I say.

Plumes of vapour escape my lips as we descend, my boots clonk against the metal steps and echo into the vast space.

'Looks like it,' Cara replies, her voice jittering. 'Did you have to bone the meat when you worked at the factory?'

I sense the disgust in her voice. Skels don't eat meat. It's for Morb consumption only.

'No, they must do it here before they send it to us,' I explain. 'Oh look, see those white containers?' I point to stacked plastic tubs. 'The cuts of meat arrive in those.'

I let my hand slide down the clean, silver rail as we near the bottom of the steep stairs. We stride across the deserted factory floor, footsteps echoing.

'There must be a door back here somewhere, a ramp to the Sky Train or something?' Cara says, rushing past me. She disappears behind the plastic sheets that separate the cold cuts.

I push through the heavy swinging carcasses in her wake.

'Cara wait!' I yell and my voice echoes back to me and fades away.

I push and shove my way through, sending meat swinging behind me, where is she?

I find her, on her hands and knees, holding her throat, dark curls bent over one of the plastic delivery tubs. She coughs, and a splatter of undigested food hits the back of the tub. I stand over her.

'Are you okay? What is it, food poisoning?'

I touch my stomach, hoping that I won't be next but she shakes her head.

Stale bread and a handful of vegetables couldn't have given her food poisoning, could it? I look around for something she can wipe her mouth with. We have to keep going. If we stay here, they'll find us and fuck knows where Kian has jiggered off to. Great help he was.

I push my way back between the hanging meat. There's nothing around, no storage, nothing, just thick plastic sheet after thick plastic sheet ... I peel back some plastic. I wonder where they slaughter the cows. I tilt my head. Are these cows or pigs? I know my farm animals. Learned about them from my grandfather. What is this meat? Fingers trembling, I place my palms on either side of the chilled carcasses hanging in front of me. The hand of fear is tight around my throat. Squeeze. The tendons in my neck are like iron. I force the two meat halves together and hear the gurgle and splatter of Cara retching up more prison food, I feel mine hit the back of my throat. Nipples, not udders or pig teats but breasts, a woman's breasts. This is a woman! A person. A Skel! Bile burns my throat. My knees weaken, legs soften, and my quivering bones collide with the hard floor. The room spins round, faster and faster. I will not vomit. I won't. I won't! My job. The meat. The grinder. I've been mincing ... the meat it's ... my stomach lurches ... it's people.

Chapter Seventeen

Drift Side

'Skyla get up!'

My arm is being tugged but the voice seems far away, yet close to my ear or inside my head. Bones soft, limbs like noodles, I'm dragged to my feet then lifted off them. Bumped along, legs dangling and in seconds the brightness behind my eyes dims, and warm air flushes my cheeks. Boots clump down stone stairs, jarring my body as we descend.

'I can't breathe.'

I open my eyes to see a blurry mess of sandy hair and a pale hand holding his pale throat. Bunce! Who's carrying me? Strong arms and tender hands lift me down until my boots touch the ground.

'Can you stand?' Kian asks, hands around my waist, steadying me.

'I think so.' I say, holding my dizzy forehead.

Bunce stands with one arm over his eyes, shielding his face from the orange glow. The sun is low; a giant angry eye of a cyclops, the red mountains his shoulders. It's dusk. Inside the prison, it felt later. I'm disorientated. I'm not sure where I am. Rock Vault is a vast network of corridors inside and looming angles of black stonework outside. It's at least a mile wide. I've never walked all the way around it. This part of the city seems dirtier than where I call home and dead rats litter the gutters, crows occasionally swooping down to peck at them.

'You're safe for the moment,' Kian says, leaning up against a pine tree. Pleased with himself. 'No one comes out here at sundown.'

I scowl at him, as if I'm aiming a thousand knives at his head.

'Did you know?'

His eyes dart to Bunce and then Cara. Dizziness abated, I round on him.

'Did you?' I ask again.

Everyone stares at the guard who used to be my most trusted friend.

'Yes,' he says, bitterly.

'Nice friend,' Cara spits.

Bunce says nothing.

'What do you want from me, eh?' Kian slides down the tree and sits hangdog, arms flopped over his bent knees. 'Should I run around the city screaming, prisoners are Morb food. What's that going to achieve? Would you have believed me, if you hadn't seen it for yourself? I got you out.' Kian shoots us all a look like we're ungrateful children. 'I'm sorry that isn't good enough.'

'You walked away and left us!' I say, anger rising in my chest. 'Left that man to die …'

Kian rises to his feet and stalks up to me, close, in my personal space.

'I was rescuing your pet!' Kian yells, 'Or should I have left him to die?'

'How can you do such a job knowing all this?' I ask, confused at what my friend has turned into, 'I don't understand how you can betray your people in this way.'

'No, you wouldn't, would you?' Kian says, grinding his words and spitting them out at me. 'It's the Sky-way or the highway, right?'

'Wrong!' I snap. 'I must have mistaken you for someone that gives a shit!'

I cross my arms, forcing him to back out of my space.

'I do give a shit!' He fires back, 'But I don't want to end up in the fucking grinder!'

'Oh right, I get it now,' I say, my voice rising. 'As long as you're all right, nothing else matters.'

'What?' He shakes his head. 'No!'

Cara and Bunce don't join the debate. They're quiet, for a moment I forget they are there.

'It's wrong, Kian,' I say, close to tears. 'Eating people … it's wrong. Don't you understand that?'

My stomach turns at the thought of my part in it. I didn't know, I reassure myself. Unlike Kian, I didn't have a clue what I was doing.

'Of course, I do!' Kian yells, running his adrenalin shaky fingers through his wavy hair. 'But there's nothing I can do about it.'

'It has to be stopped. We have to think of a way!' I say, fists clenched.

Kian grabs my shoulder with one hand and touches my face with the other.

'Yes, we do need to think of a way,' he says, 'but not today. Today you need to get away.'

I hold his hand to my face and close my eyes to stop the tears. He does understand.

'Skels don't think,' Bunce suddenly pipes up, waving his hand dismissively. 'They do what they're told to do.'

All three of us glare at the Morb, who quickly shoves his hands in his pockets and shuffles his feet, raising the dust.

'I'm going,' Kian says, turning his back on me. 'They'll notice I'm missing.'

'Wait!' I grab Kian's hand, he closes his fingers around mine and brushes my skin with his thumb. I blush. 'When will I see you again?'

The words I speak don't match my thoughts. *We might never see each other again* is what I want to say. *I miss you* is what I want him to know. But I don't say those words, even though I fear this could be the last time I see my best friend. Why can't I be honest with him? Bunce and Cara are staring at us. Bunce is calm, no longer struggling to breathe in the suffocating humidity, but his eyes tell a different story. Normally they're filled with mild amusement, as if every day is a celebration. Not now though, they're filled with despair. I drop Kian's hand and he walks away, towards the chiselled rocky steps that lead up and inside Rock Vault.

'We'd best get going before it gets dark,' Cara says.

Her eyes droop, she looks as if she might vomit again. She stands as far away from Bunce as possible, as if he's poisoned or impure.

Cara heads in the direction of the mountains, her body slowly disappearing down the hillside with every step, Bunce in her wake. I glance over my shoulder. Kian is gone. Rock Vault towers over me like a rock monster bearing down on its victim. How did we escape so easily? No one escapes. I hurry out of the shadow of the prison and back towards freedom. Bunce walks head down, awkwardly quiet, probably trying to avoid making another faux pas. I want to know his thoughts. Is he regretting his decision to come with me? Did he know about the meat? The cold corpse covered with plastic comes back into my mind; smooth and clean. No one would eat me, I think to myself. I'm covered in dirt and grime. Irrational. What's wrong with me? Stop thinking about it, Skyla. But I can't. The meat. How many people have I fed into the grinder? How many of them did I know? I find myself searching the databanks of my mind for faces I no longer saw at work, or at the market or in passing. I've been grinding people up for years, holding bits of their bodies in my hands. I feel dirty, I want to scratch off my skin. I want to go home.

'I have to stop by my cube,' I tell Cara.

'Nope,' Cara says, dismissively.

'But I need clothes, I need to wash!' I protest.

'It'll be crawling with guards, you know that.'

I do know that but I still want to go home.

On the horizon, the last rays of sunlight sink behind the mountains and a blanket of darkness drops over the city like a death shroud. The sun is gone. The danger doubles. Cara struts out in front, stick thin arms swinging. Strong enough to move a heavy door with me but otherwise weak, anyone could overpower her, so why the confidence? I don't have my knife, my security, and I'm increasingly nervous about it. I suppose Cara has nothing more to lose, except her life and that, by Gale City standards, isn't worth much.

Bunce shivers. The extreme change in temperature with the setting of the sun must be too much for his body, or else he's mentally damaged by the horrors he's seen inside Rock Vault. Either way, it seems he isn't coping. I place my hand on his shoulder. He flinches at my touch, stops walking, and throws his arms around me, burying his head into my neck. I'm taken aback, but decide to hold him. His shoulders relax, I push him to arm's length and stare into his chubby face. He's tired but not broken ... yet.

'It's gonna be okay.'

I tug Bunce by the shirtsleeve to catch up with Cara.

We walk in silence, past cube after run-down cube. Every second window is smashed, walls cracked, paint faded and peeling. This side of town makes me think of nightmares. Deserted streets, abandoned cubes, the ones who couldn't leave hide away from an unspeakable curse – venture outside and be struck down by it. Blinds twitch, residents watch as we walk towards the danger. That's how I feel right now, exposed, an outsider about to be sacrificed to the monsters and ghosts of this side of town.

Bunce flinches when doors slam shut either side of us. Lights out isn't for a few hours but it doesn't matter, I'm guessing lightbulbs are in short supply, turn on a light and have the bulb stolen. Nearly every streetlamp is smashed. This must be Drift Side. I never come to this part of town, ever, and for good reason. Every blind on every cube is closed. Cara's steps leave no sound on the pavement. I tread gently, following her example, the ex-maid has learned to be light-footed – a breeze no one notices until it has already gone by. Bunce's sneakers have a soft sole, which I'm thankful for because he walks heavily.

'Does she have it?' Bunce whispers, his shoulder bumps against me as we walk side by side.

'No,' I shake my head. 'And that's good. If she had, it would be in Central's hands now, and her head would be on the line.'

'Oh,' Bunce sighs.

We walk in silence for a few minutes. I open my mouth to explain about Bins but Bunce gets in before me.

'I'm tired,' he groans, dragging his feet.

'I know you are.'

'I'm hungry and dirty too,' he whines.

'I know!' I snap.

'It was too hot, and now it's freezing.'

'Will you stop moaning!' I growl.

'I'm not moaning, I'm ...'

He's struggling to breathe again. His white skin is grey, eyelids drooping. No, no, don't black out. Stay conscious. He's too heavy, I can't carry him. I link my arm with his and try to prop him up a bit.

'Do you want to talk about it?' I whisper.

I don't, but I need him to let go of some of it. He needs to unbottle his worries.

'Which part?' Bunce whispers back, miserably.

I'm not sure what he has seen, and I don't want to drop something on him that he doesn't already know and freak him out even more.

'What's bothering you most?' I say, softly.

'Hmm, let me see ...' he says, tapping a finger to his thin lips. 'Apart from the constant growling of my stomach, the lack of sleep, and heat exhaustion. I thought the inside of the cell was pretty bad, that is until they started manipulating my mind to the point that I violently vomited and they had to stop. Then your friend took me past a room full of instruments and a dirty, blood-encrusted operating table which left me gagging again and just when I thought things couldn't get any worse, I find out ...,' Bunce gulps. 'I have ... in fact ... been eating...' He sighs deeply. 'Morbihans are cannibals. Cue more VOMIT!'

'Shhhh!' Cara hisses over her shoulder.

Bunce's chest heaves with anxiety but he doesn't relinquish my arm. I'm not sure what to say. Then when I do say something, I wish I hadn't.

'If you think about it, you haven't been eating other Morbs, so it's not really cannibalism.'

'Oh, that makes me feel a whole lot better!' Bunce hollers, bulging cheeks flushed pink. 'Eating other people is absolutely fine as long as you don't eat your own race! Have I got that right?'

'Will you shut up!' Cara is facing us, hands on hips, curly head tilted to one side. She hisses at Bunce. 'If you keep 'ollering like that, you'll have every Mutil within a mile over 'ere and they won' hesitate to shove a stick up ya piggy arse and roast you over a fire!'

'Sorry, Cara,' Bunce hangs his head.

An unexpected smile tugs at the corner of Bunce's mouth. I send back a smirk. He has never heard Cara speak this way. She would have barely talked while in his sister's service and when she did, it would have only ever been politely. It seems she's as mad at Bunce for ruining her life as she is at me.

We pass an alley and a tingling runs through my ponytail, then a tug. I whirl around, there's nothing for my hair to snag on. I double back and flatten my back to the cube on the other side of the alley. Bunce stops and opens his mouth, about to call out, I touch my finger to my lips. He flattens his back to the cube on the other side of the black void and watches me. I peer around the brickwork. I can't hear or see anything. A rat darts out from the darkness with a squeak. Bunce squeaks like a mouse and clamps his hands over his mouth. Cara waits for us, hands on hips again. Bunce walks towards me.

'That rat nearly gave me a heart – arrrgghhhh! Skyla!'

Bunce's legs dangle above me. A giant of a Mutil holds the Morb by the scruff of his shirt. The Mutil is almost completely naked, a scuffed metal plate where its genitals should be. Almost half the monster's body is metal, but he isn't ticking. No moving parts, no sounds of organs inflating and deflating. A Mutil without the warning sounds. No wonder so many Skels are killed this side of town. Bunce's face turns purple as the collar of his shirt cuts into his throat. I need a weapon. I search the streets for a broken bottle, shard of glass, anything. There's nothing.

I tug at the huge filthy arm. Hang on it with all my weight. The Mutil tilts its head, trying to work out what I'm doing. Quick footsteps and Cara is beside the monster. She kicks it in the shin and then yelps, recoiling from the pain of her foot impacting with the metal limb. The monster lets out a war cry. More will come. Bunce coughs; he's choking. The Mutil moves one heavy step after another, carrying his meaty catch in the direction of the park. I lose my grip, fall from his arm and collapse onto the road, landing in a pothole. I've got to get the lumbering thing off its feet. Back of the knee. The one that isn't metal. I run up and drive my boot into the decaying flesh behind its knee. The beast buckles. Cara is quick to react, she reaches down and using both hands, pulls the metal leg out from under the creature. The big stupid animal falls back and slams into the ground.

Bunce is released. He gasps and scrambles away, holding his red-ringed neck. Cara strides up to the skin-covered side of the Mutil's head, lifts her foot and stamps on the Mutil's fleshy throat, crushing its windpipe. She does this several times, letting out a grunt each time her foot connects with the monster's neck. Bunce gawps at Cara like he's seeing her for the first time. Seeing the real her. Once the ex-maid has stamped the monster's face into a bloody pancake, we each offer Bunce a hand and haul him to his feet.

'Thank you,' he says in a small voice.

Cara nods, steps over the large, blistered feet of the dead Mutil and walks on as if nothing has happened. I follow her lead, Bunce close behind me. I glance over my shoulder at the corpse. I've never killed a Mutil like that. I always run from them rather than engage them in a fight. Most aren't quick enough to catch me. Sure, I've had to stab a few but I don't ever go for the kill. Cara stamped on its face and neck with such spite, as if she had a personal grudge. It unnerved me a little. To kill without a direct threat to your life seems almost evil. He was down. She could have maimed him and walked away, but she didn't. Bunce is keeping his distance, choosing to stay as close to me as possible and as far from Cara as he can. When we catch up to her, she acts as if nothing out of the ordinary has occurred.

'Okay, listen up,' she says, in a tense voice. 'My uncle's cube ain't far, he won' turn us in but he won' let us stay long. My cousin linked into a High-Host family and so my uncle might 'ave some less …' She looks Bunce up and down. '… weird clothes that'll fit you.' She turns to me. 'I have some clothes there too. Just so ya know, Glory Runners are as deadly as Mutil round 'ere, stay close and keep him out of trouble.' She jerks her thumb at Bunce.

We follow Cara around a corner and through an alleyway, which is dim but not pitch black, the rising moon expels the shadows. The ground is thick with a carpet of rats running over each other, no longer in the sewers, probably forced out by the same slurry of death I encountered in the bathing block. I think back to the exploding toilet. They must be dumping unusable body parts in the sewer. Nasty. Behind me, Bunce squeaks like a frightened mouse. I look back to see him side-stepping through the alley, trying to keep his feet from coming into contact with the scurrying rodents. Where's Cara? There's knocking, then a mumble of voices, one Cara's, the other a deep slurring. Cara's curly head appears from around a wall.

'All good, come in.'

I turn the corner and almost trip on what could be mistaken for a pile of rubbish. Bunce is so close behind me he nearly falls over me. We walk around it, both staring down at the loathsome creature.

'Anana,'

The pile of wreckage groans.

'Anana, anana.'

I crouch down to take a closer look. It's an old Mutil. Ancient. Sun spots on its bald head, grey hair migrating down sprouts from its ears and chin. A lens hangs from a wire protruding from its eye socket. Its slumped against the wall, small triangular breasts sagging, nipples pointing down. The female Mutil doesn't move when rats run over her lap like she's part of the ground. Her wrinkled lips part.

'Anana.'

'What?' I ask her. 'What are you trying to say?'

Cara appears.

'What are you doing?'

'What's this Mutil doing here?'

Cara picks up a banana skin from the floor and throws it at the old Mutil. It hits the side of her face and her decrepit hands go into a frenzy, feeling around for the skin.

'Anana!'

Shaking fingers bring the rotting peel to her toothless mouth and she pokes it in with one finger, sucking on it like a baby sucks its thumb.

'My uncle feeds it,' Cara explains. 'I've told him to stop but he won't. He's lonely, and a brain-dead old Mutil for company is better than nothing, I guess.'

The sorry creature chews on the banana skin oblivious to everything around her. Beside me, Bunce is more interested in dodging scurrying rats. Jovial yet menacing voices travel towards us, echoing through the streets.

'Quick, get inside before we're seen.' Cara beckons.

Chapter Eighteen

Running from Runners

Inside her uncle's cube is disgusting. The walls are streaky, floor crunchy underfoot, and it smells like stale vomit, piss, and shit. Cara wedges the door shut behind us. The air in the room is hazy. It's more than nauseating. The blinds at the window are closed and stained. The only light source comes from a single lamp on a small table beside the single bed. A round of light from beneath the lampshade illuminates a silver tray, which is piled with empty glory sticks. The pencil-thick, black sticks with the clear liquid measure in the centre makes my skin crawl.

Glory looks like orange sand. Some Runners have tried to dupe people by selling them sand in place of glory, but sand doesn't burn – or melt into a liquid like glory does. I don't really know what it is or where it comes from. I've never tried the stuff, not even a puff. Seeing what it does to people over time is enough of a deterrent. An arm brushes up beside me. Bunce stands with his nose and mouth buried in the crease of his elbow. Cara's uncle sits on the bed, slouched against the wall, eyelids drooping over protruding golf ball eyes. He's not asleep but he doesn't look awake either. His tight, grey t-shirt is stained with what can only be vomit, and there are rings of sweat at the armpits. Though a Skel, he is not thin. He looks a similar size to Bunce. How has he been feeding himself?

'Ere.'

Cara throws black cargo pants and a shirt at Bunce. He catches them, holding them by the tips of his fingers.

'I'm not wearing your uncle's clothes. He clearly hasn't washed in months!'

Cara raises an eyebrow.

'Don't worry, precious. These are me cousin's clothes. They're clean.'

Bunce brings the clothes to his nose. Satisfied they're clean, he darts behind the cupboard and into the kitchen area to change. Cara throws a red dress at me. I raise both eyebrows at her.

'Where'd you get this?' I ask.

'Me cousin gave it to me. Ain't never worn it. Thought it'd look good on you,' she winks.

I frown. Is she kidding? What's her game? The dress feels like rose petals in my hands. I'd love to feel the material against my body. I stop daydreaming and hand it back.

'Do you have something a little less "sell your body" and a little more "stay alive"?'

She laughs and hands me some knickers, a bra, (a size too small but it will do) black pants and a shirt. She also hands me a couple of facecloths and a slither of used soap. After a quick stand-up wash in the kitchen, which is dark enough not to feel uncomfortable handwashing our bodies in a tight space, though Bunce washes with his back to me, pants on, bending to reach between his legs and scrub his undercarriage, we're dressed and ready to go. Cara's uncle is still in the same spot and hasn't said a word.

'This is my cupboard,' Cara tells me as she dresses. 'When you're employed as a maid, they take ya cube and give it to someone else, like they do with hosts. I wanted somewhere private to keep me stuff, can't take much to the Morb complex, not that I've ever 'ad much. Me cousin gives me things he don't need, good for bartering, you know. It's 'ow we keep me uncle alive, coz he don't work or nuffin.'

'Don!'

A male voice shouts from outside and a fist slams against the door.

THUMP! THUMP! THUMP!

'Open the door, ya filthy old waster!'

The woman's voice is followed by the man's laughter.

'Shit!' Cara whispers, and pulls me into the tall cupboard with her.

'Bunce,' I say in a strained whisper. 'Get under the bed.'

Bunce looks down at the crud-encrusted floor.

'Oh gross!'

'Do it!'

I pull the cupboard door to, leaving a crack to look through. Bunce rolls under the bed as the front door crashes open and two tall figures meander into the room. The woman is muscular; a Runner, I can tell. She wears a navy jumpsuit with splits up each side, and her dreadlocks are piled high on her head. Her eyes glow bright green in the darkness, and her skin is black as flint. Sharp instruments hang from her belt. They gleam, polished, ready to torture a new victim. The man is blotchy, his skin the colour of bile. Dark rings encase his tattooed, green eyes and are mirrored in the matted, greasy ringlets hanging over his shoulders. They're gang members. Which gang tattoos the whites of their eyes green? I can't remember.

'Donald, wake up and pay up,' the man says, with a cruel smile.

Four of his teeth are filed into sharp points. My eyes widen and I'm tempted to push the door open a little more, so I can get a better look at him. Only the Mutil have filed teeth. Central do it to them before they are slung onto the streets. It helps when hunting – you cannot tear meat from your prey with blunt flat teeth. I've never seen a Runner with filed teeth. The shark-toothed man slinks towards the bed. He wears a tight navy t-shirt and black waistcoat. He's muscular but also thin, like the muscles have been stuck on to his body as an afterthought, and he carries something in his right hand, a cage with a black cloth over it. He places it on the end of the bed.

'Come now, Don,' he says sweetly. 'You ain't high because we ain't given you ya fix yet. 'Less you using other Runners, but 'choo ain't doin' that, are ya?'

A pathetic whimper comes from the pile of human wreckage slouched on the bed.

'Maybe he can't 'ear us?' says the woman. 'All that rich food and fine clothes ya son gives ya made you deaf as well as dumb? Is that it, Don?'

Cara's fear breathes through her skin and into mine. My heart beats fast too and the cramped cupboard starts to feel like an oven. The ex-maid's breasts are pressed into my back and her curls brush the side of my face as she leans over my shoulder to peer through the crack in the door. I flinch at the unexpected touch of my hand, but I allow Cara to lace her fingers with mine. She relaxes a little. I take my eyes off the intruders for a second and glance down to see one of Bunce's sneakers peeking out from under the bed. The Morb lies deathly still.

'Please ...' Cara's uncle croaks. I can't see him from our hiding place.

'Oh, so you can 'ear us,' mocks the pointy-toothed man. 'Well then, maybe he couldn't see us, huh, Sib? He didn't know it was us.'

'I think ya right, Dutch, and useless eyeballs have no business being inside a useless head,' sneers the woman called Sib, and she takes a tin from inside the pocket of her jumpsuit.

Sobs and creaks come from the bed and Cara's uncle's bald head appears at the bottom of it. Is he trying to escape? He can hardly move, let alone run. My instincts tell me to help him. I must have unknowingly shifted forwards because Cara tugs at my hand. This time I stay put. My urge to help that man in Rock Vault only made things worse.

'What'cha doin', Don? You gonna pay us after all?' asks Sib in mock sweetness.

Don collapses on his back and shakes his head. He is shivering and sweating. Glory has chewed it up his life and spat it out. He's an overdose away from death but today his dealers will finish the job. Glory Runners are not merciful, unless they think you'll find a way to pay. They may still spare his life, if we can remain undetected. If we are discovered, I don't know what will happen.

'Hold him,' says Dutch.

Sib hands over the tin, and grabs hold of Don by the shoulders, he doesn't resist. I watch as Dutch carefully opens the tin and pockets the lid, his hand returns from his trouser pocket with a pair of tweezers with which he pulls a wriggling maggot from the small round tin. Don is sobbing again. Sib has propped him up on the hard, wooden end of the bed. She holds his feeble arms down with her elbows and her long spidery fingers clasp either side of his hairless head.

'Oh my glory, Donald, when's the last time you took a bath?' she says, wrinkling her nose.

'Hold him still,' urges Dutch, as he leans over. Don squeezes his eyes shut and Sib slaps him sharply upside the face. He chokes on a sob and opens his bloodshot bug eyes. Sib forces one eye to stay open with her thumb and forefinger. Dutch drops the maggot onto Don's cornea. Don flinches. I cringe. Sure, a maggot in your eye isn't pleasant but it's not like it can burrow into your brain and kill you. What's the point? Dutch suddenly whips the black cloth from over the cage. I can't see what's in it but I hear it.

'CAW!'

The caged cry is followed by a frustrated flapping. My stomach sinks, rocks at the bottom of it. That's the point.

'Cara,' I breathe.

'No,' she whispers back.

The bird is out of its cage but still protesting. Dutch holds it tightly.

'No, no, please.' Don has finally found his voice, and it is that of a frightened child.

'My son, my son will pay you.'

'Oh, I don't doubt that, but I fink you need a little 'elp in remembering to pay on time,' says Dutch. 'Don't you agree, Sib?'

'I surely do, Dutch,' she says, her eyes wild with pleasure.

Don feebly thrashes his stubby legs and squirms as Dutch lowers the bird's beak in line with the sorry man's maggot-laced eyeball. I close my eyes. I can't watch this. How can Cara let this happen? A soul-shattering scream tears its way from the addict's lungs as the crow stabs its beak into the soft jelly of his eye, in an attempt to retrieve the maggot. Don's bloodcurdling screams compete with Dutch and Sib's loud, maniacal laughter. I can't cope with this. Hiding while someone is tortured to death is not who I am. The Runner's laughter turns to angry shouts of pain. What? A hand tears back the door and I'm dragged from the cupboard in time to see Dutch snatch Bunce up from under the bed. Blood drips from a kitchen knife in the Morb's hand. Dutch drops the crow and it flaps up to the ceiling, pushes its feathered body through a hole in the wall and disappears.

'You stupid, fat fuck! Do you know who I am?' Dutch yells, spit flying at Bunce's wincing face. 'You is too light to be this bastard's son, who are ya?'

'I'm …'

Bunce splutters and pulls at Dutch's hand. Dutch drops the Morb and collapses on the bed, holding the back of his ankle. Bunce lies in a heap on the floor.

'Look at these lovelies, Dutch,' says Sib, as she holds both mine and Cara's heads back, her fists grasping handfuls of our hair.

Bunce glances up at me.

'Sorry, Skyla.'

'Fuck! Is there nothing clean in here!?' Dutch searches around the bed area, I'm guessing for something to stop the flow of blood coming from his slashed ankle. Without looking up he replies to Sib, 'very nice, we'll take 'em to Bullet.'

'Bags of sweet glory, will he be pleased with us,' Sib grins, she's missing a couple of teeth. 'Wanna know why they call him Bullet, girls?'

'Coz he's a weapons dealer.' Cara answers, hands on Sib's, working to release the Runner's grip on her hair.

'Nuh ah, coz he fires white-tailed bullets into anything that moves.' Sib makes a violent thrusting gesture with her hips, shouting, 'BANG! BANG! BANG! BANG!' she laughs, 'he'll bang you two raw … till your insides are on the outside. Won' that be nice?'

'Da fuck he will!' shouts Don, coagulated blood and jelly spilling from the hollow where his eye once was.

BANG!

Dutch's body goes limp and drops to the floor with a thud. Don points the gun at Sib, then changes his mind.

BANG!

Cara's uncle falls backwards, the blood spray from the side of his head joins Dutch's splatters across the wall. Screaming erupts. Sib leaps over the bed to cradle her partner in crime. I rush to help Bunce up. I grab the kitchen knife beside him and once he is on his feet, I step back and scoop the gun from the bed, halfway out the door I turn back.

'Cara!'

Silent tears run down her face as she stares down at her dead uncle. I wait but I'm conscious of the Glory Runner's desperate sobs. After sorrow comes rage and Sib doesn't seem like the type to forgive and forget. Cara touches her uncle on the arm as if in loving thanks, then dashes after us.

Outside the atmosphere is hushed. The shots must have been heard but no one rushes to the scene. There are only shadows, creeping around without their owners. We hurry across the empty pothole-riddled road. I grip the kitchen knife tightly, galloping sideways, my eyes never leave Don's cube. Sib doesn't come out. I bend and slip the knife into my boot; my security comes back. Next, I check the safety on the gun and shove that under my bra strap. It's a small handgun, a pistol that senior guards sometimes carry. Where did Don get it?

Confident the Glory Runner isn't coming after us, we head north-west and a familiar feeling comes over me. I know where I am. I can see The Spiral, the central point of the city. I signal to

Cara and Bunce to keep following me. I wonder what possessed Bunce to cut open that Runner's heels? What made him pick up the knife in the first place? He's either found some courage, or he's gone crazy.

Behind me, Cara wears a calm determination, but Bunce's eyes are empty, blank, not twisted in distress from the shooting as I was expecting. He's had a baptism of fire into my world and I wouldn't have been surprised if he lost his mind but that doesn't seem to be the case. He seems stronger, mentally and physically, when only moments before he was whining like a baby. I know why though, don't I? To inflict harm on another, let their blood spill for the purpose of saving yourself or to save others, creates a shift in consciousness. Slicing Dutch's ankle open is a big deal. Morbs don't use violence to solve their problems, because they would never be in a position where they would have to. Bunce is something else, he's even managing to keep up with us.

'Why were the whites of their eyes fluorescent green?' he asks.

'They're Runners. Gang members,' I explain.

'I don't know what that means,' he says.

'They tattoo colours on their eyes to signal which clique they belong to,' I explain. The leader of the green gang pops into my mind, 'I think green Runners belong to Dra'cave.'

'Dra'cave?' Bunce says, confused.

'Named after their leader, Marcus Dra'cave,' Cara interrupts. 'Evil bastard.'

'They're all evil, aren't they?' asks Bunce, his question aimed at anyone with the answer.

'Not like him,' Cara shudders. 'He likes to skin people after he kills 'em. Makes clothes out of 'em.'

'You're not serious?' Bunce frowns at Cara.

'After all you've seen, you still don't understand how this city works?' I say, exasperated. 'Do they teach ignorance at those Morb schools or are you naturally that clueless?' I can't stop myself. 'Sitting in your safe classrooms, learning useless junk, lies Central tell you and you swallow them all, don't you? Mummy and Daddy tucking you in at night … there, there baby, monsters aren't real. Who are the real monsters huh, Bunce? The Mutils? The gangs? The addicts? Or the monsters who created them?'

'Skyla, it's not his fault.'

Cara pulls at my arm. Dragging me into the shadows. I bat her hand away and take a step closer to Bunce.

'Skels – are – treated – like – dirt. Experimented on and chopped up into food for your gluttonous race: Have you seen Frank? Yeah, I ate him yesterday.' Bunce winces, I keep talking at him. 'Most people are high on glory because they can't deal with their horrible lives. What are your lot high on, cakes?' I turn on a mock Morb accent. 'Oh, Bunce, I'm so upset, the maid forgot to order zesty cakes at the Hyper Market today, it's tragic, I know. Imagine a world without cakes, I'd kill myself!'

Cara gives me a dirty look, as if I've gone too far.

'I'm still here, aren't I?' Bunce says, wearily. 'I haven't gone running back to Mummy and Daddy, even though I'm scared out of my wits! And yes, all I really want to do is drop you and go home but like an idiot I don't. Like an idiot I would follow you to the end of the desert …'

He trails off. I purse my lips, slightly ashamed of my outburst. He hasn't quit and I should give him credit for that. I don't give him enough credit. Cara speaks to Bunce, her tone softer than usual.

'You don't wanna run into any more gangs, trust me. Especially not Dra'cave. He'd love a Bunce skin suit. Skin as light as yours he would wear like a badge of honour.'

'Cara, you're not helping,' Bunce says, dragging his feet.

'I'm tellin' ya,' Cara says, dark curls bouncing as she strides through the streets talking to Bunce in a casual manner, like they're discussing the weather. 'He wouldn't think twice about wearin' ya cock and balls on his face like he was goin' to some freakish masquerade ball!'

'Cara!' I smirk, pretending to be annoyed with her like she's a naughty child who said a swear word. Bunce's face is red. He chuckles.

'Not just that,' Cara grins, revelling in making the Morb laugh. 'I 'eard he used to go around wearing a boob hat!'

Bunce allows himself to let out a guffaw. I smile and shake my head. Cara clamps her hands over her mouth, she cannot believe she's said such things to a Morb. When the giggles subside, a weight is lifted between us. Cara seems to have let go of her resentment in losing her job with the Vables. I guess a family member giving his life to save yours can dramatically change your perspective. Our lives are now too interconnected to hold grudges. There's enough to fight against without fighting with each other.

Chapter Nineteen

Glory Den

We stick to dirty walls like flies to the dead heads above the trenches, weaving along the rows of crumbling cubes in silence. The last thing we need is to attract a hungry Mutil, or more gang members. My body aches, the kind of tired that goes deep into the bone, my legs feel like they're made of lead and my boots clomp heavily into the dark streets as if a giant owns them. Gunshots are rarely heard around the city. When a gun is fired, people scatter like birds. Tonight is no different, except unlike people, the crows perch undeterred on their favourite staring spots. Always watching, lined up on cube ledges and tree branches. The sinful secret keepers. They see Gale City as it really is and only they know everything. I wish they could tell me if Clover is still alive. I could do with some of his advice right about now.

'Skyla!'

'Tess?'

I turn around and Tess launches herself at me. I lift her up and her thin legs wrap tight around my waist, like a baby bear would around its mother. She places her head on my shoulder, and I stoke her brittle hair.

'What are you doing out here?'

'I've been looking for you.' She nuzzles into my neck.

'You shouldn't be out here alone, it's not safe.'

I pinch the flesh on her shoulder and then feel her bony arm.

'Stop that,' she says with a giggle.

'What?' I ask smiling.

'I'm fine. I'm not starving!' She holds my face in her tiny hands and looks straight into my eyes. 'I can look after myself.'

'I can see that.' I lower her down gently and start re-plaiting her unravelled braid. 'Why is it always the right one?'

Tess laughs. I reach into the pocket of her tattered dress and pull out the elastic band she should have around her hair.

'We better keep moving, that Runner could still catch up to us,' Cara says, eyes darting around the streets. I nod, and Tess weaves her tiny fingers between mine.

'How's your mum?' I ask.

'Worse. She's really sick. That's why I came to find you. You're all I've got,' she says, hugging me around the waist.

'Where's Clover?'

'I haven't seen him since our card game.' She chews the corner of her bottom lip. 'People say he's dead, taken by the guards.'

'Don't be silly …' I say, squeezing her hand. 'Clover is lucky. I'm sure he's fine.'

My words are different to my thoughts. I know what Tess says could be true. Maybe Clover's luck did run out. I can't tell Tess that. I can't upset her further. Sometimes too much truth can poison a person, and children should never overdose on harsh truths.

'Who's Clover, friend of yours?' Cara asks.

I shake my head.

'Slum Lord.'

'This little girl is an Eremite?'

I nod and Tess grins at Cara.

'Accepted by Eremites,' Cara says, eyes burning through me, impressed, 'Interesting.'

Cara starts questioning Tess about the slums. I guess she is thinking of where she'll go. Lost her job, uncle dead, the slums might be her only choice, if they agree to take her. I can't think what to do right now. I can't take Tess into The Spiral with me. I'll have to take her home. I stop and pull the group into the shadow of a Sky-Train support.

'Cara, are there any glory dens around here?'

'Why you wanna know that?'

'Clean ones, that High-Hosts visit.'

'There's one by the orchard.' She points in the direction we were heading. 'But I don't think ...'

'Don't think,' I say, 'I'll do the thinking. I got us all into this mess, I'll get us out.'

I stride away, pulling Tess along by the hand. Bunce quietly follows. Cara doesn't, she stands with her arms folded, only for a moment, then gives up being stubborn and strolls up beside me. We turn down the last alley on the block, and out of the darkness a wall of heavy, dirty, emerald material hangs down, blocking our path.

'This it?' I ask Cara. She nods. I push the curtain aside.

'I hope you know what you're doin', Sky,' Cara whispers.

On the other side of the filthy, emerald curtain is a makeshift tent. Tables, butted hard up against the alley walls, are lit with fireflies in glass jars. Glory doesn't usually have a smell, but inside the den the haze is thick and smells of burnt leaves. I lead the others towards the back. Tess holds on to my arm with both hands, her body tight up against my leg. She has good reason to feel threatened. To either side of us are High-Hosts and Eremites, some talk in low voices and puff on sticks, some are slumped over tables, gloried off their face, and some follow us with their eyes.

Repressed coughs splutter behind me. Trying to cough quietly never works, but Bunce attempts it anyway. If he draws in any more sharp breathes before he coughs he'll get high off the second-hand smoke in here. I sit our group down at an empty table, which is a broken door resting on a tree stump. Across from us is a male High-Host. He sits alone, eyelids heavy, he slowly puffs on a glory stick, smoke shooting out of his flared nostrils like that of a dozing dragon; my grandfather used to draw the mythical beasts for me alongside a woman wielding a sword. A halo of smoke circles the addict's frizzy, teal hair which he wears in two buns high on his head, the lines at his mouth deepen with each drag and the puckered, dark skin under his eyes tells me he's past his useful age; useful to Central that is. Cara stares him out as she lowers herself onto an overturned crate and crosses her spindly legs. She doesn't blink, he's forced to look away.

'I'll get us a drink.'

I reach into my pockets, then realise I have nothing worth trading. Bunce doesn't either. My guess is his backpack was confiscated at the prison and I know Cara has nothing. Beside me, a small hand reaches up, palm flat, bag charm resting on it. I smile.

'Thanks Tess, but I don't think a Central bag charm will count as tender here.'

'It's gold,' she says, still holding it out.

'Bunce.' I raise an eyebrow.

'It is,' he confirms.

'Thank you, Tess.'

She drops it onto my palm, I curl my fingers around it and make my way towards the barkeep. When I arrive at the rotting plank of wood that is the bar, I'm surprised to see a young face; cheeks hollowed by glory use but she can't be more than fourteen.

'How much you want? 'She slurs.

She leans forward and props her weary body up on the bar. Two girls lurk in the darkness behind her, one braiding the other's short black hair. The girl sitting wobbles to one side as the other one tugs her hair tight.

'I'm not using, I just want some water.'

'We don't serve water.' She throws the comment at me.

'What do you serve?'

'Octli.'

Her dry lips hardly move; every word an effort to push past her shrivelled mouth.

'Anything else?'

'No.'

I glance over my shoulder. Tess picks up a used glory stick left on a tray at our table. Cara leans over, whispers in Tess's ear and points to the tray. Tess drops the stick, a look of disgust on her face.

'I'll take three.'

I pass the bag charm across the weather-beaten wood bar. The barkeep's eyes expand at the glint of gold. She reaches out to take the bag charm that dangles from my fingertips. I snatch it back up into my hand. Another young girl arrives and slams down three glasses filled with milky white liquid in front of me. She turns away, exposing a sheath on the side of her belt.

'Any of you know where I can find Bullet?'

I swing the bag charm and the teenage addict follows it with her eyes. The other girls shrink back into the emerald material behind the bar.

'No one finds Bullet,' she says, hypnotised by the gold in my hands. 'He finds you.'

I come to the conclusion that any enquiry I make of this man will be met with the same tight-lipped answer. I nod and drop the bag charm into the girl's cupped hands. She cradles it like it's as precious as a baby bird.

'What happens now?' Cara says, as I place the three glasses onto the table at once.

'What'd you mean?' I ask her.

She picks up a glass and touches it to her lips. Bunce sniffs the white liquid and screws up his nose, but sips it all the same.

'I don't 'ave a purpose no more, I can't seek employment and I don't 'ave a home.' Cara takes a swig from the glass and sweeps her other hand through her dark hair, pulling tight curls off her face, then she reaches down and picks up the used glory stick Tess had been handling. 'Maybe I should go the same way as my uncle.'

'Don't say that!' I smack the stick from between her fingers. 'Life can turn on the tip of a glory stick. Find a new purpose.'

'Like what?' Cara snaps.

I think for a moment. Tess draws circles in spilt glory powder with the tip of her finger.

'You're Tess's new guardian.' I say, hoping Cara will be grateful for this job. Skels need to feel they have a purpose otherwise they'll end up like Don, hiding from the world in a glory-induced trance, slowly destroying themselves from the inside out. I hope Tess's needs will marry with Cara's.

'What do I know about kids?' Cara says, frowning.

Tess grins, elbows on the table, she rests her face in her hands and gazes at Cara like she's her long lost sister. Cara winks at her new red-headed responsibility and says, 'okay, but only because I can see how much this girl means to you.'

'Thank you.' I say warmly, and I mean it.

'Cara will take you home, okay?' I tell Tess.

'Where you going?' Cara asks.

Bunce doesn't join the conversation; he's busy pretending to study the glass of misty milk, while actually studying the array of junkies around us.

'To change our lives,' I reply.

I gulp down half of my Octli. It's bitterly refreshing.

'And 'ow's a Skel gonna do that?' Cara asks.

'A Skel isn't,' I reply. 'I'm a host, remember? Creator of life. I'm gonna create us a new life.'

'Yeah right!' Cara scoffs.

Cara passes Tess her glass, which has only a quarter of the alcoholic beverage left. Tess lets the liquid slide down her throat and cringes at the taste. She frowns at Cara.

'I need to go.' Tess jiggles on her seat.

'Go where?' Cara asks.

'Pee.'

'Can't you hold it?'

Tess shakes her head.

Cara begrudgingly gets to her feet. She takes Tess's hand and leads her towards the back of the den where the barkeep sits. The girl behind the bar jerks her thumb to a curtain behind her, and the two disappear behind the cloth.

'What's the plan? Where are we going?' Bunce asks under his breath.

'We're,' I point to him and then to myself, 'going nowhere.'

Bunce crosses his arms and they knock into the glasses, he quickly steadies them.

'Oh no, you're not brushing me off! Wherever you go, I go.'

'I'm going to find Bullet.'

'Are you insane?' Bunce says, his voice a few decibels higher than usual. He throws his hands up, knocking over the empty glass next to the used glory stick tray it rolls across the table. 'You heard what that foul woman said about him.'

I stand the glass back up.

'There's no choice,' I say, lowering my voice in the hope that he will copy me. 'I've heard the rumours. He's dangerous ...' I press my lips together, a bedraggled woman in a black shawl is staring at me, she looks away when I meet her gaze. I lower my voice further. 'He's more than dangerous. A dead soul is what my grandfather called him, but he's the only weapons dealer in the city.'

'What do you need weapons for?'

'I can't go into The Spiral without them.'

'The Spiral? You are insane!' Bunce hisses, veins in his neck bulging.

'I met a Morb, locked up inside Rock Vault. Old guy. Big, rimmed lenses like goggles.'

'Bins?' Bunce says, frowning. 'They questioned me about him. The guards said if I knew what was good for me I should tell them what I was doing outside his lab. They said he caused the explosion with dangerous experiments ... when I wouldn't talk, they started sweeping my mind. Oh, that was horrible ...'

'Bunce ...'

'Sorry, didn't mean to stray off-topic. Anyway, you couldn't have met Bins because he's dead.'

'He probably is now,' I say.

Bunce knocks the table with his knees. The glasses clatter together, he's determined to draw attention to us. Clumsy Morb.

'But why lie to me?' Bunce asks, 'Why say he died when really he was locked in a cell?'

'Dunno.'

'Why was he in a cell?'

Bunce lines the glasses up, away from his clumsy limbs.

'He was uncooperative.'

I pick at a stone lodged in the grooves at the bottom of my boot.

'What do you mean?' Bunce frowns.

'He refused to tell them where the serum is.' My nail splinters but the stone is out. 'Bins created the cure.'

Bunce's eyes glaze over, like he's left his body and will be back later. Why did he agree to come with me if he wasn't convinced the cure was more than a rumour? I told him not to come. I said I'd go into hiding. He could have backed out. He took one hell of a risk on something he didn't fully believe in. I click my fingers in his face.

'Bunce?'

'Wait …' Bunce places a finger to his lips in thought. 'Why would Central ask Bins to make a cure and then throw him in a cell?'

'They didn't ask him.'

I smile, thinking about the old-timer shouting at the prison walls.

'Oh,' Bunce's eyes are wide. 'He broke the law!'

'Yes,' I say, 'and so have you, more than once. Look where you are!'

Bunce fidgets. It's as if he's playing a game and me saying things out loud makes them real.

'Why not swear him to secrecy?'

I can see the cogs going around in Bunce's head.

'Control,' I say, my eyes wandering to the glory stick tray; another form of control. 'Central need to keep control of Bins, you, me, everyone. Without regulation and fear, they couldn't live in luxury. They don't do things for the good of the people. They don't do what's right for the city. They do things for the good of themselves, do you understand?'

Bunce nods.

'It's hopeless,' he sighs.

'It's not hopeless. We know the cure is real and we know where it is. We just need the right weapons and ...'

'The right weapons? What we need is an army! Plus, you already have a knife and a gun!' Bunce spits.

He crosses his arms, pressing his thin lips together until they are whiter than his skin. The way he always does when he's scared to do something.

'Look. We'll need more than a handgun and a knife. The place will be swarming with guards.'

'Like I said – Army!'

'Keep your voice down, 'I say, and slap Bunce upside the head. He moans and holds the place where I hit him. 'We don't have an army. Stop being stupid.'

'Oh, I'm being stupid? Why can't we sneak into The Spiral? We don't need weapons if we remain undetected.'

'Do you think we can breeze in and out of there like the wind?'

I cross my arms. Trying to explain something to Bunce is like trying to dig out a stubborn chunk of meat that's lodged deep in the grinder.

'No,' Bunce says. 'But we're trying to avoid confrontation, right? Not go in there, guns blazing!'

Glass shatters behind us and a fight breaks out between two female Skels. The girls keeping the bar rush out to break it up. I slap my hand down on the door table and draw Bunces attention away from the fight and back to me.

'Yes, but we need to be prepared for anything ... why am I saying "we"? You're not coming with me.'

'Can't we get weapons from someone else, a Slum Lord or something? I don't fancy dealing with that Glory Runner. Anyone that works for Bullet ...'

'No one works for Bullet. He doesn't pay Runners,' I explain. 'He uses them as and when he pleases. All I know is, if Bullet comes to your part of town, you pay him with whatever or whoever you have.'

'But if he moves around how do you expect to find him?'

'Sib said she was going to take us to Bullet. She knows where he is and she'll be looking for us.'

'You're going to use yourself as bait?'

There it is again, that voice twice as high as what's natural.

'Nah, you're the bait,' I smirk. 'You're the one who cut her mate's ankles open.'

'No way! No way in Skel Hell!'

The teenage bartenders hold the fighting addicts' arms up behind their backs and force them through the curtain and out onto the streets. The other patrons haven't noticed the commotion, too deep in their glory-induced stupors.

'Look, Bunce, if the guards find us, we're dead. If Sib finds us, we're dead. If we get caught inside The Spiral unarmed, guess what? We're dead! We'll kill two birds with one stone. Get weapons and get Sib off our backs.'

'I can't let you go in search of someone who wants to, and I quote, "bang you raw"!'

'Sib said that to scare us,' I cough. The smoke inside the den is getting thicker. 'I'm sure it's not true.'

'I can't let you do this.' Bunce coughs as well.

'Excuse me?' I croak.

'You heard me. You're not going to find Bullet. It's suicide.'

'You can't tell me what to do!' I'm getting sick of everyone trying to control me.

'But it's okay for you to tell me what to do, is it?' Bunce snaps.

'Yes, glad we cleared that up.'

'You never take me seriously,' he growls. 'Stupid Morb, what does he know about anything.'

'It's good you understand,' I say, calmly.

'All right, get yourself killed if you want to, but leave me out of it.' Bunce sighs. 'Stubborn Skel!'

'Mindless Morb!' I fire back.

'Morbihan are the most intelligent beings in this city,' Bunce says through his hands, which are clamped over his nose and mouth in a feeble attempt to keep the glory smoke out. 'But what do I know.'

'Only after you finish puberty,' I mock. 'Before that you're all as mindless as the Mutil.'

My head feels light. I'm not sure if breathing glory-vapour will have an effect or not. Last thing I need is for my senses to be impaired. We sit in silence, both holding our arms across our noses, until Tess and Cara return. I stand, Bunce leaps up and Tess rushes around the low table and wraps her spindly arms so tightly around my middle that I have to almost prise her from me so I can move.

'Cara will take good care of you, Tess.' I say, stroking her head.

Cara is already moving towards the exit, she sweeps the curtain back and steps out of the den. Out on the street she gives me a look as if she'll never see me again.

'Good luck, Sky.' There's pity in her tone rather than encouragement, she thinks I will fail, 'I don' know how ya gonna fix things ... just stay away from the Dark Angel, okay?'

I nod and let the curtain drop before Bunce has passed through; he gets caught up in the material and whips it aside aggressively. I'm angry at him for arguing with me. What does he know? Nothing, that's what! A great mountain of a man walks towards us, robes billowing. Cara pushes Tess behind her and turns into a statue, clenching her fists, ready for a brawl. Bunce freezes with fear.

'Clover?' I ask, as the big man nears.

Two figures sweep out from behind the giant, their eyes glowing green.

'Run!' I scream.

ACT II
THE CURE

Chapter Twenty

Green-eyed Gang

'That's them! Those fuckers killed Dutch!'

The Runner to the giant's right is Sib.

Cara snatches Tess up and before I can blink they've disappeared into the foggy streets. I push Bunce to follow her. He hesitates for a split second. My body language reassures him I'm coming too and he disappears into the fog. I don't follow. I told Tess's mother I would protect her and I mean to. I need to draw the gang away from my friends.

The green-eyed gang stand in front of me. I square my shoulders.

'We didn't kill Dutch.' I lock eyes with Sib.

'You callin' me a liar, bitch!'

The tall Runner, dark as night, dreadlocks down to her waist, fronts up to me. She's a clear foot taller than I am.

'Don killed your boy, not us.'

I'm hoping the others have had enough time to get away.

'Guilty by association!'

Sib pokes me in the shoulder hard, with the handle of a knife from her belt of torture.

'Looks like ya friends 'ave run off and left ya!' The giant booms.

The three thugs circle me, giant to my right, Sib in front, and a short, athletic Runner to my left. The giant would seem to be the most threatening but it's her on the left that draws my concern. There's something inhuman about her oval face. Her long lashes are red fans above diagonal eyes, elongated by a flick of eyeliner, and her burnt orange hair with golden tips is cut in a sharp bob, the breeze fans through it and I'm reminded of sand dunes shaped by a dust storm. There's an unusual weapon attached to her right hand; curled tight over her knuckles lies a second layer of skeleton, silver and bloodstained. I wonder how many people she's knocked out with that fist of metal bones.

Screams cut through the fog. Cara and Tess emerge, their bodies twisting and turning, fighting to free themselves. Several pairs of neon-blue dots blink within the mist. I do a quick count: two pairs; three, four. My heart sinks into my boots. A rival gang drag my friends along like rag dolls. No sign of Bunce.

'Lose something?'

The gruff voice belongs to a muscular body, braided beard, and piercing tattooed blue eyes. The man grins smugly, his crooked yellow teeth overlap, most are chipped and broken.

'Salvador!' Sib steps forward. 'You're on our cut.'

Salvador shakes his head, chestnut ponytail swishing.

'You have no cut. Dra'cave have no business anywhere in this city.'

Tess starts to cry. The scrawny male that holds her has a firm grip on her neck.

'Shut up, little bitch.' He raises his hand. Without thinking, I crouch, draw my knife and brandish it at him.

'Do it and die!'

I could have pulled the handgun, but I don't want them to know I have it. We're outnumbered, and if they take the gun from me we're screwed.

The gangs laugh amongst themselves. The scrawny one clutching Tess grins, a metal plate where his top teeth should be. He loosens his grip on Tess's neck.

'Give me what's mine, Salvador, and fuck off back to your cut,' Sib shouts. 'No bad blood.'

Sib keeps a firm grip on the knife in her right hand, her left touching the top of another weapon on her belt.

'Too late, Sib. There's already bad blood.' Salvador steps closer to the green-eyed gang. 'You see, Don was our client and now he's dead. That's loss of income for us.'

'So, that snivelling shit *was* doing deals behind our back,' Sib whispers to her Runners. She presses her lips together and shakes her head.

'I figure these three,' Salvador pulls Bunce up from the ground by the hair, 'and the one you got there,' Bunce yelps and holds his head, Salvador points to me, 'should cover it.

Sib frowns, as if she's contemplating the proposal. Her green eyes linger on Bunce and I remember what Cara said, *Dra'cave would wear his skin like a badge of honour.* I can tell Sib wants to be the one to deliver that honour.

A dagger leaves Sib's hand. My reaction is fast enough; blade inches from my face, I drop down and flatten my body to the ground. My heart clings to my ribs, beating against them, blood thumps in my ears. A body thuds to the ground, and below the persistent fog. The woman who was holding Cara lies still, head twisted, cheek flat against the tarmac, dagger between her lifeless neon-blue eyes.

I catch my breath before it runs away screaming, and scramble on all fours towards a set of shoes I recognise as Cara's. Tess drops down and kneels beside them. She has her hands over her ears and her eyes squeezed shut. Screams and yells break out above us, clashes of metal, punches thrown. Cara scoops up Tess and Bunce's sneakers join Cara's slip-on shoes. They run. I stand and take off after them but a hand reaches out, grabs a handful of my shirt and pulls me into the fight. A boot connects with my shin. I yelp and limp away.

The gangs haven't noticed the others are missing. They're too busy fighting with each other. Cara, Bunce, and Tess are on the other side of the road.

'Go!' I mouth, stooped over, holding the pain in my shin.

Bunce and Cara shake their heads and beckon me. Cara's eyes dart everywhere. I wave my hand at them to leave.

'Just go!' I mouth.

Cara nods and leads a reluctant Bunce and Tess away. Bunce looks over his shoulder at me worriedly, as they depart.

I limp across the road and down the street. Not too far, enough that I'm at a safe distance but can still see the gangs. I watch the five remaining gang members battle it out. I need Sib to live. I need her to take me to Bullet. Copper bob fights with grace, dancing around her blue-eyed rivals, stopping her performance every few seconds to bring that heavy fist of bones down onto an opponent. Blood spits from a scrawny man's mouth as the bone glove strikes his jaw. Sib's dreadlocks spin as she twirls around and brings two long blades down into a wooden pole Salvador is wielding. She's wild, enjoying herself way too much. Psycho! The giant no longer towers above the group, *the bigger they are the harder they fall.*

My ears are assaulted by a high-pitched noise, the sound of a hundred strangled crows – the siren. Warmth from the sewer whispers up through the grates and adds to the fogginess but the smoke isn't thick enough to conceal me. I duck into the shadow created by the overhang on a sixteen-floor cube and flatten my back against the cold wall. I stay still. Only my eyes move, sifting through the darkness. The siren stops and its wail is replaced by heavy boots. A synchronised march comes towards me. Guards are like robots; hunt, seek, destroy – they won't stop until their mission is complete, which makes me wonder why I've not yet been recaptured. I mould my body to the hard, concrete blocks. They won't capture me. I am the wall. They won't see me. I'm invisible.

The squad charges past me and the tail of a scarf brushes my cheek. They're too close, they'll find me. I don't falter, don't move. They don't find me. They don't even slow down, they march straight for the gangs. I wonder if Kian is with them. I wish he was with me. I lean out from the wall to see the mass of tan uniforms collide with the bloodied gang members. Motorised sound to my left. I pull my head in, air rushes through my hair and my ponytail slaps my face.

'Hover-cycles?' I whisper to myself in disbelief.

I touch my lashed cheek and stare wide-eyed into the road. Five electric hover-cycles zoom past me, sleek, like bullets, they cut through the fog, speeding through the streets in single file. In a flash of power, the bikes roar down the street and towards the crowd, spitting lightning sparks onto the road from beneath metal bodies. I have only seen hover-cycles once before, they're rarely used.

If curiosity was a drug, people would think me high as a kite on it right now. Why send all this force for a handful of gang members? My legs start moving and before my mind engages, I creep after the guards. I know I shouldn't. It's too dangerous but I can't stop myself. I need Sib and if the guards detain her, I'll never find Bullet.

The temperature has dipped, mist settles over everything, eerie, like the clouds are falling from the sky. I'm thankful the mist is growing thicker. I feel braver behind its veil.

I sneak up beside a tube and lean against it. It was not so long ago that I was on the other side of this glass. It must be the only tube that runs through this side of town and it leads straight to Rock Vault. I think of the surgeons inside Rock Vault. This must be their route to work. Just another day at the office, hacking people to bits. I sneak across the road, cutting through white wisps. Within the swirling cloud, an ocean of tan uniforms gathers around a handful of street rats, who have stopped fighting each other and are now fighting not to be detained. I note two hover-cycles leaned up against a cube. A woman screams.

'Filthy spooks! Let go of me!'

It's Sib. They're using hover-cycles to catch gang members? That's not right. Sib's just a scumbag Runner. Maybe the hover-cycle guards were sent to find Bullet? He would be a big prize to Central and Sib could lead them straight to him but she won't, she'd die first. I edge closer to the scene. Three heads bob up and down from within the guard circle. No sign of Coppertop; like a snake, she's slithered away. The men aren't shouting, they struggle against their captors but say nothing. Sib is the only one mouthing off.

'You're breaking my arm! Let go or I'll break your ugly fucking face!'

Dreadlocks flick forwards. A guard yells out in pain. Thud. His body hits the ground. Then Sib's grunts mix with many thumps. Her face re-emerges over the crowd, blood on her forehead, eyes wild, black pupils filling the fluorescent green. *Who headbutts a guard?* I feel a rush of admiration for Sib, brave bitch. It soon fades. She's probably more idiotic than brave, or drugged up to the eyeballs, though Runners don't often consume their stock. I need that damn Runner! Ideas bandy around in my head, all of them useless. I know what I must do but I'm already shaking at the thought.

I boldly stroll towards one of the hover-cycles and cautiously lean over to see if I can find a starter, a button, or something. Under the visor, the dash is blank. How the hell do you turn this thing on? The crowd of guards are starting to disperse, marching off in different directions, none towards me yet. I feel around the bike handles. I glance up again, nerves causing my palms to sweat. Pale moonlight pushes through the clouds and shimmers across the black paintwork. The smooth surface glints. I stroke my fingers down the cold, hard metal – a beautiful machine. What would it be like to take off on it, feel the wind in my hair, engine between my legs? An engine revs, I turn my head to see a crackle of lightning explode from beneath one of the bikes near the crowd. Oh shit! Sib is on the back of a cycle.

Sib's escort revs the engine again and the front wheel spins. *Do something, Sky!* My inner voice shouts. *Stop this!* I run. Not away from the guards, as usual, but straight for them. My lungs burn, I swing my arms and pump my legs, boots pounding on the ground until I'm going so fast my boots hardly touch the ground. The hover-cycle screams towards me – a missile with my name on it. My feet are on fire. Faster, run faster! Jump!

I leap onto the wheel arch, left leg leading, right leg swings out. CRACK! The rider's head is a football, my right boot connects with the black helmet and the guard topples. The bike swerves.

I drop down into a crouch and hold tight. My left leg slips, wind screaming past, trying to throw me off, icy fingers ripping through my hair. I cling to the windshield like a spider clings to a web. The rider tries to drag his dangling body back up to the controls. Sib does nothing, she sits with hands bound, calmly watching me, shifting her body with the swerving hover-cycle to keep her balance. Knees bent, I hold on to the windshield with one frozen hand. The other hand slips to my boot. Knife. Pull. Lift. Lunge. Drive ... Withdraw. Blood sprays from the guard's groin and over my wrist. The rider screams and his breath fogs the visor. He holds his gashed leg.

The hover-cycle is out of control, swerving dangerously. I lose my grip. Slip. Grab the glass again, knuckles taut. Bloodstained knife. Boot rim. Push. I hold on tight with both hands. The bike slows and the lightning beneath cuts out. I feel a jolt and wheels emerge from within the metal body. What's happening? I look up in time to see Sib finally move. She lifts her knee high and her boot comes down hard on the rider's chest. He falls. Thump. Bump. Back tyre rolls over his arm. The smell of burning flesh rises. Sparks from beneath the cycle must have fried his skin. He was lucky it started cutting out. He'd be burned to a cinder otherwise. I swing my body into the driver's seat. A red light is flashing and the bike seems to be slowing down, what do I do? I glance over my shoulder at Sib.

'Pedal!' she shouts.

'What?' I yell back.

'Charge it up, start pedalling!'

I look down towards my feet, sure enough, pedals. I clamp my boots to the footholds and start to push. There isn't much resistance. I pedal hard and the wheels spin over the smooth road. I lean into it and the power kicks back in. Then my legs start to rise, both pedals have shifted diagonally and I can no longer move them. I look at the dash; lights, dials, and clocks which mean nothing to me. I grip the sleek machine with my thighs, feel the weight of Sib on the back and then roll the handles. Grunt. We jerk forwards. It likes it. I twist the handles again. We take off.

I flatten myself, mould my body to the bike and Sib hunkers down behind me. I glance over my shoulder. The street is silent. I pull on the handle again, more power. There's a crackle beneath us and the lamplights either side of the road turn into smeared lines as we speed through the silent city.

After a few blocks, Sib taps my leg. I glance back. Her arm is an arrow pointing left. I lean, she leans with me and I make a rather wobbly turn down a narrow alleyway. Two lights flash up on the dash, then another and another until the entire dash of tiny lights are blinking at me. I've done something wrong. I don't know how to drive this thing! We're losing power again. The pedals don't descend this time. Shit! What is it? I jab at the lights, some turn off and others turn on. The metal body of the bike shudders beneath me and slows down. I stop trying to fight it and ease back. The hover-cycle sighs, the wheels touch the ground, and the power cuts out. Dead. I've broken it.

Sib swings down from the back of the cycle. I lift my leg over the seat and prop the bike against the dirty brick wall. Sib cricks her neck and holds out her bound hands. I reach into my boot. I cut her bonds and replace my knife. She rubs her wrists, then lunges for me. Her teeth gnashing together like a predator snapping a warning. I recoil. She lets out a breathy laugh.

'Cocky enough to stab a guard and steal his hover-cycle, but still a frightened little gutter rat.'

'I'm not scared of you.'

'Yes, you are … and you should be,' she says, darkly. 'You think saving my life changes anything?'

'No,' I say, indignantly. I know my actions change nothing. Glory Runners believe in a life for a life. If you take one of theirs they'll take one of yours, doesn't matter which one. Me, Bunce, Cara or anyone connected to us. It's all the same to them.

'So why save me?' Sib says, hands on hips. 'What's your game?'

I think for a moment. How am I going to convince Sib to take me to Bullet?

'I need weapons,' I say.

'What for?'

Words spill out of my mouth as I think of them.

'Kill that pale fucker who caused your mate's death.'

'Now why would you do that?'

'Clear Don's debt. As you say, saving you doesn't change anything. I'd rather pay with his life than mine.' I shrug. Trying to act casual.

'Is that so …'

Sib digs her finger into the back of her head and scratches between her thick dreadlocks. Our eyes lock, I try not to blink, praying she will believe my lie.

'You have a knife, what more do you need to kill a High-Host pig?' she says, dark eyes stabbing me with suspicion.

'I kill him and I'll be number one on the wanted list. I was hoping one of your gang would stab him.'

Sib narrows her eyes.

'What you talkin' about?'

'I need weapons to protect myself. He's not High-Host …' I pause, reluctant to tell the truth but I have no choice. I have to make her believe I want to kill Bunce. '… he's a Morb.'

Sib raises her pierced eyebrows, the six green dots above each brow reach almost up to her hairline in disbelief. She laughs. Deep guffaws, bent over, shoulders heaving, hands on her knees. When she's done laughing at me, she straightens up, hands on hips, she swaggers towards me.

'A Morb. Ha! Outside, wandering around the city? Pull the other one.'

'It's true.'

'That's the biggest load of shit I've ever heard! Morbs can't survive out here. Everyone knows that.' Sib sneers at me and her nose wrinkles like she can smell my lies.

'I was meant to be host for his sister,' I stutter. 'We ran away.'

'You're a host and you ran away?' Sib snaps. She digs her thumbs into her weapon belt and steps closer to me. 'Do you really expect me to believe that?'

'Did you not notice how white Bunce is?'

'Hosts bleach their skin.'

'Come on, they couldn't bleach it that light.'

Sib purses her thick lips. I shuffle my feet. The passing time becomes more of a danger with every second spent. The crazy Runner grabs hold of my shirt and pulls me to her, her hot breath on my cheek.

'Riches handed to you on a plate, yet you run away. What's wrong with you?' Sib snarls. 'Done time in Rock Vault? They screw with your brain?'

'I …'

She shoves me away hard and turns her back. I give up. She'll never believe me. She'd believe a lie before the truth. I hang my head.

'Okay,' Sib says over her shoulder. Her cruel eyes bore into my skull, desperate to penetrate my mind, read my thoughts. 'What say I buy you didn't want a life of luxury. If that's true, who were your host family?'

'The Vables,' I say.

'Seven levels of Skel Hell, you are stupid!' Sib throws up her hands.

'You know them?'

'None of us *know* them, we know *of* them. Vable is a technical engineer. A mobility scientist. He designed that hover-cycle.'

'How does a Runner know that?'

'I know many things. Knowledge is a dangerous necessity. Can't survive the streets without it.'

My thoughts. My exact thoughts, spoken from a Glory Runner's mouth. We are not so different after all. I'm frustrated at myself – at the fact I have something in common with a scummy Runner! I'm growing impatient. Time is galloping past, I don't have enough of it to waste. I need to get back to Bunce. This is taking too long.

'Will you take me to Bullet or not?'

Sib studies me. Shakes her head. Then strolls away. I hurry to catch up. Back out on the streets she takes huge strides. There's nothing this side of town, where's she going? Whimpers come from the other side of the road – someone moaning? Two figures move slowly within the shadows, a round afro of blond hair emerges from the alley. A Glo-Girl; glory stick hanging from her lips, she side-steps and leans against a doorway exposing the other figure. Back up against the alley wall, arms behind her head as if she's relaxing on the grass looking up at the stars, is a gang member, I'm sure of it. I'm too far away to see the eyes but it doesn't matter what colour they are, all Runners and gang members are a threat to me. Including the one I'm following.

Sib stops advancing at the sound of a groan. I realise there is a third figure, on her knees in front of the Runner. My jaw drops. It's rare for female clients to agree to a service on the streets, their deals are usually carried out privately in some dingy back-alley cube. The kneeling Glo-Girl's head moves between the woman's legs. I don't want to see this but I can't tear my eyes from the scene. The Runner continues to moan. Lips touch my ear, warm breath whispering into it.

'Fancy a bit of that, do ya?'

'No!' I say, red rising up my face.

Sib laughs and her long legs resume their confident stride. She turns a corner and, heart racing, I slip down the road after her. Curiosity tries to tug me back. I ignore it, even though it pulls hard. I keep up with Sib. Why would that Runner risk being caught like that? I've only ever seen men do something so reckless for a moment of pleasure. Those nightcrawlers better finish the job and get moving, or they'll all find themselves in Rock Vault.

'Down here.'

Sib flicks her head towards a dead end. I take a deep breath and follow her into the darkness. There's a scraping noise of heavy metal and then a small light appears in time for me to see Sib's body disappear down a hole in the ground.

Chapter Twenty-one

Bullet

There's a rotten smell down here, it suggests a buffet of cold cuts for the rats of this city, but the rising water keeps them away. I had no time to think, Sib was down the rungs and splashing through the water without a moment's hesitation and if I didn't want to be lost and alone in the sewers, I had to keep up. I wade through the murky water, following the ring of light around Sib. A small lamp strapped to her shoulder throws light out in front of her.

A lone rat, its fur spiked by the wet, swims for its life, holding its twitchy nose above the littered, underground water. There are no other rats down here, which isn't a good sign. We're either brave or foolish. Probably both, except I'm not feeling brave. Was it foolish to follow Sib? Is she leading me into a trap? Leading me not to meet Bullet but to the Dark Angel of death?

Something brushes past my thigh and catches on my pants pocket. I hesitantly reach down to pull the white floater from me.

'Ugh!'

I throw the slimy skeleton hand as far from me as possible.

SPLASH!

Fuck knows what else I'm walking through? Probably the same sludge that burst up through that toilet, it must have come from this river of death flowing beneath this rancid city. The water rises as we wade further down the tunnel, it laps at my crotch. Oh please, don't let it reach my knickers.

'Would you stop fucking around back there!' Sib shouts, her voice bouncing off the rounded walls.

She wades through the sewage and slurry of human remains without so much as a downward glance. I slosh quickly after her, contorting my body to avoid suspicious-looking floating objects.

It isn't long before we reach a junction. Sib turns left and climbs up a small ladder which disappears into a hole in the ceiling. I wait, not wanting to be rained on by her dripping clothes. When her boots disappear, I grip the wet rungs, my hands and soles of my boots slip as I climb. I hoist myself into the hole and water from my pants and bootlaces drips over the crawlspace. It's a dusty scrimmage. My shirt rides up and the rusting metal scratches my back. Sib drops down on the other side, her boots making a dull thud. There's light up ahead.

'You're late.'

A male voice beyond the tunnel.

'Ran into some spooks, sir. That's why I took the sewer entrance. No one saw us.'

'Us?' The voice, which must belong to the weapon's master, sounds surprised.

The tunnel widens and I pull my legs round beside me and slide down into the chamber. My boots squelch as I hit the floor.

'This Skel wanted to meet you.' Sib says.

I take two steps towards a circle of light in the middle of the room. My legs drip with the last remnants of sewer water, and around my boots a wet stain grows dark on the concrete. Intrusive stares move over my body, I recognise one person; Coppertop, purple bruise swelling on her cheek. She's the only one not looking at me. Beyond the spotlight, in the shadows, a figure sits on a throne of bones. The top of the bone throne is in darkness, the bottom is a pile of skulls, Bullet's knee-high, leather boot rests on a large skull near the centre, his other leg is bent across his lap, boot resting on his knee.

'A Skel who dares to step out of line ... way out of line. I'm intrigued,' says his slithering voice from the shadows. 'Are you hungry, little mouse?'

I stay out of the spotlight, more comfortable in the darkness.

'Yes, sir,' I say in a small voice.

'Then please, eat with us,' the voice says, soothingly. Long fingers emerge from the shadow, the light cuts off at the wrist, the floating hand points, 'it's not often we entertain guests. Never, in fact.'

I cautiously move in the direction the slender hand is pointing, towards a table lit with tall, cream candles. It looks like a sacrificial altar. A bounty of fruit graces its fine red tablecloth and golden goblets have been placed between each platter. Gang members push past me and take their seats. I hesitate, not frightened by the thought of breaking bread with these hardened criminals, free food is free food, and the throne of bones is unnerving but still, that isn't filling me with dread. What stops me in my tracks is thick, green and brown, and weaved between the platters, as if it slithered onto the table of its own accord. In one piece lies a huge baked snake, its body reaching from one end of the table to the other. I've never seen a snake so big. The clash of cutlery stops. Are they waiting for me?

I take a seat next to Sib. Not thinking, the first thing I do is poke the dead snake. My finger makes a depression in the soft, warm skin.

'Didn't ya mama teach you not to play with ya food?' Sib hisses.

Even though she brought me here, my presence seems to aggravate her.

'No. She was too busy being dead,' I hiss back.

Sib snorts and turns her back on me. Once the gang begin to eat, I grab great handfuls of grapes and berries and take huge bites from apples and bread. After a few minutes of gorging, letting the sweet juices run down my chin, I grab a goblet and chug back fresh water until I think my sides will split. I wipe my mouth with my sleeve and repress a belch. I get the feeling someone is watching me and they are. Sib looks at me in semi-disgust, neon-green eyes glowing in the flickering candlelight. I pick up a napkin and dab the corners of my mouth, and Sib goes back to chewing her food politely. A Runner with more manners than me. Great.

I search the table to see if anyone else is stuffing their face like a ravenous dog. They aren't. Big men, the size of small mountains eat slowly and in silence. Many are carving great chunks from the snake, my stomach turns. Then something else causes me unease. From the head of the table, red laser eyes lock onto me. Bullet's eyes are not green like Sib's. The other diners' eyes aren't all green either. Two hard-faced men to my right, one with a long scar across his cheek, have blue eyes, there's one green like Sib and the rest are red. Huh? Gangs don't mix with each other like this. Sib was fighting the blues and now she's having dinner with them? I'm the only one whose eyes do not glow in the dark. A scraping of chair legs across the floor and the others are back where they were standing when I entered the room. I stand and walk back towards the central light.

'Thank you for your hospitality,' I say to the shadows, in my sweetest voice.

'It's my pleasure, or at least … you will be,' the sly voice purrs. 'Come closer, little mouse.'

Now that my basic needs are met, the desire to meet my other needs is overwhelming. When hungry or thirsty, fear doesn't really penetrate. The mind and body work like a heat-seeker; stay alive, keep breathing but once this target has been met other emotions come into play. I reluctantly step into the light, standing inches from the most dangerous man in Gale City. This was a bad idea. Bunce was right.

The tall shadow stands and takes two steps towards me. Out of the darkness a broad nose appears, the light slowly sneaks over the contours of Bullet's soft bone structure, his oval face framed by long, black hair. He wears a tight jacket, no sleeves, muscular arms exposed. His high cheekbones and pointed chin offer a strange sort of handsome, almost pretty, smooth skin on one side of his face, the other riddled with scars. Sharp lines are etched in clusters on his eyebrows, cheeks, and trailing from his lips. Bullet licks the corner of his mouth, tongue darting over two fresh cuts on his plump upper lip, red pools to the surface of his malt complexion.

'Skin like dark honey …' he sighs, trailing a thin finger down my forearm as if he is brushing me with a feather. I try not to flinch at his touch. His tongue darts out to lick the same corner of his mouth, tasting the blood.

'Hair like golden sand …'

His knee-high boots click against the concrete as he slinks around me. His fingers sweep through my hair. It tingles. I shudder.

'And brown eyes as deep as tree roots, connected but with a need to break free …?'

I'm not sure whether to answer him or if that was a rhetorical question. I stare into the blood red, which should be white and his pupils burn through me. He steps back, vanishing behind the darkness surrounding the spotlight.

'Perhaps your place is with us?'

I blink and Bullet faces me again. I flinch. He moves quick, hardly a sound. It's no wonder he's evaded capture all these years. His tongue darts back out, a peculiar tic; like a seductive serpent with an unquenchable thirst for blood.

'Is that why you're here?'

'She's here for some weapons, sir,' Sib's voice sounds in the left corner. 'Says she wants to kill the fucker that slashed Dutch's ankles. Not sure I trust her.'

'What is trust, if not something to lull your prey into a false sense of security?' replies Bullet, smiling sweetly. 'You are not her prey. You need not give her your trust.'

He gives his attention to me. His eyes drink me in, he looks upon me like I'm the most beautiful creature he's ever seen. I don't like it.

'Tell me, little mouse. What's your birth name?'

I clear my throat and keep my voice steady.

'Skyla.'

I don't give him my first name. I never give anyone my first name. It was my mother's and mine to keep. Central knows my real name, but most other people don't and I intend it to stay that way.

'Skyla. Pretty. Too pretty a name for such a dirty little girl,' Bullet whispers.

'About the weapons,' I say, in an attempt to keep things professional. 'I can't pay you but …'

'Hush, you're too twitchy, in too much of a hurry,' Bullet whispers, his fingers finding my topmost shirt button. The button drops to the floor and my shirt pops open.

I glance down to see two small knives on his fore and index fingers. I work to control my trembling, I must ignore the frightened little girl inside me.

'You can relax. You're not required to pay me now.'

He flicks off another button, exposing the top of my breasts, which are squashed into Cara's bra. The butt of the handgun is visible. Bullet doesn't look concerned. Fearless man. He runs a sharp finger knife down my bare skin and between the soft flesh of my breasts and drops his gaze down my shirt. I retain my composure. The sharp point doesn't break my skin. He tilts his face up towards mine and his almond-shaped, lustful eyes once again bore into me.

'For you are not ripe.' He coos.

I keep my face stern, I mustn't look as if his craziness is disturbing me, but it is. What does he mean I'm not ripe? I'm not growing a pair of melons in my bra. I don't ask. I honestly don't want to know. I want to get out of here alive and in one piece.

'So, I'll pay you later, then?' I say, sheepishly.

'Oh yes,' he says, grabbing my chin and turning my head. I feel wet on my jaw. Bullet licks the length of my face and then moans into my ear like the taste of my skin has caused him to climax. He whispers, 'I name the price and the price is high. When I call on you, you'll come …' he releases his grasp on my face, 'or die.'

I will my arms still, they don't listen and tremble uncontrollably. Unnerved by his words, yet seduced by his scent. I breathe in his skin, sweet spices. I want to lick him back. The urge ebbs when Bullet sits back on his skull throne, the bones are probably of his enemies, I wonder how many skeletal thrones he has hidden around the city, how many people has he killed? I clasp the top of my shirt, never taking my eyes off this strange man. This man who agreed to give me weapons in return for I don't know what and I don't know when, but I don't have a choice. I need his help.

'Bring her what she wants,' Bullet orders.

There's movement around me, footsteps, everyone leaves except Sib and Coppertop. Metal hinges squeal and a rusty door clatters. I don't look to the sound, I watch Bullet's dark outline. His knife hand at his face, he slowly drags the finger blades through an unscarred inch, slicing it open, drawing deep lines on his skin. He sucks in air through his teeth and groans it out as he cuts himself. I swallow hard. I try not to look at the bloody-faced king of Gale City's underworld in case he flips and decides to bang me raw, as Sib put it.

Strange urges rise in my chest. I frighten myself. I'm fearful I might want him to touch me – want him to run those knives across my bare skin. I stare at the door, draped in darkness at the back of the room where the gang exited, sweat beading my top lip. Ambiguous feelings fight with each other, crippling anxiety and curious arousal, like eating something new for the first time. It could be poisonous or leave a bitter taste, but I'm hungry and maybe it is delicious and filling and maybe … no! It's the devil's fruit! *Take a bite. I dare you.* A moan of pleasure leaves Bullet's lips. I'm sure he licked his finger blades. My nipples harden. Control yourself, Skyla! This guy is sick! Maybe I am too? No. He'll fuck you and kill you. Fuck you with those finger knives!

'Choose.'

A tall, muscular woman with neon-blue tattooed eyes and a face full of piercings holds open an oversized, leather briefcase in front of me. I snap out of my trance, fold my arms over the top of my exposed breasts and peer into the black case. A revolver – lame. A mace – weird. Who uses those? A miniature pickaxe – I don't want that. The blade is too thin and swinging it would leave my body open to attack. I know he has better weapons than this. Is this all I'm worth? Wait, a silver shape catches my eye.

Knuckledusters. I could use those, I guess. I reach in and pull them from their foam bed. They're heavier than I expect. I slip them onto my fingers, a snug fit, it's as if they were made for me. I curl my fingers around the moulded metal. A trigger clicks. I flinch and jump back from my own hand as two shiny metal blades extend from either side of my knuckles, one facing up and one down. Not just dusters, a type of knuckle-knife. I twist my wrist, admiring the craftsmanship.

'You like blades.'

Bullet's seductive voice travels straight to me and I'm suddenly aware that I'm smiling. I salivate. I do like blades. Yes.

'It's all I know,' I shrug. Opening my fingers, the knives retract and I stow the weapon into my pants pocket. Then something else catches my eye. 'What's that?'

The woman holding the case doesn't reply. I step around the case full of weapons and run my fingers down the smooth, cold black of what looks like a semi-automatic rifle, slung over the woman's shoulder. I've seen something similar, on a touchpad my grandfather used for work but he also kept digital books on there about all sorts of things, there was one about the land wars my grandfather would to pour over, trying to make sense of the carnage. I glance back to ask the weapons master if the rifle is up for grabs. Bullet's boots have disappeared from the throne. He's gone. Sib steps into the light next to me.

'Haven't you seen a Galva before?'

I shake my head. She unclips the rifle from the shoulder strap and points it towards the woman holding the case. She doesn't move, or even look at the Runner pointing a gun at her face. Sib backs up, arm pushing me to move back with her.

'Galvanic rapid fire 12-gauge launcher,' she says, as if reading from a list. 'Electronic projectile ammunition. Accuracy up to one hundred feet.'

A rattling burst of gunfire echoes around the chamber.

Burning breath draws sharp to the back of my throat as I witness the woman's head explode like a watermelon.

The briefcase hits the ground with a clatter, followed by the woman's body, the case spills its contents as she spills her blood. The headless body convulses, current running through it. All too soon the body is still. Hairs stand up on the back of my neck. Sib's face is emotionless, as if demonstrating a Galva by killing an associate is a regular occurrence. Maybe she did it not as a demonstration, but as revenge for the fight and losing the giant's life to the blue-eyed gang. Coppertop is polishing her fist of bones with a blood-stained rag, she doesn't look over, face like stone, not a twitch. Skels don't kill each other. We see as much death as anyone, it's an unavoidable part of life, but we would only ever kill someone in self-defence, usually Mutil and we would definitely not take a life as freely as Glory Runners, Eremites, and Mutil do.

'Feel the weight,' she says, dumping the gun on me. 'You can fire one bullet or many. Just flip this switch.'

I grasp the cold metal with both hands and turn the gun on its side. I flick the switch to single fire. My hands jitter. I think them calm, close one eye, and look through the scope. I squeeze the trigger. A bullet explodes from the barrel with a push to my shoulder. It penetrates the belly of the dead body sprawled across the floor. The meat twitches, giving it jolting false life. A smoky smell ascends. I exhale.

'We done?' Sib asks.

'We're done,' I reply, bending to scoop up a small oblong case on the floor, which I hope holds extra bullets.

I throw the gun strap over my head and follow Sib and the red-headed Runner to the back of the room. Sib pushes open the door then blocks me when I try to pass.

'Down here we don't pay debts with labour. You better kill that Morb.'

I tug at the shoulder strap until the gun is central to my back.
'I will.'

'Good.'

Chapter Twenty-two

She's Missing

I fall asleep in the open air, holding the Galva, cradling it like a new-born baby. The security of my new weapon allows my tired body to peacefully slumber. Birds call to each other – not the crows – the smaller ones that stay away from bigger birds; their song rouses me. I've slept later than I wanted. A Sky Train shelter is not a safe place to sleep. I lick my dry lips, stale taste in my mouth, tongue furry. The sun taps on my eyelids with its golden fingers and when I finally lift them, I'm met with an orangey-pink sunrise. I peel my throbbing back from the bench, indentations of wooden slats aching in lines across it, I squint up at the sky. Candyfloss clouds ripple through the blue. One looks like a hover-chair. I hope Bunce, Tess, and Cara got away safely.

My stomach pinches me. Even after Bullet's banquet, I'm still hungry. If only I could eat the clouds. Candyfloss reminds me of my mother, I have never eaten it but I'm sure it existed because I read about it in a picture book. A battered, old picture book made from a tree with pages you turn rather than swipe. My grandfather had read it to my mother as a girl and years later it was one he read again, but to me. It was about a place called a 'fair.' A wondrous place for families to go and be happy. I wanted more than anything to be part of the story, to eat the candyfloss, ride the rides, to play the games. I wanted to feel the excitement, breathe in the happiness, step inside the pages and be safe forever.

My grandfather and other elders would tell me it was once so, that fairs existed and that there was a time when people worked but were also free to do as they pleased. They were respected members of society like the Morbs. Apparently, Skels were once scientists, doctors, and engineers. I want to believe it, but in my heart,

I know it's a lie. Not real. All the stories told to children are made-up to bring comfort. Some even make up stories to bring comfort to adults. Skels are subservient because they think they're going to a better place when they die. That's not true either. You get one shot at life, and finding the cure will free me, Bunce, his race and mine. I'm sure of it, but I'm also frightened of what I must do to make it so. My nerves are all but shot, yet the magnificence of the dawn is empowering me. It's time. The Spiral beckons.

I shift my weary bones from the bench and stretch the stiffness from my legs. I can't walk around in the light of the day with a rifle on my back, and I'll definitely be higher up on the 'wanted list' for throwing that spook off his hover-cycle. *Spook*. I'm even starting to think like a street rat. I hurry down the station steps and use the receding shadows as cover. The streets are deserted but they won't be for long. My footsteps are loud against the quiet. Boots dropping onto the concrete like rocks down a dried-up well. I step lightly but cannot seem to hush my heavy soles. The marmalade-dusted slums are in my view quicker than I expect. The vector ring is still live. This time I know, because I can hear a faint hum of energy. It sounds as though the field is buckling under the pressure of being constantly in use. I check over my shoulder, pull up the grass cover and duck into the dirt tunnel.

'Skyla! You're not dead!' Bunce says.

I duck out on the other side of the tunnel. Has he been sitting here waiting for me, all night?

'Not yet,' I say, reaching down to help him up. He takes my hand.

'I wanted to go back for you, but Cara said Tess was our priority.'

'She's damn right.'

Although Bunce looks happy to see me, his face is oddly contorted.

'Have you been waiting here the whole time?' I ask.

'I'm on watch,' Bunce says proudly, like he's been trusted with something important. He hasn't. If a Mutil gets in, it will be his screams as it bites into him that alerts the others. He's nothing more than cannon fodder.

'On watch? Was there another Mutil?'

'No, it's Kareen, she …' He twiddles the end of his black shirt in his thick fingers.

'Bunce,' I interrupt, and force my lips into a reassuring smile. 'Tess's mother was dying. People die young out here …'

'It's not that!' he says, and locks me with a sorrowful stare. I cross my arms and wait.

'Kareen was murdered.'

'And?' I shrug.

I'm sorry the woman died, I really am, but people get murdered all the time. I witnessed a murder a few hours ago. Gangs are constantly killing people and it's somewhat normal for Eremites to kill off their dying. I can see how Bunce would be shocked, but he needs to toughen up and get over it.

'And …' Bunce says tight-lipped. 'Tess is gone.'

'What! How? Where's Cara?' I yell, my blood boiling. They had one job, one job! Keep Tess safe. Is that so damn hard?

'Cara was knocked unconscious. She's gone looking for Tess.'

'Knocked unconscious by who?' I growl.

'I don't know.'

Bunce rubs the back of his neck. His fidgeting is starting to grate on me. If he doesn't stop twitching, there's going to be another dead body to add to the count.

'Where were you in all this?' I shout.

I should lower my voice but I'm livid. How could they let this happen?

'I was asleep,' says Bunce, chest heaving.

'How can you sleep through someone being murdered?' I yell.

'She was smothered with a pillow!' Bunce yells back at me. 'Cara didn't wake up right away either. What were we meant to do, stay awake all night?'

'If that's what it took!' Bunce stares at his sneakers. 'I don't have time for this, I have to find Tess.'

I turn back to the tunnel and Bunce grabs my arm before I can duck through the hole.

'Cara is looking for her, she can't have gone far. It's imperative we … what's that on your back?'

'A Galva,' I say, turning to face him. 'Now let go of me!'

'A Galva?'

Bunce peers around me cautiously, as if touching the rifle will cause it to go off.

'Is that really necessary?'

I sigh. I'm going to have to take him with me this time. He can't stay in the slums without a minder. The Eremites have tolerated both him and Cara, for Tess's sake but with her gone, there's no need to feed an extra mouth. I reach into my bra, the top of my breasts popping out from behind the rifle strap. Bunce drops his gaze, as Bullet did, except he quickly looks back up at my face, cheeks flushed.

'I haven't got time to fuck about,' I hold out the gun. 'Here, you take the handgun.'

He doesn't take it from me.

'Where shall I keep it?'

I push the gun to his chest and his body stiffens.

'Shove it in your back pocket.'

'It might shoot my ass off,' he says, horrified at my suggestion.

The sun is higher in the sky, it warms my skin, we have to leave now. If we leave it any longer the streets will be teaming with guards and Skels.

'It won't shoot your bloody ass off!' I yell at Bunce, 'but I might if you don't shut up.'

Chubby hands shaking, Bunce places the gun in the back pocket of his tie-dyed jeans.

'Where'd you get those jeans?'

Bunce swings his backpack into my line of sight.

'That guard friend of yours …'

'Kian?'

'Yes. He left my bag at Tess's.'

I exhale, thinking. I can't be in two places at once. If I go looking for Tess, I delay finding the serum and Central might be close to breaking Bins. Every second counts.

'Cara will find Tess, won't she?' I ask Bunce.

I know he doesn't have the answer to my question, but I need to hear some reassurance.

'I believe she will.' He nods.

I should have done more to protect her. I hope she wasn't snatched. Maybe she ran off, upset. I decide that's more likely.

'We should focus on the bigger issue,' Bunce says, he touches my arm tenderly. 'There's no way back, we have to press on.'

'Right,' I say, pulling nervously on the Galva strap. I hold up my hand. Bunce grabs it like we're about to arm wrestle. His grip is firm. 'Let's do this.'

I duck into the tunnel, Bunce leans in close to the back of my head.

'Today we live,' he whispers.

'Or die trying,' I whisper back.

Chapter Twenty-three

The Spiral

We move like spiders through the hazy city streets, clinging to walls and creeping around corners. The early risers – street sweepers and tree pruners – are too busy to notice us. Our streets aren't immaculate like the Morbihan side of town but they aren't as dirty as Drift Side. I wonder why the Skels on our side get up and tidy up and the ones on Cara's side don't bother? The Sky Train thunders overhead, casting its snaky shadow across the pavement, and as I lead Bunce to our doom, I think about Tess's mother. Why would anyone kill Kareen? I don't think she was eating and if she was, it wouldn't have been much, so food supply was not the issue. There are plenty of people who want me dead, but there's no motive for anyone to sneak into Kareen's shack and smother her. It doesn't make sense.

'How do you suppose we get past the guards?' Bunce whispers.

'Shut up and walk,' I whisper back.

'Skyla.'

'Bunce?'

I stride on, irritated. He's already slowing me down but I couldn't leave him in the slums. The Eremites were using him as bait for Mutil, he'd only need to eat more than his fair share of food and they'd kill him on the spot.

'Before we get there,' he stutters, 'that is, before we probably get killed … I want to say thank you.'

'For what?' I ask, confused. I adjust the gun strap to stop it sticking into my breasts, I pull it up across the top of my chest and hold it in place at my hip.

'For helping me.' Bunce says.

'What?' I ask. I have no idea what's he's going on about. I need to get things straight in my head and I can't formulate a plan with him jabbering on.

Ouch. There's a stone in my boot. I lean my shoulder against the warm cube wall, hiding in the overhang shadow. Bunce copies me. I tug at the laces and slip off my left boot and tap the base. A small stone falls onto the ground.

'Bunce, let's get something straight,' I say, tugging my boot back on. 'I'm helping myself, and as much as I like you ...'

'You like me?' Bunce says, his smile almost touching his ears.

I roll my eyes. This Morb hangs on to even the smallest show of affection.

'Sure,' I say. 'We're friends, aren't we?'

Bunce nods. Good. I need him to think that we are. We're not, but I don't totally hate being around him, I hate that he slows me down but I don't hate him. He's starting to grow on me, I guess, like moss does on a rock.

'So,' I say, moving out of the shadows, 'let's concentrate on the task and leave the thanking until we get through this, okay?'

'Okay,' he says and follows me.

Once through the densely cubed area called Central Side, we hit the boundary. There's no real boundary, it's imaginary. Like drawing a line in the sand and pretending no one can cross. Skels never cross the boundary into the Morbihan side of town, unless they already work there. Come to think of it, I've never seen anyone cross the line. Eremites, Mutil, gang members, Runners, Glo-Girls – no one crosses the line. How odd. We're about to break that unwritten law. With our backs to a towering Morb apartment, we edge along in its shadow and past the back entrance to City Hall. We take a flight of stairs up and over a tube that crosses the boundary and which also leads to the City Hall Sky Train stop. As we march down the other side of the stairs and around a corner, the sun strikes a diamond above me. I look up, lifting my hand to my forehead to shield my eyes. The Spiral – Central headquarters, a glittering evil eye on the city. Deep breath in, blow it out. *You can do this*. No, I can't. I'm walking Bunce to his death. *No, don't think like that. You can do this. I can. Anything is possible. Look how far we've come already.* We round the corner and …

'Shit!'

I back into Bunce.

'What is it?' He whispers.

His hand hovers over his right back pocket, where the gun is. He's jumpy. I need him not to be so jumpy.

I peer back round the wall. The glass-fronted entrance doors to The Spiral are swarming with dozens of guards, like bees round a hive.

'Is that Kian?' I crane my neck. There are a few, tall guards with black wavy hair.

'Couldn't Kian let us in?' Bunce whispers. I duck out of sight when a guard eyes the wall. I hope she didn't see me.

I grasp Bunce's arm and whisper to him.

'You think the other guards will accept that? Just rock up to Kian, hey, buddy, let us in.' I puff out an over-exaggerated sigh.

I peer around the wall again and Bunce peers with me. I touch the Galva strap. It's a bad idea to start firing randomly at the group of guards but what choice do I have?

'How many do you think you could take?' I ask him out of the corner of my mouth, eyes locked on the scene.

'None.' Bunce replies, aghast.

'Be serious!' I snap.

'I am!'

'Look …!'

The swarm of guards disappear inside Central headquarters.

'And then there were two,' I say, smiling.

'Two outside!' Bunce says, 'How are we going to get past those inside?'

'One problem at a time, Bunce,' I say, studying the building.

The Spiral is a long, silver cylinder reaching into the sky with a giant sphere on top. When I was a child, elders told stories of an extra moon that fell from the sky and became The Spiral. Many children couldn't tell that this was a lie, I knew it was, yet part of me still wanted to believe it could happen. My eyes are drawn skyward, the top of the sphere is blocked from view by the surrounding trees and two drones buzz in to my line of sight, they whizz past in the direction of City Hall. Sometimes drones carry recording devices. I don't think they clocked us. I reach down beside me and scoop a stick from the ground. I twirl my long, sandy hair into a bun, and shove the dry stick through the middle to hold it in place. A crow caws. In the nearest tree, a lone black bird sits fluffing its feathers. He looks at me, studying my face.

'Glider?' I whisper.

Glider's head jerks towards me. He glances from left to right, stopping with every slight turn of his neck, as if his eyes are taking panoramic snapshots of the city one frame at a time.

'Who are you talking to?' Bunce asks.

'Shhhh. We don't want to spook him.'

Bunce falls silent and adjusts his backpack. Pinned to the front of his bag is a small badge, Gale City emblem on it. I snatch it from the fabric.

'Hey! You could have ripped my backpack.' He whines.

'Be quiet,' I hiss.

I wave my hands around, trying to get the bird's attention. Shiny badge in my fingertips. His head cocks, black beady eyes on the prize. Crows frighten me, they're unpredictable creatures. Much like Kian, I guess. It's no wonder they worship him. The black bird's wings spread and he floats down onto my hand, sharp claws gripping the soft flesh of my fingers. I wince at the pinching pain. I'm hoping the bird will realise I'm Kian's friend and help me. Although possibly not, if the bird recalls that heated exchange at the pond.

'Drop it on the guards,' I coo, and point to the doors.

Glider tilts his head and snatches the tin badge in his beak, then lifts off. I rub my scratched hand and watch him glide back up into the tree.

'No,' I say, in a quiet but firm voice. 'The guards!'

His sleek, black beak turns away and I'm faced with black tail feathers, and over the branch, the crow shits out a splatter of green and white onto the pavement below and takes off.

'Damn crows!'

'You didn't really think that was going to work, did you?' Bunce asks.

I pop my head back around the wall.

'I was hoping … hey, look!'

Glider is perched on a ledge above the guards' heads. I grin and wink at Bunce. Bunce shakes his head dismissively, he must think I'm crazy.

'Get ready,' I say, looping my fingers through the knuckle knife in my pants pocket.

Glider drops the badge and it clicks on the ground in front of the guard's boots. They murmur to one another and glance up in time to see Glider swoop away, then one bends to pick up the badge.

I dash out from behind the wall, ducking under one of the huge support beams that slope down from the main structure, my boots scuff across tiny bricks arranged into a picture of the Gale City emblem; a huge mosaic crow holding the sun. Before they know what's happening, my fist is planted in the standing guard's face, top edge of the knuckle knife smashing into his temple. He drops like that woman did when Sib shot her in the head with the Galva. The other guard grabs my ankle and yanks me off my feet. My back cracks against the hard ground. I groan and roll into the foetal position. A hand is at my neck, squeezing, his knee presses hard into my thigh, pinning me to the ground. I thrash around, blood rushing to my face. I plunge my knuckle-knife up into his fleshy side, hoping I've hit an organ; he grunts and falls backwards.

Sun-glinted metal flashes past my face. Bunce has pulled the guard's sword from its sheath. Panicking, the Morb slices it through the air with all his might and practically severs the guard's left hand, leaving it hanging off by a thread of skin. His screams are muffled by his crimson scarf, which I pull tight around the back of his head before punching him in the face, the knuckle-knife connects, crack, nose broken. His head drops backwards. Thud. Two down. Bunce drops the sword and it clatters to the ground. The Morb stands beside me, shaking and slack-jawed. I wipe my knife on the guard's leg, smearing his blood across his tan pants, retract the blades and pocket my knuckle-knife. I like my new weapon.

'Hide the bodies round there.'

I point to the edge of the building, next to some tall trees. Bunce nods, dazed but functioning. Arms beneath the armpits of one of the guards, he drags him away. I'm impressed with Bunce, he stepped up, though I'm more impressed with how sharp that blade is. I pick up the delicate, blood-smeared sword. I contemplate keeping it. I decide against it and throw it next to its owner, step backwards and study the front doors. No surveillance, they must think guards are enough security. Palm-pad to the right of the doors. Dammit! If only Kian was out here, Bunce's words seem less silly. Boots scrape across the ground as Bunce hauls the other guard towards the corner of the building, bloody hand trailing red along the dusty concrete.

'Hold on!'

I stoop and pick up the almost severed hand, press my boot to the guard's wrist and pull. It rips away. Droplets of blood spray my toecaps.

'What are you doing?' Bunce asks, a green tinge to his face.

I step up to the front doors and press the severed hand to the palm-pad. The doors swish open. I cautiously step in to the building, Bunce hurries to follow. I press the oozing hand to his chest. He snatches it and flings it out the door behind him like it's a hot rock.

'Gross!'

Below my boots, words spit at me from an embroidered mat: 'The System Works!' I hate those words. In my head, I rearrange them into *Works the System!* and that's exactly what I intend to do, starting now. The entrance hall is quiet, haunting. I breathe in its strange synthetic air. I can only liken it to opening a box of new plastic containers at the factory.

Beneath my boots, the blue carpet feels like sponge. I resist the urge to take off my boots and walk across it in bare feet. I gaze around the walls, no surveillance cameras in here either. I don't get it. I knew Central were arrogant, but to think they can't be touched, that's more than arrogant. Disgusting despotic bastards, they actually believe they don't need security because no one would dare challenge them. How wrong they are. Still, no matter what I think of them, I'm definitely afraid of them; the fear of being caught prickles over my skin and dries out my mouth. I *am* frightened of the repercussions of being discovered inside this Central haven. The last public display of punishment was a warning to all. There hasn't been another since. I block the frail and wrinkled body from my mind and try to picture my grandfather's smiling face, but all I can see is blood running from his grey hair into his grey eyes. Will I follow in his footsteps, humiliated, tortured, and eventually executed in the middle of Market Square?

'Skyla.'

Unaware I've stopped moving, I flinch when Bunce touches my shoulder. My instinct is to place my hand on top of his. I won't. I can't accept his comfort. I've told him we're friends but we're not. I'm using him to better my life. I can't let him get too close. Present time knocks on the door to my mind. I open it.

'I'm fine, let's go.'

I keep expecting to be caught, anticipating a guard or a Central to appear at any moment, but they don't. I wouldn't know a Central even if I did see one. Are they even human? Inhuman monsters are all I can picture in my mind's eye. My ears are pricked for the sound of guards coming after us or the wail of the siren. Nothing. It's eerily silent as we creep down the stretch of hallway that seems never-ending. The silver-painted walls are lined with framed quotes. 'We stand united for the greater good.' Another: 'Some must kneel so others may stand in glory on their shoulders.' *On* glory on their shoulders, I think to myself. The last one I read makes my skin crawl. 'We the givers, we the takers, we the peace and harmony makers.' Do they really believe their own bullshit?

At the end of the hall, we arrive at what looks like a shaft. There isn't a palm-pad. As we near, the doors automatically open. We cautiously step inside the round, mirrored chamber. The doors swish closed, coming together with a light kiss. Me and Bunce exchange dark looks. This is it. The panel next to me shows a vertical line of round lights. Each has a symbol on them but I don't know what they mean. I try to remember what Bins told me: third floor? No, third door and my age is the floor, number twenty. I count the lit-up buttons until I get to the twentieth. I push my finger against it. A robotic voice sounds from above. I jump back.

'Clone archives. Please step into the footholds and grasp the handrail.'

Clone archives? What's that? Handrail? I see it.

'Shh-iiit!'

My legs fly up above my torso. I cling to the handrail, fighting against the force pulling my feeble body towards the lift roof. Bunce has his feet in the footholds, and one arm looped under the rail, but his other arm is flapping about uncontrollably. The skin on my face feels like it's tearing away from my skull. The lift slows. My legs float for a moment and then fall with a thud. I'm a puddle on the floor. The doors swish open.

'Clone archives. Please exit with care.'

I crawl out of the lift. Bunce offers me his hand. I launch up into his arms. He's also shaken but manages to steady me. I cling to him for a moment and take in the short corridor. Same blue carpet underfoot, same silver walls, except the picture frames are replaced with doors to the left and right of us. No people around. Thousands live in this city but outside of the Morb complex the place often feels constantly deserted. It's as if people live their lives avoiding each other. I never noticed it before.

'It can't be this easy,' I whisper in Bunce's ear.

'Maybe Central is a myth? They don't exist,' he says out of the corner of his mouth.

'No,' I shake my head, 'there's someone in charge of the city, and what about the guards from outside? Where are they?'

'No one has ever done anything like this before,' Bunce tries on a soothing tone 'My guess is they aren't expecting us.'

'I know, but surely there should be someone around.'

Bunce shrugs and points his finger from left to right.

'Which door?'

'Bins said third from the lift,' I say, in my smallest voice.

'Third from the left?' Bunce asks.

'No, third from the *lift*,' I reply.

'There are two doors third from the lift, right or left?'

I bite my nail. No longer perfectly shaped and polished, they're chipped and dirty. In worse condition than when I worked at the factory.

'He didn't say.' I glance from one door to the other.

Bunce squares his shoulders, and points to the third door on the left.

'I'll take this one, you take the right.'

I nod and we edge past doors one and two. I slide my back against the smooth, cold wall next to door three and before I can shout 'no!' Bunce presses his palm to the pad. I wait for his screams. They don't come. It doesn't burn. Theory tested. Scare tactic only. This means we can open any government door we like! I didn't need that severed hand. I wait for the metal door to swish closed behind Bunce, then press my hand to the palm-pad for my door. The metal door clicks open and disappears into the wall with a swoosh. The room is bathed in a spring-green light. I step inside, eyes everywhere, heart pounding.

'This is an office?'

The emptiness doesn't answer. The large room isn't empty, exactly, there's a lot of space and at the far end are towering columns. A room lost in time. Forgotten about, yet still maintained. My boots echo on the black, marble floor and as I approach the columns they become clear; not columns but dozens of glass-cylinders glowing with lime-coloured liquid. They're at least ten feet high and as wide as I am tall. I walk towards the nearest one. Drawn to something pickled inside it.

'What the hell?' I gasp, and step back.

Floating inside the huge jar is a creature I've never seen before. White skin bleached green by the liquid lime, huge body like lumpy dough, tiny skeletal limbs; distressed expression on its under-developed face. I move to the next over-sized jar. Same green skin, slits for eyes, skeletal body one side, arms and legs blown up to an enormous size on the other, same painful expression on its distorted face. My stomach churns, the same feeling as when I found bodies hung up like cattle in Rock Vault. Even so, I can't stop myself from wanting to know – wanting to see. What are these things? I walk across the marble to a smaller cylinder on the other side of the room, to another body, a baby. Cheeks grown over the eyes, an explosion of rolls upon rolls of tissue, skin covered in scales. *SICK! What kind of fucked-up experiments were they doing in here? How much suffering did these mutant creatures endure before they died? Mutilation is bad enough. Don't they have any respect for life!*

Tears roll down my face. I can't beat their system. *What am I doing here?* I back away, eyes scanning each watery grave. Next thing I know my hand is behind my back, on the Galva, I pull it in front of me and grasp it with both hands and aim. My finger trembles on the trigger. *No Skyla, don't. They'll hear it.* I squeeze my eyes shut, tears running down my cheeks in despair.

I sigh, sling the gun back over my shoulder and run from the room. Heart like a sledgehammer, it thumps pain into my chest. I can't breathe. I can't breathe … the door automatically slides out of my way and I hurl myself back into the hallway. *No one is safe. Morbs, workers, we're all the same to Central. They're evil. They'll turn us all into mincemeat or monsters! I can't stay here. I have to go. Have to get out! Bunce.* I press my palm to the pad on the opposite door, it opens and I fly through it. Thump. I slam into a body.

'Skyla?'

Someone grips my wrists.

'Bunce! Run! Run far away!'

Tears sting my eyes. Everything is a blur.

'Calm down.' he says, pulling me to him. Strong arms almost wrap twice around my slight frame.

'Bunce, get out of here!' I stammer.

'Lower your voice.'

A hand strokes my hair. Why isn't he running away?

'No, no. You don't understand. No life is sacred to them, not even Morbs.'

Tears spill from my eyes. I can't stop them. I wipe my wet face on the strong arm.

'Have you got a death wish? I get you out of Rock Vault and you come here? How the hell did you get past security?'

I breathe in the faint smell of dirty city streets masked with soap.

'Kian, where's Bunce?'

I glance around, I'm in some sort of meeting room. Tables and chairs in rows, vision screen on the far wall.

'Bunce?'

'He should be in this room!' I say. Standing on tiptoe, I peer over Kian's broad shoulders. Bunce is nowhere to be seen.

Kian pushes me away. I stumble backwards into a chair and almost fall down into it. I wipe the tears from my eyes and I stare into Kian's angry face, puzzled.

'Unbelievable! Is it the thrill of something dangerous, is that what turns you on?' Kian says, his stare cold, as if I am his enemy.

'What?'

'Oh, come on, Sky. I'm right about you two, aren't I? You're fucking him.'

My jaw drops open, eyes wide with fury.

'What! Kian, he's a Morb!' I say, louder than I should.

'Galva, huh?' Kian crosses his arms and nods to the Galva strap. 'I only know of one person with those kind of weapons.'

'So?' I say, defensively. Why is he being such a prick? He's been acting weird since the day of the lab explosion.

'Fuck Bullet, you'll fuck anyone,' he says, casually.

'Fuck Bullet?' I hiss, fists clenched. 'You actually believe I'd prostitute myself for a few weapons?'

'How else did you get them? Bullet isn't charitable.' Kian shoves his hands in his pockets. 'Seems you'll give a ride to anyone … except me.'

'Is that what's important to you, Kian?' I say aghast, 'Who's inside me, and the fact it isn't you?'

'That's not what I meant!' he says, hurt replacing the anger in his eyes. 'I don't want anyone touching you.'

'Too late,' I say throwing words away, 'I've already fucked my way through the entire city.' I cross my arms. How dare he!

'I'm serious, you're special to me.'

'Am I?' I raise my eyebrows, 'Sorry, but would you care to tell me how else "you're fucking him" and "you'll give a ride to anyone" is meant to be interpreted? Did I mistake those words for I love you?'

The silence that follows is uncomfortable. I wait. I need to find Bunce but I also need to sort this, whatever *it* is, out with my 'friend' or else he will blow everything for me. Bye-bye cure. Will Kian tell me he loves me? Does he? I know he cares about me more than anyone has ever cared about me, but he has a funny way of showing it. His eyes water. I've never seen him cry and I don't expect to now. Most of Kian's family are dead, taken by illnesses Central don't care to treat. He's had no one to teach him love. His frustrations are ruling his head.

'I care about you, Kian.' I say softly, 'but you're not the only person in my life. You have to accept that.'

'What about Bunce?' he says, jealously, he's jealous of a Morb! This is ridiculous. 'Do you care about him?'

I don't know how to answer. I think I do care what happens to Bunce. I've never been good at lying and I've never lied to Kian. I shrug.

'I see.' Kian says, miserably.

But Kian doesn't see. I've never had many friends and I've been through so much with Bunce. I *am* fond of him. Kian should accept that. Instead, he turns his back on me like he does every time he experiences a situation he can't control, or emotions he doesn't care to share.

'Where are you going?' I say.

'To find that Morb and break his fucking neck!'

Kian strides towards the lift, I hurry after him.

'No! Kian please, I need him!'

Kian stops, one foot in the lift, one on the carpet.

'What about me? Do you need me?'

I sigh. Kian is my oldest friend but he isn't *my* Kian anymore, he belongs to the city. The city emblem on his shoulder turns me cold, the mark of a puppet. I'm reminded guards are traitors. They do Central's bidding.

'I need a friend, not a guard,' I say.

'I need a link.' He says, 'We could have been happy at The Hub ... now that's all gone.'

I'm surprised when a single, angry tear escapes and runs down his clenched jaw. He wanted to be my link, why didn't he tell me? Kian doesn't say another word. He steps back and the doors close. I lunge, scratching at the metal, clawing at it.

'Kian! Stop! Wait!'

I push my fingers into the join and try to prise the doors open.

'Shit! Shit!'

I slap my hand against the cold silver. Ouch. My palm throbs.

The doors spring open again. Kian is gone. I step into the empty chamber with a heavy heart. No idea which button to press, wondering if this is all worth it. I count up again and realise I started from one instead of 'G' for ground floor. This must be the nineteenth floor. Maybe Bunce realised the same and went up a level. He could already have found the serum and be on his way back to get me. I press the button above the one I pressed last time, the symbol on it resembles a slanted chair. The electronic voice rings out.

'Central Offices. Please step into the foot holds and grasp the handrail.'

This time I'm quick to comply. The jolt is over fast. I've advanced one floor. According to the panel, there are only two more, but stepping out onto the next floor, it doesn't feel like I'm anywhere near the top of this building. A figure appears at the far end of the corridor and I flatten my back to the wall as the lift doors swoosh closed behind me. There's nowhere to hide. I'll be seen. The figure doesn't notice me. Is it Bunce? I squint. No, too tall and thin. I count three doors on the right, none to the left. I sneak along, the bouncy carpet muffling the sound of my steps. I press my palm to the pad; the door slides open and I slip inside.

Chapter Twenty-four

The Serum

The door swishes shut behind me with a quiet click. I step forward and bump into a leather couch, forcing it slightly to the left. Ouch. I lean against the smooth, rolled arm and rub my stinging thigh. I touch the leather with my fingertips, was this once a human arm? The thought repulses me and I snatch back my hand fast, as if the couch gave me an electric shock. I take stock of the room; leather chairs, leather desk top, leather brief case. People sacrificed. I take two steps into the centre of the office and stand with my arms tight to my sides, not wanting to touch anything.

There's a cabinet behind the desk next to a slit of a window. It's the only item of furniture not covered with skin. I sidestep around the back of the desk, breathing in, so no part of me touches the leather upholstered chair. Then, fingers trembling, I open the clear cabinet doors and feel around for a secret compartment or a catch. I knock over a commemorative plate, stand it back up and read the fancy gold scroll: *For diligence and devotion to duty.* I roll my eyes and keep searching. There's no compartment. Next, I open the filing cabinet. I thumb through files, tempted to peek inside at the documents but I don't, I have to be quick. Nothing there, either. No secret panel or box, no serum.

What was that? My muscles lock with fear and I give my hearing priority over my other senses. There's a murmuring outside the door; idle chit-chat. *Hurry, Skyla, hurry!* I drop to my knees and search under the desk, the smell of the polished leather chokes me and panic tightens my chest. I find nothing under the desk and crawl out, glance up. What's that? I get up off my knees and examine a large painting, which is hung on the wall, dominating the room. The picture is split into three panels. I trace my fingers over the top one. An outer space backdrop, the sun in one corner and in the other there are large, silver rectangles with rays of sunlight beaming between them. The rectangles seem to be reflecting the sun's rays down onto a red planet. The picture beneath is of a desert landscape; blue skies, domed colonies, smokestacks pumping out great plumes, and people in spacesuits. The paint is faded in places, I wonder how old it is and who painted it. There's no signature at the bottom, and any thought of the artist is suddenly forgotten when I realise what I'm looking at. The last picture is of a city. My city. Gale City.

I don't understand what this artist is depicting. I reach my arms to either side of the masterpiece and lift it off the wall. I need to know more. Perhaps there's a description on the back. I turn it over, stiff board, no signature. I haven't got time for this, it's art, it doesn't have to mean anything. I turn the painting back over and hurry to replace it on the wall. My eyes catch an imperfection in the discoloured square where the painting was hung. I lower the painting, prop it up against the wall then scrape my finger over the mark, plaster falls away. This can't be, this place is immaculate and an inferior wall would never pass building inspection ... no it wouldn't, because it wasn't this way when the building was constructed, was it? Someone did this recently.

I frantically scratch at the wall, plaster driving under my nails. It comes away so easily. With both hands, I claw until the carpet has dandruff and the hole is big enough for me to reach my hand inside. My fingers close around a small object. I pull it from the wall. I hold out my shaking hand and slowly spread my fingers like the bud of a flower opening to the sun. In my palm is a dust-covered, velvet drawstring bag. I smile, overcome with emotion. I don't know whether to laugh or cry.

'The serum,' I whisper to myself.

'I'll take that.'

Thick fingers snatch the bag from my hand. No! In a flash I'm on my feet, ready to take down this Central bastard. I'll fight … I'll …

'Clover?'

The mountain of a man, my rock in bad times, smiles warmly as he sits down behind the desk. My mouth hangs open in shock. He's wearing a suit, his bulging arms almost splitting the seams. Silver sparkles at his wrists; cufflinks brandishing the Gale City emblem.

'Hello, Sky.'

'Clover?' I say again, frowning, staring. What's going on?

'Please, take a seat.'

I lean away from the chair, in my mind's eye someone's skin is being stripped off. The room warps. I hold my thumping forehead with one hand, my sickening stomach with the other.

'I'll stand,' I say, puffing out the stress. I compose myself.

Clover crosses his fingers over the velvet bag on the desk. He's still grinning. That pearly white grin I used to know; once reassuring, now like a wolf bearing down on its prey. A wolf in sheep's clothing, as my grandfather used to say but Clover isn't a sheep, he's a large predator in a smaller predator's clothing. My confusion is soon replaced by anger. It creeps in and closes my fingers into fists. I clear my mind, I focus my hatred.

'Surprised to see me?' Clover asks, his deep voice almost jovial.

'No,' I lie, and roll my eyes to the ceiling.

'Come, come, Skyla, let's not play games.'

'Look who's talking? You're a fucking Central!' I snap, and fold my arms.

Clover unlocks his thick fingers and pulls the small bag apart, he reaches inside and gently removes a vial of dark green liquid. It looks like pond scum. I fix my eyes on the vial, words are tumbling from Clover's plump lips, I catch every second word until he says something that attracts my full attention.

'The painting was created in 2056 by a well-respected and prominent artist who was born to an Earth city in Russia. Do you like it?'

I shrug. I'm confused. Earth City in Russia? Who talks like that? The Russian cities, the ones not already under water, were destroyed in the land wars, like all the others.

Clover rests the vial on the velvet bag and gets up from the desk. Confident. Certain I won't try and snatch it. My fingers twitch but don't move. I watch as strong arms lift the painting up and place it over the hole in the wall, back in its position as if it had never been removed.

'Gramps was a keen artist, wasn't he? He would have appreciated this, don't you think?' Clover smiles. I don't return it.

'My grandfather ...' I pause, jaw clenched. *Gramps*, why would Clover call him that? Only people that knew him best called him that. I try not to show that his mention of my grandfather in such a casual way has rattled me. '... was going to teach me to paint. That day never came.'

Clover doesn't reply, doesn't say sorry, he doesn't say that executing my grandfather was not in his control. He doesn't say these things because I know it was in his control. He's responsible for my grandfather's death. He let that happen. Rage surfaces as I stare at Clover, whose dark eyes search my face, empathetic in their gaze. A Central with empathy for a Skel? Not likely. He doesn't care what happens to me or anyone. Clover points to the top picture and continues his happy lecturing.

'Paintings tell stories and this painting tells a particularly special story. It depicts an important historical event for the human race, one that would change our existence forever.'

I stare at the painting. What does he mean? This is a work of fantasy painted by an artist with an overactive imagination.

'In what way?' I ask.

'It shows how the human race managed to save itself from the brink of extinction.'

Clover's speech is euphoric. This painting excites him the way a Runner arriving with glory excites an addict. I'm conscious that the longer I keep him talking the longer I will stay alive. I try to think of a good question.

'The human race survived because there was no one left to fight. The cities are under water or in ruins. Gale City is the last city on Earth, and we're not exactly thriving, the population is small.' I say, feigning interest.

'It won't stay small for long, and allow me to correct you,' he licks his full lips, 'Gale City is the first city, not the last.'

I have no idea what he's blabbering on about, and I'm starting to wish he would either kill me or send me back to Rock Vault.

'Whatever you say.' I cross my arms.

'What's this?'

Clover points to the top-most picture; the one of the sun's rays reflected onto the red planet by giant mirrors.

'A planet,' I say, flatly.

'Mars. The first planet humans set foot on outside of Earth.'

'People went to Mars?' I'm suddenly interested.

'STRATA-K was the first ship to successfully land on Mars. Missions A-J failed, half of them were unmanned. K was our last hope and the first successful human mission, and once settled on the red planet, a specialist team studied DNA samples from inside the Martian mountains, set up infrastructures, mostly caves for mining and greenhouse gas emission plants and ...'

'If that's true, why aren't there people on Mars now?' I interrupt.

I look over the three-section painting again and Clover's words plant a seed in my mind.

'There are,' he says. 'STRATA-K was a one-way mission. No going back. The team were terraformers. The planet's atmosphere thickened over time, and with the help of the mirror system and greenhouse gasses, the air became breathable. When the land wars erupted people were evacuated from Earth, well, what was left of it after accelerated global warming took hold.'

'Mars was colonised?'

The seed sprouts.

'Mars *is* colonised,' Clover corrects.

I study the second picture; domes and smoke billowing into the sky and people in spacesuits. My eyes drop to the third picture. The one of Gale City surrounded by red desert. My gaze flits to the window. Through the open horizontal blind, the red sand stretches to the darker mountains cut into the clear blue sky. Clover's lips spread into a smile.

'They're not strictly human,' he says, thoughtfully.

'Who?'

'The Morbihan ... Tell me, Skyla, what do you think Morbihan stands for?'

'I don't care.' I say dismissively, shock prickles over my skin, he can't be saying what he's saying.

I do want to know, but I don't want him to think I'm interested in anything he has to say. Why is he telling me stories? Why isn't he dragging me off to prison? Is my life a game to him? I've forgotten how intuitive he can be; he can feel my curiosity and feeds it without permission.

'Martian Organism of Raised Biological Intelligence with Humanoid Attributes and Nature.'

I don't speak for a moment. I didn't hear anything past MARTIAN! Like little green men?

'Martian?'

The word escapes before I can stop it.

'The Morbihan are part indigenous, unlike us,' he says with an air of satisfaction. 'They have more right to Mars than we do.'

'What are you talking about?' I snap, 'this isn't Mars, it's Earth!'

Clover walks back round to the desk and sits down.

'Are you sure?' he asks, brown eyes wide, wild with delight at my ignorance. I glance back out of the window. I say nothing. I'm not sure of anything anymore.

'Humans have not inhabited Earth for thousands of years, Skyla,' he says, still staring at me, his eyes narrow and unnerving.

He's not an Eremite, I tell myself. He's a Central! I can't believe anything he says. He's trying to scare me.

'But the elders ...'

'What they teach, and what is truth, are two different things. History tells us that some people couldn't let go of their old life. They struggled with the fact that Earth was a wasteland and that they could never go back home, so they made up their own reality, a new Earth and that carried through generations.'

'That doesn't make sense!'

'Sometimes, a lie is told so often that it becomes truth,' Clover raises his dark eyebrows. 'The elders believe this is Earth and generations of inaccurate accounts of history have preserved this falsehood.'

'I don't believe it. This is rat-shit! Mars is a small, red planet way out in space. I've read about it. It's a desert planet with no life, a bunch of abandoned rovers on it and ...'

My blood freezes, veins turning to icicles under my skin, the light hairs on my arms shiver. There aren't any other cities; there's no communication from beyond the wall. If there were land wars here, the Skels who do come back from their desert missions would have seen ruins, or told stories of abandoned cities or oceans far and wide. *Nothing but sand for miles* is all they say. I sigh. Maybe I've always known, maybe Clover's right and like them I allowed myself to believe the comforting lie. Then there'd always be a chance I could leave the city, in the hope of finding other civilizations out there, people who survived.

'Okay, say I believe you. Why clone people? There are enough Skels in this city. We don't need Morbs, and why not clone animals, huh? The city is overrun with rats and crows and parasites but you can't clone some sheep or cows?' Clover frowns. 'Yeah, I know about what you do to prisoners, as if mutilation wasn't bad enough!'

Clover shakes his head and holds up his hand to stop me from asking any more questions. He acts as if I've said nothing out of the ordinary.

'Cloning is not as simple as all that. That's the reason Showcase was created. When you clone a person or an animal they don't turn out quite the same. The Day of the Bird is a prime example. Sloppy cloning and quick breeding.

There's a thud against the window. I gasp and turn my head to see a crow slide down the glass. Maybe they know we're talking ill of them and they're trying to get in and peck our tongues off. I shudder. I can't stand those feathered freaks.

'As you can see ...' Clover points to the window, a black feather stuck to it, 'they're not as they should be. We don't know why they're not right. Cloned animals survived the process but then died within days but some survived long enough to breed and their genetic defects carried over. Tests were done and it was concluded that cloned animals aren't safe to consume.'

'Yet people are?' I spit.

'Skels are not clones.' He says patiently.

'So why clone at all, if it's that problematic?' I say, crossing my arms, thanks to these Central idiots we have a city swarming with deranged birds.

'Scientists have always been obsessed with the past, they even tried to bring back dinosaurs, reinstating the white skinned was another challenge for them.'

'Did white humans become extinct like dinosaurs?' I ask, I have heard of these beasts, they once roamed the Earth but were wiped out by an ice age.

'The loss of the lighter skin pigmentation due to centuries of interracial relations, coupled with the rising sea levels and floods which triggered the land wars in which many perished, caused the white skin to become rare,' Clover explains. 'There were a few whites transported to Mars, but not enough to rebuild this type of human. Scientists had pre-empted this problem, and insisted a stock of human and animal DNA was transported to the new home planet.'

My expression stays blank. Who cares about what colour people are? I don't. My mind wanders, searching for a solution to this dangerous situation, for a way out of the room. I pretend to pay attention while thinking of an escape plan.

'Central started the cloning programme to avert the extinction of the white races. They tried many cloning methods, but the subjects kept dying like the animals did. They soon realised that they needed something to bind them to the environment.'

A fire lights in my mind. The flames flicker until I can see a picture in them.

'Those giant cylinders! You did that! You created those deformed people, didn't you?'

I feel like a bucket of cold water has been poured down my back. This is all too much. Clover strokes the vial.

'Not me personally, Sky,' he says calmly. 'I wasn't around back then. I've read the logs. After many failed attempts, a strand of Martian scrab DNA delivered the best results; an entirely new race of people. The scientists must have thought they were so damn clever, until the side-effects occurred.'

Clover is thrilled recounting his ancestor's discoveries. I'm disgusted anyone would interfere with nature in this way, and what the hell is a scrab? More scientific terminology that I don't understand.

'You know ... I walked straight into that room. The one with all your precious research, pickled people, and scientific instruments. I could have destroyed everything in there!' I say, spitefully.

'But you didn't.'

Clover reaches behind him. My eyes flick to the vial. He grabs a glass bottle filled with bronze liquid.

'Drink?'

I shake my head. He unscrews the top and pours himself a measure. He swirls the liquid inside the tumbler in his great fingers. I walk around the desk to face him.

'I didn't destroy it, because I thought it couldn't be that important. The door wasn't locked or guarded.'

'Not everything of importance is locked away or guarded. If that was the case, we would all guard our lives by locking ourselves away.'

'Central do,' I say, indignantly.

'Not all of us,' Clover grins.

I look at Clover though different eyes. I would have trusted him with my life. Yet all the time he had the power to change my fate and didn't do a thing. He knew the lies told to us about this planet yet he keeps the population blind to it. I want to shoot him in his smug face! He hasn't had me dragged back to Rock Vault yet, so I figure I'll press him for more information. Maybe if I can keep him drinking, he'll get falling-down-drunk and I can grab the cure and run.

'Why was making a white race so important?' I ask.

Clover leans back, tips the tumbler and lets the liquid slide down his throat. He holds his hand out, offering me the chance to sit. Again, I shake my head and stand tall. He clears his throat.

'No single colour stands out as superior when you are marvelling at the beauty of a rainbow,' he says, pouring himself another glass. 'But to lose or to have never seen any one of those colours would be a shame, don't you think?'

'People are best with their colours mixed,' I say, folding my arms.

'You're entitled to your opinion,' he says, knocking back his second drink. 'That's all anyone is entitled to.' He pours a third. 'In my opinion, it's important to keep diversity alive and preserve all the colours of the rainbow. Had we not created the Morbihan, we would all be the same colour.'

'I don't see the problem,' I say.

'No, you wouldn't. You believe we should all look and behave the same. Yet you couldn't be more different from other Skels.'

Clover puts down his glass and picks the vial back up. He tips it upside-down. The black-green liquid ripples down the sides.

'Why don't you behave differently?' I say, heat rising up my face. 'Cure the Morbs, change things for the better.'

'Because I don't believe that would make things better.'

I clench my fists. There's no point in arguing with someone who doesn't care to see your point of view. He's never experienced the life of a Skel. He'll never understand, and even if he does, there's no way Central will swap their luxury, power, and privilege in order to empower and improve the lives of gutter rats. They don't have to, so they don't.

'A stroke of genius,' Clover says, holding up the vial. 'No doubt about that, but it was created by a foolish genius. The contents of this vial will only lead to misery. Surely you know this?'

My muscles tense. I don't agree. I watch the vial in his hands. Be patient. Don't let the rage out. Don't do anything rash. My emotions take charge of my head.

'Clearly I don't know shit!' I yell, slamming my fists down on the desk. 'If I did, I would have realised what damn planet I lived on. I would have known that you were too clean to be a Slum Lord, too well spoken, too compassionate!'

The small office is starting to make me feel trapped. I need to get outside. Earth, Mars, whatever. I need to get out of here.

'Compassionate?' Clover sounds surprised. He grins. 'You think I care about people?'

'Not anymore! I think you're a cun–'

'Tut, tut … careful, Sky.' Clover raises his voice. 'I've kept you alive this long, you wouldn't want to ruin it now.'

Kept alive? Without the cure, he can kill me now. What am I going to do? Go back to the Vables with Bunce? They'd never have me back, and Bunce – they'd probably disown him.

'You've been useful,' Clover smiles slyly. 'I need more people like you around. You led me straight to the serum. As I knew you would.'

'What?'

'Did you think you could breeze in and out of here like the wind,' Clover laughs.

I said that to Bunce, before we came. Bunce – where is he? Clover clearly admires the sound of his own voice.

'I allowed you to leave Rock Vault with Bunce and his sister's maid, just as I allowed you to enter this building.' I gawp at Clover. 'I know every move you're going to make before you make it.'

The vector ring, the floodlights, he wasn't spying on the Eremites, he was spying on me!

'So, all these years pretending to be a Slum Lord, pretending to look out for me, you were actually spying on me?'

Clover pauses. He seems lost for words. As if he wants to spill some top-secret information but can't, or won't.

'Yes, and yes, and I'm going to continue to watch you, Sky. I know you have more to show me and I know you got that weapon from Bullet.'

I touch the gun strap.

'If you know where he is,' Clover says, firmly. 'It would be wise to tell me.'

'I don't. He moves around.' I say.

'That he does, but I warn you,' Clover leans forward. 'He doesn't forget a debt, so if you have any idea of his whereabouts …'

'I told you I don't!' I say sharply.

I wouldn't tell him, even if I did know where Bullet was, I might have before, when I thought he was an Eremite. Clover leans back. Calm. Like nothing is ever a problem for him. I stare at the man I used to trust. I feel betrayed. Used. Lied to. But all I've really been is deceived. Clover isn't family. I have no family. He isn't even a friend. He was there for me when times were tough. I actually believed he cared about me, like Ms Grouse and the elders at the factory. They looked out for me too. Why do I feel hurt by his deception? Everyone in Gale City has an agenda. Why am I so surprised? How many others is he keeping an eye on? Who else is on his radar? Kian? Tinny certainly wasn't. Cara and Bunce? Maybe. Clover was watching, and waiting for someone to lead him to the serum, and that someone was me.

Clover gets up from the desk and walks towards me. He holds out the vial. I touch my Galva. Clover touches the breast of his suit jacket.

'Do you think your draw is quicker than mine?'

I let my hand drop. In the time it would take to ready my gun, Clover would have riddled me with bullets. I have to do something. I take a chance and lunge forwards, reaching out to snatch the vial. Clover grabs my wrist and forces my arm up behind my back, my other arm locked beneath it. I'm thrust down to my knees. He's strong, too strong. I'm rendered powerless.

'Now, we are going to put an end to this and you are going back where you belong.'

He kneels behind me, his muscular arm clamps across my shoulder and his large hand grips my jaw. I struggle but it's useless, he presses my back to his chest, my arms pinned.

'No! Stop!' I gasp.

A glint of glass catches my eye. Thick fingers pinch my nose, I instinctively open my mouth to take a breath and a bitter taste hits the back of my throat. I gurgle and choke on the gloop, forced to swallow it. My body is released. I cough and retch, heaving on all fours. The serum, it's gone, down into the pit of my stomach like a slimy serpent. It's over. I glare up at Clover; the traitor, the liar. Why has he done this to me? Clover gives me his hand. Begrudgingly I take it, he helps me up and in my pocket my other hand weaves its fingers through four holes. Clover releases my hand and I release my pent-up aggression onto his face.

WHACK!

Knuckle-knife connects with his jaw. The uppercut knocks him into the desk. Blades shoot out either side and I bring one side down with all my strength, plunging it into his fleshy thigh. The fake slum lord shouts in agony. I lift my blade from the meat and it drips with Central blood, peppering the blue carpet.

'Didn't know I was going to make that move, did ya?' I spit.

Clover slumps against the desk, holding on to his lacerated leg with both hands.

'Too bad about your flashy suit, nothing gets blood out!' I smirk.

I grin. His eyes are squeezed shut with the pain.

You don't control me. No one does. The moves I make are my own.

Chapter Twenty-five

Crownado

Out of the room, I run towards the lift. Then think twice. Every guard in this building will head for the lift. I look right and then left, there's a door, not automatic, an emergency exit. I crash through it – stairs. A spiral of steps encased in a continuous glass window. I'm inside the eye. The siren sounds and I start my ascent, leaping two steps at a time. The city surrounds me, dipped in grey; the clouds look sprayed on. Any further up and I could touch the stratosphere. I want to stop, take in the Martian plains, contemplate my very existence but I can't, so I don't. Instead I bound around and up the spiral stairs at speed. Not fast enough, my footsteps soon have company. I stop, catch my breath, pull on the strap and clasp my Galva, hoping there aren't too many. A fleck of tan uniform appears. I aim and squeeze the trigger …

BANG!

Kick to my shoulder as the bullet leaves the barrel. Agonising shouts of pain. I scream at the shocking sight of the guard's exploded face. Eye socket blown out, skull and teeth visible where the skin has peeled away, wet flesh spilling down his neck. The body drops and my thoughts turn dark. I've killed a guard. Will his body be butchered? Am I providing a hunting service for the Morbs' food supply? Two more guards appear in my peripheral vison, and before the first has a chance to hit the ground writhing, I shoot the second guard in the chest. Bone chilling screams echo off the glass, before a third guard lunges and grabs my waist, wrestling me down. I fall backwards and yelp in pain as the hard edge of the steps judder my skeleton; bruising my shoulders, back, and legs. I lift my head and shoulders and aim the gun between my legs. I flick the switch. One eye closed, I look down the scope.

Bruuuuurakkkk!

The third guard's body is blasted backwards, riddled with bullets. This time I don't scream. Third kill brings no emotion. The guard's nose, eyebrows, and bits of skin explode from his skull and smear the crystal-clear glass behind him, his intestines spill out like a string of sausages. The headless body drops down beside the others. I force myself to my feet, arching my stiff back. My spine cracks. Then I reach into my pocket. No ammo and the magazine is gone. Damn. I whip the strap over my head, throw the gun behind me and into the mess of blood and disfigured bodies. I leap up two steps at a time, ignoring my protesting muscles and bruised back.

The trapdoor at the top swings open with a clatter as the wind takes it from my hand. I climb up and the cold wind slaps my cheeks. Strands of hair whip around my frozen face. Behind me is the lightning rod which sits on the top of The Spiral; overhead, a storm creeps across the sky. This is the worst place I could be right now, but – there's Bunce! What's he doing up here? And why is he so close to the edge? I move closer. I see Kian, too. Wait. Something's wrong.

'Kian, what are you doing?' I shout, but I know what he's doing. He's edging dangerously close to the edge of the building.

'He thinks he can come along and take you away from me!' Kian yells angrily, 'Steal you from my life!'

'What?' I shout.

'Says you're in love,' Kian spits. 'That I should stay out of it.'

'You're not making any sense!' I yell.

Then it dawns on me. Kian thinks I'm with Bunce. He isn't making throwaway comments, he actually believes we're together. What would have given him that idea? I stare at Bunce. He frowns like a naughty child who's told a fib but doesn't want to admit it. Why would he do that? Morbs aren't attracted to Skels … even if they were, they'd never tell anyone. Wait, did Bunce want to find the serum because he's into me? Urgh, men!

'This is stupid! More guards are coming,' I shout, frustrated that they're fighting over me at a time like this. 'Kian, are you listening?'

'Kian's dead!' he replies, darkly.

His eyes are as black as stone, they don't belong to Kian; those cruel eyes belong to someone else. I've seen them before. That terrible day, the day that came to be known as *The Day of the Bird.* An image of eighteen-year-old Kian comes to me, surrounded by dead bodies sprawled on the ground – people who had been pecked to death by an angry murder of crows. They attacked without warning. I'd been watching from inside the meat factory. The noise was like a hurricane from hell, flapping gales laced with screams. It brought the whole workforce to the windows.

We could do nothing but watch, as hundreds of people were slaughtered by the winged murderers. Everyone was dead in a matter of minutes, except Kian, who stood in the middle of the carnage, spattered with blood and black feathers. Untouched, unharmed, unhinged. He was soon nicknamed Crow and was thereafter known as an Augur or Avian – the birdman, a charmer of birds. I remember the fear everyone felt around him afterwards. They questioned why he was spared. Not to his face, many were too scared to question Kian himself, in case he brought the birds' wrath down upon them. Not even Central could explain why the birds attacked. It was put down to a freak weather occurrence. A once-in-a-hundred-year storm that drove the crows crazy. But I've often wondered if there was more to it than that and Clover has suggested there is, with all that talk of cloning gone wrong. A part of me thinks Kian has always had a connection to birds, and that day he took it too far. That day he changed from charming them to being one of them. Birds attacking guards as well as worker Skels is a big problem for Central. Who will protect them if the guards are compromised? They poisoned three-quarters of the bird population that day. The birds haven't attacked since, but that doesn't mean that they won't ever do it again.

A few crows circle above us. Bunce's eyes are tired and terrified, dark clouds beneath them; red, forked lightning across the whites of his eyes. Undeterred by the strong gales whipping his dark hair into a frenzy, Kian takes another step back. The wind's whistle sounds like laughter, jeers daring him to take that last step, teasing him as it flaps around his tan shirt and pushes his body towards the deadly drop. Kian holds Bunce tight by the scruff of the neck. He yells over the howling wind.

'Morbs can hover, but can they fly? Shall we find out, perhaps he'll die?'

Emotion is void, his face blank. More guards will be here any moment. Death surrounds us. I can feel it. The Dark Angel is waiting to steal our last breaths.

I take a small step towards the two most important people in my life. It would be so easy to join them at the edge, give up now that the cure is gone but that's probably what Clover wants and I won't do what he wants. I can't give up. I'll fight. Kill every last scumbag guard if I have to. I've killed three already. Sure, they're trained in combat and they'll have knives, batons, swords, and I have … I have a blade in my boot and my knuckle-knife in my pocket.

'Fuck it,' I whisper. Crow moves his foot out over the edge, and lets it dangle in mid-air. He means to do it. He's going to dive off, with Bunce …

'Skyla!' Bunce's screams pour fear into my heart.

'No!' I shout.

I run towards the edge and grab Bunce. I'm not strong enough to pull his large frame back towards the building. The stick falls from my bun and my hair falls over my face, my long ponytail pushed around by the wind. Heavy boots stamp behind me, but not quick enough. The guards are too late. Kian releases Bunce from his grip, lifts his arms out as if he will be caught by a circle of trusted friends and calmly falls backwards.

'Kian!' I yell.

I slip and my voice breaks into a rushing scream.

Bunce hollers beside me as we career off the roof of The Spiral and plummet towards the ground.

Air rushes past me, my body hurtling around in the downdraft. My eyes stream with water from the wind chill and my stomach takes up permanent residency in my mouth. I'm struggling to breathe – rushing air burns my throat and nose. My pant legs blow up like mini parachutes and my shirt rides up, flapping around my goose-pimpled midriff. The flapping of wings becomes louder and louder, deafening. Feathers lash my face and claws scratch at my exposed skin. My momentum starts to slow, what's happening? I force my eyes open.

'This can't be!' I say, breathlessly.

Below me is a dark tunnel – a twisting, undulating vortex of black feathers surrounds me. My limbs flail as crows push me around the safety net they have created. There's someone ahead of me, legs straight, bare back, arms by his sides. He's like an arrow racing to the ground. It's Kian. I glance around as I ungracefully tumble within the bird funnel. Where's Bunce? There's a pull, like a noose around my stomach, and my body is hurled out into the elements. My back slams into something hard. My bones groan. I'm still moving but not in the same way. It's disorientating.

Something lands behind me with a thud and a sudden jolt throws me forward, my legs swinging into the air. I summon the strength to roll back onto the cold metal surface. A few feet from my face is the beating sound of hundreds of wings. I open my eyes to a tornado of crows spinning from the top of the carriage in front of me. I'm on top of the Sky Train. My heart pounds. I tilt my head back – the twister reaches as far up into the sky as I can see. The birds start to disperse. Their numbers thin, and clusters of black wings soar up into the grey clouds, like burnt paper sailing up from a fire. As the tornado disappears, a bare-chested man is left standing at its core. His fists are clenched and his pectorals and biceps twitch. He remains standing even though the propulsion of the train should have thrown him off. He stares at the sky, eyes black as coal. This is a powerful man. A man reborn – Crow.

Chapter Twenty-six

Failed

My attention is diverted from Crow, who turns and strides across the top of the carriages, to Bunce, who hollers with fright. I grab hold of the lump of flattened meat that is Bunce and grasp his elbow tight; to prevent him from rolling off the roof and to centre myself as the train starts to slow. A boulder lands on his head from above, he groans and pulls it under his arm; it's not a boulder, it's his backpack. The dark clouds above spit rain onto my skin, threatening to turn on the tap and soak us.

A battered sign states we have arrived at Park Side. My eyes dart back to Crow, he's gone. Bunce's arm slips through my fingers and he slides down the side of the carriage. I scramble across the train roof combat-style. I go to grab hold of him before he falls to his death, but when I get to the edge, Bunce is descending the ladder. I follow and my boots clonk on the metal rungs. The train is tall, it's about twenty rungs until we reach the ground.

I search for Crow in the downpour. The rain stings my scratched face and drips into my eyes. My vision won't clear, no matter how much water I blink away. I hurry down the platform, water smacks under my boots with every step, I reach the front of the stationary train. Skels disembark, weaving around me. The train's headlamps shine into the gloom and light up the rushing rain. Bunce is dry beneath the shelter, he watches me, wondering what I'm doing. Soaked through, clothes clinging to my cold skin, hair dripping, I shiver. I have to find Crow.

The train engine roars to life and bands of rain scream across the great metal body as it picks up speed. I search the roof and my gaze catches on a profile blurred by water racing across the window. It's Crow. He's inside the train. He doesn't look for me, he doesn't glance towards the outside world, he stares straight ahead, I blink, he isn't there anymore and neither is the train. I stand in the pouring rain, watching the tail of the Sky Train bend down the track and disappear. It doesn't just disappear with my friend. It disappears with my hope. I trudge back down the platform.

'Skyla.' Bunce shivers under the shelter, eyes skyward, searching the part where the crow tornado had been.

'Yeah.'

'What was that?' he asks, innocently.

'I dunno,' I say, but I do know.

It was Crow who did that. He created that feathered twister. For years I've pushed Kian to use his strange power over the birds and now I wish I hadn't. Whatever that was, it wasn't what I had in mind.

'We should go,' Bunce says, teeth chattering.

I'm at a loss. There isn't much point in going on but I can't let Bunce freeze to death either. Where can I take him? Where's safe? Nowhere is safe in this city and especially not now I know Clover is watching us. The battered white station sign sways in the rain and wind, my eyes trace over each letter in the words 'Park Side.' This station borders my side of town, and the park.

'I know a place we can dry off.'

I lead Bunce down the steps and back out into the sodden city streets. Lamps are lit, the showers ease and misty rain dances across beams of light in a bid to become one with the puddles below. Night falls and the darkness turns my thoughts to despair. Choice is a luxury few can afford and for the amount of choice I can afford, it isn't worth having. Sometimes your only choice is death; yours or theirs. Right now, the easiest thing to do would be to leave this world hand in hand with the Dark Angel. Kian, surrounded by a vortex of crows, enters my consciousness. Not Kian. Crow. I guess now even he accepts this nickname. There's no going back to the way things were.

Before he was dubbed Crow, Kian had always been daring, determined to learn all he could from others and experience as much as possible. If kids were climbing trees, he'd climb to the very top. He never fell. His confidence was his superpower and he was treated like a superhero, and after he survived the massacre that's what people believed he was. Actually, he was not so much a hero, more a villain gone straight. A protector but also recognised as unstable, someone who could snap at any moment. The Day of the Bird was a mixed blessing for Kian. His life was spared but he would never be the same, and ours will never be the same now either.

I hold open the silver gates, stretching the locked chain-link to its limit so Bunce can squeeze through, then I slip in behind him and the gates clatter back together. I wondered why they didn't use a modern gate or Vector Ring, my grandfather says it's to do with nostalgia, designers like to mix the past with the present. The rain evaporates, giving way to an intermittent breeze. It struggles to keep momentum, too scared to follow us, too scared to wake them. This is foolhardy, I think to myself. I would never have brought Bunce here if I didn't have to. I need time to gather my thoughts, and with guards hunting us we need a place they won't think to look for us. I can't stop time, no matter how much I wish for it but if we are set upon, time will stop for us – forever.

The park used to be a gathering place for families. A place of beauty and relaxation, Skels would visit the park on their recoup day but as the number of Mutil increased so did the need to control where they resided. They were eventually forced off the streets, and into the park. Families don't come here anymore, and even though the Mutil are mostly nocturnal, Skels are still afraid to set foot in the park, even during the day. Children sometimes dare each other to put a leg through the bars, but no more than that. They know the dangers. Tonight, the park is dark and quiet. A bad combination. Although the rain has stopped, the ground is soggy, the grass struggling to drink any more. This means we can't run the gauntlet. It's too slippery. We need to reach the hilltops beyond the tree line, and all that lies between us and safety is this grassy open area. The Mutil could be hiding anywhere. Some will be roaming the streets, but a good number remain in the park, hunting rats, snakes, and crows.

'You okay, Bunce?'

Bunce doesn't answer. His cheeks aren't hollow yet, his bulk disguising how malnourished he is.

'Bunce?' I whisper, taking his hand. His cold fingers close around mine. 'We need to move faster… Bunce! Are you listening?'

I stop talking, my voice stolen by the sight of a figure standing in the distance. Mutil hunt in the shadows, they don't stand in full view. I drop Bunce's hand and slowly creep forwards, mindful of the dense pine trees to my right. This could be a trap, are Mutil that cunning? I've never heard of them setting traps before. A twig snaps behind me and I raise my hand for Bunce to halt. I glance over my shoulder and he stops.

Moving freely in a wide-open space feels alien to me, unnerving, unnatural. Cautiously, I step towards the lone silhouette, the low moon lights up the glistening grass, and as my shadow grows closer to the stranger, a fretfulness grows inside me. The figure has its back to me. It holds a battered, dirty, red umbrella high above its head, which wouldn't be much shelter from the rain, broken and bent with half the material ripped from the spokes. As my shadow stretches nearer, I notice the stranger is smaller than me, a lot smaller, a child.

Panic races and stabs me with a painful thought. If I don't get this child out of here the Mutil will kill and eat it. I can't protect a child out in the open like this. I could take on two, maybe three Mutil, but the park is home to hundreds. I step closer and it feels like the surrounding trees are giving me a wide berth, leaning away in fear. I'm soon close enough to grab the kid. Moonlight shines over dripping wet, braided hair. There's only one girl I know with hair long and red. Half-unravelled right plait.

'Tess?' I whisper to the back of her head.

Tess moves her head to the right. She doesn't turn around or speak.

'Tess, what are you doing out here?' I say, bending down to her level.

She still doesn't answer. What's wrong with her? Can't she hear me?

'Come on, I'll take you home.' I whisper in her ear.

I grip Tess's thin wrist and she instantly drops the umbrella. She doesn't move when I tug her to come with me.

'Tess …' I say, nervously, bending down.

In a whirl of red braids, Tess turns and lunges at me, biting down hard into my shoulder. I scream in pain. What the fuck? Teeth rip through the fabric and blood seeps through my top. I push back on Tess's head, forcing the young girl's face to the moonlight. I gasp. Her eyes! One is white, blind, and the other is clicking – it's mechanical! I force her head back further and her jaws release me. A wave of fright crawls down my back and I throw the raggedy body to the ground. Thundering footsteps splash towards me, Bunce arrives at my side, panting.

Tess hisses at him, Mutil mouth stained with my blood. Her discoloured teeth have been filed, tips dripping red. She leaps to her feet and strikes, sinking her pointed, yellow teeth into Bunce's arm.

'ARRRGGGGH! Get her off me!' he yells, trying to prise the ten-year-old's jaws from his forearm by yanking at her braids with his other hand.

'Oh, Tess, what have they done to you?' I say, lips trembling. 'I'm sorry, oh sweetheart, I'm so sorry.'

Tears fall thick and fast down my cheeks. My knees fold and I slowly collapse, like plastic shrivelling in a fire.

'This can't be happening!' I yell into the grass. Water splashes my face as I thump the ground with my fist.

'Kill her!' Bunce screams.

'It's all my fault,' I sob hysterically. I can't control my sorrow. It would hurt less if she was dead. But I can't kill her.

'Sky! Please!'

Bunce flails around while Mutil Tess grunts and snorts, shredding and devouring his flesh. I can't deal with this. Acid swirls in my stomach. I dry-heave. She's only a girl. What crime did she ever commit to deserve this? I won't kill her. I won't! I squeeze the tears away, grab the handle poking out from the top of my boot. Pull. Grip. Sweep the blade across her leg. The child's high-pitched scream pushes the birds from their branches in a feathery black cloud. Bunce falls back, arm released. Any Mutil hiding within the trees do not respond to the young girl's cries. They're not like us. They don't come running to a child's aid, not even one of their own.

Bunce shuffles backwards, holding his bloody arm. I grip the knife smeared with Tess's blood and stand over her tiny, trembling body. She hasn't been altered as much as most Mutil but her brain is as damaged as the others are. She's no longer my little Tess.

'What are you doing?' Bunce yells. 'Put her out of her misery!'

'I can't,' I cry. 'Please don't ask me to do this. I can't.'

Before I have to make that dreadful choice, Tess's body goes limp. Oh no, she's dead. Surely, I didn't kill her with one slice to the leg? My thoughts send pain into my heart. I struggle to breathe. I take a step closer to the girl I promised to protect. A hand grabs my ankle. I scream and jump backwards. Tess's artificial eye snaps open and she growls at me, clambers to her feet and limps off into the night like a wounded animal.

'Why did they do that to her?' I weep, angrily. 'What's she done to anyone?'

'What do you mean?' says Bunce, breathlessly. 'She did that to herself.'

I turn around, and my long ponytail slaps the side of my face with the momentum.

'What do you mean … *did that to herself*?' I say, bearing down on the Morb.

'You know, mutilated herself. So, she could be like the Morbihan.'

Now I'm angry.

'What the hell are you talking about?' I yell, fists clenched, nails digging into my palms.

Bunce grasps his bloody arm like it will fall off if he doesn't keep hold of it. Pain etches across his cloud-white face, but I don't care. He'd better explain himself. My instincts are pushing me to leave him in the park to bleed to death. It's hard to care about someone when they represent every loathsome characteristic of the Morbihan.

'I … culture class. They … some Skels want so badly to be Morbihan that they mutilate their bodies to be like us …' Bunce trails off, obviously realising he has been lied to.

'WHAT?' I scream.

I can't contain my rage. Let the Mutil hear me! Let them come! Right now, my adrenalin could kill them all.

'They talk about self-mutilation on the news too. How was I supposed to know it's not true?'

I stare at the Morb in disbelief, how could he believe that? Tears escape down Bunce's round cheeks. In pain physically and now mentally, too. He's guessed about the torture rooms in Rock Vault, knows Tess was snatched and turned into that creature by Central. The truth hurts, a lot.

'It's not your fault, Central lies to us all,' I say, but I'm still mad at him for being so naive.

I take Bunce's bleeding arm from him. The wound is brutal. He could easily say he'd been attacked with a saw and no one would question it. I need to find something to dress his wounds. I touch my shoulder. My injuries are minor in comparison.

I help Bunce to his feet and we carry on across the green, under the watch of the full moon. The rocky hills are black, except for the edges that face the moonlight. I secure Bunce's backpack over my shoulders and scamper up the rock while he painstakingly climbs with one hand. He stumbles and trips a few times but soon we're at the top. I take a moment and gaze out over the horizon. Beyond the wall, orange sand deepens to the rustic red of the mountains. The light fades when rain clouds shift over the small circle in the sky but the moonlight isn't completely blocked, and it's because there's a second moon, smaller, not much brighter than a star but it's there. Why have I never noticed it before? Bunce stands next to me for a moment and we watch as the bigger moon reappears.

'Phobos and Deimos,' Bunce says, nodding to each speck in the sky. His eyes roll back and I hold his shoulder to steady him. He recovers.

'I've never noticed the second moon before,' I say, captivated.

'How strange,' Bunce says, flatly.

The rain begins again, this time in great drops that splatter angrily onto the rocks. My hair becomes heavy and strands of blond stick in wet lines across my face. I peel it away and push Bunce up a steep incline. His sneakers slip and slide but he manages. I really hope it's still here and Central hasn't found it and filled it in. I feel around the bare rocks, where is it?

'What are we doing up here, Sky?' Bunce asks, breathless.

He's shaking. Droplets of rain hang and shiver from the tips of his sandy hair and pale nose. Is he going into shock or is it just the chill of the rain? I have to get him inside now.

'Aha!'

I shake off Bunce's backpack and push a medium-sized rock to the left. I throw all my weight into it. A little more. My shoulder twinges. *Ignore the pain, Skyla.* Heave. My palms scrape across the jagged, wet rock, my skin stings. Crunch. I peer into the dark hole, turn, kneel, and stretch my right leg down into the blackness. My foot finds a rung. I descend, looking up at Bunce as I disappear into the hillside. Raindrops pelt my head until my feet hit the bottom.

'Watch out!'

Bunce's voice echoes down from the top, there's a thud near my feet – his backpack. His large frame follows, blocking the moonlight and rain. He struggles down using his good arm and is soon beside me in the darkness. He leans up against a wall, breathless.

'You okay?' I speak into the darkness.

'Nauseous and dizzy,' he rasps.

'Hang in there. Now … if I were a slimy little Slum Lord,' I mutter to myself, feeling across the damp jagged walls with my hands, for a shelf or a hook 'Where would I keep the …'

'Matches?'

Bunce's face glows orange. A small flame flickers over his shining eyes. He found matches! Relief washes over me and leaves just as quickly. He holds the match in his left hand, obviously unable to strike it with his right. His arm oozes. How am I going to heal that great gaping gash? Fire first. Arm next.

'Here,' I say, pointing to a ring of stones in the middle of the room.

The fire is made up. The leaves are shrivelled and dry, waiting to be lit but the fire maker never returned, because Clover killed him. Bunce crouches and lowers the lit match to the pile. It doesn't take. He attempts to strike a second match after the first singes his fingers. I snatch the box from his limp hand and strike two matches at once. I light the leaves and kindling in several places and the fire starts to crackle. Soon flames leap, casting their fiery shadows over the rocky walls, and now the room is lit up enough, there's more wood in a corner. Bunce sits back against the stone wall and examines his torn flesh. The rain has cleaned the wound, but it's still oozing.

'I don't feel well,' he mumbles.

I scan the den. There's not much here. A bucket, some crude shelves with blackened pots and chipped plates, and a filthy mattress in the corner. I chuck some thick logs on the fire, warmth quickly fills the small cave but Bunce still shivers, cradling his arm.

'Let me see,' I say, kneeling next to him and turning his forearm towards me.

Blood pools with the motion. It's worse than I thought. I'm not sure it will close without stitches. Bunce winces as I rest his arm on his leg.

'Don't suppose you've got any bandages or needle and thread in that bag of yours?' I ask, knowing the answer.

Bunce shakes his head.

I unzip the rusty-orange backpack and take out a flask, it's Tess's, maybe her mother's. It's full. I hand it to Bunce, who pulls the stopper from the top with his teeth and chugs, water spilling from the sides of his mouth.

'Slow down,' I say, taking the flask from him. 'It has to last.'

'Why?' he says, 'I drink the serum in the morning and we get out of here, right?'

I don't answer. My tongue swells in my mouth.

'Right?' he says again.

'I don't have the serum,' I mumble.

'Pardon?' he asks, voice jittery.

'I ran into Clover.'

'Clover? The Eremite? I don't understand.'

Bunce gives me a look like he's trying to figure out a difficult maths equation.

'He's not an Eremite. He's a traitor, a Central,' I say with a sigh. 'He pretended to be a Slum Lord to spy on people.'

'Really?' The confusion on Bunce's face makes me worry his head might explode. 'Is that what Central do?'

'How do I know?' I snap.

'Has he hidden the serum away somewhere else?'

'He, um …' I stammer, embarrassed of what I'm about to say, 'he made me drink it.' I hang my head. I don't know why I feel ashamed. It wasn't my fault.

Bunce's cheeks flush.

'You drank it?'

'He made me!'

Blood runs in lines down Bunce's forearm.

'Then that's it. It's over!' he says, angrily.

'No, it's not.' I hold out my arm and pull the knife from my boot. 'If you drink my blood it may ...'

'Drink your blood?' Bunce looks at me in disgust.

'It might transfer the cure to you and ...'

'Sky! I've been eating people. EATING PEOPLE!' he yells in my face. 'I'm not drinking your blood!'

'But ...'

'NO!'

I flop back, defeated. Bunce sits, seething, his chest heaving. I shove my knife back in my boot and distract myself from hopelessness by rummaging through Bunce's backpack. I pull a brightly-coloured shirt from the pack. The sleeves are pink, the back is orange and the front two panels are green and blue. I raise my eyebrows at Bunce, trying to relieve the tension. A reluctant smile tugs at his lips.

'Morbs don't wear dark clothes.'

'I know,' I say softly, but I'm a tad taken aback by his informal tone. That's the first time he's shortened the word. I pull a white t-shirt from the bag, in the upper right corner is an embroidered logo, the city emblem. Those words I hate embossed in gold. *The System Works.*

'It doesn't though, does it?' Bunce stammers, pain, cold, and despair bullying his body.

'No, it doesn't, not for us,' I say miserably.

The system didn't work for Tess either, I think to myself. My poor Tess. Bunce looks above my head, as if he's reading my thoughts in a speech bubble.

'It's not your fault, Sky.'

'It is.' I say, staring at the floor. 'I failed her and I've failed you.'

'Don't do this.'

Tess's face flashes in the flickering fire, the flames her red hair. Clockwork eye, teeth like razors. How many people has she killed?

'What should I do, huh?' I say, brandishing the shirt logo at him. 'Pretend everything is rosy? Should I have taken my host duties gladly and turned a blind-eye while my people are forced to work themselves to death, so others can live like kings?'

Bunce doesn't respond. He stares at me. His face resembles that of a youngster coming home from their first day of work, realising the world is not as their parents painted it. I can't stop the poison spilling from my lips, I need to purge it.

'La la la, I'm so happy living in my utopian complex where nothing can ever harm me. While others are mutilated so my people can have new organs. Skels butchered to sustain the Morbihan existence, and those left are forced to serve us. I don't care about anything but me and my comfort. I've got the perfect life so the rest of you can go fuck yourselves!'

'Have you lost your mind?' Bunce says, eyes bulging.

His face is having a fight with the pain caused by his shredded arm. He's trying to keep from wincing – trying to ignore what must be agony. Red drips through his fingers, which are firmly clamped over his wounded arm. I fix my eyes on his round face. Let him bleed, I think. He's probably never spilt a drop of blood in his entire life.

'Maybe I sound crazy to you because I speak the truth. And the truth is so ugly that you won't allow yourself to see things for what they really are!'

'How can I see things that others have blinded me to?' he says, panting.

'You let them blindfold you,' I say, calmly. Having spat out my grievances I feel lighter, but I have to make Bunce understand. Make him see things as I do. Lift his blindfold.

'Your world is nothing but a dream. Created by Central and sustained by people like me who live the nightmares so you don't have to. Do you understand?' I ask, but I don't wait for an answer. 'If Morbihan don't start sharing the burden of the darker side of life, it will find a way to balance things out. Ever heard the saying, "too much of a good thing is bad for you"?'

Bunce shakes his head. I heave a sigh. 'Your people float through life, kept buoyant by Skels. They don't know how to swim because they've lived in the safety of the boat for so long, but one day, Central will tip it up and the Morbs will drown.'

By the look on Bunce's face, I'd swear the Dark Angel had squeezed his shoulder and whispered in his ear, *you're next.* I've shown him the truth and now I sort of wish I hadn't. He'd have been happier ignorant, living a comfortable life inside his protective bubble. Now look at him, he's sitting in a cave, probably got pneumonia, half-starved with a great chunk missing from his arm. I'm disgusted with myself. I'm so damn selfish. I'm just like that bastard, Clover. I've made Bunce's life worse, so I can feel better.

I pull my knife and stab the t-shirt viciously, tearing it into shreds. Bunce doesn't speak. The Bunce I first met would have protested at destroying his clothes, he would have been horrified. This Bunce doesn't even look up. He cares about nothing and I did that to him. I've given him a life worth losing when he had a life worth living. The guilt ties a knot around my throat and pulls.

I kneel down before the only friend I have left, who probably won't want to be my friend for much longer.

'Ouch, don't be so rough,' Bunce complains as I wrap the fabric tight around the open wound. Red immediately seeps through. I wrap more of the shirt strips around it and tie off the ends. It will have to do. I reach up and start to unbutton Bunce's shirt. He grabs my wrist with his blood-stained hand. I look up and his eyes swim into mine. My heart beats faster as he squeezes my bony arm with his strong hand. The pain hasn't taken his strength. He pulls me closer until my nose is almost touching his. He leans in. I gasp. Is he going to kiss me? Soft words spill onto my lips.

'I can dress myself, for now at least.'

He lets go of my wrist. Cold stare. Resentful eyes. He does blame me. I pull back, deflated. Confused. I want his affection? Now he's withdrawn it, I want it. Why would I want a Morb to kiss me? It's hardly the time or the place. Surely, I'm not that desperate? I search my feelings. I frown as Bunce struggles to take off his shirt using his one good arm. I avert my eyes from his exposed chest. He's so pale. Curiosity? I've never been with anyone so pale. Multi-coloured shirt on, I glance back at him, at his pink lips. An urge to lean over and taste them takes hold of me. I push it to the back of my mind. I can't do that.

Bunce told Kian we were in love. Why? Is he in love with me? Is he more than a friend? No. But the more time I spend with Bunce, the more attached to him I become. I can't pretend that I don't like him. In fact, I liked him the moment we met. I liked him a little more when we formulated the plan to find the cure, even more when he was bold enough to run away with me, and even more when he was brave enough to cut open that Runner's ankle. A ball of guilt rolls around inside my gut. Here I am telling him how ignorant he is, when until a few hours ago, I didn't even know what planet I lived on. I swallow my pride and ask the question burning inside of me.

'What planet are we on?'

Bunce frowns.

'Excuse me?'

'This planet we're on now, what's it called?' I ask.

'Mars.'

The answer is effortless.

'You know that, at least.'

I cringe at my own words. I should admit that I didn't know that. I should say, *hey actually, I was blindfolded too, and that's why I didn't know about both moons or that we live on Mars*. I should come clean. My ego won't allow it. Instead I let my thoughts drag me back to better times spent in Bunce's company, times that might have continued had I let things unfold naturally instead of forcing my will.

I think about how Bunce used to meet me every day before class. Once, after walking me back to his sister's apartment he was allowed to sit in my room with me. We talked for hours. He showed me a popular digi-mag. I read well enough but the mag made no sense to me. I remember the title, *YM Magazine!* Inside were the most bizarre stories and articles. One page was devoted to young people's problems. Morb problems, of course, because they really weren't problems at all, not to me anyway, or any Skel. I stare at the flickering fire, cast my mind back and retrieve the memory. 'Ask Lyca', a column where Morbs under the age of twenty-one submit their dilemmas and Lyca would solve them. *'Dear Lyca, I'm attracted to girls and guys and I know sex for reproductive purposes isn't allowed, but can I have sex with girls?' 'Dear Lyca, what's a boner?' 'Dear Lyca, I'm being bullied because I'm smaller than everyone else. I can't seem to put on weight. I've tried eating more and exercising less but that does nothing. Why hasn't puberty started for me? I'm seventeen! Will I ever become a fully-grown Morbihan? Help!'*

We both laughed, but it was clear Bunce thought these were 'real' problems. He could never comprehend what I might ask Lyca; *'Dear Lyca, I'm tired of being a slave to the system and being told what to do, having a curfew, being told what to wear, how to act, what to say or not say. I'm tired of working twelve-hour days, six days a week in a cold factory, but I guess I can cope with that because I still have my recoup day. What I'm most aggrieved about is becoming a host. I don't want my body used and abused in order to breed more over-privileged Morbs. I want a better life, one without the fear of being chucked into Rock Vault and mutilated or executed, my head skewered on the line for all to see and judge, or worse, my body used to sustain Morbihan life. I want to feel safe on the streets and at home. I want my parents not to be dead. I want to hug my grandfather. I want Tess not to be a Mutil. I want Crow to be Kian again! I ...'* I don't want to cry. I'm stronger than this. The backpack is a good distraction. I delve back in and find some apples in the bottom of it and hold them up.

'I didn't put those in there.'

'Kian, probably,' I say, and hand one to Bunce.

He takes the green apple begrudgingly and bites into it. I take a huge bite of mine and the crisp taste reminds my stomach that I'm hungry. I gnaw at the fruit, chewing fast, it's gone in seconds. I chuck the core into the fire. Bunce leans against the wall, emotionally and physically exhausted, his eyelids droop. The half-eaten apple threatens to fall from his left hand.

'Bunce.' His eyes snap open. Dreamily, he listens to me.

'Do you know your host mother?'

'You mean Nadina?'

'Is Nadina the woman who pushed you into the world?' I say, trying to coax some sense from his sleepy head.

'Yes,' Bunce nods, 'we see her once a year.' He yawns. 'She has her own family now.'

I think for a moment. Bunce said that so easily, as if it was natural for Morbihan to mix with High-Hosts, so why is it unnatural to engage on the same level with Skels?

'Do you have any feelings towards her?' I ask.

'Like what?'

'I dunno, some sort of bond? You lived inside her for nine months.'

'No, not really,' Bunce says, more awake now. 'We don't have a lot to do with her. Some families are more involved with their hosts. They celebrate special occasions with them and stuff.'

I'm starting to think maybe I was wrong and Kian was right. It would have been easier to accept my host duties. Why do I always have to complicate things? I make everything so difficult for myself. If I'd just stuck to the rules we wouldn't be in this mess.

'Interesting,' I say. 'So, how does the host's link come about?'

'Arranged,' Bunce says, in a matter of fact tone.

'Arranged?' I snap. 'Can't the host choose their own link partner?'

Bunce laughs.

'Don't be silly.'

'Why is that silly?' I say, indignantly.

Bunce's tone changes.

'It isn't, I don't know why I thought it was. It is terrible and hosts should have the right to choose their link, whoever it may be,' he says quickly.

I smile. Even after all we've been through he still manages to retain his cheeky sense of humour. Bunce yawns again and I catch it. I press my palm to my gaping mouth.

'Get some sleep,' I say, nodding to the mattress.

'What about you?' he asks in a sleepy voice.

'I'm good here.'

I prop his backpack up like a pillow and lean my head against it. Bunce heaves himself to his feet and shuffles over to the mattress in the corner. He lowers himself onto the lumpy pile. Flat on his back, arms placed carefully by his side.

'This mattress stinks! Couldn't you have found something better?' he grumbles.

'It's not mine.'

'It isn't?' Bunce turns his head to look over at me. 'Whose is it?'

'Tinny's,' I say, closing my eyes.

'Tinny's!' Bunce yells. 'This isn't your hideout?'

'Nope.'

'It belongs to that Slum Lord who tried to cut my throat?'

'Yep.'

'Gross! I can't sleep here, who knows what he's done to this mattress!' Bunce sits bolt upright and starts examining the mattress. 'There's probably piss and jizz all over it!'

'Jizz?' I laugh at the word, but also at Bunce swearing. He never swears and it sounds funny coming out of his mouth.

'It's not funny, Skyla. I can't sleep on someone else's jizz stains.'

'You can sleep on your own, then?'

I'm laughing so much, my stomach aches.

'You're twisting my words,' Bunce smirks.

It feels good to laugh, even though the future looks bleak. I need the feeling that laughter brings. We can't give up yet.

I have to keep Bunce's spirits up. There must be another way that we can make things better for both of us.

'You don't need to worry,' I say, kicking off my boots. 'Tinny only ever used this place to hide from guards. He wouldn't have felt relaxed enough to … ruin the mattress.'

'How do you know?'

'I followed him once, found his hideout and he swore me to secrecy. In exchange, I could use this place when I needed to. He was pissed off about it, though, he never really liked me, said I was a dabbler.'

Bunce raises his blond eyebrows.

'You know,' I say, reaching behind my head and untying my hair, the damp locks fall over my shoulders. 'Living in two worlds, a Skel but also a law-breaker.'

Bunce slowly lies back down.

'You're more than a law-breaker now. We're both fugitives,' he sighs. 'What's going to happen to us?'

'I don't know, but I'm not giving up on you,' I say, and I won't.

'I'm not giving up on you either.'

With those words, Bunce closes his eyes and I close mine, but inside my head his words remain. What does he mean? Is he saying he's not going to give up pursuing me? My thoughts explode into a vision of Tess's smiling face, and then the mutilated one. I open my eyes and gaze upon my sleeping Morb, his chest rising and falling, peaceful. Bunce says he's not giving up on me. Well, I'm not giving up on Tess. I'm going to help her. I watch the entrance, rain lashes the rocks outside, a few raindrops find their way through the hole, causing a puddle to form at the bottom of the ladder. I hope the puddle doesn't grow any bigger. I don't want to wake up submerged in water. I let my eyelids close. I sail into slumber, listening to the snap and crackle of the dwindling fire and the plink, plink, plink of water dropping into the pool beneath the entrance.

ACT III
THE CHOICE

Chapter Twenty-seven

Love and Lies

I wake to a ticking noise that I hope is something else. The sound sends pins and needles over my skin. I open my eyes. Pitch black. Fire dead. No light shining through the entrance. It's blocked. I can't see a thing.

All I have is my ears. I weigh heavy on them, my eyes wide in the thick darkness, trying to break through it but I don't even see shadows. I listen, making my breathing shallow so I can home in on which direction the rattling breath and lolloping steps are coming from. I don't move. Aware of my stillness, my heart trembles and trips over its own beat. The kitchen knife is in my boot. My boot is not within reach. My knuckle-knife is. I quietly slip my fingers through the cold metal loops.

Wait … Wait …

Grunt. Sniff. Sniff. It's close. Strong body odour flairs my nostrils. A mixture of sweat, shit, piss, and puss stirred in a jar and then spread over the skin, this is the stench of a Mutil. I take a breath and choke on it. This creature doesn't have lenses, red eyes would have been a help in locating it but then the stench is enough of a giveaway, I could smell this beast a mile off.

Wait …

I launch an uppercut hard and strong. My fist pushes through muscle and then bones – ribs. I cut through, slicing open the flesh with one side of the retracted blade. The Mutil screeches in pain. Female. Tess? I'm lifted into the air by my throat. Not Tess. I kick and thrash about. The dawn streams in and slices through the blindness, the cave bathed in a murky orange. I can see – just. Two figures stand a few feet away. Is one Bunce? I'm thrown, air rushes for a second before my back slams into the shelves, plates crashing to the floor, pots clattering on the stone ground.

'Bun—'

I yell, then stop myself. They can't see well. Don't give away your position. I rub my throat, more to rub the stink from the Mutil touching me than to sooth the strangulation marks.

BANG … BANG!

THUD!

Shots fired. Body sprawled at my feet. The rising sun warms the left side of my face. My eyes adjust, dirt-encrusted bare feet slap towards me. I turn my weapon and plunge the slender knife upwards, piercing something soft. The scream that erupts is like nothing I've ever heard. The cave envelops the noise and the walls vibrate around me. I pull back my hand. A mess of innards spill down the blade and over my clenched fist, I retch and flick the gunk off me. The beast falls to its knees; its face exposed in the dusty light, or rather, what's left of its face. Swollen, infected gums housing crumbling teeth are exposed through a disintegrated cheek, the flesh eaten away by some parasite. I get to my feet. The Mutil, still on its knees, cups his ruptured scrotum. I grasp what little hair is left on its head, and in one swift motion I carve a red smile across its neck and let the body drop.

I turn to the mattress. Bunce sits on the edge, gripping Don's handgun with both hands. I wipe my knife over the beast's thin rags.

'Spot of breakfast?' Bunce says calmly, he lowers the gun.

I retract the blades and shove the knuckle-knife into my pocket. I step over the bodies and crouch to wash my hands in the puddle at the entrance. Dirt floats in the water. I'm exchanging one set of grime for another. I clean as much residue off my skin as is possible, and glance over at Bunce. No fear in his eyes, boyish innocence gone; now there's a cold lake harbouring a sea monster beneath its steely waters, desensitised to violence, death a way of life. He's becoming more like me. A product of my world rather than the one he was born to. I drop down onto the mattress and take Bunce's injured arm in my hands. His words were complacent but his body gives him away, he shakes with adrenalin from his first kill. I decide not to talk about it. Taking a life is always hard, even in defence. I turn his arm over. The makeshift bandages are soaked with orange and red, it's infected.

'I'll find us something to eat after I've cleaned up this mess,' I say, pointing to the two dead Mutil.

Bunce smiles weakly and his thick fingers softly push my limp hair behind my ear. His touch is electric. I get up quickly.

Cleaning up the mess was harder than I thought. I'm not strong enough to pull the bodies up the ladder on my own; Bunce climbs to the top and yanks them up with one arm while I push. I cringe, trying not to let their rancid flesh touch me. I heave them up the ladder far enough so that Bunce can grab hold and drag them into the daylight. We pile the male and female Mutil a few feet away. The bodies will deter others from venturing near the entrance, but we'll soon have to deal with flies and crows and rats and all the bottom feeders that live in the surrounding park.

Exhausted and feeling faint, Bunce goes back into the den while I venture down the rocky hill. I don't go far and I don't have to. I spot fruit trees at the back of the park.

Three days pass, melting into one another. Sun up, sun down, moons up, moons down. The fruit trees at the edge of the park keep us fed, oranges and apples aplenty. They must be the only fruit trees Central don't control. I wonder why they allow this fruit to grow unchecked and unclaimed? Maybe it's deemed unclean due to Mutil contamination. Strange since the Mutil wouldn't choose to eat fruit. They hunt for meat, any meat. Rats, birds, snake, people. It's all the same to them, I guess it's all the same to Morbs too, if they're even aware of what's in their food, Bunce wasn't. I also find fresh water by way of a small creek. This must be what's keeping the Mutil alive. I start my trek back to the hill, fruit-laden pack on my back, flask of water in my hand. The decomposing carcasses piled on the hilltop act as a deterrent. Albeit unsightly and the smell repulsive, it does repel other Mutil and anything or anyone else who seeks to infiltrate our resting place.

I think about Bunce as I reach the entrance to our camp. He's recovering well. His wound is healing, but only after the maggot therapy. He was more than reluctant about it, kept squirming every time I tried to drop the wriggling flesh-eaters into the wound. Two days of rain had filled a crevasse on the rocky hilltop which made a good place to wash. After cleaning away the congealed pus, the infection persisted. Maggots started to spill from the female Mutil's eye socket. I scooped them up, washed them and placed them in the gash on Bunce's arm, then wrapped the wound loosely in the last of the t-shirt bandages. It didn't take long for the therapy to work. The infected skin was soon stripped away. Carnivorous wrigglers flushed out, it should heal but he'll be left with a nasty scar. His first scar. A reminder of how dangerous it is out here and how different it is inside the Morb complex.

And there's something else. Somewhere I've been going in secret. Every time I climb back down the ladder I wonder if he'll sense my guilt. If he'll see I haven't been telling him the whole truth. I can't tell him. He wouldn't understand.

When I reach the hideout entrance, I always check my surroundings before I climb down to make sure I'm not being watched. I never climb down all the way, I jump from the third to last step. Boots splashing into the small pool of rain water at the bottom.

'Where've you been?'

The fire has dwindled and I can't see Bunce's facial expression, which is hidden in the gloom, but I can feel his stare, feel his cold eyes accusing me.

'You know where I've been,' I say, throwing the backpack down beside him.

'You've been gone for hours, what's taken you so long?' he says, coolly.

I poke the fire with one of the larger sticks and add a few more twigs and small logs. Bunce's sour face is illuminated, his dressings spotted with blood. I sit down next to him on the hard floor and reach for his arm. He pulls away from me.

'It needs air to heal properly.'

'You didn't answer my question,' he says, brows knitted.

I snatch his arm from him and start unravelling the loose dressings. He allows me to nurse him.

'I have to stay out of sight,' I lie. 'There were more Mutil to dodge than usual.' I try and sound casual but I can hear the lack of truth in my tone.

'I see,' he says, flames dancing on the glazed surface of his eyes.

'See what?' I say, irritated.

I hate these mind games. If he knows what I've been up to, then he should say it. I turn my attention to his wound. No sign of infection – the maggots worked. Hopefully with the air getting to it, it'll start to scab over soon. No wincing, he's obviously not in much pain. Bunce looks down at the wound and then up at me. His soft features twist.

'It's obvious you're sneaking off to see him,' he snaps, his lips purse as if angry with his mouth for forcing words through them.

'Who?' I ask, confused.

Bunce isn't on to me. He really doesn't know where I've been. He shakes his head and gives me the cold shoulder. I raise an eyebrow. What's he talking about? Then it dawns on me.

'Are you talking about Kian?'

'I'm talking about Crow, the bird whisperer,' he says, over his shoulder.

'Kian is Crow!'

'Kian is gone! Look what he did with those crows, he created a ... a ... crownado!' Bunce stammers. 'He's dangerous and unstable. I don't like you seeing that lunatic behind my back.'

'Behind your back?'

I tug on his shoulder, he has no choice but to look at me.

'You know how I feel about you,' he says heatedly. 'At least have the common decency to tell me you're seeing him. I thought we were friends.'

'Friends don't tell each other who they can and can't see, or is that another thing Morbs feel is justified?'

'My race has nothing to do with this. Morbs are honest.'

'Honest. Ha! You told a lie the very first time I met you, and look at all that bullshit you spouted out about the Mutil.'

'Central fed us those lies, you know that, and I wasn't telling big lies. Morbihan value honesty above all else.'

'I value people,' I say, angrily. 'So, you think lies are fine as long as they're not *big* ones?' I've been visiting Tess, all right? Taking her food, like I always have. I promised I would protect her. I promised her mother.'

I clench my jaw, seething. Empathy swallows Bunce's jealousy.

'You can't save her, Skyla,' he says softly. 'You can't save everyone.'

'I don't want to save everyone,' I snap. 'Central can go fuck themselves.'

'Well, you can't save everyone who deserves saving. You couldn't save your grandfather, you can't save Tess and you can't save me. The point is, it's not your job to save the world.'

'Well whose job is it then? Who's going to stop this nightmare? You? Kian? I'm not trying to save the world, Bunce. The old world is lost. We need to rebuild civilisation. Save the city.'

'Why? You hate this city.'

I'm suddenly lost for words. He's right, I do hate this city.

'There's nowhere else to go. We're trapped here. If there were other cities beyond the wall I'd leave, but there aren't and I can't go on living in this screwed-up system, it has to change. There's no justice.'

Bunce holds his head in his hand.

'No, there isn't. Life has no justice system so why do you think we should live in a world of justice? Stop fighting, Sky. There's nothing to fight for.'

'Then there's no point in any of it.' I say, bitterly.

'Of course, there is, there are some wonderful things to live for. Things worth enduring this fucked-up existence for.'

'You're starting to sound like Kian. The one person you hate.'

'I don't hate Crow. I hate that you love him and you don't love me.'

My heart stings at the sight of Bunce's sorrowful face. He's right, I don't love him, not the way he wants me to, and not the way he seems to love me, but he's wrong about Kian. He's my best friend, not my boyfriend. I care what happens to Bunce, I do. That's a kind of love, isn't it?

'If I didn't care about you,' I say, 'I'd have told Kian to leave you in Rock Vault to rot.'

'You used me. You only allowed me to tag along so you could feed me the serum and change your life.'

'Things are different now.'

'Are they?' Bunce says, sarcastically. 'I thought you were beginning to like me, that maybe we could be ...' he blushes, 'more than friends.'

'I ...'

Bunce talks over me.

'But now you know there is no cure for me, that I'll eventually be hover-chair bound, you've stopped yourself from getting too close, from ever falling in love with me. You've shut me out.'

I'm speechless. I try to respond.

'That's not true ...'

'Yes, it is!' he yells. 'And who could blame you? I'll never be the man you want. Even if you could love me, you hate Morbs.'

'But I don't hate you, Bunce,' I say.

My lip trembles as I realise what he's saying, who he thinks I am. I've always thought of myself as a crusader for the poor and repressed. A truth-seeker, a believer in justice but I'm not. If the Skels suddenly switched places with the Morbs, would I care about the Morb's plight? Would I bother to seek justice for them? I want to cure Bunce, not just for my own selfish needs any more, for him too, but do I care about the rest of them? I swallow hard. Bunce is right, I'm a hypocrite.

Shadow is cast over me as Bunce gets to his feet and reaches for his backpack.

'Wait, where are you going?'

'Home. Where I belong,' he says, bitterly.

'Don't go,' the words fall from my lips. 'I don't want you to go.'

Bunce drops the backpack and kneels down in front of me. His ocean blue eyes crash waves of passion into mine. I don't want him to go but I can't tell him I love him.

I cup his face with my hands, his skin soft under my fingers. I do feel something more intense than friendship alone. I dust my thumb across his lips, he closes his eyes and I replace my thumb with my mouth. He pulls back, staring at me like he's seeing me for the first time. I half-smile and he doesn't hesitate, he leans forward and his hand reaches behind my head. He kisses me like it's his last dying wish. I return the passion, tasting his lips the way I'd savour a ripe strawberry. I feel his longing, his need, his desire. It penetrates my heart and a tear escapes and runs down my face. Everything is lost yet I'm happy in this moment, in his arms. My mind empties, nothing matters but his touch, nothing is real except our entwined bodies. The world drops away along with my clothes.

Bunce's hands are warm. He slides his soft fingers nervously up the inside of my thigh and towards the crease of my leg. My body tingles with anticipation. It's been so long. I need this. I slip my tongue past his lips and between my legs he slips his fingers up and past mine, thick, warm, and now wet and rhythmic. My nipples harden. We're going to do this. I'll be his first. *Can I do that and walk away? I care for him but I honestly don't know if I could ever love him. What is he expecting of me?* My thoughts evaporate with his movement, a tingle across my right nipple as he gently sucks and kisses, his fingers tracing the other one. I arch my back. How has he never done this before?

His kisses move down my stomach and I suck in air through my teeth. Bunce's hands glide over my legs, parting them. I run my fingers through his hair, grab a handful, and squeeze my breast with the other hand. His breath is hot, his tongue soft and his lips touch all the right places. Shock waves ripple through me and I moan with pleasure. Who is this guy and where's Bunce? I gently tug his head up by the hair, he smiles, moves up over me, leans in and kisses my neck. I push him over onto his back and launch my body up onto his. He gazes up at me, his eyes filled with *I love you.*

He's lovesick, I might end up hurting him. Should I be his first? He's not mine, my first was five years ago and there've been a few since then. He wants me to, even though I'm not of his people, even though he knows how I feel about the Morbihan, he wants this. He may never get another chance and I need the release.

I slowly lower myself onto him, and he closes his eyes. I lean on his chest lightly enough that my movement gently rubs my nipples over his bare skin. I start to grind. I kiss him, his neck, his ears, his shoulders, his lips. He's deep inside me, hard, strong. The excitement grows. I move faster, throw my head back and moan, scream his name as climax comes to take me. It's coming, it's close, I'm coming, I'm coming! Bunce groans, and shivers, his hands clasp my buttocks, pushing me to move faster still. Yes! I follow his lead, faster, faster … My thoughts escape into words.

'Bunce … I'm coming …'

Bunce answers.

'Sky, oh … Skyla!'

I feel it, the hot explosion. I slow down, smooth, gentle, from a gallop to a trot. I freeze, eyes wide.

That sound.

The siren, they've found us!

Chapter Twenty-eight

A Cold Stone for a Heart

'Bunce, come on!'

'I can't run as fast as you, slow down!'

I tear through the tree line, dicing with death. I don't lead Bunce further into the trees, instead we stay at the edge of danger. If we run across the open grass the guards will see us, but in the thick of the trees, the Mutil will snatch us. We run down the fine line between two enemies. I stumble and slip on something smooth beneath my feet. I roll over on my ankle, tripping on fallen branches. I manage to keep my balance and look down, not branches, bones! Strips of moonlight reveal skulls and tibia and ribs. Bunce shouts, 'gross!' I keep running, my boots crunch and slip on the collection of skeletons scattered around the tree roots. I'm glad I didn't venture this way while out looking for food and water.

The siren has stopped; its wail not enough to disturb the wildlife but the marching rumble of the guards' approach is. The ground vibrations push crowds of crows from their perch, they fly to safety. I duck into a moonlit shadow. Bunce is a few feet behind me. He clings to a tree.

'Skyla, there's nowhere to run,' he pants, 'we might as well give ourselves up!'

'You might as well, they'll execute me.'

'Not if I say I forced you to help me escape or something, maybe they'll be lenient.'

'I killed three guards in The Spiral. Not to mention the two we maimed at the front doors.'

'We can tell them it was self-defence, right?'

I sigh. Has Bunce learned nothing after all he's witnessed? Why does he think I'll be treated the same as him? He's seen for himself that we aren't equal, yet deep down he still believes the system works.

'I'm going to the wall.' I say.

'The wall? Why?'

'There's an ingredient in the desert that I need to make more serum.'

'What ingredient?'

'I don't know, Bins said people died to bring it to the city.'

'So, let me get this straight in my head,' Bunce says in a patronising tone, 'you want to go into the desert, to find an ingredient to make more serum, but you don't know what the ingredient is, where to find it, or how to make the cure?'

'Yes, but ...'

'And you say people died to bring it to the city?'

'I know but what else can we do? If we go to the wall, maybe there'll be a clue, we could torture information out of one of the watch guards, I don't know! It's better than sitting around waiting to be caught, isn't it?'

'No, Sky. It's a horrible idea.' Bunce kicks a skull to one side and almost trips over it.

'Any better ideas?' I ask.

'Yeah,' he says. 'How about we shoot each other in the face.'

'Don't joke.'

'I'm not! That's a much better plan than yours. This way we die without suffering, dehydration, and starvation first.'

Boots thud past and Bunce disappears behind a tree. I shrink back too. When I'm sure the guards are far enough away, I move off, beckoning for Bunce to follow.

'I'm going into the desert. I'm doing it. End of,' I say.

'Da fuck you will!'

I look round at Bunce. Confident smile. Twinkle in his eye. I can't help but laugh at the use of Don's words and the Skel accent he put on.

'Using me dead uncle's words now, are ya.'

Cara stands before us, hands on bony hips. Ripped shorts, so short they could be mistaken for knickers, her black shirt is missing some buttons, tied up at the waist with a three-string woven belt.

'Why you in 'ere? Don't ya know this is Mutil territory?'

Framed by curls, Cara's eyes show no sign of guilt. I smile sweetly, and jab my fist hard into her face.

'Damn, Skyla!' Cara yells, cradling her swelling cheek. 'What the fuck?'

Bunce rushes to Cara's aid, but she pushes him away and approaches me.

'Is this about losing ya little friend, Tess? I've been looking for her for days, I 'aven't stopped, and this is 'ow you repay me! I should snap ya fucking neck!'

'You shouldn't have let her out of your sight!' I yell.

'Ssssseye.'

'What was that?'

Bunce spins around.

'Sssseye, ssseye.'

The voice slithers through the darkness, crawls around the bark, and shuffles through the leaves. Flash of red hair. A small frame darts out and back into the shadows.

'Tess. Come out,' I say.

'Tess?' Bunce says, backing away.

'Tess, you shouldn't 'ave run off like that, I'm glad you're okay ...' Cara trails off as the small girl steps into the light. Tess's mouth is closed, hiding her pointed teeth. The two moons light up the young girl's brown skin, freckles flecked across her nose and cheeks, she almost looks like the same little Tess, her mismatched eyes the only discrepancy. She wants more food. I don't have any. I left it all back at the den in my haste to get away. She doesn't like the fruit but she eats it. I kneel down and take her hands.

'Don't touch it! Are you crazy?' Bunce squawks.

'Shut up, Bunce!' I snap.

I can't let him spook her. She's been accepting food from me for days. I've earned her trust. Cara doesn't say a word.

'I don't have any food right now. You'll have to climb the fruit tree. Okay?'

'Ssseye. Seye.'

She doesn't understand. She keeps repeating my name. I meant to show her how to feed herself. I was going to these next few days.

'Listen, Tess,' I coo, pulling her closer. I lean forward and the handgun drops from my bra strap onto the bone littered ground. I don't pick it up. Sudden movements scare Tess. 'You have to go get fruit from the trees.'

I point behind me. She turns and looks to where I'm pointing and then stares back at me with a blank expression.

'Sky, stop this,' says Bunce impatiently. 'We have to go.'

I ignore him and smile warmly at the helpless little girl I swore to protect. Tess reaches her small arms around my neck. I close my eyes and embrace her. My lip quivers. Eyes open again, Bunce is striding away. Cara follows him, but glances back at me, worried. Yank at my ponytail.

'Ouch!'

I pull away.

'Tess, you're hurting me!'

I reach up and try to prise her small fingers apart. I peel one back and it clamps back down. She won't let go of my hair. She growls. Jagged teeth sink into my neck. I howl in pain, my heart racing.

'Stop! Tess, stop it!'

This time she means to kill me. Why is she doing this? I search the ground around me, my fingers touch slimy things, hard things, who knows what; all the while I'm still trying to prise her off with my other hand. The pain. The PAIN! My fingers find the gun, I bring my arm up, place the barrel to her head and squeeze the trigger.

BANG!

Her blood and brains splatter the side of my face and I taste her exploded flesh on my lips. I let her limp body drop to the ground. I wipe the wet from my face and then clean my bloody fingers with the front of my shirt. Her tiny lifeless body is draped over the bones and skulls. I step over it and walk silently past Bunce and Cara. A cold stone where my heart once was.

Chapter Twenty-nine

The Wall and Back

I wake to sunlight creeping through the canopy of leaves. My deep sleep was filled with a warm tingling feeling, and only the glorious dawn is enough to persuade me to leave my slumber. I don't normally dream, and if I do, it's always nightmares. Usually about being eaten alive by a large, male Mutil, or nightmares about crows pecking me to death, about my mother's death, the public end to my grandfather's life, and now Tess will be added to the horrors. The line between the world of nightmares and reality is blurred. The memory of Tess sinking her teeth into me for a second time, before I was forced to blow her brains out, will stay with me forever. I tell myself she is better off dead. I try to convince myself that what I did was for the best, that her mutilation wasn't my fault but the sinking feeling is overwhelming and the monster that lives inside my head tells me otherwise, that I murdered her.

Once I'm fully awake, Tess stalks my mind. I touch my neck and shoulder, where she bit me. I can't picture her as she was before the mutilation; actually, I can hardly picture her at all. She presents as a disfigured shadow, a girl with no face. She's a phantasm plaguing my thoughts. I expected nightmares of Tess, but last night she did not enter my dreams. I slept soundly. I haven't slept as deeply since before Selection and I've never dreamed in such vivid colour as I did last night, not since I was a small child. Kian was the centre of this dream. Before he became someone else, back when he was my trusted friend. Although *friend* doesn't do our relationship justice, we have always been more than friends, more like family. Will he still want to be my friend, now his fears have come true? I don't think he'll ever speak to me again if he finds out about me and Bunce. Everything is so messed up.

I dreamed of Kian as he once was, before he became a guard, before he became Crow. He made me feel safe. I wish he was with me. Do I wish for his company instead of Bunce's? If there is one thing Bunce doesn't do which Kian does, it is make me feel safe. Even as cold and harsh as he can be, Kian equals safety, whereas Bunce equals uncertainty and probably death. I think of my life before Showcase. Things used to be simple. I wish I was back in the past, on one of my recoup days, enjoying the freedom. All Skels are permitted one day of leisure. A day to rest before another working week. Tired workers are not productive. Kian and I had the same recoup day and we would always spend it in each other's company, either at the pond or climbing trees or wandering around Market Square. It didn't matter what we did, as long as we were together.

Central provides Skels with rations, a horrible gruel for breakfast, lunch and dinner, so many people grow vegetables and trade them. Skels also make things to trade at the market for other useful things. Neither Kian nor I had much of anything to trade. Both of us were without parents, which meant we were poorer than most, Kian more so than me with three younger brothers to care for. The boys would entertain themselves during the day, but would always turn to Kian for nourishment and Kian would always turn to the market.

Last night's dream was of our second meeting. Unlike other young Skels, who liked to browse in groups, I'd always go to market alone; that is, before Kian.

Thanks to my dream, the day I bumped into Kian at the market is as fresh in my mind, as if I'd lived it yesterday. The warm air was pulsing with spices and smoked meat but what came through thickest was the smell of rain, that damp smell that smothers everything even before the first drop has hit the ground. I love that smell. It was the start of monsoon season and even though charcoal clouds threatened overhead, Skels remained determined to get in one last day of trading before the relentless downpours lashed the city.

I remember walking past many stalls that day, perusing the wares, weaving in and out of people busily swapping and bartering. There were so many things to trade for; pots, bowls, spoons, lucky rocks painted to represent different symbols of the Glory in the Sky; all making promises to hold off the Dark Angel, promises I know a rock (painted or not) cannot keep. There were fruit and vegetable stalls and sometimes bread. I always gave a wide berth to the meat stalls. Plucked birds and skinned snakes hung up under the canopy, swaying when gusts of wind rushed through. Clear bags filled with liquid were dotted around to keep the flies away. Anything flies were most interested in never interested me. Skels don't eat meat but Eremites do and they often exchange rare and lavish items for it. Once I tried to catch a snake with thoughts of selling it. I lunged, it slithered away fast and I was left with my face in the dirt. I never tried to catch animals again.

Instead, I tried to trade my hair fasteners – which were nothing more than forked sticks with the bark stripped away. No one ever wanted them, except Ms Grouse. Sometimes she took pity on me and traded a small pumpkin for three sticks and an apple, which I'd stolen at great risk. It was easier to climb a tree and risk getting caught, than waste a whole recoup day chasing snakes. I remember running my fingers along Ms Grouse's table of wares, I stopped to pick up a small smooth fruit. My mind unlocks a conversation with Kian.

'You gonna trade for that?'

I snatch my fingers from the edge of the wooden table and drop the fruit. Kian smiles at me; soft boyish face, small frame, athletic arms folded across his puffed-out chest.

'Yeah,' I say, smiling back, nose in the air.

'With what?' he laughs. 'Those sticks?'

I glance down at the fasteners gripped tightly in my hand. He won't want these and I haven't any apples. What's he doing watching Ms Grouse's stall? Why would he help that old woman? He told me his parents were dead and Skels don't take other people's children in. 'Charity begins at home, look after your own' is the chant of our people.

'Helping Ms Grouse, huh?' I say, accusingly.

'Yeah, she's sick. I get a few melontines out of it, though,' he shrugs.

A couple of melontines isn't worth losing a whole recoup day. Hybrid fruits are disgusting anyway, the melon/clementine mix being one of the worst in my opinion. I swipe the yellow fruit from Kian's fingers and the piled-up figs on the wobbly wooden table roll towards me. A few drop to the ground. I quickly shove my collection of sticks onto the table, making a barrier to stop more fruit from falling.

'How many sticks will it be, then?' I ask, smugly.

Kian raises his thick eyebrows and nods to the figs on the floor. I waste no time in scooping them up, using the bottom of my snood as a makeshift bag. I hold the frayed material tight so the figs can't escape. Without warning, water drops in great sheets from the heavens and I scream when the cold rain runs down my back. I duck under the stall with Kian, who hugs me to his side. We watch as other stallholders struggle to hold on to their wares, and cloth roofs blow inside out with the howling wind. Ms Grouse's stall is sturdy and many market-goers stumble towards us, heads down. They shout to Kian over the squalling wind. Kian nods for them to take shelter with us.

From that day on, we spent nearly every recoup day together. Being with Kian made my life worth living. I lived for the end of my working week but it was never enough. I always wanted more. More freedom. Less fear. More safety. Less fights. More rights. More justice. It never came and now it looks as though it never will.

A breezes rushes through the trees and spots of golden sunlight sparkle through the leaves. I think about waking Bunce. I should have taken him home, I could have dropped him off outside the door to the complex but he insisted on coming to the wall with me, as did Cara.

I sit for a moment, twirling the info-card Cara gave me between my fingers. She got it from Crow. I may as well start calling him that now he has officially accepted this name. Crow gave the card to Cara when she ran into him while looking for Tess. He didn't ask about me, didn't even care to ask if I was alive or dead. All he said was my name and handed Cara the card. No explanation. I shove the plastic into my pocket.

I'm emotionally drained and I know Bunce is exhausted but we must keep going. We managed to escape capture in the park, the guards must have been tipped off about the two Mutil bodies piled on the hill, but we're exposed out here by the wall. Guards don't patrol the edge of the wall but there's a station every few hundred metres. Clover will hunt me until I'm safely locked away in Rock Vault and can cause no more trouble, or perhaps he will let nature take its course and I will eventually cause my own demise. Maybe the siren and the patrols aren't actually for us, perhaps we aren't a priority now the serum is gone?

We don't eat breakfast because we have no breakfast. Before we left Tinny's hideout I managed to pick up the flask of water, which Cara carries, and I also grabbed the gun but that's all.

'What kind of creature does Crow want you to catch, then?' Cara stands over me, her shadow stealing my warm sunlight.

'Why are you still here, Cara?' I ask. Not bothering to mask the irritation in my voice. What the hell is she blabbering on about, catching a creature for Crow?

Cara stares at me blankly and then as if the thought had suddenly occurred to her, she takes out a small rectangular object from her pocket.

'I got nowhere else to go, and I should give you this,' she says, reaching into her pocket. 'Crow gave this to me, too. I was gonna keep it and use it as a bargaining chip, since you obviously hate me after what 'appened with Tess but I want you to trust me. Here.'

She hands me a metal square and I look at her wrist, remembering the one embedded there. It's still there but cracked, she must have tried to remove it. I tap the screen and six words appear: A few scales should be enough.

'I don't get it?' I whisper to myself.

'Well, info-cards are locked, only guards and Central have access to the technology that opens them and tiny touchpads are not locked. Anyone can read them or watch holo-news on them, I'm guessing the note is cryptic-like and the info-card has some secret on it.'

'I get that, Cara.' I say, but why give these things to me?

'If the creature 'as scales, I'd say it's a snake,' she says, ignoring my question. 'Let's grab one and get going.'

Cara has obviously read the note and come to her own conclusion.

I stand and stretch the stiffness from my legs. If we were set upon by guards, I would not be able to run, my muscles are heavy as rock. Bunce is on his feet, staggering close to the wall. I sprint to catch up, forcing my muscles to unlock. My thoughts race along with my steps. I don't know who I am anymore, what am I fighting for? It used to be I'd fight for myself. I would help others, as long as there was something in it for me. Even when helping Tess I had an angle; access to the slums, the pond, and a hiding place from guards and Mutil. The fight for life – that was always for my life. I'd never fight for Crow like I've fought for Bunce. Why? Maybe Bunce needs me and Crow doesn't? Urgh. Fuck Bunce. I kick the orange sand. That's right. I did fuck Bunce. I let that happen. I took his virginity and I can never give it back. I snatched it greedily, because *I* needed a thrill, I did this knowing he cared more for me than I for him. Right now, all I want to do is run away, look after myself and no one else but if I leave him to be captured, he'll probably be tortured and mutilated. Why do I care what happens to him? I just want to go, disappear forever.

I recoil at my thoughts, my head is trying to eject my demented mind. Seven words use my brain as a trampoline. *Why does anyone even bother with me?* I don't have an answer. Maybe the answer is right in front of me? Bunce is ten feet away and on his knees, holding his head.

'Bunce?' I yell to him.

He doesn't move. Sand creeps into the city from under the wall. It lies beneath Bunce's knees, turning his blue jeans orange. I crouch beside him and lift his head; droplets of his sweat run between my fingers. His hair is saturated.

'Bunce, what's wrong? Talk to me.'

His face is pale. It's always pale but now he has the look of shiny porcelain.

'I think I'm sick,' he rasps.

'No shit!' Cara says, she holds out the flask.

I take it and I press the water to Bunce's lips. He sips and struggles to swallow.

'Can you stand?' I ask.

Bunce shakes as he tries to pull his heavy frame up on to his feet. He leans against me, my legs buckle, I lift his arm up over my shoulder and Cara does the same on his other side. We walk slowly, the sun blazing down. It beats us, hot fists pounding my back. Is it too hot out here for the Morb? Maybe he's going through the change. What if he blobs out right now. Cara and I couldn't carry a full sized Morb. I glance sideways at the young guy slumped around my shoulders, feet dragging through the dust. His frame seems slighter, lighter. I stop abruptly. Bunce groans.

'We have to get you home.'

'No,' Bunce croaks at me.

'Yes. There's something wrong with you, what's the use of finding the ingredient if you die out here?'

'No. I'm staying with you. I ... I want to stay with you.' his eyes plead.

Cara helps me prop him up against the wall. She walks ahead a few feet, kicking up dust over her worn slip-on shoes, all the while staring up at the wall, probably wondering if it can be scaled without climbing equipment.

'Whoa!' Cara suddenly yells, 'look at the size of this!'

She holds up a sheet of shredded snakeskin. It's as long as she is tall and wider than her. She throws it to the ground like it's diseased and carries on looking for a weakness in the wall.

I turn my attention back to Bunce, he reaches for me, hands shaking. I crouch and take his hands in mine.

'I know you don't love me,' he whispers.

'I …'

'Don't say it,' he rasps. 'Don't say it just because you think I'm dying.'

'I won't say it,' I assure him. 'I don't know what that kind of love looks like.'

I was quick to judge Kian for not knowing how to love, thinking I did because I loved my grandfather and he loved me but that's a different kind of love and I have never been in love.

'It doesn't look like anything …' Bunce smiles at me like I've said something daft. 'You feel it.'

'I do feel something,' I say, and I do. 'I care about you.'

'But you don't love me, even now, even after we …'

Bunce's eyelids droop. I shake him.

'Bunce.'

He opens his eyes.

'I'm fine… just tired.'

'Listen, I don't know how to feel about anything,' I say, propping myself up against the wall beside him. 'Now that Tess is dead, Clover is a traitor, and Kian isn't Kian, I feel like my heart can't take any more punishment. I care what happens to you. You're all I've got left. I don't want to lose you.'

Bunce stares at me in shock. I stare back as shocked as he is, did I just say those words? Did I mean them? I did. As much as I want to run away from everyone, be alone, and only have them in my life when it suits me, I don't want to be utterly alone. I don't want to be without him in my life.

'He needs to see a Verity.'

Cara throws the words at the wall but they are meant for me.

'What's a Verity?' I shout over to her.

'A healing mistress, you know, a Morb who can see truth,' she says, walking towards us.

'How's that going to help?' I ask, confused.

'A Verity can see truth in your mind but also within your body,' rasps Bunce, his eyelids flicker. I hope he doesn't pass out.

'They can sense what ails you,' Cara adds.

'Yes, Cara,' Bunce pleads with his eyes. 'Take me to Lyca.'

'Take you to Lyca?' Cara spits. 'Do I look like my brain's been mutilated?'

'She won't turn us in,' Bunce wheezes.

'She's a Morb, 'course she'll turn us in.' Cara rolls her eyes.

'No, M orbs don't betray each other.'

'We ain't Morbs, Bunce,' she reminds him.

'To betray you is a betrayal of me,' he says. 'I promise you, she won't turn you in.'

Cara shrugs at me. She doesn't know if that's true and neither do I, but there's no choice. I nod, we peel Bunce from the wall and heave his body up over our shoulders. With our aid, he's able to walk – just.

'Where do we find this Verity?' I ask Cara, talking across Bunce.

'You're not going to like it,' she replies.

'Where?' I insist.

'The Barracks,' she says, and she's right I don't like it. I don't like it one bit.

It takes us twenty minutes longer to reach the guard station than it would have if Bunce could walk unaided. We sneak around the back of the Barracks. Cara says the Verity works out of an underground healing shop on the other side of the towering stone pillars. The home to guards is a great fortress, grey stones the same as historic castles used to look before they were all destroyed or swallowed by the sea, and inside these walls there'll be training grounds and dorms and an armoury filled with weapons. Above us, the Sky Train hammers over the manned turrets. Being this close to the Barracks causes nausea to pull at my stomach. Cara helps me half-carry Bunce around the back of the stone enclosure. Behind the brickwork, higher ranked guards yell, while lower ranks march and scramble and run. The sounds create a vision in my head and I wish I could see in, find out how accurate the picture is that my mind has conjured.

After a few minutes, I stop and prop Bunce up against the wall. He doesn't weigh any more yet he's getting heavier with every step and sweat pours down his temples. I catch my breath but it's stolen again by a horrible bone-shaking noise, a low growl, followed by a gruesome bark, like a wild animal is throwing up the bones of someone it ate last night. My skin prickles like bird feathers stroked the wrong way. Cara holds her midriff, she pants and puffs, trying to speed up her body's recovery from carrying Bunce. There's a crack in the wall. I lean in and peer through it. A person thrashes about on the ground, limbs flailing, he hollers while two huge beasts attack him. Guards laugh and the man on the floor shouts, 'Enough! Call them off!' A whistle sounds and the beasts release the guard on the floor and sit to attention. The guard gets to his feet with the help of another then pats the dust from his protective suit.

The awful creatures that attacked the guard in a padded suit are called dogs but they're more like wolves; they've been enhanced in every way possible. Bigger, stronger, and part bionic. I like them less than the Mutil. These evil creatures have a keen sense of smell, they're fast and have been known to outrun hover-cycles. Their teeth are metal daggers and they can see just as well in the dark, as in the day. They aren't used regularly because Skels fear them, we call them Ruinous because they can ruin a person in minutes. We don't see these creatures often because Central can't have their workers walking around in fear, it's unproductive.

I can't help but feel I'm the cause of all this stepped-up activity. My mind has a tug of war with the idea. I go on the run, taking a Morb with me, killing guards, and screwing up the system and now security has been increased. How can one girl cause all this hysteria? I've always fantasised that I would one day bring the city to its knees, but never really thought that I could. Cara chews at her bottom lip nervously, she's fearless but not stupid, Ruinous scare her. She picks up Bunce's right arm and I resume my place on the left. We continue trudging.

Even though Cara shoulders half of the weight and Bunce is looking thinner, he is heavier than ever. I hold his lank arm draped over my shoulder and every so often I check for a pulse. He's hardly breathing.

We edge around the side of the building but there's not enough shadow; daylight exposes us. Two Skels, carrying what could be mistaken for a High-Host male whacked out on glory. That is dodgy enough. Two Skels, dragging a sick, twenty-year-old Morbihan. People would freak out. Bunce's bright shirt is like a beacon saying here we are, come and get us! I'm surprised we haven't been spotted already, but perhaps Clover is still watching me, allowing me safe passage, hoping I'll lead him to Bullet. I won't. I'm never going near that psycho again.

'Here it is,' Cara drops Bunce's arm, 'come on.'

I buckle under the weight. Bunce groans. The ex-maid leads us down a narrow flight of stone steps, I look down at my boots to assure my footing. Each step has smooth edges. I imagine water rounded the steps, floods during monsoon season. I hitch Bunce up, my arm around his waist. He clings to me.

Cara stops dead and my face collides with the back of her curly head. I back up, lean sideways and peer past her. There's a line of Skels in front of us. At the bottom of the steps is a secure door. Cara turns around to face me.

'Jump the line?' she asks.

The lined up Skels look pretty downtrodden. Frail, stooped over, and broken. Skels don't like confrontation, elders especially.

I'm confident we can skip to the front of the line without incident. I nod to Cara and she goes to step past the first Skel, an elderly man.

The city speakers crackle to life, not with the siren this time but with an announcement. Cara stops advancing. I cringe at the merry jingle I know so well and soon the chirpy voice of Delia Gold springs forth in an echo of sickly sweet optimism, spouting the usual greetings.

'Citizens of Gale City, good day to you. I hope this announcement finds you in good health and high spirits. Workers are the backbone of our beloved city and we at Central want you to know how much we appreciate your hard work and dedication.'

No one moves. Even though we have somewhat broken our programming, neither Cara nor I move a muscle. When an announcement is made, no one ever moves. Everyone stops work and listens. The city holds its breath and waits for Delia's shrill voice.

'We want to assure you once more, that the deployment of the GDU is to protect and serve you in this difficult time of gangs and Glory Runners'.

GDU stands for Guard Dog Unit, they should call it RDU: Ruinous Death Unit. The voice with no face suddenly becomes deeper and Delia's counterpart, Chester Stout, chimes in to deliver the next part of the announcement. The insanely smug tone in his voice always manages to grate on my nerves no matter what words come out of his mouth.

'Delia and I hope you will feel safe under GDU protection and enjoy carrying out your daily duties as normal. Once again, our gratitude is given for the splendid job you are doing in ensuring the city is run efficiently. We want you to know your safety is paramount to us. You are the heart of Gale City. Never forget.'

Both announcers' voices sing out in unison, *'The system works!'*

Cue irritating jingle, followed by the crackle of the station break. So, Central are telling Skels the Ruinous are there to protect them. Skels will believe this, too. I've never believed the announcements, there's always some underlying angle, and this one is us, the dogs are to find us, not Bullet or Glory Runners, they have always operated in the city. The guards have to be seen to be doing something about them but many are doing back alley deals with Runners. Some guards are dodgy as hell.

Like clockwork dolls fully wound again, the Skels start to move. The elders in front cough, and shuffle from one foot to another. I sidle down the steep incline, dragging Bunce, excusing my way through while Cara barges past without a polite word. The elders, as expected, remain quiet. Cara reaches the secure door and it swishes open, a warden steps out, Cara darts backwards, narrowly avoiding collision. The High-Host is dressed in long, flowing, plum-coloured robes, her hair of the same colour is straight like vertical blinds. Four purple butterflies flitter from the corner of her right eye down her cheek; a hologrammatic tattoo, the glittery wings flutter every few seconds. The purple woman glares at Cara.

Chapter Thirty

The Verity

'Next!' she shouts past Cara.

'We're next!' Cara says in a cocky tone.

The warden tilts her head gracefully towards Cara, letting her unnaturally straight purple locks fall down her right shoulder.

'You're not Mr Sprinton.' Her eyes flick up to me and Bunce. 'Isn't that the missing Morb? He's all over the news.'

She points at Bunce. The Skels turn their heads to us, worried. I shake my head.

'You must be mistaken,' I say.

'Wardens don't make mistakes, dearie,' she says to me and then smites Cara with a narrow stare.

'Well,' Cara says, stepping forwards, 'let me explain ... oh to hell with it!'

Cara shoves the warden through the doorway. The purple High-Host stumbles backwards and is about to protest when the door swooshes shut.

'Don't kill her!' I yell desperately into the thick slab.

The Skels mumble to each other but no one intervenes. Not one tries to stop us. There's a scuffle behind the door. Whispers. Silence. The door slides open.

'Next!' Cara hollers.

I step inside the holding chamber. Bunce steps in too, clinging tight to me. The warden lies on the floor. Feet and hands bound with strands of Cara's woven belt. The purple princess goes to speak, Cara lifts a finger to her lips.

'Remember what will happen to you if you speak.'

The warden purses her lips and lies in infuriated silence.

'Go through,' Cara raises her hand towards a second door. 'I'll stay and keep an eye on her.'

We slip past Cara and walk over to a small sanitation station. I rub sanitizer over our hands and drag Bunce through a second door which is open. A coldness, like crashing through a wall of ice, startles me. Bunce is rejuvenated by it and manages to hold his head up, relieving the pressure on my sore shoulders and aching back. He pulls my arm from around his waist and staggers forwards. I instinctively wrap my arms around my shivering bones and scan the room. I don't know what to concentrate on first. The curious chamber overflows with trinkets, amulets, crystals and spices. It's as if the market has been compacted and stored inside this underground cavern.

Whimsical music flitters around us as we move further in and I get a strange sensation, like we're surrounded by tiny fairies, fluttering about wearing tiny bells. The walls are draped in purple silk and every shelf is overloaded with fetishes. A sparkle of silver catches my eye. I lean closer to a round table where a silver and white glistening tree looks to have grown up through the middle of it. I reach out, fingertips about to brush one of the crystal branches.

'Don't touch that.'

A silvery voice with a spike of warning drifts towards us. I search for its owner. Find her. An old Morb, with jewels in her long flowing hair, sits on a podium in a hover-chair encrusted with gemstones. She has a regal air about her.

'Welcome, Bunce.'

'Good morning, Mistress Lyca.' Bunce croaks.

Lyca? A bell rings in my head.

'As in *Ask Lyca*?' I say.

She doesn't answer me. I follow Bunce to the podium and notice Lyca's eyes have no pupils or lenses, just large white spheres in a large white face.

'It's a pleasure to finally meet you,' Lyca says to Bunce in a warm voice. 'Though I sense you are a little unwell, my boy.' She wheezes. 'I really think the hospital is best.'

Her face points towards Bunce, but with no pupils shifting around, I wonder if she's blind.

'Mistress, the pleasure is all mine,' Bunce steps up to the hover-chair and shakes Lyca's hand, then he kneels. 'Please, can you help me?'

'You're hungry. Help yourself to the bowl before we begin. My other clients will wait.'

Bunce bows in thanks and takes a handful of grapes and two pears from a golden bowl beside the Morb queen. He avoids the wrapped meat products. He passes me the pears and I put one in my pocket for Cara.

'It is possible that being out in the elements has harmed your health,' Lyca says, stifled by her overworked artificial lungs. 'Your family are worried about you. Morbihan should not be outside.'

'That's your opinion,' I say, biting through the skin of the pear. I bring my hand to my mouth, to contain the juices as they run down my chin.

This time she answers me.

'And it is a good one. Maybe you should keep yours to yourself.'

'And maybe you should get on with it,' I snarl, stepping up beside Bunce. 'Can't you see how sick he is. Help him!'

'You should learn to hold your tongue. I've been more than hospitable to you, Skel,' says Lyca. Raising her painted-on eyebrows, she draws a sharp breath. 'Maybe I should alert Central to your presence?'

'Do what you want,' I shrug, sucking the sweetness from the pear. 'Maybe then Central can tell you a few home truths. Like what's in your food, for a start. You wouldn't be so cosy with them then!'

'Skyla!' Bunce says.

'I'm curious,' I say, dropping the pear core on the floor and kicking it under a round, silk-covered table, 'what's a highly respected Morb of your skill level doing working out of a dingy cluttered pit like this?' I mock. 'Why aren't you in a luxury boudoir inside the complex?'

'Verity cater to all who need us,' she rattles. 'Morbihan don't often need us, but guards,' she takes a breath. 'Skels,' another breath. 'And sometimes even outlaws like yourself, come to me. Now,' She clasps her meaty hands together, 'speak out of turn once more, outlaw, and I'll bind your tongue.'

'You can sense illness and disease but can't sense you've been digesting human flesh all these years?' I scoff.

'How is it that you know about that?' Lyca says, amusement playing on her purple lips.

Why isn't she shocked at my admission? I open my mouth but no words come. Lyca softens her tone and talks down to me as if my IQ is lower than that of a Mutil.

'I'm a healer, child. We know everything about the body.'

'But it's cannibalism!' I yell.

Bunce coughs.

'You said it wasn't, because we weren't eating other Morbs.'

'Shut up, Bunce!'

'Our bodies need meat,' Lyca rasps. 'Not enough grows in a desert city to sustain us. The choice is, eat the meat available or die.'

'I'd rather die!' I shout.

Lyca clutches an amulet around her neck with her thick fingers. Her eyes close. I wonder what she's doing, but then my tongue starts to swell, filling every corner of my mouth. I'm choking! I fall at her feet, clutching my throat; tongue twice its normal size hanging out of my mouth. Bunce shoots an alarmed look at the Verity. She lets go of the amulet.

'Yes,' she says, resting her laced fingers over her huge stomach. 'You used to believe that.'

My tongue shrinks back like a salted slug and I cough, gasping for air. I stare up into the Verity's white eyes. They say the eyes are the windows to the soul. I can't see into hers, like I can't see a bird inside an egg but I feel her eyes are looking right inside me. I get to my feet and take a few steps back, fearful she might try to suffocate me with my own tongue again, or worse. She's right, I no longer hold death as a desire.

Lyca beckons to Bunce and he leans closer to her hover-chair. She places her oversized hand on his chest and closes her eyes again. It looks like she's listening to his heart through her palm. She snatches back her hand.

'So, is he dying from that gash in his arm or a lack of human flesh consumption?' I ask, less cockiness in my voice.

'Neither, my dear,' Lyca says, breathlessly. 'Bunce is cured.'

'What?' Bunce and I say, in unison.

I can't believe it. Is she telling the truth? But then, why would she lie?

'His body has been in shock. It had to partially shut down in order to cope,' Lyca says.

'But he can't be cured,' I say.

'Skyla drank the serum, not me,' Bunce explains.

Lyca gestures for my hands. After what she did to me without touching me, I'm not sure I want to get any closer to her. I reluctantly step forwards and place my hands in hers; they feel like silk, she's never worked a day in her life. Her eyes close for a third time. After a few seconds, the warmth of her thick fingers pass into my cold bones. Her eyelids spring open and the white eyes stare at me. She smiles warmly.

'My goodness! This is a first.'

My cheeks flush, Bunce looks away.

'What is?' I ask but I think I know.

'Morbihan linking with a Skel.'

I gasp.

'But how did you ...'

'I know, because Bunce is cured, yet you drank the serum. Somehow it was transferred and at the front of your mind is a connection with Bunce on a level deeper than friendship. It can only mean one thing, you transferred the cure in an act of passion ...' I stare wide-eyed at Lyca as she continues, 'but you no longer have the power to cure another, only Bunce does. I assume that because he is Morbihan, unlike you, the serum has stayed in his system. He could cure everyone, if he so wished.'

Lyca winks at Bunce.

'Are you asking to be cured?' Bunce says plainly.

'Oh child,' Lyca laughs and her entire body wobbles. 'You know we do not have those hungers. Libido is something Morbihan lose once through puberty, scientists are still trying to figure out why, at twenty-one, it's gone. It's probably why we are such peaceful people.' She takes a breath and smiles. 'We have no need to chase after each other to fulfil sexual desires.'

'So why do those desires develop in the first place?' I ask, confused.

'My guess is, and I am not a scientist, but I think it's to do with procreation.'

'If young Morbs have sex they can produce offspring, naturally?' I ask.

'It's possible and probable,' she nods.

'So why take Skels as hosts?' I say, irritated. 'If those under twenty-one can keep the Morb population going, you don't need us.'

Lyca fixes me with her white-hot stare.

'One so young could never make the permanent decision of choosing the right link partner, so we encourage them to stay as pure as possible.' Her artificial lungs groan. 'Never to risk pregnancy with someone that may end up as incompatible. In addition, we don't know what problems a post-childbirth body could face, research into the change is ongoing. There was talk of a young Morbihan who was poisoned by her pregnancy but there aren't any records to support this. Better to err on the side of caution.'

'But it's okay for young Skels to be abused in this manner?' I say hotly.

'I've never heard any Skels use the word "abused" to describe becoming a host,' Lyca frowns.

'I'm not just any Skel,' I say, crossing my arms.

'I can see that,' Lyca says, her voice saccharine. 'But my dear, you must understand that only a fully-grown adult can make such decisions about the future. Young minds are flooded with hormones, they aren't equipped.'

'I disagree,' I say coolly. 'This city is run by 'fully-gown' adults and it's a mess. Why don't you show a little faith in young people? Let them make their own choices and see what happens? And how about telling them the real reason behind Skels becoming Mutil.' I lower my voice, trying to keep my emotions under control. 'Why don't you fill the news channel with the truth, rather than lies?'

Lyca stares at me like it's me that has Martian DNA in my genetic makeup.

In a rush of air, Lyca is beside me, she can't move her hover-chair much further for the trinket stacked tables blocking the way.

'Look at me, young Skel ...' she says soothingly. I meet her white eyes. 'You cannot change your role in the system. You can only change the system's role in your life.'

The words open in my mind like a lotus flower opening to the sun, and a smile is at my lips before I can stop it. With these few words, Lyca has gained my respect and diminished my hatred of her.

'Thank you,' I say, and I mean it. 'You've answered all of my *Ask Lyca* questions in one sentence.'

'Go quickly, my dears,' she says, 'The city's future is in your hands. Embrace change, for without it we'd be forever stuck in a timeless place, and if change stops, life stops.'

Lyca bows her huge head. I bow back and follow Bunce out of the small room, handing Cara the pear as we walk past her.

Cara unties the warden's arms and legs and whispers, 'sorry about that.'

Bunce strides tall and strong up the stone stairs, face tilted to the sun. Cara and I hurry after him. He looks better, skin glowing golden, blond hair shimmering.

'So, what's he got?' Cara asks, when we reach the top.

'Nothing.' I say.

'But what's wrong with him?' she asks, irritated.

'Nothing.' I repeat.

Chapter Thirty-one

Ruinous

When we reach Central Side, Bunce leads us down an alley and we relish the cool shade of the towering Morb apartments. Cara leans back against the wall and turns her attention to the ripe pear, taking a large bite. Bunce leans over me, one hand on the wall and with the other he gently brushes the back of his fingers down my cheek. His eyes shine happiness into my soul. He leans in and our lips meet. He kisses me tenderly, like we're lovers about to link forever. I kiss him back, softly, gentle. He's happy, I can feel it radiating off him, brighter than the sun. I wind my arms around his neck and stroke the back of his head. I forget the world. I forget everything, until Cara gasps beside us and the pear drops to the ground.

'What in Skel Hell?'

We pull apart and I wipe my mouth with the back of my hand.

'I guess we got carried away,' Bunce says, smiling.

'Got carried away?' Cara shouts, eyes big as saucers. 'I don't, I can't … I 'ave no words. No words!' She turns on her heel and storms off.

'Cara!' I shout.

'Stay away from me, Sky. You fuckin' sicko!' she yells, as she breaks into a run, footsteps echoing into the distance.

'Sky, let her go,' Bunce says, taking my arm. I snatch it away.

'You don't understand, do you?'

'Understand what?'

'Even if by some miracle Central let us live, even if they allow us to be together, that's the kind of reaction we're going to get, day in day out, and worse. Do you think people are going to accept us?'

'Yes.'

'No! Would your family accept you linking with a Skel?'

Bunce sighs.

'What shall we do then, eh? Isn't this what we wanted? What's done is done.'

I wring my hands.

'Let's take it one step at a time. Being cured is a big enough bombshell without letting on that we …' I stop, I can't think of a good word. I don't want to say, "are lovers" or "want to be linked" because I'm still unsure of my feelings.

'One step at a time sounds good to me.'

Bunce takes my hand and kisses it.

'Do you feel any different?' I ask. 'I mean … I know you feel better but how does it feel to be cured?'

Bunce tugs at his baggy shirt, and hikes up his trousers.

'I feel strong. Invigorated,' he says, clenching his fists. 'Like I could take on every guard in the city single handed.'

I smile.

'This isn't going to be easy.'

'Nothing worth fighting for ever is.'

I stare at Bunce's slender face, cheeks no longer round and boyish, his eyes look more defined, his nose seems thinner. He's handsome. I feel more attracted to this face. Hell! Am I that superficial? I am. I want to kiss him again. Rip his clothes off. Bunce stares back at me.

'Do you think I'll lose any more weight?'

'Dunno,' I say, and I don't know.

'I don't want to get thin and weak.'

I narrow my eyes.

'Like me, you mean?'

Bunce's eyes widen.

'No, I mean I don't want to go too far the other way and get sick again. You're strong and beautiful. You would be, no matter what.'

'Thanks,' I say, but I don't mean it. I mean, *you jerk!* Men are all the same. Me strong, you weak. Bunce is as bad as the rest of them.

'I mean it, Sky,' he grabs my hands. 'Scrawny, chubby, dark skin, light, scars, chipped teeth, whatever. It's not about what you see. True beauty is how someone makes you feel when you're around them.'

'Yeah right, that's not how things work, Bunce.'

'It is for me,' he says stepping closer. 'Beauty flows from within, no matter what face you're given.'

I kiss his cheek and pull him by the hand to walk at my pace. He drags his feet until we are moving so slowly a snake would overtake us. I'm not used to being talked to the way he talks to me. It makes me uncomfortable. I change the subject.

'I'm going to my Cube.' I say, trying to ignore the fact Bunce has swept my hair aside. 'Get a change of clothes.' Kisses trail down my neck and I melt into Bunce's arms. 'You can wear some of my grandfather's old clothes for now.'

Bunce pulls away and frowns at me.

'They aren't old-man clothes!' I say, rolling my eyes. 'Though we're not fashion victims, like you lot.'

'I didn't mean to offend you,' Bunce says, hands caressing my shoulders.

'It's fine, it takes a lot more than a frown to offend me,' I take his hand. 'Come on.'

We slip through an alley that separates the slums from the park and head out onto the street. We walk in the direction of my cube: Park Side, Road Four, Cube Block H, C-1. The city is a system of grids, like living on the circuit-board that powers the train riding over the top. Skels know the grid so well they need not use their eyes to find their way. They don't even glance up as they scurry about, hurrying to fulfil their duties.

Bunce and I walk close to one another, so no one can see our laced fingers. The misplaced euphoric feeling doesn't last; it abates when the sun is smothered by grey cloud. The trees shudder, leaves trembling in the wind. *'There's a storm coming ...'* The wind whispers. I know what's coming and no amount of

Bunce's love can stop it. A never-ending hurricane is on its way, a maelstrom we created which could destroy everything, including us.

The cure is both a blessing and a curse. If Bunce and I go home to his family, we won't be greeted with open arms. What will Central do when they find out? What will Clover do? I think of all the people who will lose their High-Host privileges, all the lives this will change for the worse. If I'm honest with myself, I know I'm as good as dead. By curing Bunce, my choices haven't changed, unless Bunce agrees to cure others. He stares at me, eyes brimming over with love. He won't agree.

'Are you going to cure others?' I ask, sheepishly.

'Huh?'

Bunce holds his jeans up with one hand, to keep them from falling down. He looks like a boy playing dress-up in his father's clothes. It seems more possible in my mind that his clothes have grown, rather than his body shrinking. I double back to stand beside him. The wind picks up around us.

'Your classmates,' I say loudly. 'If they want it, will you cure them?'

'Skyla, I think we've established I'm not gay.'

'I meant the girls.'

'No,' Bunce says firmly, walking away. I jog to catch up.

'But we agreed when we left the complex that ...'

Bunce cuts in.

'We didn't agree that you should drink the cure,'

'I was forced.' I cross my arms and purse my lips. Infuriating!

'I'm not going to have this conversation with you, Sky.'

'Think of what you're saying.' I stress.

'In my shoes, would you do it?' he asks.

I don't even have to think about it. I would do it. Fuck a few Morbs, or die horribly once Central catches me? No contest.

'Other people will want to be cured too.' I try my best to explain things to Bunce in a way he'll understand. 'Bins created the cure for Kally. Shouldn't she be able to live her dream?

Especially, after her grandfather gave his life for her happiness. And you heard Lyca, only you can do it.'

'I won't do it. I hate Kally!' he says, staring straight ahead.

'Someone else then, after that you can leave it to them to spread the cure.'

'No!'

'Why not?'

'Because it's my choice, and I choose you!' Bunce grabs my shoulders. 'You and you alone. I never want to be with anyone else.'

The firmness of his voice cements his words, the wind rips through his hair, giving him a rugged look. I can't help what I say next.

'But it's your duty.'

Bunce scowls at me and I instantly want to take my words back.

'Was it your duty to sleep with me, then? Pathetic Morb who'll never experience sex!' he rants. 'Here's a sympathy fuck!' Bunce turns his back and walks off. I run to catch up.

'You know it wasn't like that,' I say, pushing my wind-frenzied hair from my face so I can see where I'm going.

'Wasn't it?' he says, marching ahead with no thought as to where he's going.

'Don't play games!' I say.

I'm annoyed he thinks I would have sex with someone because I feel sorry for them. I have more respect for myself than that. Healing society is different to having sex with people because you feel sorry for them. If that were true I'd have slept with half the city by now.

'You're the one playing games!' he says, hiking up his jeans which keep slipping down. 'Not sure if Crow will ever come back for you so you'll settle for me until you know for sure.'

'Now you're being idiotic.'

'Am I? What would happen if Crow suddenly appeared to rescue you like he always does?'

'I'm not some helpless damsel in distress. For your information, I've helped Kian out of a whole heap of shit in the past. That's what friends do, help each other. And I don't care where he is or what he does. I don't care what you do, either,' I say, but I do care. I lied to Bunce, twice. I turn my back on him. 'I'm going.'

'It's not your cube anymore. They gave it away, you heard Cara.'

We walk along, arguing. All the while, the storm builds, spurred on by our raised voices. Rain spits down on us.

'I'm going to get my stuff?' I say.

A rumble tears through the clouds above.

'They probably burned it.'

Flash of lightning.

'Thanks for that.'

The sky grows darker.

'Be realistic, why would they keep it?'

The next roar of thunder is closer.

'Why would they burn it? I just want to go home, all right?' I shout.

I stand, hands on hips and drops of rain patter onto my cheeks.

'Neither of us has a home anymore!' Bunce yells.

'I don't accept that.'

I shake my head but I know it's true and the truth hurts.

'Then accept this,' Bunce gazes into my eyes. 'I don't care how you feel about anyone else, it's how I feel about you that matters. You will, always and forever, have a home in my heart.'

Again, I find myself lost for words. Shocked at how sure he is of his feelings, even more shocked that I find myself wanting a home in his heart. I blink the raindrops from my eyelashes.

'Forever?' I whisper.

Bunce takes my hand back and weaves his fingers with mine.

'Forever,' he whispers back.

I squeeze his hand. I'm not waiting for Crow like he says. Maybe Bunce is my forever. I guess we could live in Tinny's old hideout, but the guards are probably monitoring that by now.

Or we could go find the ingredient in the desert, which is what I was going to do in the first place. The flaw with that idea is that Bins is dead. Who will make the cure now? I wouldn't know where to start. I idly shove my hand into my pocket and feel a sharp plastic edge, wait ... the info-card. I bet it holds the formula for making more serum. I mean, what else could it be?

We run through the lashing rain and when we arrive at my cube, I stare at my front door longingly. No guards, no ruinous, no one around. Overhead, the grey clouds have multiplied, swallowed the sun and the blue sky. The rain grows heavier.

'Why isn't anyone guarding my cube?' I say to Bunce.

'It's not your cube anymore, that's why,' Bunce replies, 'a sane Skel wouldn't come back to a cube that's no longer theirs.'

I roll my eyes and slip inside, Bunce follows close behind me. The air inside is clogged with pungent smells but at least we're dry. Bunce shakes the wet from his hair like a drenched rat would from its fur. I wrinkle my nose, the Skel who's taken up residence here must not have emptied the bucket for a few nights. Gross! I scan the tiny square space. Nothing much has changed. I want to lie on my bed, go to sleep and forget the world, but Bunce is right, it isn't my bed anymore or my home. I walk a few steps and yank open the wardrobe door. My clothes are crumpled up at the bottom, I kneel down and rummage around, some of my grandfather's stuff is still here, I fling a pair of black pants at Bunce and he hurries to put them on. Clothes pushed out of the way, I lean into the wardrobe and feel round the edges for the loose panel. My fingernails scrape the wood, a piece flips up and a dark hole appears.

I reach inside and remove a small wooden box from the dust and cobwebs. It holds my keepsakes. I thought about taking the box to the complex, but didn't because I deluded myself into thinking it was all a mistake. I wasn't really selected and they'd realise I was the wrong girl once I arrived and send me back home.

I push back the lid and slide the smooth orange pebble and red ribbon to one side, treasures I'd found as a child. A glint of gold peeks out and I pinch my finger over it and pull out the necklace given to me by my grandfather before he died – the real treasure. I hold it up and admire the shiny pendant. It spins, catching on the fork lighting flashing through the window, golden spectrums dancing over my palm below it. I've never worn the necklace for fear of it being stolen, lost, or confiscated. The pendant is a solid gold coin, something that used to be called money.

My grandfather tried to explain it to me once. He said people worshipped money and that my pendant was "old" money. It didn't occur to me to ask what new money might be. He said money often came in the form of numbered paper and people would fight over it. I don't know why anyone would worship paper that isn't filled with words. During the land wars, people worshipped the sun. Praying it would give them enough energy to heat and light their homes, that it would stay strong during the winter months. My grandfather explained that before people realised they could harness the sun's rays efficiently, they used to dig down into the ground to release gas, sunlight trapped in rocks. The drillers would sell it to people at high prices and that's how the war began, when every inch of land was filled up and the planet sucked dry, and the seas too high, that's when nations turned on each other, fighting over land in order to create their own food reserves and renewable energy. No one can own land but those people back then didn't understand that. None of us own any part of Gale City. Central controls it but no one owns it.

I fasten the necklace around my neck and shut the box, placing it back beneath the dusty panel.

'Where'd you get that?'

My grandfather's trousers fit Bunce, tight across his thighs but better than the baggy ones he was wearing.

'My grandfather gave it to me.'

'I thought Skels didn't like possessions,' he says.

'Oh, we like them but they aren't available to us,' I say, admiring the gold around my neck. 'Anyway, this is special, not some junk you might buy at a Morb store.'

'We don't value junk.' Bunce says hotly. 'We're not that different. You act like the Morbihan are aliens.'

Aliens. I smile. They are Martians but then I guess all colonists are, me included. Bunce offers me his hand. I grab it and he pulls me onto my feet. I cup Bunce's less round, more angular face. He touches his nose and forehead to mine. The front door swings open and crashes into the wall. Startled, my heart skips a beat and I cling to Bunce. The outline of a tall, dark figure is cut out against the grey outside.

'Don't cha' know the difference between kissing someone and killing them?'

My heart sinks. Sib. I reach into my pocket and thread my fingers into the four loops of my knuckle-knife.

Before I can blink, two strapping men covered in tattoos enter the cube and take a hold of Bunce.

'Hey!' I shout and grab at Bunce's arm, but it's no use, they've come to repay the debt after he inadvertently caused Dutch's death.

'Let go of me.' Bunce struggles, the men hold his arms tighter.

'Nice place you got here.' Sib mocks.

My eyes lock on to her as she steps into the room. Shadow lifts from her face to reveal a twisted smirk and cold, green stare surrounded by long dreadlocks. She moves forwards until she's in my personal space.

'You lied to me.' Her breath is stale. I swallow my fear and hold her stare.

'And?' I say boldly, but I don't feel bold.

Unlike the guard at the complex, I don't think I can take Sib and I'm concerned about the burly men restraining Bunce.

'And?' Sib says, thick lips spreading into a toothless grin. 'That's why I did what I did.'

I stare into her tattooed eyes, wishing looks could kill.

'What are you talking about?' I ask, confused.

Bunce struggles in the corner of the room, but there's no getting away. Sib's lackeys hold him to the spot with little effort.

'Repaid your debt with interest,' she beams.

My body feels as if it's been injected with icy water. Bunce is still alive. What did she do? Then I realise. Kareen. She killed Tess's mum.

'Kareen. You murdered her,' I say.

'Yes,' Sib says, walking around me like a wolf circling its prey. 'But the genius was in framing your little friend.' My face twists in disbelief. Sib's softens. 'Oh, don't worry, I pumped that little princess so full of drugs, she wouldn't have felt a thing on that operating table. If they took a knife to her quickly, that is.'

The laugh that follows chills me to the bone. Sib took Tess. She gave her to the dodgy guards at Rock Vault. I shake with rage. Thunder rolls over the top of the cube block, loud, like it's cracked the sky. I clench my fists.

'You bitch!' I yell over the roaring rain, which pelts the window like a spray of bullets.

Sib smiles at me like I've given her a compliment. If they opened her up on the mutilation table, they'd find an empty space where her heart should be.

'Anyway, back to the reason I'm here,' Sib says, as if she's heading a meeting. 'Dra'cave wants the Morb and Bullet wants you. Get moving.'

Sib motions to the big men and they drag Bunce towards the door.

'No!' I shout. 'You went too far. Now you owe me.'

Sib raises an eyebrow.

'Owe you?'

'I had to kill Tess,' I say through gritted teeth. 'That's your fault. You took two lives for one. Now it's you who will pay.'

I have nothing in mind. Why did I say those words? I wait for Sib to reply.

'Killed one of your own, huh?' She says, stroking one of her dreadlocks. 'You could be useful to our gang, but you still have to pay the price for the weapons. Perhaps there'll be something left of ya to salvage after Bullet's finished with you.'

I don't wait to find out what the price is. My anger at Sib for having Tess mutilated boils over. Arm muscles locked, I strike. Swipe. My knuckle-knife finds the soft flesh of Sib's stomach. I yank the blade free and lunge for her neck. I miss and plunge the other side of the knife into her shoulder. She screams and staggers backwards into the small dining table. It collapses and Sib crashes to the floor. Stupid Runner. She watched me take the weapon from the case. I lost my Galva but I still have my blades. Why didn't she think of that?

My eyes flick to the men holding Bunce. They don't rush to Sib's aid. Can't risk letting go of the top prize that is Bunce. Sib's back on her feet, she holds her stomach. I know I haven't hit any major organs because she can still stand. My arm is straight as an arrow by my side, I grip the bloodied knuckle-knife tight. The weapons usually dangling from Sib's belt are gone. What's she gonna fight me with?

'ARRRGGHHHH!' She screams towards me.

I'm slow to react. I yelp in pain and gasp for air, my body curls over, reeling from the punch to my ribs. I stagger to one side, bumping into the bed. I straighten up in time to see a second fist fly towards me. Sib brings it down hard into my chest. I fall back into the wardrobe, winded. Metal clatters against the floorboards. My knife! The room swims.

'Skyla!' Bunce calls out and his sneakers scuff against the wooden floor. I can't let her beat me. Sib's arm draws back.

'Fucking bitch!' Sib growls, 'Should have killed you when I had the chance.'

I stand as straight as my bruised body will allow. Swaying, I clench my fists, swing my right leg high and bring it down hard, a grunt escapes my lips as my foot connects with the Runner's head. She lets out a yelp and I drive my left knee into her body, she doubles over. Adrenalin spurring me on, I stab my elbow into her back, driving my bodyweight down onto her. She draws back. I turn and drop to my hands and knees, searching the floor for my knuckle-knife. Mistake. I glance back. Thump! My cheekbone shatters. Blood sprays from the corner of my mouth, red splattering down my lips and jaw. I spit the metallic taste, a tooth with it. Dizzy. My body falls forwards and connects with the hard floorboards, the side of my face throbs against the smooth wood. My eyes roll back. She's won. There's a voice, it sounds like it's disappearing down a well.

'Skylaaaaaaa …'

My eyeballs roll around. The lids stutter, I can't open them. I lie there, blood seeping from my mouth like drool. My limbs are heavy, unable to move, unwilling to try. My face throbs. The floor vibrates. Thundering steps. Scratching sound. Smell of wet fur. Distant screams. A woman's screams? Growling. My eyelids flutter open and a blurred image reaches me. Someone writhing on the floor, grey masses darting around, red, grey, and brown blurs. Sharp teeth, snouts covered in blood. More screaming, boots knocking against the wooden floor. I make out a grey tail, hear a grunting sound. My body lifts from the floor and into someone's arms, I'm carried like a small child. I blink several times, it doesn't clear my vision … shiny guard boots? Yes. Bunce's sneakers follow, Sib's lackeys' dirty boots are next. They're being escorted away by guards. I will my eyes to focus, they won't, they're shocked with head trauma.

The dark mass on the floor isn't moving anymore and all I can hear are slurps and snorts. My eyes focus seconds before I'm carried away. Sib lies on the floor, a faraway look in her tattooed green eyes. Her insides are on the outside, Ruinous feed on her – the two dogs rip meat from her ribs in a frenzy, like they've been starved for weeks. I hold back the urge to vomit and two words enter my mind. *Tess. Justice.* Grey gathers at the edges of my eyes. Darkness.

Chapter Thirty-two

Back to Rock Vault

I open my eyes. Above me, the ceiling flickers with candlelight shadows. I close my eyes and re-open them. I'm awake but not yet alert. Where am I? I spread out my arms and clasp the huge duvet that surrounds me like a cocoon. After years of sleeping on a lumpy mattress and more recently, wherever I could lay my head, the enveloping softness of this cushioned bed feels strange. Am I dead? Maybe there is a heaven and I'm curled up on a cloud. No. I've felt this before. I sit up too fast. The room spins. Palm to my forehead I wait till it stops. Confident I'm not going to pass out, I move my hand down and place it over my heart. Beneath the thin cotton covering my skin, my fingertips feel the round shape of the gold coin. They didn't take my necklace.

I wonder what time of day it is? The large window is sealed off with a steel blind. The room is lit with salt rock lamps lined up like little deities on a concave shelf in the wall behind the bedhead. Their glow is meant to evoke a sense of serenity, but my bruises tell the truth – this is far from heaven. I'm a prisoner again, only this time I'm not in Rock Vault. I don't know whether to feel relieved about that or not.

I throw off the squashy duvet and, holding my injuries, I slowly get up. The icy floor shocks the soles of my bare feet. This is a Morb apartment. I'm in a host room. My old host room? I spot my dresser. How long was I out? My body aches, bruises still fresh. I've been here hours rather than days. I touch my hand to my chest where Sib landed that second punch. I pull at the material, I'm wearing a white gown. I grasp my hair and bring a strand to my nose, it smells of flower petals. I'm clean. My fingers touch my lip and run over a bumpy scab. Someone has treated my wounds. I hobble over to the door holding my ribs and stomach, which are tender to the touch. I press my palm to the pad. Nothing happens. I'm locked in. Why am I here and not strapped to a mutilation table, or waiting for my head to be severed and skewered on the line over the trenches?

The wall next to me vibrates with sound. I shuffle closer. A voice. Bunce? It sounds like him but I can't make out what he's saying. A woman starts talking, straining her low voice to reach a higher tone. It's Mistress Vable, I'm sure of it. I lean closer to the clean white wall and her shrill voice vibrates through.

'I hope you're happy! *My brother*, the first Morbihan to contaminate himself and cause a crisis! You've polluted your body and ruined your future.' Mistress Vable rants without stopping to breathe, her artificial parts must be struggling to keep up. 'Do you have any idea of the ramifications of what you've done? Well, do you?'

I press my ear to the wall but I can't make out what Bunce murmurs back. The shouting continues, his reply is obviously not what his sister wanted to hear.

'How could you be so selfish? We've been worried sick wondering where you were. Worrying you might be dead. And did you spare a thought for us?' She pauses to take a breath. 'Did you stop to think what would happen to our way of life, our very existence? Look at the state of your arm!'

Silence. Then a vibration comes back to the wall.

'Mother and father are too traumatised to see you right now.'

Silence. Bunce must be talking. I strain to hear him.

'Absolutely not!' His sister bellows, 'You can never see her again!'

Another silence.

'The authorities have agreed that you will remain here with us under lock and key, literally.' Mistress Vable explains.

I press my ear hard to the wall. Her voice softens. 'That way it will be impossible for you to run away again. The Skel is to be reassigned.'

Reassigned? Dread slithers up the back of my neck. If I'm not staying here and I'm not going back to the factory, where are they sending me? Mistress Vable bleats on.

'I don't know why they spared her life, I really don't. And you ...' She sobs angrily. 'You will be test subject one-four-seven.'

'THE HELL I WILL!'

Bunce's voice crashes through the wall loud and clear.

'How dare you speak to me like that!' Mistress Vable's voice goes up an octave. 'You don't have a choice! People can't see you like this. You look terrible, skeletal! People will talk. It's a disgrace.'

Bunce doesn't reply, or if he does, I can't hear him. I press my cheek even harder against the cold concrete, jamming my ear to the wall.

'You are not to leave this room.'

After a few moments, I hear the door swish shut. I tap on the wall.

'Bunce ...' I whisper to the plaster and then realise he won't hear that. 'BUNCE!'

'Sky?' A muffled voice comes back.

'Yeah, it's me, you okay?'

'Apart from feeling betrayed by my family, I'm fine, are you okay?'

'Bruised but in one piece, how are we going to escape?'

The wall stops talking.

'Bunce ... I said ...'

'I heard you ... We're not going to escape.'

'What?'

'Skyla, you almost died back there and ...'

Heavy boots outside my door.

'Someone's coming,' I hiss into the wall.

'Sky, don't do anything foolish ...'

'I won't, just hang in there.' I whisper back.

I leap back into the bed and throw the duvet over me, the door slides open. A masked guard steps into the room in full uniform and the door closes behind him. He steps closer to me and my body tenses. The guard then sits down at the end of the bed, removes his helmet and drags down the red scarf covering his lower face.

I scramble down the bed and throw my arms around his neck. I weep into a broad shoulder.

'It's okay, Sky,' Crow coos, and strokes my hair.

I can't stop blubbing. The tears keep coming. *Stop it, Sky. Suck it up, you damn baby!*

'I thought I'd never see you again,' I sniff.

'You aren't seeing me now, Sky.' Crow says.

'What do you mean?' I speak into his shirt, a little scared of the response.

'You look upon me as Kian, I'm not him anymore, I'm different,' he says.

I look skyward and search his green eyes, they're no longer black like they were on top of The Spiral, but they also no longer shine like emeralds. They're dull. Free from emotion.

'How different?' I ask.

'This is the real me,' he says, emotionless.

I cup Crow's warm cheek and search his eyes for any trace of my friend. I don't find him. Is he really the strange bird whisperer that everyone says he is?

'That bird tornado, you do that?'

Crow shrugs.

'That happened because I accepted who I really am, and you must accept your fate … for now, at least.'

I pull away. Crow isn't here to help me, he's here to escort me.

'What do you mean?' I ask accusingly.

'You've been reassigned,' he says, a heaviness to his words. 'I'm taking you to your new quarters at Rock Vault.'

'I'm not going back there!' I yell, and back up, towards the head of the bed. 'No way!'

'You are and you must.'

Crow fixes me with an authoritative stare. He stands, places his beaked helmet back on his head and pulls up the scarf. His muffled voice speaks into the cloth.

'Get dressed, we leave in ten.'

I stand on the high platform, dressed in clean but tatty, second-hand city issue uniform, and wait for the Sky Train that will carry me to my fate. The sun has almost set, its orange glow mixes with the onset of night, forming purple swipes across the sky, like someone has run a paintbrush between the colours. Crow stands beside me. He doesn't speak to me, he doesn't crack jokes, he hardly moves. The last time we were on this platform together he was seeing me off to become a host, smiling and happy. I wasn't happy but I wasn't as miserable as I am now.

Down the track, the bright headlamps of the train shine through the dark, mauve sky; two eldritch eyes judging me from the distance. So, this is it. I tried to change my life for the better and did the complete opposite. The rushing wind sweeps strands of blond out from the tight knot on my head and the loose wisps dance around my hairline. The engine grinds to a halt and a sigh of pressure releases from the great metal guts. I lace my cold fingers with Crow's warm ones.

'Come with me?' I ask.

Deja vu.

'I have to come with you, I'm your escort,' Crow says.

The doors slide open, he steps inside the train, pulling me into the carriage with him. Inside it's warm and quiet. To my right, a small Skel sits watching holo-news on a device in the palm of his hand. He's a rail worker, his safety helmet is visible over the projected images. There are two news channels for Skels, the official one and the unofficial one. I know he's watching *Central Times* because no Skel would watch the other one in plain sight. It's circulated by Slum Lords.

The only other commuter is an elder. Her black uniform is frayed and faded. She stares in to space, her face beaten and tired. I scoot up close to Crow. Normally, an escort guard would stand over me, but it seems Crow isn't one for rules, just as Kian wasn't. The train grunts to life and the sudden propulsion knocks our shoulders together. I link my arm through his. He doesn't object but neither does he respond.

I turn my face to the glass. My reflection looks ten years older than it did a few months ago. Out of the window, the platform shrinks away and the lights from Morbihan apartments throw spectrums through the dimly lit train carriage. I'm on the last train and it's probably the last train ride I'll ever take. No longer a factory worker and never really a host, my new title is 'sanitationist' or 'scrub' as the guards like to call them; the lowest of the low. I've been assigned as a prison cleaner, and since the prison really isn't that clean, I have no idea what my job will entail but I know I'm not going to like it. I think of Bunce. I wonder what he's doing now. I wonder if he has it worse than me. Test subject one-four-seven doesn't sound like fun. I hope they don't torture him. The test tubes inside The Spiral flash before my mind's eye. This is all my fault.

Chapter Thirty-three

Inked

Crow marches me up to the main entrance to Rock Vault. The wooden planks leading over the trench water are rotten and uneven beneath my boots. Crow strides over them confidently, while I stumble along in his wake. The scarf that Crow gave me is pulled tight up over my nose and mouth. The vile trench water bubbles with death. A dozen sleek black crows are perched on the overbearing building, as if to greet their master upon his return. Their cold stares lock on to me like guns pointed at my head. I know they hate me and they'd hurt me, if it wasn't for the bird whisperer at my side. We pass under the single streetlamp and fear stabs into my gut. I can't go back into this palace of torture. I stop walking and Crow turns around when he notices his steps echo alone.

'Sky?'

'Don't make me go back in there,' I say, desperately.

'Please, Sky, I didn't bind you because you said you wouldn't resist.'

'I know I said that but …'

The towering black double doors bear down and the bolts seem to grin at me – a sinister smirk. This time you'll be trapped forever! Adrenalin races through me and panic takes over. I turn, I run. I sprint, my calves tight. Thoughts scream inside my head. *Move faster! Run … Run … RUN!*

'CAW … caw, caw, caw … CAW, CAW!'

Flapping surrounds me. I hold on to my bruised ribs and pump my legs harder.

Feathered missiles fly at my head.

'Get off me!'

I throw my arms over my face to protect myself. Tug at my neck, my scarf is stolen. Nip at my ear. I scream. Claws dig into my hair, pulling at the bun, others scratch at my clothes. I flail my arms around to warn them of. A jab to my lip, old wound opened up. There's a triumphant screech from the black beak which drew my blood. Panic knots in my chest. I bury my mouth in the crook of my arm to shield it from another attack.

'Crow!' I holler. He doesn't answer.

Murderous creatures, they'll kill me. I drop to my knees, arms tight over my head, tuck in. Feathered wings flap around me and from all directions, sharp beaks stab at my soft skin, trying to force me to uncurl from my protective ball. Is Crow ordering them to do this? My throat constricts. My breathing quickens. Get them off!

'GET THEM OFF!' I scream.

It stops …

I'm lifted. Red drops fall from my lacerated lip. I uncurl, turn and thump the guard's chest with both fists, but he doesn't let go of me. He throws me over his shoulder and hauls me back towards the black doors of doom. I shout for help but no one comes to my aid. The doors open as we approach, like a great gaping mouth, ready to swallow me whole. I lick the blood from my lips and a familiar bitter taste swims over my tongue. Tears of despair run down my cheeks. My head hangs helplessly as I'm carried like carcass into the depths of Rock Vault.

Once inside, Crow slams me down on my feet. He doesn't steady me. He drops me like a sack of potatoes and strides away. I watch his silhouette as it grows smaller and his steps quieter along the dank passage before me.

'Crow!' I yell after him, my voice echoing. He doesn't respond.

Behind me the giant front doors are closed. There's no point in trying them. I know they won't open. Above are long beams of cobweb laden lights and around me the walls are depressingly grey. To my right is a square, glassless window. Under it, on a shelf, is a peculiar device; a trapezium shape (I think) with a clear disk on the front and a bent bar placed on the top. Not knowing what I'm meant to do, I take a step towards the object on the table. My tired eyes reflect in the plastic disk, face surrounded by the numbers 1-9. I move my head, checking over my reflection. I look like a Glo-Girl who's taken a beating from a client. Bruised cheek, lip split in two places, and my hair looks like one of those killer crows tried to make a nest in it. Look how far I've come in improving my life. Go me!

'Hello?' I call through the dark hole in the wall. 'Anyone there?'

Silence.

I poke my fingers into the round holes on the disk and accidentally pull back on the number four. It spins, making a clicking noise. I lean closer. What do these numbers mean? A ringing noise erupts from the object, and the banana on the top vibrates. Panic. I didn't mean to break it. The ringing echoes loud in the corridor. How do stop the sound coming out? I try the finger holes again, the disk spins around but the ringing doesn't stop. I grab the top, it lifts off and the ringing cuts out. I stretch out the curly cord attached to one end. How odd. There's noise coming from the round end. I put it to my ear.

'Hello.' A quiet, electronic voice says.

'Hello?' I say, uncertainty shaking my voice.

'Megan Skyla,' the robotic voice replies. 'Take your ID card to room nine immediately.'

'What ID card?' I ask.

The voice doesn't answer. It's replaced by a strange flat tone. I lower the voice receiver back onto the hook. Then jump back at the appearance of an outstretched arm through the dark window. I take the card from its fingers and immediately the arm withdraws back into the shadows. I step sideways and trip over my knapsack. Crow must have dropped it, along with me. I can't believe he walked off and left me. Asshole! I stoop and sweep my bag from the dirty floor, then make my way down the ominous passage, treading quietly. Two rodents scurry along the edge of the wall as if they own the place, stopping only to squeak at each other.

Rock Vault is a stark contrast to The Spiral, I think to myself. I run my hand along the dark crumbling walls, dirt building up on the tips of my fingers. Deeper into the prison, I pass doors that look younger than the walls. Have people tried to break out and they had to replace the broken doors? These doors look brand new and new things would never be wasted on Skels. The Mutil are often thought of as having more strength then regular people. Elders say if sight is impaired, the other senses become stronger, so if you take away the mind does the body get stronger? Maybe they hold Mutil behind these doors before they sling them out on to the streets.

I flip my ID card between my fingers. On it is a small-scale map of my palm print, my name and assignment: Megan Skyla. Sanitationist. I fucking hate this card. It says nothing about me.

In a few short strides, I reach door number nine. It's ajar. I knock once and then slip inside. The room I find is not what I'm expecting. Clean, sterile. A whimper comes from a reclined chair in the centre of the room. I approach it. Next to the chair is a small table. On the table is a tray and on the tray, is a bloody, black-smudged cloth and some tiny bottles. A bright light shines down on the young girl holding her arm by the wrist as if she slit it. Her face is hidden by a mess of dark braids. Her quiet sobs drop tears onto her wrist, no cuts, just black lettering surrounded by inflamed, irritated skin.

'Hey,' I say softly. 'You okay?'

'I'm not dead, so I suppose that means I'm okay.'

The girl doesn't look up at me. She continues to weep.

'Andia,' a deep voice bellows into the room, followed by a tall muscular man wearing his guard scarf tied tight around his bald head. He tosses a tattoo gun onto the tray then lifts the girl's wrist and wraps it in a clear film, 'You can go. Follow the corridor to the end and turn left. The other sanitationists will see you to your sleeping quarters.'

Andia nods and gets up, her eyes downcast. She glances in my direction for a split second but doesn't recognise me and I hardly recognise her. Last time I ran into Andia was at Showcase. She was smiling and happy and ... how did she end up in here? I don't get to ask her. She picks up her bag and tears out the door. Her sobs and staggered steps slowly fade away as she moves down the passage. The bulky guard is staring at me.

'Er ... do you want this?' I ask, handing him the ID card.

'Take a seat,' he replies, snatching the card from me.

I sit down in the reclining chair but I don't lean back. I feel awkward and stiff. I scan the tray, drawn to the tattoo gun. My eyes settle on the needle. I hope it's clean. The guard perches on a stool opposite to me, it buckles and shifts, too small for his muscular backside.

'Try not to tense up,' he says in a disturbingly silky tone, like he's about to give me a massage. 'The tenser you are, the more it will hurt.'

He gives me back my ID card. I pocket it and gingerly place my arm on the table. He grips my wrist and wipes the skin with what I can only assume is a sterilised cloth, at least I hope it is.

'Why do I need a tattoo?' I ask, before the needle touches my skin.

'So we know where you belong,' he replies, matter-of-factly.

I want to yell at him, slap his face and say, *this isn't where I belong!* But I don't.

'You don't brand city Skels like slaves,' I say, instead.

Impatience clenches his prominent jaw.

'Skels move around in different jobs. Some become hosts or guards, scrubs never leave.'

'Never leave,' I say, deflated.

'You've been saved from the Dark Angel.' He grunts. 'You owe Central your life. Be grateful for that.'

Owe Central my life? Ha! What life? I want to spit in his face but it's not wise to spit in the face of someone holding a fine needle to your skin. The needle starts to buzz. The pain scratches, then stabs down to my bone, my voice catches in my throat and I'm unable to utter another word. I wasn't tense before but I am now. Holy fuck! I grip the chair with my free hand, the other one twitches and my fingers flinch as if my tendons are being pinched. What's he trying to do, tattoo it on my veins? A cloth wipes across my wrist at intervals. I close my eyes and will my mind to block out the pain. When the buzzing stops, the guard speaks.

'You're done.'

I open my eyes. The guard wraps my wrist in the clear film then releases my inflamed arm. I shake with fretfulness. Not because of the pain or because I'm scared to be back in prison where people are tortured, mutilated, killed, and chopped into Morb food, but because not only will I probably never see the light of day again – I'm now marked for life. The last of my freedom removed by the permanent black symbol on my skin, in a place where I can't cut it out without bleeding to death. The linked black lines resemble an R and a V for Rock Vault. A least, I think that's what it means. I stare at the black ink and realise it's more than that, the way the letters are linked together suggests the 'R' is a person kneeling, hands tied to the bottom of a rock, the 'V' is made up from the bottom part of the R and the top of the 'V' has a line swept to the right like a ledge, symbolising the rock. The same emotions that took hold of Andia take hold of me. I will always be identified as a scrub. This is my forever home, not inside Bunce's heart, but inside this prison.

'I have other duties, you know.'

I snap out of my trance and struggle out of the chair. Eyes glued to the clear wrap covering the swollen markings on my arm, I mindlessly reach down, scoop up my knapsack and hurry out of the door.

'Follow the corridor to the end and turn left. The other sanitationists will see you to your sleeping quarters,' the guard grunts at me.

The passageway is cool, the walls retain no heat. I'm glad of it because my dry mouth is starting to drive my instincts.

Hunter-seeker. I need water. My boots drag anxiety across the concrete floor. Water. Andia. Sleeping quarters. Duties. My stomach makes a popping sound and hunger is added to the list. I turn the corner. Thump! I collide with a body, topple off my feet and fall backwards onto the cold floor.

'I'm sorry,' a soft voices drifts down to me, 'I didn't see you.'

A hand reaches down and I grab it. The stranger pulls me to my feet and the shock of the fall is nothing, compared to the shock of white hair and milky complexion I'm faced with. Penetrating pink eyes smile back at me. A faded yet deep scar traces around the right eye and down a lily-white jaw. I'm motionless for what seems like a decade. The stranger still has hold of my hand. He turns my wrist over and notes my tattoo. I instantly tug away from the creature's grip. He doesn't seem offended. He grins at me.

'Actions speak louder than words,' he coos with a voice too soft for his sharp features. 'Yet your eyes tell you to ignore my gesture of kindness.'

For a moment words fail me. He thinks I'm being rude, when all I really am is shocked.

'Er … thank you for helping me up.'

The strange albino man bends and scoops my ID from the dusty floor. He examines the card in his colourless hands.

'Hello … Megan,' he says, smile widening, cherry pink lips stretching into the whiteness of his cheeks. I snatch the card from him.

'It's Skyla,' I snap. 'No one calls me by my first name.'

'Leave her alone, Dove,' a deep voice booms down the corridor, accompanied by the sound of heavy boots, clomping clumsily towards us.

A tall, weighty man in uniform stops beside us. I recognise him, no mistaking that crooked nose, probably been broken a few times by other guards for touching their personal Glo-Girl or by the Glo-Girl herself for taking without paying. This guard was sat next to Crow at Showcase, the one who laughed at my exposed breasts. I address the pale stranger.

'Your name's Dove?'

Dove nods.

'He doesn't know how to talk to people,' says the guard, dismissively.

My back finds the cold wall. I've unknowingly backed away. The guard leans over me. My cheeks burn a little. He runs his fingers down my shoulder and around the shape of my breast. I let his fingers wander while I try to think of a way to stop him from doing anything more to me.

'Have you still got that pretty dress you wore to Showcase?'

His fingers reach my thigh. His lips close to mine, hook nose almost touching my cheek. He smells like he's run a marathon through dog shit. I turn my face, his fingers push between my legs, he rubs them up and down.

'You like that?' He breathes heavy on my ear. He rubs my leg, not where he intends. Dumb oaf. I clench my jaw. I want to break his fingers. If only I had my knife!

The guard has no thought of Dove being right there. No permission from me and he doesn't care. I wonder if he'll try to rape me with Dove idly watching. The threat is real. This guard has no moral compass. When I was a small girl, I used to hide under my blanket at night thinking it would protect me from monsters. Now, I feel trapped with only my fear for company, a monster has hold of me and I'm without my protective blanket. I'm at the mercy of the guards and I've never seen them show much of that.

'I do,' says Dove unexpectedly.

'Do what?' the guard stops rubbing my inner thigh and rounds on Dove, angry at being interrupted while playing with a new toy.

'Know how to talk to people,' Dove says, smiling.

'Don't talk much sense though, do you?' grunts the guard. He turns back to me. Reaches for my breast but is put off again by the white man in the corridor with us.

'I do.' Dove says, simply, 'I'm talking sense now. What's this if not a sensible conversation?'

'See! He's impossible,' says the guard, shaking his head at me.

I get the feeling Dove only speaks when it's absolutely necessary, and it seems he felt it necessary to save me from this guard's advances.

'Fingers!' A male voice echoes off the walls.

'On my way!' the guard named Fingers shouts back. He points his thumb at Dove. 'He goes days without talking and when he finally does open his lily-white lips, the biggest load of bullshit comes out! Watch out for this one. He's a fucking basketcase.' I nod. 'I'm sorry he ruined our moment; next time I'll take you somewhere we won't be watched,' he grins, uneven teeth, a crocodile's smile. He cups both my breasts and squeezes, I freeze and resist the urge to knee him in the balls, 'Mmmm, they feel as good as they looked at Showcase,' he releases me and walks off, looks over his shoulder and winks, 'See you around.'

Once Fingers is out of sight, relief washes over my body and I breathe out the tension. He'll be back for me though and next time he'll catch me alone. I make a mental note never to go anywhere in here on my own. No knife, one guard I could take, more than one, no dice. I add the name Fingers to the hit list in my head, right next to Clover.

Even though I think Dove tried to help me, he puts me on edge; his freakish eyes stare through me. He has a lunatic vibe about him. Dove doesn't say anything about what just happened. His expression remains vacant. I've never seen anyone so pale. His eyelashes are invisible, his pink eyes are unnaturally far apart and his eyebrows are hidden under a mop of white hair. He looks other worldly; the Morbihan are not this light. What's wrong with him? I want to ask him so many questions. Why are you so white and not in a hover-chair? What are you doing in here? What's going on with your eyes? Only gang members tattoo their eyes to show which part of the city they belong to, and none of them have chosen pink as their gang's colour. Plus, gangs tattoo the whites of their eyes, whereas Dove's irises are pink.

'So,' I say timidly, 'did your parents give you that name?'

Not the question I most wanted to ask, but it is the politest I can muster. Dove shrugs.

'Are you Morbihan?'

Dove frowns and shakes his head. I sigh. I have a feeling this is going to be like trying to pry glory from an addict's hands. I change the subject.

'Do you know where the sleeping quarters are?'

Dove nods.

'Can you take me there?'

Dove nods. I wait for him to move but he doesn't. I raise my eyebrows.

'Can you take me there now?'

Dove nods again, but still doesn't move.

'Let's go then,' I say softly, like I'm talking to a child.

Dove turns his back on me and I follow him a little way along until we reach a dead end. I peer around for a door. Nothing. I turn back to my guide to find he has disappeared. I frown. *Where'd he go?* I feel around the back wall with my hands, maybe there's a secret palm-pad. All I find is dirt. I clap it from my palms and glance down. I'm standing in a hole. We've walked down an incline. I crouch and find a crawl space. I can't see what's at the other end. It's the only place Dove could have gone. I kneel on the gritty floor, my knees complaining about the hardness of it. I crawl through the tight space. It stinks. If rock and brick could sweat, this repugnant odour would be the result. When I reach the other side, Dove is waiting for me, smiling, like he's brought me to the fair. I take in the room. It couldn't be less like the fair in my childhood book. I didn't think I would ever find a place worse than a prison cell. I was wrong, and this is it.

Lights shine in pockets around the enormous, high-ceilinged, humanoid warehouse. On both sides, giant metal structures tower above us, mile-high ancient metal ladders providing access to beds stacked virtually on top of each other. Except to me they're not beds – they're cages.

'New sanitationists reside in block one,' says Dove, finding his timid voice again.

I follow him into the pit of despair. The stale air and odour of sweaty feet makes me retch. Eyes follow me and I try not to connect with any. I pass dirty face after miserable dirty face. This place is a graveyard for hope and happiness. We arrive at the back of the room in front of an almost empty and dilapidated block of beds. The rusty ladder looks as if it will crumble as soon as I step on it.

'If you need to relieve yourself,' Dove points to a hole in the floor in the far corner, behind our bunk block. 'Do it there.'

I put on a fake smile.

'Thanks,' I say, and Dove bows his head, he turns to leave, I catch his arm. 'Really ... thank you.'

Bow lips smile back at me, and I'm sure he understands I'm thanking him for sticking around when the guard groped me. I watch his messy white locks as he strides back towards the entrance.

I study the rickety, giant cages and spot Andia on the second bunk. I don't want to be too high up, but I don't want the bottom bunk either. Visions of rats crawling over my body and the structure collapsing on top of me dance maliciously through my mind. Third bunk it is. I sling my knapsack over my shoulder and start to climb. The rickety rungs wobble with my ascent. I pass Andia, but her light is off and her face is buried in a pillow. I reach my sleeping quarters and climb onto the bed. It's lumpy, as if the thin mattress has been stuffed with sand and broken glass. My pillow is flat and smells of mothballs, and the city issue blanket is riddled with holes and tears. At the end of the bunk are some makeshift shelves. I don't bother unpacking the few possessions I have. I can't allow myself to believe I'm staying in this hellhole. I throw my boots and bag onto a shelf and flick on the dim light above my head. I lie in silence, listening to whispers coming from other blocks. I peel the clear film from my wrist and stroke my finger over the tattooed slave symbol. The ink might be permanent but I'm not going to be. I reach up and click the switch. Lights out.

Chapter Thirty-four

Scrubs

I'm woken by a collection of sounds; voices, footsteps and running water. I sit up, rub my eyes and will them to focus. My tired body tells me I haven't slept for more than an hour; this feeling is not helped by the lack of windows, which makes it feel like it's still night. My body might not agree but the bustle and chatter indicates morning has broken. There's a long snaking line of scrubs behind the bunk block directly opposite me. When my eyes properly adjust, I notice they're all lined up chest to back, genitals to buttocks, completely naked.

'Sky,' I feel a jab through the thin mattress, 'is that you up there?'

I lean over the bunk, hair dangling. I'm met with Andia's worried face.

'What are they doing?' I ask, nodding towards the line.

'Showering, I think.'

My stomach throws acid up my throat. I don't want to stand naked in that line. It comes down to which I would rather be, embarrassed because I smell bad or embarrassed because my body is exposed? I sigh, grab the comb from my bag and scramble down the bed. I swing my left foot onto the first rung and my toes don't touch metal as I expect. Black material is draped over the rung. I reach down and lift it. It's a new uniform, an ugly black jumpsuit. I quickly remove my necklace and shove it in the jumpsuit pocket. I wonder why I still have it. They didn't check me for weapons or contraband. Strange. I guess they expect the guards to do that before escorting new scrubs to Rock Vault. Crow didn't bother.

Once at the bottom of the ladder, Andia and I use the bottom bunk as a washing basket and dump our clothes there before joining the queue. I cross my arms over my breasts and shuffle along. This is degrading, worse than Showcase.

'What do you think we'll be doing today?' Andia whispers over my shoulder.

'I don't know.' I say and I don't.

As we reach the front of the line, my overwhelming anxiety about using the communal shower is not in keeping with the task at hand. A male scrub with dark rings under his eyes hands me a slither of soap, dripping water over my arm as he leaves the shower. I resist the urge to look down, consciously keeping my eyes on people's faces. I don't know why I feel inclined to check out men's genitals and compare other girls' breasts to mine, but I do. I step into the spray. I squeak when the rust-tinged water hits my skin, it isn't freezing, but I wasn't ready for it to be so cold. I rub the soap in my hands, then lather and rinse my goose-pimpled body as fast as I can, mindful not to knock my elbows into the female next to me.

Once clean, I follow those already showered to a dry area. Wet footprints walk in but don't walk out. I stand next to Andia, wondering why there are four of us lined up along the wall. A shaft of air hits us, hotter than desert wind. I gasp and a few of the female scrubs smirk at me. The heat feels as if it will flay my skin from my bones. It stops just as quickly as it began and we shuffle away to make room for the next lot. Andia and I tug on our scrub jumpsuits. I brush my stringy, soap-washed hair into a high ponytail.

'Greetings,' Dove strolls towards us, he's the only person in the whole place who consistently wears a smile.

'Morning,' I say in unison with Andia, who grins at me, before she remembers where she is and her frown returns.

Churning and popping noises come from her direction.

'Where do we have breakfast?' Andia asks Dove, holding her stomach to stop its protest.

'Breakfast? What's that?' Dove says.

'The first meal of the day, you know, breakfast?' says Andia, blue eyes wide with alarm.

Dove stands with his hands by his sides, shoulders square, his face plain.

'We – don't – eat – breakfast,' he says, in a tone that suggests Andia is hard of hearing.

'What do we eat, then?' Andia asks, confusion tracing lines across her brow.

'Vegetables,' Dove replies.

'I mean, when? I'm starving!' she blurts out.

Dove looks Andia up and down and says.

'You are not.'

I can't help but find this exchange amusing. Dove answers everything robotically. Is he some sort of cyborg? Instead of mutilating people they're being turned into a new type of artificial intelligence?

'Are you in charge?' Andia asks, heavy frown on her brow.

'No. Central are in charge,' Dove replies, wry smile on his pink lips.

Andia clenches her fists. The happy-go-lucky laid-back Skel is losing her patience. Her frustration abates with the sudden commotion around us. Everyone is dressed in their jumpsuits and standing in rows of ten. Dove nods to us and we move to the back of the group and stand perfectly still. Dove stands at the front.

'Affirmation!' he shouts.

The scrubs link arms in one movement and I hurry to copy. They hold their tattooed wrists and a chorus of droning voices echoes into the shower-soaked air.

'I am here because Central has spared me. Saved my life from the clutches of the Dark Angel. I belong here. I live to serve my city. United for the greater good. We kneel so others can stand in glory on our shoulders. The system works.'

I glance at Andia, her face twists with shock. I can see her thoughts as if they are written on her forehead: *Seriously?* The scrub on my left drops my arm. My jaw sets. The system can suck my ...

'Come on, Skyla! Dove's leaving.'

Andia drags me by the arm to the front of the crowd. The other scrubs do not push or curse as they are squashed forwards. They shuffle like zombies, ignoring everything and everyone around them. One by one, we crawl through the hole and out into the dark corridors. The scrubs file off in different directions. We follow Dove, his white hair like a beacon in a sea of darker heads.

Guards stride past, chests puffed up, inflated sense of importance sneering though their smug faces. They barge through the crowds, forcing scrubs out of their way. Anyone who doesn't move fast enough is thrown up against the wall. I stick close to the dirty walls, I don't want to bump into that guy Fingers. I can guess why that's his nickname and the last thing I want his fingers all over me again or worse, inside me. Head down to avoid unwanted attention, I glance up at intervals, checking the face of every guard that passes, hopeful. Not Crow. Not Crow. Not Crow. Sigh.

The mass of bodies moving around disorients me. I'll never find my way back to the sleeping quarters and really, I don't want to. I want to find a way out.

Every passage looks the same as the last but soon my surroundings feel familiar. We turn another corner and Dove waits outside a door. A door I've seen before. I don't want to go in, the swinging corpse of a woman hanging like a gutted pig is still fresh in my mind. I swallow hard. I'm starting to wonder if I actually survived Sib's attack. Maybe I didn't, maybe this is Skel Hell. I thought my life was bad before. What's that saying? 'Out of the desert and into the quicksand.' That's what's happened and I'm slowly sinking.

'On Sunday, the butchers take their recoup day, which allows us to do a deep clean.'

Dove speaks in such a way that anyone would think we are taking a tour of beautiful gardens, instead of cleaning up the carnage from the savage butchering of human bodies.

'Do we get a recoup day?' Andia asks, a hopeful look in her deep-blue eyes.

'No.'

'No,' I mutter. This place is Skel Hell, for sure!

The illuminated factory hasn't changed since I threw up over by the back benches. My legs turn to elastic as Dove leads me, Andia, and seven other scrubs down the metal staircase. My teeth chatter and my breath creeps out in wisps of smoke. There aren't any hanging cuts of meat. There's a large, white door on the far wall, the "meat" must be in there. I submerge in a hot bath of relief. Dove passes out latex gloves. The scrubs snap them on and hurry over to a nearby cupboard. They grab buckets filled with bottles and cloths and sprays. They split up and set to work, while me and Andia struggle to wiggle our fingers into the gloves.

'Follow me.'

We walk with Dove towards the other end of the cold factory. He stops in front of a tall metal cupboard. The door squeals and moans as he pulls it back. A strong smell of ammonia leaks out. Dove sets down three buckets. I watch him fill each one with supplies; spray bottle, mask, brush, cloths, and a large bottle with a skull and cross bones on it. Each time Dove drops something into the bucket his white arms flash at me. Neither wrist is marked.

'Why aren't you branded like the rest of us?' I ask.

I'm hopeful he won't clam up today. He seems talkative. Well, as talkative as he probably gets.

Dove thrusts a bucket handle at me. I take it and my arm is yanked down by the weight; it's heavier than I expected.

'There's no need to mark my skin,' he calmly explains. 'I would be instantly recognised if I set foot outside.'

'You've never been outside?' I ask, astonished.

'Oh, you're surprised? How nice to see that emotion,' Dove smiles so wide I can see his pink gums above his crowded teeth. 'I was born of two normal-skinned Skels, they were surprised too … so I'm told.'

'Where are your parents?' I ask.

'Dead, and yours?'

'Dead.'

'Mine might as well be dead,' Andia says, joining the conversation only after she'd familiarised herself with the items in her bucket. 'I'll never see them again and even if I did, they wouldn't speak to me. Not now.'

'What did you do to land yourself in here?' I ask.

Andia rubs her arm and averts her eyes.

'I had a fight with a host.'

'You had a fight?' I smirk.

Andia in a fight, I'd never have believed it.

'It was an accident!' She crosses her arms.

'An accident?' I smirk, 'How can a fight be an accident?'

'It was!' Andia says, exasperated. 'I didn't get selected and so I asked to try on my friend's MHF outfit, and she refused,'

'MHF?' Dove asks.

'Meet the host family,' I explain. He nods to signal he understands.

'We fought over the dress,' Andia says, eyes still on the floor. 'It got damaged and … she got accidentally punched in the face.'

I laugh.

'Yeah, I accidentally punch people in the face all the time.' I mock, trying to keep my sniggers from developing into a guffaw.

'I didn't mean it.' Andia wrings her hands, 'It was my first offence. They couldn't decide what to do with me. The girl's nose was broken, not fixable, I'd ruined her pretty face and so her host family didn't want her anymore, damaged goods, they said. She lost her host privileges and I was sent here.'

Andia hangs her head and mopes off to make a start on the back benches. Andia has always been passionate about becoming a host, too passionate for her own good, it would seem. I give my attention back to Dove.

'Why aren't there more like you?' I ask.

I hope I'm not being intrusive. Dove is odd but seems kind. The last thing I want to do is offend him.

'It is unknown what causes this skin pigment. If I were to procreate, my children would probably be the same colour as you, or your friend over there,' he points to Andia.

'What if you reproduced with a Morb?'

Dove stops digging out supplies in the cupboard and stares at me. My bucket becomes heavier the longer I hold it, I hoist it up in my arms.

'That is forbidden. My skin may be light, but I'm still a Skel. Your hair is light,' he nods towards my head, 'lighter than any Skel I've seen, maybe you are like me.'

'I'm not like you!' I say with a sharpness I didn't intend. 'My grandfather said I was always outside as a small child, my hair bleached in the sun.'

Dove's stare shoots straight though me, he thinks I'm lying to him. He slams the cupboard door shut.

'They wanted me to reproduce,' he says, carrying on as if the previous words about hair colour were never spoken, 'as an experiment ... unfortunately, my seed is dead.'

Dove leads me over to the bench next to Andia, who scrubs in a circular motion, arm bent; she presses down hard and I remember she used to clean down some of the machines at the factory; she worked various jobs, unlike me. I wasn't interested in knowing how to do everything. Dove takes out the spray bottle and a cloth. I copy.

'Your seed is dead?' I ask.

'Yes, I cannot reproduce.'

'Oh.'

Lucky you, I think. If I couldn't reproduce, I wouldn't be in this mess right now. I soon wonder what kind of mess Dove had got himself into in the past. He's so compliant, I couldn't imagine him breaking laws. Yet the scar on his face, from temple to chin, would suggest otherwise.

'Why are you in here?' I ask, hoping he will explain the scar.

'They believe my skin would burn and blister outside. It's safer for me in here.'

Dove continues to scrub. Head down, I'm faced with the top of his messy white hair. What he said doesn't ring true. I think of another question to try and get him to look me in the eye.

'Why don't the guards blab about you?' I say, spraying my half of the bench top, more than I need to.

'People who don't question, never find answers,' he says, without looking up.

'I don't understand,' I say and I really don't.

'They believe that I am High-Host. I'm told High-Host families have been known to bleach their skin,' Dove says. Putting away the sprayer, he rummages through his bucket. Unsuccessful in finding what he's looking for, he walks round to me and pulls a scrubbing brush from my bucket. I grab his wrist.

'Yes, but a host could never get their skin this white …' I reach out and touch Dove's arm with my other hand, running my fingers down his milky skin. He doesn't back away. His arm is so soft, like silk, as if it is made from the feathers of a dove. How is that possible when he works in a place like this? He should be covered in rough skin, shouldn't he? 'My friend, Bunce, is sensitive to sunlight,' I say, releasing his wrist. 'He was never in direct sunlight for long and his skin quickly got used to the outside, but then he's not nearly as white as you.'

'Skels and High-Hosts aren't sensitive to sunlight,' Dove says, as if he already knows this to be true.

'Everyone needs shade from the sun,' I explain. 'Anyway, he's not a Skel, he's Morbihan.'

White eyebrows lower, pinching together like a fluffy cloud above Dove's pink eyes.

'You're mistaken, the Morbihan have never ventured outside.'

'This one did.' I shrug. I don't expect him to believe me.

'I don't sense that you are lying,' he says.

'Why would I lie?'

Dove studies my face, pink retina like a laser scanning for deceit.

'What happened to him?' he asks.

'He changed.'

I spray more of the strong chemical on the bench surface and begin scrubbing a large bloodstain.

'He didn't change, did he?' Dove's soft voice becomes the lightest of whispers, 'he was cured.'

I stop scrubbing and stare at him.

'What makes you say that?'

'Bins,' says Dove. I flinch at the sound of the old Morb's name. 'He talked in his sleep about a serum to cure the obesity or rather, stop it before it starts, everyone thought he was crazy … It exists, doesn't it?'

'It did, it's gone now.' I reply.

'I see.'

Dove pours something the same consistency as sand onto a dark mark on his side of the bench and uses the wire brush to gently work it into the stain. I change the subject. Talking about the serum could get me into trouble.

'Why would they choose to keep the Morb race going, rather than clone you? The Morbs can't even walk and they rely on artificial organs, it's a struggle to keep them alive.'

'I am but one man. The DNA samples they used to create the Morbihan included many different sequences, it would not have been the same with me.'

'So, if they cloned you, the white race would all look the same?'

'Yes, all like me. Morbihan were a triumph for Central. They're highly intelligent and that's useful but tampering with nature always comes at a price.'

'How do you know all this?'

'The walls whisper …' Dove says, his lips turn up at the corners. 'This place holds many secrets but the walls don't keep them. Walls have never stopped secrets from being told.'

I watch Dove scrub a black smudge in a circular motion. The toxic chemical smell brings water to my eyes. Head full of fuzz, I slip my mask over my nose and mouth and continue to scrub my part of the bench top. I'm struck by a burning question.

'Would you leave this place if you could?' I mumble through the mask.

Dove shrugs.

I probably won't get any more information out of him today. I sense he's told me a lot, by his standards. I weigh Dove up. He is older than Crow, not by much, early thirties maybe, and he's a little unstable ... not that Crow isn't. Dove's smile doesn't seem fake. I'm not sure ... a forced optimism? More than twenty years without ever seeing the world outside would make anyone crack up. There's a reason Dove took me under his wing. He wanted me to bump into him, I know it. Did the walls whisper to him about me? Did they tell me I'd escaped once before?

My ears are assaulted with the high-pitched screech of the siren. Andia clamps her hands either side of her head. I pull down the mask and shout over the noise, but my voice gets lost, swept away with the wailing. It's louder than ever. Dove shakes his head. He can't hear me. A dozen guards spill down the metal steps and surround us. I search for Crow, craning my neck above the huddled scrubs. The black arms and legs of a jumpsuit flail above a dozen guards, the body is carried high above their heads like a sacrifice. The siren drops away, replaced with a girl's screams. My ears are ringing but I can still hear her cries.

'Please! Please! I won't do it again. I promise. I promise ...'

I vigorously rub my finger against the outside of my ear until it pops and the muttering surrounding me becomes crisp. Deep voice close to my cheek.

'I will come to you on the fourth night.'

Crow has already started walking away, marching in rhythm with the rest of the guards, up the steps and out of the door, carrying the young girl with them. My eyes meet Dove's.

'Sometimes they scream that they haven't done anything.'

'Where are they taking her?' I ask.

'One of three,' Dove says, eyes downcast.

'What's that?' I say, but I think I know. I exchange dark looks with Andia.

'Mutilation, murder, meat,' Andia replies for Dove.

Dove nods.

'Does this happen often?' I ask.

Dove scrubs harder, taking his anguish at the girl's removal out on the bench.

'Once is too often.' he replies.

Chapter Thirty-five

Rogue Guard

Alone light shines small in the huge scrub hall. My light. Everyone is asleep. Around me, several scrubs snore and snort; mattresses creak with restless tossing and turning, and the occasional dull cough echoes from someone in a far bunk block. I've been here four days and already I feel like a zombie. Tired and drained, my back hurts, my feet throb, and my spirit is breaking. I lie, quiet as a mouse, staring at my shrivelled hands. The gloves don't help much. Chemicals still manage to seep through and blister my skin. I pick at my flaking fingers; my eyes are heavy but I don't close them. No windows, no clocks, but I know it's midnight. Midnight calls to me, a tiny reminder inside my head whispering, *you should be asleep.*

'You should be asleep,' says a familiar voice.

I lean over the edge of my bunk to see Crow standing at the bottom of the ladder, his face dipped in darkness, the outline of his wavy hair level with that of a sleeping Andia.

'What took you so long?' I say, climbing down.

'Sorry, I'm not meant to be on prison duty tonight. I had trouble persuading Fingers to swap with me. He couldn't work out why I would want to take a Vault shift. We all hate it here.'

I'm glad that bastard hates it in here. It increases my chances of not running into him again.

'At least you don't live here,' I say, tugging at my sleep shirt, a cue for him to look at the awful rag and pity me.

'You don't live here, either,' he says.

I point to my wrist.

'Argue with that.'

We sit down on the bottom bunk. It sinks and I'm dragged into the centre of the bed. I hold on to the rim of the mattress with both hands. Crow sits close to me, our thighs touching. I find myself wanting to be close to him, wanting to feel his arms around me again. If only I could turn back time, go back to how safe he made me feel at the edge of the pond. It wasn't a great life but I wasn't a prisoner. I wish my choices were different. I wish I'd taken the easy road and agreed to be a host. The tears fall fast. So fast, I don't realise I'm sobbing.

'Hey, what's wrong with you?'

I sniff and wipe my eyes with the back of my hands.

'I just … I can't stay here.'

'And you won't,' Crow says, almost sweetly, almost Kian. He wipes a tear from my cheek with his thumb, 'I freed you once, remember?'

I want to believe that he can get me out of here, but I know he didn't do it last time. Clover did.

'You're not under Clover's orders anymore, are you?' I ask.

'How do you know I was taking orders from Clover?'

I look away.

'He told me he had been controlling my life so that I would lead him to the serum.'

'I did it to keep you safe.'

'I know,' I coo, touching Crow's hand. 'And I'd have done the same for you, but this time you can't help me.'

'I can't, no,' he says, taking my hands in his.

'No one can,' I tug my hand from him, stand and place my foot on the ladder. 'Now, if you don't mind, I'm going to bed.'

Crow grabs me by the waist and pulls me to him. I get a surge of unexpected excitement.

'I do mind,' he says, his grip is firm. He leans in and kisses me gently on the lips. 'I'd rather you were in my bed.'

'One-track mind, much?' I raise my eyebrows.

He winks.

Whatever transformation Crow has gone through he hasn't changed his feelings about me. I don't know whether to slap his face for that remark or answer with 'let's go!' Bunce climbs into my consciousness, guilt into my stomach.

'You don't make things easy for yourself, do you?' I laugh. 'I'm sure there are plenty of girls not locked up in prison who would love an invitation to your bed.'

'Since when was anything easy worth doing ... or having?' he raising one eyebrow.

'I'm not a fucking possession, Crow!'

'I never said you were. And anyway, why would I want to possess something that causes me so much grief?'

He laughs, and turns to walk away.

'Wait!' I hiss under my breath, not wanting to wake the others.

Crow stops but doesn't turn around.

'Are you going to help me get out of here or not?'

'I can't help you but I know someone who can,' he turns his head so I can hear him clearly but doesn't look back, 'find two others willing to come with you and meet me in the morning by the main entrance.'

'Two others?' I ask. 'Like who?'

'I don't care,' Crow says, his boots echoing against the concrete floor as he strides away. 'Just make sure they're trustworthy.'

I climb back up to my bunk and shut off the light. Pitch black. I close my eyes and then open them again, same darkness. Nothing to see. I wish I could turn the light off inside my head. Who will I take? Andia, of course. I only know her and one other person, Dove. No one else has spoken to me. Not one word from anyone, just stares, hating me for not having suffered in here as long as they have. But can Dove be trusted? Will he come with us?

I don't remember falling asleep. My eyes are slits. I feel like I've only just closed them. The room is sweat-stained. Mouldy, even. I'm amazed the scrubs don't get sick and die with no fresh air. They should be dropping like flies off the vector ring. There are a few vents in the ceiling but not nearly enough. What I wouldn't give for an open window, to feel the breeze on my face. Andia is already showered and dressed. I grab my comb and clothes and slide down the ladder, throwing them and my night-shirt on the bottom bunk. I'm not quite last in line. Once dressed, necklace secured around my neck, we stand in rows the same as we did yesterday and the day before that and the day before that, arms linked ready for 'Affirmation'. The same dull words drone from the scrubs' mouths. I mutter along eyes on Andia who is two rows ahead of me, Dove is at the front. The sea of slaves starts to move. I wriggle my way through the hunched-over bodies.

'Andia!'

She stops.

'Sky, I don't think I'm working with you today ...'

'Shhh, listen. We're not going with the others, come with me.' I tug on her arm. She resists.

'What? Why?'

'We're getting out of here.'

I pull her through the tightly-packed bodies, shuffling to the front of the room.

'We can't.' she says.

'Yes, we can. I have help.'

'They'll kill us.' She lowers her voice, glancing around at the other scrubs but they're not interested, it's like they're drugged or something, 'No second chances for scrubs. You saw how they took that girl away on the first day.'

I stop shuffling forwards.

'I don't have time to argue. Stay here, then.'

Andia winds one of her tight plaits around the tip of her finger.

'I'll come,' she nods.

'We need Dove too,' I say quickly.

'What for?'

'There needs to be three of us, I don't know why.'

'He might turn us in.'

'We have to take that risk.'

Andia falls on the floor, writhing.

'Oh no, I think I twisted my ankle!' she shouts, unconvincingly.

I stare down at her, amused.

'You're a shitty actor.'

'Shut up … oh, ouch, I can't get up.'

I roll my eyes and try not to laugh. Her trick works. Dove is soon crouched down beside her. The rest of the scrubs steer their scrawny bodies around us like robots fitted with obstacle detectors, no need to look up, their bodies will automatically avoid a collision. Dove gently lifts Andia's ankle to examine it.

'Did you fall?'

'No,' she whispers. 'Sky has a plan to escape.'

Dove drops Andia's foot and she winces at the painful and unexpected impact of her ankle bone with the floor. Dove stares up at me.

'Will you come?' I ask, hoping upon hope he won't turn us in.

Dove seems to consider the invitation, pink eyes searching the floor for an answer. After a few seconds, he looks back up at me.

'Only two things in life are certain, death, and change. I have not experienced change and death will soon come for us all … I will go with you,' he says.

'We have to leave now,' I say to him.

He nods and helps Andia to her feet. She flicks her braided hair over her shoulder.

'Where?' Dove asks, quietly.

'Main entrance.'

Dove lifts his white eyebrows at Andia.

'Keep up the pretence. If you were really injured, the ID office is where you'd be taken. They won't suspect anything untoward. Skyla, get under her other arm.'

I do as Dove says and we help Andia to the crawlspace. Once on the other side we keep up the act. My heart races as we turn down the passage towards freedom. A figure waits for us in the middle of the corridor. Crow stands tall in his uniform; handsome and confident as always. I expect Andia to show an interest in him but she doesn't even give him a second glance. Crow opens the door to the room where we received our tattoos. We file inside and he follows, shutting the door behind him.

'No cameras in here, so we're safe. Your uniforms.' he says.

He hands me and Andia a guard uniform each. When he gets to Dove, he stops.

'Dove?' he says to me.

'Yeah, so?' I say. 'You said three people.'

'How am I supposed to hide his skin? He'll give us away the moment we get outside the door!'

Dove opens a drawer and pulls out some black latex gloves.

'Guards don't go around wearing latex gloves, and what about your face!?' Crow growls.

Dove smiles.

'Once I complained about a hole in my shoe, and then I met a man with no feet.'

'This is crazy!' Crow throws his hands up. 'You couldn't find someone normal?'

I shrug and pull my belt tighter. The uniform is a little big.

'What is normal?' Dove says, smiling. 'Normal is as normal acts, my friend. If it is normal to murder and mutilate innocent people when following orders, then no, I'm not normal, but you are.'

'I'm not your friend, freak,' Crow grunts. 'For someone who has a reputation for being mute, you're extremely chatty, and I've heard you're a dirty snitch.'

'I only talk to people worth my words and I can only snitch on a person who is in the wrong. I can't snitch on people who do the right thing, don't you think?'

Crow scowls, thrusts a uniform at Dove and turns to help Andia adjust her helmet. I help Dove wrap the red scarf around his face before placing the beaked helmet on his head.

'What now?' I ask Crow, though it's clear what his plan is.

'A friend of mine risked her neck to set this up. The job is a consignment of parts from factory to Morbihan residential.'

'You know what?' Andia says. 'I would probably understand that better if you said it in Japanese, and I don't speak Japanese.'

Crow sighs.

'Jumpsuits in that cupboard.' He points to a dark corner of the room. Dove collects up the discarded scrub uniforms and takes them to the cupboard. Crow settles his gaze on Andia, 'We're taking an important package from one place to another. Got it?'

'Got it!' she nods, and gives Crow a shaky two thumbs up. She's jittery, this is way out of her comfort zone.

'Once outside, move as I move ...' Crow barks instructions, 'do as I do, and don't speak until the package has been delivered and we're safely out of sight.'

'Won't someone be suspicious that it wasn't sent using drones?' I ask. Crow's jaw clenches and a vein pops up in his neck. 'I mean, what's in the package that it needs a four-guard service?'

'I don't know.' Crow shakes his head, irritated. 'It's not my business to know. I trust my friend's judgement, and anyway, there wasn't much time to hash things out. I could hazard a guess that since it's going to Master Vable, it must be important engineering parts.'

The fine hairs on the backs of my arms prickle. Back to the Vables. To Bunce.

Getting outside was surprisingly easy. Crow pressed his palm to the pad. The doors opened and we walked out. I don't know why I thought the front doors would be bolted with extra locks and chains or something. What wasn't so easy was the way Dove reacted to the light. Early in the morning, with the sun only just peeking above the buildings should have been the best time for him to experience the outside, but even that is too much. Dove struggles to keep up, blinded by the light, overwhelmed by the sounds and sights, his pink eyes dart around, trying to take everything in. He gasps and shakes. I lift my head and take in huge gulps of fresh air as we march across the bridge. Freedom tastes good.

A crow flaps past Dove's head and he ducks in fear. I march close to him and gently touch his arm. His body relaxes. The bird settles on Crow's shoulder and turns its feathered head to stare at me through suspicious, beady eyes. I'm sure it's Crow's pet, Glider, and I can tell the bird hates me. My grandfather once told me crows recognise individual human faces and can hold a grudge if you treat them badly. I don't know if I have ever treated a crow badly. Maybe it thinks I treat Crow badly and sees me as a threat?

We march down an alley and wait outside a factory door. Crow goes in and is soon back with a long, rectangular box that looks as if it might be filled with broom handles. 'FRAGILE' is written on the side in black, capital letters. The bird that hitched a ride on Crow's shoulder sits perched in a nearby tree, eyeballing me. We take our places one behind the other, hoist the long box up onto our shoulders and march across town. I wonder why we don't take the Sky Train. My guess is that whatever is in the box might interfere with the train's controls. We finally reach the entrance to Bunce's apartment block. Crow presses his palm to the pad; the door opens and we follow him into the holding chamber. The same smarmy man who gave me access when I was a host greets us. I'm overcome with a strange feeling. Not nostalgia; a familiar foreboding mixed with anxiety and regret.

'One guard only from this point,' the repulsive man says.

'I was told four guards were needed,' Crow says.

'Only one from this point,' the man repeats.

Crow nods at me.

'We'll go to the Barracks,' he says. 'You see the package safely to Master Vable.'

I nod, and glance at the others who look petrified at the thought of leaving without me or, more to the point, leaving with Crow.

As my friends march through one door, I prop the package up against the wall and scrub with the burning chemical. Then I enter the door opposite, grasping the package with both throbbing ha... It isn't heavy, just awkward because of its length. I hold it tight against my shoulder like a solider carrying a shotgun. The last thing I want to do is drop it. Inside the complex, the cool air wraps around me and dries the sweat running down my temples. Apprehension creeps up on me as I walk the same stretch of corridor I did the first time I met the Vables. Not as unsteady on my feet as last time, my boots easier to walk in than those stupid heels.

Halfway down the corridor, the realisation hits me. Bunce. I can get him out of here. Is that why Crow insisted I go on, to free Bunce? That doesn't make sense. He hates Bunce. I guess it's because I'm the only one who can go on. Crow needs to help the others find somewhere safe to stay. As a fugitive, I can't do that, and I'm also the only person who knows which apartment belongs to the Vables. This one. Number twelve. I knock. They must be expecting me. Although not *me* personally, that's the last thing the Vables would expect. The hum of a hover-chair glides towards the door. I keep my head down, beak covering my face.

'Ah thank you, my good ...'

My eyes meet Master Vable's shutters.

'Ms Skyla?'

I nod and place the package inside the doorframe.

'They've got him locked up in the attic space,' he blurts out, sharp intake of breath. 'He's allowed out to attend the education facility and to undergo tests, but after that he is locked away again.' Another forced breath.

'It's okay.' I say, in a soothing voice.

'No, it's not. Nothing is. This wasn't what was meant to happen.' He sniffs. 'They're making him ill, Ms Skyla, the tests are abrasive, he can't take it.' My former master coughs and splutters. 'All our hard work for nothing. Bins, Hatti, Lyca. I've failed them all, but most of all, I've failed you and Bunce.'

'Hatti?' I say, a vision of the eccentric top-hatted Morb floats into my head. Now I'm confused. 'I saw him on the vision screen saying the serum was destroyed.'

'Yes, he's good at propaganda, is Hatti.'

'Are you saying you know about the cure?' I frown.

'Of course I do,' his mechanical eyes blink, 'I set Cara up as the decoy. Oh, that poor girl but sacrifices had to be made.'

'Who intercepted the drone?' I ask, somewhat taken aback.

'Flair, a lovely High-Host. Works for Lyca. She snuck into an office inside The Spiral,' he speaks quickly, taking sharp breaths between every fifth word, 'made a hole in the wall behind the painting, placed the cure inside and covered it over with putty, it was the one place we knew they'd never suspect.'

'The warden.' I whisper. She must have let Cara overpower her.

'What are you doing?' Mistress Vable's wicked voice stings the air. 'Shut the door!'

'Coming, my love.' Master Vable sings out.

'I'm sorry,' I say, and I am. 'It's my fault Bunce was captured. I should have listened to him.'

'None of us could have predicted this,' he says, emotion in his voice making up for the lack of it in his lenses. 'And the more I think about it, the more I admire you both.'

'For what?'

'Taking a risk. Taking control of your life.'

I try to smile, but I have never felt more out of control in my whole life.

Master Vable pushes a button on his hover-chair. A lid flips up and he plunges his thick fingers into the hole, pulling out something shiny.

'The attic isn't guarded, it's locked with this.'

He hands me the curious object; gold with a loop at one end, a long stem and a jagged edge at the other.

'It's an old way of locking doors. Put it in the keyhole in the attic door and turn,' he takes a breath. 'Then use the handle and the door will open. Please help him, Ms Skyla. He's miserable without you. I'm concerned for his health.'

'Okay,' I say.

I touch Master Vable's plump hand and then march off to the sound of his stifled breathing. I head for the servants' stairs. I push everything Master Vable confessed to the back of my mind and remember all the emotions I felt when I was with Bunce. I can't wait to see him. We can finally be free. I make plans in my head. We'll leave the city, escape into the desert, there must be something out there. I leap the stairs two at a time, joy driving me. Joy! I haven't felt like this since I was a little girl, and what's this key? What a strange object. I hold it tight and its curves imprint on my palm. I arrive at the attic door out of breath and elated. I push the key into a small slot under the handle and turn. It takes a little brute force … then it moves and click, I turn the handle and throw the door open.

'No!' I scream. 'Oh please, no!'

I fall to my knees, shock spilling out onto the floorboards in floods of tears. My beaked helmet drops from my head and clonks against the hard wood. The room spins. I hang on to the floor, it feels like it's falling away beneath me. I crawl on all fours, I have to get to him. I take a deep breath, hold on to my dizzy head and I get to my feet. Trembling all over, I pick up the overturned chair, carefully climb onto it and pull the dagger from the guard belt. The ceilings are low and the makeshift noose has been tied off over an exposed beam. I grasp the rainbow-stripe tie with one hand and start cutting. His body brushes against me as I saw into the fibres. I keep sawing at the cost of the overstretched tendons in my arm. The last thread snaps and the body falls to the floor with a heavy thud. I climb down from the chair, shoving the knife into my worn boot. I kneel beside the body. His face is grey, eyes closed, swollen purple. I want to lift the lids but I know he won't look at me, he won't suddenly come back to life simply because I lift his eyelids.

'Oh, Bunce, why?' I whisper, and force my fingers under the strained material at his neck. It's too tight. I can't get it off.

My tears rain down on his cheeks and it's as if he cries with me. I lay my hand on his chest, over his un-beating heart. Bunce touched my heart. He saved my soul and I brought him death. I'm the reason the Dark Angel took him. I notice he's wearing their words. *The System Works* is stitched in bold white cotton below the embroidered city emblem. My fingers curl around the badge beside his right lapel. About to rip the logo off, I feel a solid edge beneath. I peel back Bunce's blazer, slip my hand into the breast pocket and pull out a mini touchpad. My hands tremble as I tap the screen. Black lettering appears, paragraphs I know I don't want to read, but I must, because they're for me.

Dear Skyla,

I hope this letter finds you. It probably won't but if it does, I want you to know I love you with all my heart. I've loved you from the moment I met you and I don't regret going with you.

I scroll down, the screen is small and my finger has to pass over several times to read each line.

My brother-in-link told me you've been reassigned to prison work, that you'll be locked away forever. I hate to think of you back in that awful place. They keep me locked up in the attic. I'm only let out to attend the education unit or when they want to run tests on me. The tests make me ill. Constant headaches and my stomach feels like a fireball lives inside it. They've taken so much of my blood. I'm sure they mean to kill me. I won't go on their terms. I say when the Dark Angel comes for me!

I want you to know I did what you said. I agreed to cure Kally, in secret. She didn't come alone. She tricked me. There were three of them. They all wanted to be cured. I said no. They wouldn't listen. Every time I close my eyes I hear them laughing. I feel their hands grabbing at me. It makes me sick to the stomach. All people do is take. Strip you down until there's nothing left. Everyone wants their pound of flesh!

You said you wanted to save the city. You can't save something that's dead. Gale City is dead. Curing Morbs will only make things worse. We are a selfish, greedy, insular race, you were right. And if by some miracle you manage to escape Rock Vault a second time, please Skyla, leave this place and never come back. As for me, I don't want to live without you.

Remember, your home is in my heart.

Forever.

Bunce.

I stare until the words melt together in a black smudge. Tears drop on the small screen and distort the words. I read over the second to last word again.

'Forever.'

I close my eyes, freeing more salty tears. I shove the screen into my pocket and press my lips to Bunce's cold forehead. I snatch a pillow from the bed in the corner and gently lift his head to place the soft pillow underneath. He's finally at peace but I'm enraged. Hot anger rises in my chest. Those bitches think they can take what they want and get on with their new lives. He'd come so far, grown so much and now he's dead.

I step over Bunce's body and up to the window. Adult Morbs hover along and youngsters stroll through the spaghetti of tubes oblivious to what's gone on in this attic, ignorant to my reality. I study each pale creature. *Which of you did it?* The sky is as dark as my thoughts but Mother Nature is nothing compared to the storm brewing inside me. A long grey cloud sails over the city, swallowing everything in its path. Palm trees bend and quiver in the rushing wind. A thunderclap startles the crows settled in the nearest trees at the edge of the Morbihan side of town, their fretful caws dispel into turbulence above. Thunder and gales are a warning of danger, but there'll be no warning about me. *I am the storm and they don't know I'm coming.*

I will avenge Bunce.

Birds are pushed from the trees by a blink of lightning, they disappear into the grey horizon like ashes scattered to the wind. Thunder crackles and a jagged line tears across the darkness in a luminous flash of silver.

I step back over Bunce, scoop my guard helmet from the floor and press my palm to the alarm on the wall. The siren immediately screams, filling the building with its whining.

'Rest easy, Bunce,' I coo to my dead lover. 'Your suffering is over.'

Back out the door, I hurry down the steps and dash down the corridor, rush down more steps. I need to get out before the guards come pouring in and find Bunce. I need to get across town.

I run down the tube at top speed. My legs charge onward with little effort from my brain, no need to push myself to keep going, emotional power courses though me. I burst from the Morb complex and smack into a wall of thick, humid air, rain lashes my body, guard uniform instantly soaked, right through to my skin. The storm rages and I march into the desolation, water running off the front of my beaked helmet in a waterfall. I think of Bunce, of Bullet, Dove, Andia, of Crow, of Clover and Cara and Tess; they rush through my head like a kaleidoscope of lost souls. I march on, into the eye of the storm.

People think there are choices. They think they have life and a reason to breathe. They don't but now I do. My choices are black and white. Remain inside the darkness or walk into my light. Live for revenge or die for nothing. I live. They die. That's it.

Acknowledgements

There are so many people to thank. Too many to list, so I'm going to do the best I can and if I have forgotten anyone then I hope they'll remind me to mention them in book two.

To my husband, Chris and our wonderful daughters, I could not have done this without your patience and understanding. I love you to Mars and back. I want to 'thank' my cheeky cat, Rupert, for generally being a nightmare; furry backside in my face while tapping his paws on the keyboard pretending he's the writer.

Right, here comes the mega list of awesomeness that is my writing support network.

Thank you to Betsy and Fred at Bloodhound Books for taking a chance on me, I'm forever grateful. Thank you to Nebojsa Zoric, who designed the fantastic cover. Thank you to my editor Emma Mitchell and to Eileen Wilson for last minute proofreading and tips. Big hugs to the rest of the Bloodhound gang for all your support.

I want to thank my agent, Vicki Marsdon, for always believing in me, and my brilliant band of beta readers who have been valuable beyond words, I could not have done this without them, they are: Shel Thomson, Heather Gower, Leah Porter, Nick Jackson, Jade S Bokhari, Liv Brennan, Prachi Percy Sharma, Sandy McPeak and Cliona Gibson. I also want to thank Elinor D. Perry-Smith for being the first to edit this novel when it was in its infancy. I learned a great deal from your notes.

I want to thank my mentors: John F McDonald and Lucy V Hay. I give thanks to John for his great advice over the years and to Lucy for being my guide. I cannot thank Lucy enough for all she has done. I want to thank Samantha Shannon and Gemma Todd, they are amazingly talented writers who I've learned a great deal from, thank you for your advice and for being an inspiration. Thank you to Derin Attwood and Lee Murry for giving me the courage to carry on.

That brings me to Carmen Radtke and Racheal Howard who encouraged me to enter competitions and offered ongoing support, along with all the Bang2writers and Create50 writers who exchanged feedback with me. I want to thank Chris Jones for encouraging me to shoot for the stars, and a big thank you to Niki-Mark Hadden for being a guiding light in the darkness. I also want to mention Sarah Hardy and Sumaira Wilson for holding my hand through this process, and Libby and Chris for all their help with the launch. Thank you to all who leave reviews. These are the biggest gifts.

I thank my parents, ma and pa, and the rest of my extended family for always believing in me, not forgetting my lovely grandmother for being my biggest cheerleader. I also want to thank all my friends. My besties, my online community and everyone from the village. Thank you for always supporting my writing career and celebrating in every success while also being there when my work was rejected. Special thanks to Emma Keating, Olga Ghosh, Debbie Thorton, Joanna Horne and Emma Cooke for listing to me ramble on about writing. An extra special thank you to Rita and Richard Bishop who provided me with the most beautiful and inspiring space in which to write. Lastly, thank you to all those who bought this book. Readers are amazing people. Thank you for connecting with me.

Glossary

Air-Soles: Connective strips applied to the bottom of shoes enabling the wearer to glide through the air rather than walk/run.
Augur: One who studies birds.
Avian: Relating to birds.
Bathing Block: Where Skel's go to wash/use the toilet.
Central: The ruling elite of Gale City.
Central Side: A city suburb.
Crownado: A tornado of crows.
Cube: A small one room dwelling with kitchenette.
Cube Block: A block of one room dwellings.
Drift Side: A city suburb.
Eremites: Skel's who have opted out of the system.
Gale City: The name of the city.
Galva: A type of rifle, shoots electrifying bullets.
Glo-Girl: A prostitute who works for drugs.
Glory: A dangerous street drug.
Glory Runner: A drug dealer.
High-Host: A Skel who has finished her birthing duties.
Host: A Skel chosen to carry Morbihan babies.
Hover-Chair: A life support for Morbihan which hovers from A to B.
Hover-Cycle: An electrically charged bike.
Hyper Market: A place where Skel's order groceries for their masters.
Knuckle-knife: A knuckle duster with two retractable blades.
Link: A lifelong lover.
Melontines: A hybrid fruit. Melon and clementine.
Morbihan/Morbs: Martian Organism of Raised Biological Intelligence with Humanoid Attributes and Nature. Cloned race.

Morb Complex: Where the Morbihan live.

Mutil: A mutilated Skel.

Octli: A drink made from fragmented plant sap.

Palm-pad: A locking system of which most pads are deactivated.

Park Side: A city suburb.

Rock Vault: The city prison.

Ruinous: Bionic dog/wolf hybrid.

Serum 574: The cure for the Morbihan obesity.

Showcase: A ceremony for selecting hosts.

Skel: A skeletal looking city worker.

Skel Hell: Torturous afterlife for evil souls.

Sky Train: A monorail.

Slum Lord: An Eremite who rules over the city dump.

STRATA -K: A spaceship.

The Barracks: The guard training grounds and residence.

The Dark Angel: Death AKA the Grim Reaper.

The Day of the Bird: A day recognised after the crows of Gale City murdered hundreds of Skels.

The Glory in the Sky: Heavenly afterlife for good souls.

The Hub: Where the High-Hosts and their link partners live.

The Spiral: Central Headquarters.

Tube: A clear walkway/hoverway connecting buildings.

Vector Ring: An electrically charged barrier encircling the dump.

Verity: A spiritual healer who can feel what ails a person, sometimes also an agony aunt.

Vision Screen: A television which projects holograms.

25657506R00220

Printed in Great Britain
by Amazon